"This is more than simply an anthology: it is also a history lesson...a substantial and important volume, a landmark anthology that all lovers of well-written horror fiction will want have on their shelves."

—*Black Static*

"A darkly shining beacon of hope in an unimaginative world."

—Neil Gaiman

"Every story here is worth re-reading, and you are sure to make rewarding new discoveries or rediscover old favourites."

—*Supernatural Tales*

"An invaluable resource for all of us who believe in the genre."

—Clive Barker

"A good summation of what contemporary short story writers have produced in the horror area."

—*SF Site*

"An essential record, invaluable and irreplaceable, of modern horror fiction in all its range and variousness."

—Ramsey Campbell

"The best horror anthologist in the business is, of course, Stephen Jones."

—*Time Out*

"An essential volume for horror readers."

—*Locus*

THE BEST OF
BEST NEW
HORROR

THE BEST OF
BEST NEW HORROR

VOLUME ONE

Edited by
STEPHEN JONES

With an Introduction by
RAMSEY CAMPBELL

DIP

THE BEST OF BEST NEW HORROR
VOLUME ONE

Originally published in slightly different form as *The Mammoth Book of Best of Best New Horror: A Twenty-Year Celebration* by Robinson Publishing.

Front cover illustration by Norman Saunders.
Originally published on *Strange Stories from Another World* #5, February 1953.
Back cover illustration attributed to Al Avison.
Originally published in *Witches Tales*.

A Stephen Jones Book for PS Publishing Ltd.

This trade paperback edition published in April 2020
by Drugstore Indian Press, an imprint of PS Publishing Ltd.,
by arrangement with Stephen Jones.

2 4 6 8 10 9 7 5 3 1

ISBN 978-1-786365-74-3

Design and Layout by Michael Smith
Cover design by Smith & Jones

Printed and bound in England by T. J. International

PS PUBLISHING
Grosvenor House, 1 New Road
Hornsea HU18 1PG, England

editor@pspublishing.co.uk
www.pspublishing.co.uk

Contents

ACKNOWLEDGEMENTS

THE EDITOR WOULD like to thank Peter and Nicky Crowther, Mike Smith, Marie O'Regan, Ramsey Campbell, David Saunders, Michael Marshall Smith and all the authors, editors and publishers who contributed to the series over the first twenty years, for their help and support.

This volume is dedicated to
NICK ROBINSON
KENT CARROLL
and
HERMAN GRAF
for their trust and vision thirty years ago.

And also for
RAMSEY CAMPBELL
for his continued guidance and
inspiration during all those years.

EDITOR'S FOREWORD

OKAY, LET'S GET something absolutely straight from the beginning—despite what the title of this book says, this volume does not necessarily represent the ten finest stories that appeared in *Best New Horror* during the title's first decade.

For a start, those first ten volumes contained more than 230 stories by 115 authors and, given the nature of any "Year's Best" series, *all* the stories in those books can be considered to be the "best" in some form or another—at least according to the criteria of those who compile them.

Back in 1992, in the third volume, my co-editor Ramsey Campbell and I pointed out that: "*Best New Horror* does not purport to be a collection of the year's best horror stories. Instead, we hope to present a varied selection of fiction—loosely connected by various notions of horror—that illustrates the range of themes and ideas currently being explored in the genre, by top names in the field and exciting newcomers".

That policy statement could just as well be applied to this current compilation as well.

We decided very early on that it would be presumptuous to claim that Best New Horror contained a definitive selection of the year's best horror stories. After all, such definitions are totally subjective and differ widely between each individual. So instead, as Ramsey and I explained those many years ago, these anthologies over the years have attempted—based on the material seen—to present an annual "snapshot" of some of the best horror fiction writing to be published in a particular year.

With so many superior stories and talented authors to choose from, and with the number of tales necessarily constrained by the word-length of a single book, I decided to limit my choice for this anniversary edition to what I considered to be one of the best stories from each volume.

When it came to my definition of "best", I considered whether a particular story was the most effective, stylish or simply influential in any individual volume. As a consequence, this led to some juggling of titles and authors until I felt that I had achieved a representative selection of ten superior horror stories (and don't expect me to define my "various notions" of what constitutes "horror" here—this book speaks for itself).

Unfortunately, because I also decided to only allow one story per author, by necessity some very fine tales and their creators have had to be left out of this anthology.

As a result, many excellent writers who have regularly contributed to the series over the years—including Poppy Z. Brite, Dennis Etchison, Stephen Gallagher, Charles L. Grant, Brian Hodge, Graham Joyce, Joel Lane, Tanith Lee, Thomas Ligotti, Kelly Link, Nicholas Royle, David J. Schow, Steve Rasnic Tem, Karl Edward Wagner, Cherry Wilder and Gene Wolfe, to name only a few—are not represented in this current volume.

There is nothing to say that these and other equally talented writers could not be included in another compilation using the same criteria at a later date. There is certainly a wealth of talent and some extraordinarily powerful material to draw upon throughout the distinguished history of this anthology series.

But until then—like the series itself—this current volume should be considered a representative sampling of some of the finest work that was included in *Best New Horror* during the anthology's first ten years.

Is it actually the *best* of the *Best*? I'm not so sure . . . but I do know that these tales and the authors who crafted them represent the pinnacle of the horror genre between 1989 and 1999. And that can't be a bad thing for any "Best of" compilation.

—Stephen Jones

INTRODUCTION

BETTERING THE BEST

THIRTY YEARS! THEY'VE seen horror dwindle almost to nothing under the pitiless light of the marketplace, tottering away only to grope, however tentatively, back into the open. I'm reminded of the 1950s, when I discovered the field. The great pulps were dead or dying, and almost no horror was being published as such. All horror comics had been banned by the British parliament, and yet two years after the ban came into force, the august Faber & Faber published *Best Horror Stories* with a gleefully lurid cover. The genre was largely being kept alive—underground, if not in its grave—by enterprising small presses and short-lived magazines. In time it struggled to its feet, and by the mid-1970s it was prancing and showing all its many teeth. Like any monster, it was eventually overwhelmed, but we know monsters never really die. Perhaps we're back in that stage of its eternal gestation where I began, with an undead hibernation behind us and an uncertain future to come.

Of course things and even Things have changed. One is the onset of the Internet. Whereas when we began *Best New Horror* our readers were protected from the slush pile, unless they worked in publishing, these days the kind of material that made editors blench can be read online. Just because everybody uses language, that doesn't mean that they can write even tolerable prose. If some of the stuff out there has any merit, it's to show people the kind of thing that editors protect us from.

We begin this first "Best of" volume as we mean to continue, with the unexpected. 'No Sharks in the Med' is one of Brian Lumley's occasional tales that have no fantastic or supernatural element. Perhaps there's just a hint of revenge from beyond the grave, but the tale draws its power from its vivid evocation of the kind of Greece we tourists seek and from the classically gradual revelation of the dark that lurks beneath it, all this in the kind of Mediterranean sunlight we might think inimical to shadows. It was originally published in *Weird Tales*, a magazine that broke its pact with weirdness by reprinting, in one of its last issues of the 1950s, Merle Constiner's 'The Skull of Barnaby Shattuck', a Western novelette first published in *Short Stories*. As a young horror fan I read the tale and waited for the wretched skull to scream or do a jig or put on any kind of a show at all, but no such luck. Brian's story wouldn't have disappointed me, however, in delivering horror.

1990 brought us Michael Marshall Smith, and it's quite an event. You may be reminded here and there of Bradbury's small-town lyricism or Steve King's way with a flavoursome phrase, but Mike's voice is already unmistakable. Though his prose has grown leaner over the years, it's just as strong when it's well-fed, like the tiger in the story. For myself, I wouldn't have less of it, and I'm delighted to renew my acquaintance with his fine first publication. It may owe some of its enviable fluency to having been written in a single day. Sometimes a debut feels as if a flood of talent has been undammed, as here.

Of my own tale, which Steve has been kind enough to include, I've little to say. When I wrote it I'd forgotten that John Ware had written one called 'Spinalonga' for the thirteenth *Pan Book of Horror Stories*. That volume was graced by David Case's novella 'The Dead End' but also suffered from the rot that had set into the series. Amid the parade of child-burnings and dismemberments and mutilations that the book trots out for its fun-loving customers, Ware's leprous anecdote seems tasteful—sufficiently so to have slipped my mind by the time the family and I went to Crete a decade later. Ever since the Gothic novel, horror fiction has been inspired by landscapes, and that island off Elounda was too tempting a location to waste. Incidentally, I've just discovered that my yellowing copy of the Pan book contains a souvenir from an earlier owner—the counterfoil of a postal order bought at Bank on December 13, 1977 and sent to Cooking for Outline of Purfleet. On the back the owner has listed the contents of the anthology with an observation about each, including "Sort of comment", "Dead boring!!" and "Whoop-peee?!!" Mysteriously, the only tale not listed is 'Spinalonga', which is replaced by something called 'Max!' that's summed up as "Rotten!!"

I digress. I do, you know. Perhaps I'm delaying thoughts of Norman Wisdom, though not of Christopher Fowler's tale. In 2007 Sir Norm was rehoused in a nursing home on the Isle of Man. I'm sure his fellow tenants could never have imagined that their last days would be filled with memories of his routines—perhaps some old folks' final moments may consist of them. This fate befalls several of the characters in Christopher's splendid tale, which is both horribly funny and oppressively disturbing. Its portrait of nostalgia turned sour rings all too true, and the narrator is a memorable addition to fiction's gallery of psychotics. One feels one may easily meet him.

Now behold the irrepressible Harlan, a man with a talent so large they might have named a county after him. He dislikes the word horror as applied to fiction, but several of his tales are splendid examples of it: 'Shattered Like a Glass Goblin' for certain, and 'The Whimper of Whipped Dogs' and 'I Have No Mouth and I Must Scream', and equally the novella herein. His stories don't often reach this length, but it sustains the blazing intensity of his best work without faltering. Several decades ago Harlan was kind enough to reminisce about a visit to San Quentin for a novel I was writing. He lent my chapter vividness but by gum, it's nothing compared with his own use of the place. Read his tale, which (in the best sense) reads like the writing of a man possessed.

Even more than Harlan, Paul J. McAuley is more usually associated with science fiction than with horror. The gulf is less wide than it's sometimes perceived to be, however. Where Brian Aldiss cites *Frankenstein* as the first work of modern science fiction, other commentators—Lovecraft, for instance—claim it for horror, and so it's entirely appropriate that Paul's tale should evoke Mary Shelley's seminal novel. He recalls James Whale's gay romp *Bride of Frankenstein* as well (in which, it seems to me, the title applies to Dr. Pretorius, who seduces Frankenstein away from an unconsummated marriage to help him give birth to a creature). Paul brings to this story all the attention to detail that makes his science fiction so vivid and convincing. Its terror and pathos are worthy of the original *Frankenstein*. I would happily have helped to choose it for that year's volume of *Best New Horror*, but 1994 was the year I fled as editor, leaving stalwart Steve to sift the mounds of rubbish with which the field was laden. There was plenty of first-rate fiction, but the task of reading the worst of the rest was just too dispiriting. Whose gravestone graces the cover of that year's book? Whose skeletal hand claws at it from the earth?

1995 brought us the fantastic Neil Gaiman—brought him to horror, that is, where he intermittently perches before soaring away on another flight of wonder. Can I take a little credit? Ten years before, as a young journalist he'd interviewed me in the resoundingly empty house to which my family and I were about to move. In 'Queen of Knives' he's drawing on much earlier experiences, though. Like his superb work in comics, poetry enables him to say a great deal in enviably few words. What exactly has been said seems to shift and grow with every re-reading. Note the appearance, as in the Fowler tale, of a British comedian from the past. Comedy and horror intersect in many ways.

I can certainly congratulate myself over Terry Lamsley—over putting out the word about him, at any rate. Having picked up his first collection, *Under the Crust*, at the 1993 Ghost Story Society convention in Chester, I was on the phone days later to Steve Jones, enthusing about a new master of the spectral. Soon I wrote the introduction to Terry's next book, *Conference with the Dead*, from which 'The Break' is taken. Like Neil's piece, this story finds weirdness in a family holiday. Not that in many cases it needs much finding; after all, one of the strangest places most of us are likely to end up is our own child-hood. Often the point of the child's viewpoint in a horror story is not just to enhance the terror but to remind us what it was like. 'The Break' is a fine example of a tradition that began with Machen's masterly 'The White People'.

In his great novel *I Am Legend* (thrice indifferently filmed) Richard Matheson showed us the world overtaken by vampires, and his prophecy has come to pass, at least in terms of copies on the shelves. Series of books proliferate everywhere: erotica (*Muffy the Vampire Layer*), same-sex erotica (*Duffy the Vampire Gayer*), dog stories (*Wuffy the Vampire Bayer*), stories of a seaside donkey (*Gruffy the Vampire Brayer*), a football saga (*Cloughie the Vampire Player*), tales of the priesthood (*Stuffy the Vampire Prayer*), dietary aids (*Puffy the Vampire Weigher*), memoirs of feisty old folk (*Toughie the Vampire Greyer*) ... Sequels to *Dracula* are a genre in themselves, ranging from the hilarious *Carmel* (written by a bishop, it gives us the tip that vampires don't stutter and includes the line "Imagine my horror when he pulled a decapitated head from the carrier bag he was holding—and asked 'Do you recognise it?'") to Caitlín R. Kiernan's fine tale here. Its poetic compression gives it the substance of a novel in fewer than twenty pages. Like her friend Poppy Z. Brite, she brings lyricism to horror and to the theme of vampirism.

1998 is Peter Straub's year. I'm especially happy to be associated with an anthology in which he appears. Back in the 1970s I did my best to tempt him into *New Terrors* but (like Harlan Ellison and Anthony Burgess, among others) he couldn't be lured. Herman Melville's 'Bartleby the Scrivener: a Story of Wall-street' is central to his tale that follows, 'Mr. Clubb and Mr. Cuff'. In 1957 Melville's story appeared in the Faber book I cited at the outset, *Best Horror Stories*, preceded by the editor's admission that many readers might not call it horror. I'd say it was, but all the same, it might lead you to expect Peter's story to be a little staid. You'd be wrong. When he wrote *Floating Dragon* he set out to encompass all horror, but as you'll see, he didn't exhaust his imaginative capacity for it. 'Mr. Clubb and Mr. Cuff' is as intensely grisly as anything he has yet given us, and brings this first volume of our celebration to a triumphant close.

—Ramsey Campbell
Wallasey, Merseyside
February 27, 2020

BEST NEW HORROR

Stephen Gallagher
Richard Laymon
Thomas Ligotti
Brian Lumley
Robert R. McCammon
Kim Newman
Thomas Tessier
Karl Edward Wagner
Ian Watson
Robert Westall
Cherry Wilder
Chet Williamson
and others

Edited by Stephen Jones
and Ramsey Campbell

[1989]

I N 1989, PUBLISHER Nick Robinson decided to create a
companion volume to Gardner Dozois' excellent *The Year's Best
Science Fiction* series (retitled *Best New SF* for the UK market).

So when he asked me if I would be interested in editing an annual
"Year's Best" horror anthology, containing a selection of stories chosen
from those initially published in the preceding year, I immediately
agreed. However, I had a couple of stipulations.

The first was that I ask Ramsey Campbell—in my opinion one of the
most intelligent and knowledgeable authors in the horror field—to co-
edit the book with me. The second was that I check first that it was
okay with our old friend Karl Edward Wagner, who was currently
editing *The Year's Best Horror Stories* series for DAW Books. (Ellen
Datlow and Terri Windling had started *The Year's Best Fantasy and
Horror* for St. Martin's Press a couple of years previously, but I did not
consider that direct competition as half the book was made up of
fantasy stories.) Karl graciously gave us his blessing (which is why the
first volume was dedicated to him), and Ramsey and I started reading
everything we could get our hands on.

That first volume contained twenty stories, and marked the only
time we used tales by Robert Westall and Richard Laymon, who both
passed away far too early. Our Introduction, which was an overview of
horror in 1989, covered just seven pages, and Kim Newman and I

carried our Necrology column over from the defunct film magazine *Shock Xpress*. It ran one page longer than the Introduction.

In our summation, Ramsey and I expressed concern that the 1980s horror boom could not be sustained and, to survive, the genre would have to move out of the mid-list category. In retrospect, we were depressingly prescient.

For the cover, the publisher chose Les Edwards' iconic painting of 'The Croglin Vampire' (if you want to see where *Buffy the Vampire Slayer* got its inspiration from for The Gentlemen in the classic 'Hush' episode, look no further). The only thing Robinson did not have was a logo, so I quickly knocked up a concept using a sheet of Letraset transfer lettering. To my surprise, they used it on the final book.

In the UK, Robinson Publishing issued that first volume of *Best New Horror* in trade paperback with gold foil on the cover. For the US, Carroll & Graf decided to do it as a hardcover (without the foil), which they then reprinted as a trade paperback the following year.

When it came to selecting a story from that inaugural edition, it was not difficult. For me, Brian Lumley's 'No Sharks in the Med' has always been a powerful slice of psychological (as opposed to supernatural) horror, and a perfect example of one of my favourite sub-genres—the "fish out of water" tourist who stumbles into a situation over which they have no control...

BRIAN LUMLEY

No Sharks in the Med

BRIAN LUMLEY produced his early work very much under the influence of the *Weird Tales* authors, H.P. Lovecraft, Robert E. Howard and Clark Ashton Smith, and his first stories and books were published by the then "dean of macabre publishers", August W. Derleth, through his now legendary Arkham House imprint.

Lumley began writing full time in 1980, and four years later completed his breakthrough novel *Necroscope*® featuring Harry Keogh, a psychically endowed hero who is able to communicate with the teeming dead. *Necroscope* has now grown to a series of books, published in numerous countries and many millions of copies. In addition, *Necroscope* comic books, graphic novels, a role-playing game, quality figurines, and a series of audio books in Germany have been created from the popular series.

Along with the *Necroscope* titles, Lumley is also the author of more than forty other books, and his vampire story 'Necros' became one of the first episodes of Showtime's erotic horror anthology TV series, *The Hunger*.

He is the winner of a British Fantasy Award, a *Fear* Magazine Award, a Lovecraft Film Festival Association "Howie", the World Horror Convention's Grand Master Award, the Horror Writers Association's Lifetime Achievement Award, and the World Fantasy Convention's Lifetime Achievement Award.

A regular visitor to the Greek islands for many years, Lumley drew on first-hand experience in the following story to weave a terrifying chiller that just *could* happen.

"Ever since I spent three years on Cyprus in the mid-1960s," he explains, "I've been in love with the Greek islands. There is something about the air, the light, the sea. Over the next five decades I would still go out there at least once a year to an island similar to the one in my story—but not *too* similar—to enjoy the company of Greek friends, and to spearfish and hunt octopuses.

"And before anyone gets upset, I never shot anything I couldn't eat; most of my catch went into a freezer in the local taverna, ending up on a plate the same night."

C USTOMS WAS NON-EXISTENT; people bring duty frees *out* of Greece, not in. As for passport control: a pair of tanned, hairy, bored-looking characters in stained, too-tight uniforms and peaked caps were in charge. One to take your passport, find the page to be franked, scan photograph and bearer both with a blank gaze that took in absolutely nothing unless you happened to be female and stacked (in which case it took in everything and more), then pass the passport on. Geoff Hammond thought: *I wonder if that's why they call them passports?* The second one took the little black book from the first and hammered down on it with his stamp, impressing several pages but no one else, then handed the important document back to its owner— but grudgingly, as if he didn't believe you could be trusted with it.

This second one, the one with the rubber stamp, had a brother. They could be, probably were, twins. Five-eightish, late twenties, lots of shoulders and no hips; raven hair shiny with grease, so tightly curled it looked permed; brown eyes utterly vacant of expression. The only difference was the uniform: the fact that the brother on the home-and-dry side of the barrier didn't have one. Leaning on the barrier, he twirled cheap, yellow-framed, dark-lensed glasses like glinting propellers, observed almost speculatively the incoming holidaymakers. He wore shorts, frayed where they hugged his thick thighs, barely long enough to be decent. *Hung like a bull!* Geoff thought. It was almost embarrassing. Dressed for the benefit of the single girls, obviously. He'd be hoping they were taking notes for later. His chances might improve if he were two inches taller and had a face. But he didn't; the face was as vacant as the eyes.

Then Geoff saw what it was that was wrong with those eyes: beyond the barrier, the specimen in the bulging shorts was wall-eyed. Likewise his twin punching the passports. Their right eyes had white pupils that stared like dead fish. The one in the booth wore lightly-tinted glasses, so that you didn't notice until he looked up and stared directly at you. Which in Geoff's case he hadn't; but he was certainly looking at Gwen. Then he glanced at Geoff, patiently waiting, and said: "Together, you?" His voice was a shade too loud, making it almost an accusation.

Different names on the passports, obviously! But Geoff wasn't going to stand here and explain how they were just married and Gwen hadn't had time to make the required alterations. That really *would* be embarrassing! In fact (and come to think of it), it might not even be legal. Maybe she should have changed it right away, or got something done with it, anyway, in London. The honeymoon holiday they'd chosen was one of those get-it-while-it's-going deals, a last-minute half-price seat-filler, a gift horse; and they'd been pushed for time. But what the hell—this was 1987, wasn't it?

"Yes," Geoff finally answered. "Together."

"Ah!" the other nodded, grinned, appraised Gwen again with a raised eyebrow, before stamping her passport and handing it over.

Wall-eyed bastard! Geoff thought.

When they passed through the gate in the barrier, the other wall-eyed bastard had disappeared...

Stepping through the automatic glass doors from the shade of the airport building into the sunlight of the coach terminus was like opening the door of a furnace; it was a replay of the moment when the plane's air-conditioned passengers trooped out across the tarmac to board the buses waiting to convey them to passport control. You came out into the sun fairly crisp, but by the time you'd trundled your luggage to the kerbside and lifted it off the trolley your armpits were already sticky. One o'clock, and the temperature must have been hovering around eighty-five for hours. It not only beat down on you but, trapped in the concrete, beat up as well. Hammerblows of heat.

A mini-skirted courier, English as a rose and harassed as hell—her white blouse soggy while her blue and white hat still sat jaunty on her head—came fluttering, clutching her millboard with its bulldog clip and thin sheaf of notes. "Mr. Hammond and Miss—" she glanced at her notes, "—Pinter?"

"Mr. and Mrs. Hammond," Geoff answered. He lowered his voice and continued confidentially: "We're all proper, legitimate, and true. Only our identities have been altered in order to protect our passports."

"Um?" she said.

Too deep for her, Geoff thought, sighing inwardly.

"Yes," said Gwen, sweetly. "We're the Hammonds."

"Oh!" the girl looked a little confused. "It's just that—"

"I haven't changed my passport yet," said Gwen, smiling.

"Ah!" Understanding finally dawned. The courier smiled nervously at Geoff, turned again to Gwen. "Is it too late for congratulations?"

"Four days," Gwen answered.

"Well, congratulations anyway."

Geoff was eager to be out of the sun. "Which is our coach?" he wanted to know. "Is it—could it possibly be—air conditioned?" There were several coaches parked in an untidy cluster a little farther up the kerb.

Again the courier's confusion, also something of embarrassment showing in her bright blue eyes. "You're going to—Achladi?"

Geoff sighed again, this time audibly. It was her business to know where they were going. It wasn't a very good start.

"Yes," she cut in quickly, before he or Gwen could comment. "Achladi—but not by coach! You see, your plane was an hour late; the coach for Achladi couldn't be held up for just one couple; but it's okay—you'll have the privacy of your own taxi, and of course Skymed will foot the bill."

She went off to whistle up a taxi and Geoff and Gwen glanced at each other, shrugged, sat down on their cases. But in a moment the courier was back, and behind her a taxi came rolling, nosing into the kerb. Its driver jumped out, whirled about opening doors, the boot, stashing cases while Geoff and Gwen got into the back of the car. Then, throwing his straw hat down beside him as he climbed into the driving seat and slammed his door, the young Greek looked back at his passengers and smiled. A single gold tooth flashed in a bar of white. But the smile was quite dead, like the grin of a shark before he bites, and the voice when it came was phlegmy, like pebbles colliding in mud. "Achladi, yes?"

"Ye—" Geoff began, paused, and finished: "—es! Er, Achladi, right!" Their driver was the wall-eyed passport-stamper's wall-eyed brother.

"I Spiros," he declared, turning the taxi out of the airport. "And you?"

Something warned Geoff against any sort of familiarity with this one. In all this heat, the warning was like a breath of cold air on the back of his neck. "I'm Mr. Hammond," he answered, stiffly. "This is my wife." Gwen turned her head a little and frowned at him.

"I'm—" she began.

"My *wife!*" Geoff said again. She looked surprised but kept her peace.

Spiros was watching the road where it narrowed and wound. Already out of the airport, he skirted the island's main town and raced for foothills rising to a spine of half-clad mountains. Achladi was maybe half an hour away, on the other side of the central range. The road soon became a track, a thick layer of dust over pot-holed tarmac and cobbles; in short, a typical Greek island road. They slowed down a little through a village where white-walled houses lined the way, with lemon groves set back between and behind the dwellings, and were left with bright flashes of bougainvillea-framed balconies burning like after-images on their retinas. Then Spiros gave it the gun again.

Behind them, all was dust kicked up by the spinning wheels and the suction of the car's passing. Geoff glanced out of the fly-specked rear window. The cloud of brown dust, chasing after them, seemed ominous in the way it obscured the so-recent past. And turning front again, Geoff saw that Spiros kept his strange eye mainly on the road ahead, and the good one on his rearview. But watching what? The dust? No, he was looking at . . .

At Gwen! The interior mirror was angled directly into her cleavage.

They had been married only a very short time. The day when he'd take pride in the jealousy of other men—in their coveting his wife— was still years in the future. Even then, look but don't touch would be the order of the day. Right now it was "watch where you're looking," and possession was ninety-nine point nine percent of the law. As for the other point one per cent: well, there was nothing much you could do about what the lecherous bastards were thinking!

Geoff took Gwen's elbow, pulled her close and whispered: "Have you noticed how tight he takes the bends? He does it so we'll bounce about a bit. He's watching how your tits jiggle!"

She'd been delighting in the scenery, hadn't even noticed Spiros, his eyes or anything. For a beautiful girl of twenty-three, she was remarkably naïve, and it wasn't just an act. It was one of the things Geoff loved best about her. Only eighteen months her senior, Geoff hardly considered himself a man of the world; but he did know a rat when he smelled one. In Spiros's case he could smell several sorts.

"He . . . *what*—?" Gwen said out loud, glancing down at herself. One button too many had come open in her blouse, showing the edges of her cups. Green eyes widening, she looked up and spotted Spiros's rearview. He grinned at her through the mirror and licked his lips, but without deliberation. He was naïve, too, in his way. In his different sort of way.

"Sit over here," said Geoff out loud, as she did up the offending button *and* the one above it. "The view is much better on this side." He half-stood, let her slide along the seat behind him. Both of Spiros's eyes were now back on the road . . .

Ten minutes later they were up into a pass through gorgeous pine-clad slopes so steep they came close to sheer. Here and there scree slides showed through the greenery, or a thrusting outcrop of rock. "Mountains," Spiros grunted, without looking back.

"You have an eye for detail," Geoff answered.

Gwen gave his arm a gentle nip, and he knew she was thinking *sarcasm is the lowest form of wit—and it doesn't become you!* Nor cruelty, apparently. Geoff had meant nothing special by his "eye" remark, but Spiros was sensitive. He groped in the glove compartment for his yellow-rimmed sunshades, put them on. And drove in a stony silence for what looked like being the rest of the journey.

Through the mountains they sped, and the west coast of the island opened up like a gigantic travel brochure. The mountains seemed to go right down to the sea, rocks merging with that incredible, aching blue. And they could see the village down there: Achladi, like something out of a dazzling dream perched on both sides of a spur that gentled into the ocean.

"Beautiful!" Gwen breathed.

"Yes," Spiros nodded. "Beautiful, thee village." Like many Greeks speaking English, his definite articles all sounded like *thee*. "For fish, for thee swims, thee sun—is beautiful."

After that it was all downhill; winding, at times precipitous, but the view was never less than stunning. For Geoff, it brought back memories of Cyprus. Good ones, most of them, but one bad one that always made him catch his breath, clench his fists. The reason he hadn't been too keen on coming back to the Med in the first place. He closed his eyes in an attempt to force the memory out of mind, but that only made it worse, the picture springing up that much clearer.

He was a kid again, just five years old, late in the summer of '67. His father was a Staff-Sergeant Medic, his mother with the QARANCs; both of them were stationed in Dhekelia, a Sovereign Base Area garrison just up the coast from Larnaca where they had married quarter accommodation. They had met and married in Berlin, spent three years there, then got posted out to Cyprus together. With two years done in Cyprus, Geoff's father had a year to go to complete his twenty-two. After their last year in the sun ... there had been a place waiting for him in the ambulance pool of one of London's big hospitals. Geoff's mother had hoped to get on the nursing staff of the same hospital. But before any of that ...

Geoff had started school in Dhekelia, but on those rare weekends when both of his parents were free of duty, they would all go off to the beach together. And that had been his favourite thing in all the world: the beach with its golden sand and crystal-clear, safe, shallow water. But sometimes, seeking privacy, they'd take a picnic basket and drive east along the coast until the road became a track, then find a way down the cliffs and swim from the rocks up around Cape Greco. That's where it had happened.

"Geoff!" Gwen tugged at his arm, breaking the spell. He was grateful to be dragged back to reality. "Were you sleeping?"

"Daydreaming," he answered.

"Me, too!" she said. "I think I must be. I mean, just *look* at it!"

They were winding down a steep ribbon of road cut into the mountain's flank, and Achladi was directly below them. A coach coming up squeezed by, its windows full of brown, browned-off faces. Holidaymakers going off to the airport, going home. Their holidays were over but Geoff's and Gwen's was just beginning, and the village they had come to *was* truly beautiful. Especially beautiful because it was unspoiled. This was only Achladi's second season; before they'd built the airport you could only get here by boat. Very few had bothered.

Geoff's vision of Cyprus and his bad time quickly receded; while he didn't consider himself a romantic like Gwen, still he recognised Achladi's magic. And now he supposed he'd have to admit that they'd made the right choice.

White-walled gardens; red tiles, green-framed windows, some flat roofs and some with a gentle pitch; bougainvillea cascading over white, arched balconies; a tiny white church on the point of the spur where broken rocks finally tumbled into the sea; massive ancient olive trees in walled plots at every street junction, and grapevines on trellises giving a little shade and dappling every garden and patio. That, at a glance, was Achladi. A high sea wall kept the sea at bay, not that it could ever be a real threat, for the entire front of the village fell within the harbour's crab's-claw moles. Steps went down here and there from the sea wall to the rocks; a half-dozen towels were spread wherever there was a flat or gently-inclined surface to take them, and the sea bobbed with a half-dozen heads, snorkels and face-masks. Deep water here, but a quarter-mile to the south, beyond the harbour wall, a shingle beach stretched like the webbing between the toes of some great beast for maybe a hundred yards to where a second claw-like spur came down from the mountains. As for the rest of this western coastline: as far as the eye could see both north and south, it looked like sky, cliff and sea to Geoff. Cape Greco all over again. But before his memories could return to that:

"Is Villa Eleni, yes?" Spiros's gurgling voice intruded. "Him have no road. No can drive. I carry thee bags."

The road went right down the ridge of the spur to the little church. Halfway, it was crossed at right-angles by a second motor road which contained and serviced a handful of shops. The rest of the place was made up of streets too narrow or too perpendicular for cars. A few ancient scooters put-putted and sputtered about, donkeys clip-clopped here and there, but that was all. Spiros turned his vehicle about at the main junction (the *only* real road junction) and parked in the shade of a massive, ancient olive tree. He went to get the luggage. There were two large cases, two small ones. Geoff would have shared the load equally but found himself brushed aside; Spiros took the elephant's share and left him with the small-fry. He wouldn't have minded, but it was obviously the Greek's chance to show off his strength.

Leading the way up a steep cobbled ramp of a street, Spiros's muscular buttocks kept threatening to burst through the thin stuff of his cut-down jeans. And because the holidaymakers followed on a little way behind, Geoff was aware of Gwen's eyes on Spiros's tanned, gleaming thews. There wasn't much of anywhere else to look. "Him Tarzan, you Jane," he commented, but his grin was a shade too dry.

"Who you?" she answered, her nose going up in the air. "Cheetah?"

"*Uph, uph!*" said Geoff.

"Anyway," she relented. "Your bottom's nicer. More compact."

He saved his breath, made no further comment. Even the light cases seemed heavy. If he was Cheetah, that must make Spiros Kong! The Greek glanced back once, grinned in his fashion, and kept going. Breathing heavily, Geoff and Gwen made an effort to catch up, failed miserably. Then, toward the top of the way Spiros turned right into an arched alcove, climbed three stone steps, put down his cases and paused at a varnished pine door. He pulled on a string to free the latch, shoved the door open and took up his cases again. As the English couple came round the corner he was stepping inside. "Thee Villa Eleni," he said, as they followed him in.

Beyond the door was a high-walled courtyard of black and white pebbles laid out in octopus and dolphin designs. A split-level patio fronted the "villa", a square box of a house whose one redeeming feature had to be a retractable sun-awning shading the windows and most of the patio. It also made an admirable refuge from the dazzling white of everything.

There were whitewashed concrete steps climbing the side of the building to the upper floor, with a landing that opened onto a wooden-railed balcony with its own striped awning. Beach towels and an outsize lady's bathing costume were hanging over the rail, drying, and all the windows were open.

Someone was home up there, maybe. Or perhaps sitting in a shady taverna sipping iced drinks. But downstairs, a key with a label had been left in the keyhole of a louvred, fly-screened door. Geoff read the label, which said simply: MR. HAMMOND. The booking had been made in his name.

"This is us," he said to Gwen, turning the key.

They went in, Spiros following with the large cases. Inside, the cool air was a blessing. Now they would like to explore the place on their own, but the Greek was there to do it for them. And he knew his way around. He put the cases down, opened his arms to indicate the central room. "For sit, talk, thee resting." Then he indicated a tiled area in one corner, with a refrigerator, sink-unit and two-ring electric cooker. "For thee toast, coffee . . . thee fish-and-chips, eh?" He shoved open the door of a tiny room tiled top to bottom, containing a shower, wash-basin and WC. "And this one," he said, without further explanation. Then five strides back across the floor took him to another room, low-ceilinged, pine-beamed, with a Lindosian double bed built in under louvred windows. He cocked his head on one side. "And thee bed—just thee one . . ."

"That's all we'll need," Geoff answered, his annoyance building.

"Yes," Gwen said. "Well, thank you, er, Spiros—you're very kind. And we'll be fine now."

Spiros scratched his chin, went back into the main room and sprawled in an easy chair. "Outside is hot," he said. "Here she is cool—*chrio*, you know?"

Geoff went to him. "It's *very* hot," he agreed, "and we're sticky. Now we want to shower, put our things away, look around. Thanks for your help. You can go now."

Spiros stood up and his face went slack, his expression more blank than before. His wall-eye looked strange through its tinted lens. "Go now?" he repeated.

Geoff sighed. "Yes, go!"

The corner of Spiros's mouth twitched, drew back a little to show his gold tooth. "I fetch from airport, carry cases."

"Ah!" said Geoff, getting out his wallet. "What do I owe you?" He'd bought drachmas at the airport in London.

Spiros sniffed, looked scornful, half-turned away. "One thousand," he finally answered, bluntly.

"That's about four pounds and fifty pence," Gwen said from the bedroom doorway. "Sounds reasonable."

"Except it was supposed to be on Skymed," Geoff scowled. He paid up anyway and saw Spiros to the door. The Greek departed, sauntered indifferently across the patio to pause in the arched doorway and look back across the courtyard. Gwen had come to stand beside Geoff in the double doorway under the awning.

The Greek looked straight at her and licked his fleshy lips. The vacant grin was back on his face. "I see you," he said, nodding with a sort of slow deliberation.

As he closed the door behind him, Gwen muttered, "Not if I see you first! *Ugh!*"

"I am with you," Geoff agreed. "*Not* my favourite local character!"

"Spiros," she said. "Well, and it suits him to a tee. It's about as close as you can get to spider! And that one *is* about as close as you can get!"

They showered, fell exhausted on the bed—but not so exhausted that they could just lie there without making love.

Later—with suitcases emptied and small valuables stashed out of sight, and spare clothes all hung up or tucked away—dressed in light, loose gear, sandals, sunglasses, it was time to explore the village. "And afterwards," Gwen insisted, "we're swimming!" She'd packed their towels and swimwear in a plastic beach bag. She loved to swim, and Geoff might have, too, except...

But as they left their rooms and stepped out across the patio, the varnished door in the courtyard wall opened to admit their upstairs neighbours, and for the next hour all thoughts of exploration and a dip in the sea were swept aside. The elderly couple who now introduced themselves gushed, there was no other way to describe it. He was George and she was Petula.

"My *dear*," said George, taking Gwen's hand and kissing it, "such a *stunning* young lady, and how sad that I've only two days left in which to enjoy you!" He was maybe sixty-four or five, ex-handsome but sagging a bit now, tall if a little bent, and brown as a native. With a small grey moustache and faded blue eyes, he looked like someone who might have piloted Spitfires in World War II! Alas, he wore the most blindingly colourful shorts and shirt that Gwen had ever seen. But charming... oh, he was that!

Petula was very large, about as tall as George but two of him in girth. She was just as brown, though, (and so presumably didn't mind exposing it all), seemed equally if not more energetic, and was never at a loss for words. They were a strange, paradoxical pair: very upper-crust, but at the same time very much down-to-earth. If Petula tended to speak with plums in her mouth, certainly they were of a very tangy variety.

"He'll flatter you to death, my dear," she told Gwen, ushering the newcomers up the steps at the side of the house and onto the high balcony. "But you must *never* take your eyes off his hands! Stage magicians have nothing on George. Forty years ago he magicked himself into my bedroom, and he's been there ever since!"

"She seduced me!" said George, bustling indoors.

"I did not!" Petula was petulant. "What? Why he's quite simply a wolf in...in a Joseph suit!"

"A Joseph suit?" George repeated her. He came back out onto the balcony with brandy-sours in a frosted jug, a clattering tray of ice-cubes, slices of sugared lemon and an eggcup of salt for the sours. He put the lot down on a plastic table, said: "Ah!—glasses!" and ducked back inside again.

"Yes," his wife called after him, pointing at his Bermudas and Hawaiian shirt. "Your clothes of many colours!"

It was all good fun and Geoff and Gwen enjoyed it. They sat round the table on plastic chairs, and George and Petula entertained them. It made for a very nice welcome to Achladi indeed.

"Of course," said George after a while, when they'd settled down a little, "we first came here eight years ago, when there were no flights, just boats. Now that people are flying in—" he shrugged, "—two more seasons and there'll be belly-dancers and hotdog stands! But for now... it's just perfect. Will you look at that view?"

The view from the balcony was very fetching. "From up here we can see the entire village," said Gwen. "You must point out the best shops, the bank or exchange or whatever, all the places we'll need to know about."

George and Petula looked at each other and smiled knowingly.

"Oh?" said Gwen.

Geoff checked their expressions, nodded, made a guess: "There are no places we need to know about."

"Well, three, actually," said Petula. "Four if you count Dimi's—the taverna. Oh, there are other places to eat, but Dimi's is *the* place. Except I feel I've spoilt it for you now. I mean, that really is something you should have discovered for yourself. It's half the fun, finding the best place to eat!"

"What about the other three places we should know about?" Gwen inquired. "Will knowing those spoil it for us, too? Knowing them in advance, I mean?"

"Good Lord, no!" George shook his head. "Vital knowledge, young lady!"

"The baker's," said Petula. "For fresh rolls—daily." She pointed it out, blue smoke rising from a cluster of chimneypots. "Also the booze shop, for booze—"

"—Also daily," said George, pointing. "Right there on that corner—where the bottles glint. D'you know, they have an *ancient* Metaxa so cheap you wouldn't—"

"*And*," Petula continued, "the path down to the beach. Which is... over there."

"But tell us," said George, changing the subject, "are you married, you two? Or is that too personal?"

"Oh, of *course* they're married!" Petula told him. "But very recently, because they still sit so close together. Touching. You see?"

"Ah!" said George. "Then we shan't have another elopement."

"You know, my dear, you really are an old idiot," said Petula, sighing. "I mean, elopements are for lovers to be together. And these two already *are* together!"

Geoff and Gwen raised their eyebrows. "An elopement?" Gwen said. "Here? When did this happen?"

"Right here, yes," said Petula. "Ten days ago. On our first night we had a young man downstairs, Gordon. On his own. He was supposed to be here with his fiancée but she's jilted him. He went out with us, had a few too many in Dimi's and told us all about it. A Swedish girl—very lovely, blonde creature—was also on her own. She helped steer him back here and, I suppose, tucked him in. She had her own place, mind you, and didn't stay."

"But the next night she did!" George enthused.

"And then they ran off," said Petula, brightly. "Eloped! As simple as that. We saw them once, on the beach, the next morning. Following which—"

"—Gone!" said George.

"Maybe their holidays were over and they just went home," said Gwen, reasonably.

"No," George shook his head. "Gordon had come out on our plane, his holiday was just starting. She'd been here about a week and a half, was due to fly out the day after they made off together."

"They paid for their holidays and then deserted them?" Geoff frowned. "Doesn't make any sense."

"Does anything, when you're in love?" Petula sighed.

"The way I see it," said George, "they fell in love with each other, and with Greece, and went off to explore all the options."

"Love?" Gwen was doubtful. "On the rebound?"

"If she'd been a mousey little thing, I'd quite agree," said Petula. "But no, she really was a beautiful girl."

"And him a nice lad," said George. "A bit sparse but clean, good-looking. And I rather suspect they were both a bit well off. Wasting their planned holiday wouldn't much matter...they certainly weren't wasting time!"

"Indeed, they were much like you two," his wife added. "I mean, not *like* you, but like you."

"Cheers," said Geoff, wryly. "I mean, I know I'm not Mr. Universe, but—"

"Tight in the bottom!" said Petula. "That's what the girls like these days. You'll do all right."

"See," said Gwen, nudging him. "Told you so!"

But Geoff was still frowning. "Didn't anyone look for them? What if they'd been involved in an accident or something?"

"No," said Petula. "They were seen boarding a ferry in the main town. Indeed, one of the local taxi drivers took them there. Spiros."

Gwen and Geoff's turn to look at each other. "A strange fish, that one," said Geoff.

George shrugged. "Oh, I don't know. You know him, do you? It's that eye of his which makes him seem a bit sinister..."

Maybe he's right, Geoff thought.

Shortly after that, their drinks finished, the newcomers went off to start their explorations...

The village was a maze of cobbled, white-washed alleys. Even as tiny as it was you could get lost in it, but never for longer than the length of a street. Going downhill, no matter the direction, you'd come to the sea. Uphill you'd come to the main road, or if you didn't, then turn the next corner and *continue* uphill, and then you would. The most well-trodden alley, with the shiniest cobbles, was the one that led to a hard-packed path, which in turn led to the beach. Pass the "booze shop" on the corner twice, and you'd know where it was always. The window was plastered with labels, some familiar and others entirely conjectural; inside, steel shelving went floor to ceiling, stacked with every conceivable brand; even the more exotic and (back home) wildly expensive stuffs were on view, often in ridiculously cheap, three-litre, duty-free bottles with their own chrome taps and display stands.

"Courvoisier!" said Gwen, appreciatively.

"Grand Marnier, surely!" Geoff protested. "What, five pints of Grand Marnier? At that price? Can you believe it? But that's to take home. What about while we're here?"

"Coconut liqueur," she said. "Or better still, mint chocolate—to complement our midnight coffees."

They found several small tavernas, too, with people seated outdoors at tiny tables under the vines. Chicken portions and slabs of lamb sputtering on spits; small fishes sizzling over charcoal; *moussaka* steaming in long trays...

Dimi's was down on the harbour, where a wide, low wall kept you safe from falling in the sea. They had a Greek salad which they divided two ways, tiny cubes of lamb roasted on wooden slivers, a half-bottle of local white wine costing pennies. As they ate and sipped the wine, so they began to relax; the hot sunlight was tempered by an almost imperceptible breeze off the sea.

Geoff said: "Do you really feel energetic? Damned if I do!"

She didn't feel full of boundless energy, no, but she wasn't going down without a fight. "If it was up to you," she said, "we'd just sit here and watch the fishing nets dry, right?"

"Nothing wrong with taking it easy," he answered. "We're on holiday, remember?"

"Your idea of taking it easy means being bone idle!" she answered. "*I* say we're going for a dip, then back to the villa for siesta and you know, and—"

"Can we have the you know before the siesta?" He kept a straight face.

"—*And* then we'll be all settled in, recovered from the journey, ready for tonight. Insatiable!"

"Okay," he shrugged. "Anything you say. But we swim from the beach, not from the rocks."

Gwen looked at him suspiciously. "That was almost too easy."

Now he grinned. "It was the thought of, well, you know, that did it," he told her...

Lying on the beach, panting from their exertions in the sea, with the sun lifting the moisture off their still-pale bodies, Gwen said: "I don't understand."

"Hmm?"

"You swim very well. I've always thought so. So what is this fear of the water you complain about?"

"First," Geoff answered, "I don't swim very well. Oh, for a hundred yards I'll swim like a dolphin—any more than that and I do it like a brick! I can't float. If I stop swimming I sink."

"So don't stop."

"When you get tired, you stop."

"What was it that made you frightened of the water?"

He told her:

"I was a kid in Cyprus. A little kid. My father had taught me how to swim. I used to watch him diving off the rocks, oh, maybe twenty or thirty feet high, into the sea. I thought I could do it, too. So one day when my folks weren't watching, I tried. I must have hit my head on something on the way down. Or maybe I simply struck the water all wrong. When they spotted me floating in the sea, I was just about done for. My father dragged me out. He was a medic—the kiss of life and all that. So now I'm not much for swimming, and I'm absolutely *nothing* for diving! I will swim—for a splash, in shallow water, like today—but that's my limit. And I'll only go in from a beach. I can't stand cliffs, height. It's as simple as that. You married a coward. So there."

"No I didn't," she said. "I married someone with a great bottom. Why didn't you tell me all this before?"

"You didn't ask me. I don't like to talk about it because I don't much care to remember it. I was just a kid, and yet I knew I was going to die. And I knew it wouldn't be nice. I still haven't got it out of my system, not completely. And so the less said about it the better."

A beach ball landed close by, bounced, rolled to a standstill against Gwen's thigh. They looked up. A brown, burly figure came striding. They recognised the frayed, bulging shorts. Spiros.

"Hallo," he said, going down into a crouch close by, forearms resting on his knees. "Thee beach. Thee ball. I swim, play. You swim?" (This to Geoff.) "You come swim, throwing thee ball?"

Geoff sat up. There were half-a-dozen other couples on the beach;

why couldn't this jerk pick on them? Geoff thought to himself: *I'm about to get sand kicked in my face!* "No," he said out loud, shaking his head. "I don't swim much."

"No swim? You frighting thee big fish? Thee sharks?"

"Sharks?" Now Gwen sat up. From behind their dark lenses she could feel Spiros's eyes crawling over her.

Geoff shook his head. "There are no sharks in the Med," he said.

"Him right," Spiros laughed high-pitched, like a woman, without his customary gurgling. A weird sound. "No sharks. I make thee jokes!" He stopped laughing and looked straight at Gwen. She couldn't decide if he was looking at her face or her breasts. Those damned sunglasses of his! "You come swim, lady, with Spiros? Play in thee water?"

"My...*God!*" Gwen sputtered, glowering at him. She pulled her dress on over her still-damp, very skimpy swimming costume, packed her towel away, picked up her sandals. When she was annoyed, she really *was* annoyed.

Geoff stood up as she made off, turned to Spiros. "Now listen—" he began.

"Ah, you go now! Is Okay. I see you." He took his ball, raced with it down the beach, hurled it out over the sea. Before it splashed down he was diving, low and flat, striking the water like a knife. Unlike Geoff, he swam very well indeed...

When Geoff caught up with his wife she was stiff with anger. Mainly angry with herself. "That was so rude of me!" she exploded.

"No it wasn't," he said. "I feel exactly the same about it."

"But he's so damned...persistent! I mean, he knows we're together, man and wife...'thee bed–just one.' How *dare* he intrude?"

Geoff tried to make light of it. "You're imagining it," he said.

"And you? Doesn't he get on your nerves?"

"Maybe I'm imagining it too. Look, he's Greek—and not an especially attractive specimen. Look at it from his point of view. All of a sudden there's a gaggle of dolly-birds on the beach, dressed in stuff his sister wouldn't wear for undies! So he tries to get closer—for a better view, as it were—so that he can get a wall-eyeful. He's no different to other blokes. Not quite as smooth, that's all."

"Smooth!" she almost spat the word out. "He's about as smooth as a badger's—"

"—Bottom!" said Geoff. "Yes, I know. If I'd known you were such a bum-fancier I mightn't have married you."

And at last she laughed, but shakily.

They stopped at the booze shop and bought brandy and a large bottle of Coca-Cola. And mint chocolate liqueur, of course, for their midnight coffees...

That night Gwen put on a blue and white dress, very Greek if cut a little low in the front, and silver sandals. Tucking a handkerchief into the breast pocket of his white jacket, Geoff thought: *she's beautiful*! With her heart-shaped face and the way her hair framed it, cut in a page-boy style that suited its shiny black sheen—and her green, green eyes—he'd always thought she looked French. But tonight she was definitely Greek. And he was so glad that she was English, and his.

Dimi's was doing a roaring trade. George and Petula had a table in the corner, overlooking the sea. They had spread themselves out in order to occupy all four seats, but when Geoff and Gwen appeared they waved, called them over. "We thought you'd drop in," George said, as they sat down. And to Gwen: "You look charming, my dear."

"Now I feel I'm really on holiday," Gwen smiled.

"Honeymoon, surely," said Petula.

"*Shh!*" Geoff cautioned her. "In England they throw confetti. Over here it's plates!"

"Your secret is safe with us," said George.

"Holiday, honeymoon, whatever," said Gwen. "Compliments from handsome gentlemen; the stars reflected in the sea; a full moon rising and *bouzouki* music floating in the air, even if it is only recorded. And—"

"—The mouth-watering smells of good Greek grub!" Geoff cut in. "Have you ordered?" He looked at George and Petula.

"A moment ago," Petula told him. "If you go into the kitchen there, Dimi will show you his menu—live, as it were. Tell him you're with us and he'll make an effort to serve us together. Starter, main course, a pudding—the lot."

"Good!" Geoff said, standing up. "I could eat the saddle off a donkey!"

"Eat the whole donkey," George told him. "The one who's going to wake you up with his racket at six-thirty tomorrow morning."

"You don't know Geoff," said Gwen. "He'd sleep through a Little Richard concert!"

"And *you* don't know Achladi donkeys!" said Petula.

In the kitchen, the huge, bearded proprietor was busy, fussing over his harassed-looking cooks. As Geoff entered he came over. "Good evenings, sir. You are new in Achladi?"

"Just today," Geoff smiled. "We came here for lunch but missed you."

"Ah!" Dimitrios gasped, then shrugged apologetically "I was having my sleeps! Every day, two hours, I sleeps. Where you stay, eh?"

"The Villa Eleni."

"Eleni? Is me!" Dimitrios beamed, straightened up. "*I* am Villa Eleni. I mean, I owns it. Eleni is thee name my wife. And you must be, er, thee Hammonds, yes?"

"Yes," Gwen told him. "And your wife's name is beautiful."

"And the villa's nice too," said Geoff, beginning to feel trapped in the conversation. "Also George and Petula. They told us about your taverna."

"Good, good!" Dimitrios beamed. "And you are eating? Excellent! Now I show you."

Geoff was given a guided tour of the ovens and the sweets trolley. He ordered, keeping it light for Gwen who had gone back to their table. "And here," said Dimitrios when all was done. "For your lady!" He produced a filigreed silver-metal brooch in the shape of a butterfly, with his logo, "Dimi's," worked into the metal of the body. Gwen probably wouldn't like it much, but politic to accept it. Geoff had noticed several female patrons wearing them, Petula included.

"That's very kind of you," he said.

Making his way back to their table, he saw Spiros was there ahead of him.

Now where the hell had he sprung from? And what the hell was he playing at?

Spiros wore tight blue jeans, (his image, obviously), and a white T-shirt a little stained down the front. He was leaning over the corner table, one hand on the wall where it overlooked the sea, the other on the table itself. Propped up, still he swayed where he bent over Gwen. George and Petula had frozen smiles on their faces and looked frankly astonished. Geoff couldn't quite see all of Gwen, for Spiros's bulk was in the way.

What he could see, of the entire mini-tableau, printed itself on his eyes as he drew closer. Adrenaline surged in him and he began to breathe faster. He barely noticed George standing up and sliding out of view. Then as the *bouzouki* tape came to an end and the taverna's low babble seemed to grow to fill the gap, Gwen's outraged voice suddenly rose over everything else:

"Get . . . your . . . filthy . . . paws . . . *off* me!" she cried.

Geoff was there. Petula had drawn as far back as possible; no longer smiling, her hand was at her throat, her eyes staring in disbelief. Spiros's left hand had caught up the V of Gwen's dress. His fingers were inside the dress and his thumb outside. In his right hand he clutched a pin like the one Dimitrios had given to Geoff. He was protesting:

"But I giving it! I putting it on thee dress! Is nice, this one. We friends. Why you shout? You no like Spiros?" His throaty, gurgling voice was slurred: waves of *ouzo* fumes literally wafted off him like the stench of a dead fish. Geoff moved in, knocked Spiros's elbow away where it leaned on the wall. Spiros must release Gwen to maintain his balance. He did so, but still crashed half-over the wall. For a moment Geoff thought he would go completely over, into the sea. But he just lolled there, shaking his head, and finally turned it to look at Geoff. There was a look on his face which Geoff couldn't quite describe. Drunken stupidity slowly turning to rage, maybe. Then he pushed himself upright, stood swaying against the wall, his fists knotting and the muscles in his arms bunching.

Hit him now, Geoff's inner man told him. *Do it, and he'll go clean over into the sea. It's not high, seven or eight feet, that's all. It'll sober the bastard up, and after that he won't trouble you again.*

But what if he couldn't swim? *You know he swims like a fish—like a bloody shark!*

"You think you better than Spiros, eh?" The Greek wobbled dangerously, steadied up and took a step in Geoff's direction.

"No!" the voice of the bearded Dimitrios was shattering in Geoff's ear. Massive, he stepped between them, grabbed Spiros by the hair, half-dragged, half-pushed him toward the exit. "No, *everybody* thinks he better!" he cried. "Because everybody *is* better! Out—" he heaved Spiros yelping into the harbour's shadows. "I tell you before, Spiros: drink all thee *ouzo* in Achladi. Is your business. But not let it ruin *my* business. Then comes thee *real* troubles, eh?"

Gwen was naturally upset. It spoiled something of the evening for her. But by the time they had finished eating, things were about back to normal. No one else in the place, other than George and Petula, had seemed especially interested in the incident anyway.

At around eleven, when the taverna had cleared a little, the girl from Skymed came in. She came over.

"Hello, Julie!" said George, finding her a chair. And, flatterer born, he added: "How lovely you're looking tonight—but of course you look lovely all the time."

Petula tut-tutted. "George, if you hadn't met me you'd be a gigolo by now, I'm sure!"

"Mr. Hammond," Julie spoke to Geoff. "I'm terribly sorry. I should have explained to Spiros that he'd recover the fare for your ride from me. Actually, I believed he understood that but apparently he didn't. I've just seen him in one of the bars and asked him how much I owed him. He was a little upset, wouldn't accept the money, told me I should see you."

"Was he sober yet?" Geoff asked, sourly.

"Er, not very, I'm afraid. Has he been a nuisance?"

Geoff coughed. "Only a *bit* of one."

"It was a thousand drachmas," said Gwen.

The courier looked a little taken aback. "Well it should only have been seven hundred."

"He did carry our bags, though," said Geoff.

"Ah! Maybe that explains it. Anyway, I'm authorised to pay you seven hundred."

"All donations are welcome," Gwen said, opening her purse and accepting the money. "But if I were you, in future I'd use someone else. This Spiros isn't a particularly pleasant fellow."

"Well he does seem to have a problem with the *ouzo*," Julie answered. "On the other hand—"

"He has *several* problems!" Geoff was sharper than he meant to be. After all, it wasn't her fault.

"—He also has the best beach," Julie finished.

"Beach?" Geoff raised an eyebrow. "He has a beach?"

"Didn't we tell you?" Petula spoke up. "Two or three of the locals have small boats in the harbour. For a few hundred drachmas they'll take you to one of a handful of private beaches along the coast. They're private because no one lives there, and there's no way in except by boat. The boatmen have their favourite places, which they guard jealously and call 'their' beaches, so that the others don't poach on them. They take you in the morning or whenever, collect you in the evening. Absolutely private...ideal for picnics...romance!" She sighed.

"What a lovely idea," said Gwen. "To have a beach of your own for the day!"

"Well, as far as I'm concerned," Geoff told her, "Spiros can keep his beach."

"Oh-oh!" said George. "Speak of the devil..."

Spiros had returned. He averted his face and made straight for the kitchens in the back. He was noticeably steadier on his feet now. Dimitrios came bowling out to meet him and a few low-muttered words passed between them. Their conversation quickly grew more heated, becoming rapid-fire Greek in moments, and Spiros appeared to be pleading his case. Finally Dimitrios shrugged, came lumbering toward the corner table with Spiros in tow.

"Spiros, he sorry," Dimitrios said. "For tonight. Too much *ouzo*. He just want be friendly."

"Is right," said Spiros, lifting his head. He shrugged helplessly. "Thee *ouzo*."

Geoff nodded. "Okay, forget it," he said, but coldly.

"Is...okay?" Spiros lifted his head a little more. He looked at Gwen. Gwen forced herself to nod. "It's okay."

Now Spiros beamed, or as close as he was likely to get to it. But still Geoff had this feeling that there was something cold and calculating in his manner.

"I make it good!" Spiros declared, nodding. "One day, I take you thee *best* beach! For thee picnic. Very private. Two peoples, no more. I no take thee money, nothing. Is good?"

"Fine," said Geoff. "That'll be fine."

"Okay," Spiros smiled his unsmile, nodded, turned away. Going out, he looked back. "I sorry," he said again; and again his shrug. "Thee *ouzo*..."

"Hardly eloquent," said Petula, when he'd disappeared.

"But better than nothing," said George.

"Things are looking up!" Gwen was happier now.

Geoff was still unsure how he felt. He said nothing...

"Breakfast is on us," George announced the next morning. He smiled down on Geoff and Gwen where they drank coffee and tested the early morning sunlight at a garden table on the patio. They were still in their dressing-gowns, eyes bleary, hair tousled.

Geoff looked up, squinting his eyes against the hurtful blue of the sky, and said: "I see what you mean about that donkey! What the hell time is it, anyway?"

"Eight-fifteen," said George. "You're lucky. Normally he's at it, oh, an hour earlier than this!" From somewhere down in the maze of alleys, as if summoned by their conversation, the hideous braying echoed yet again as the village gradually came awake.

Just before nine they set out, George and Petula guiding them to a little place bearing the paint-daubed legend: BREKFAS BAR. They climbed steps to a railed patio set with pine tables and chairs, under a varnished pine frame supporting a canopy of split bamboo. Service was good; the "English" food hot, tasty, and very cheap; the coffee dreadful!

"*Yechh!*" Gwen commented, understanding now why George and Petula had ordered tea. "Take a note, Mr. Hammond," she said. "Tomorrow, no coffee. Just fruit juice."

"We thought maybe it was us being fussy," said Petula. "Else we'd have warned you."

"Anyway," George sighed. "Here's where we have to leave you. For tomorrow we fly—literally. So today we're shopping, picking up our duty-frees, gifts, the postcards we never sent, some Greek cigarettes."

"But we'll see you tonight, if you'd care to?" said Petula.

"Delighted!" Geoff answered. "What, Zorba's Dance, *moussaka*, and a couple or three of those giant Metaxas that Dimi serves? Who could refuse?"

"Not to mention the company," said Gwen.

"About eight-thirty, then," said Petula. And off they went.

"I shall miss them," said Gwen.

"But it will be nice to be on our own for once," Geoff leaned over to kiss her.

"Hallo!" came a now familiar, gurgling voice from below. Spiros stood in the street beyond the rail, looking up at them, the sun striking sparks from the lenses of his sunglasses. Their faces fell and he couldn't fail to notice it. "Is okay," he quickly held up a hand. "I no stay. I busy. Today I make thee taxi. Later, thee boat."

Gwen gave a little gasp of excitement, clutched Geoff's arm. "The private beach!" she said. "Now that's what I'd call being on our own!" And to Spiros: "If we're ready at one o'clock, will you take us to your beach?"

"Of course!" he answered. "At one o'clock, I near Dimi's. My boat, him called *Spiros* like me. You see him."

Gwen nodded. "We'll see you then."

"Good!" Spiros nodded. He looked up at them a moment longer, and Geoff wished he could fathom where the man's eyes were. Probably up Gwen's dress. But then he turned and went on his way.

"Now we shop!" Gwen said.

They shopped, for picnic items mainly. Nothing heavy, small things. Slices of salami, hard cheese, two fat tomatoes, fresh bread, a bottle of light white wine, some feta, eggs for boiling, and a litre of crystal-clear bottled water... and as an afterthought: half-a-dozen small pats of butter, a small jar of honey, a sharp knife and a packet of doilies. No wicker basket; their little plastic coolbox would have to do. And one of their pieces of shoulder luggage for the blanket, towels, and swim-things. Geoff was no good for details; Gwen's head, to the contrary, was only happy buzzing with them. He let her get on with it, acted as beast of burden. In fact there was no burden to mention. After all, she was shopping for just the two of them, and it was as good a way as any to explore the village stores and see what was on offer. While she examined this and that, Geoff spent the time comparing the prices of various spirits with those already noted in the booze shop. So the morning passed.

At eleven-thirty they went back to the Villa Eleni for you know and a shower, and afterwards Gwen prepared the foodstuffs while Geoff lazed under the awning. No sign of George and Petula; eighty-four degrees of heat as they idled their way down to the harbour; the village had closed itself down through the hottest part of the day, and they saw no one they knew. Spiros's boat lolled like a mirrored blot on the stirless ocean, and Geoff thought: *even the fish will be finding this a bit much!* Also: *I hope there's some shade on this blasted beach!*

Spiros appeared from behind a tangle of nets. He stood up, yawned, adjusted his straw hat like a sunshade on his head. "Thee boat," he said, in his entirely unnecessary fashion, as he helped them climb aboard. *Spiros* "thee boat" was hardly a hundred per cent seaworthy, Geoff saw that immediately. In fact, in any other ocean in the world she'd be condemned. But this was the Mediterranean in July.

Barely big enough for three adults, the boat rocked a little as Spiros yanked futilely on the starter. Water seeped through boards, rotten and long since sprung, black with constant damp and badly caulked. Spiros saw Geoff's expression where he sat with his sandals in half an inch of water. He shrugged. "Is nothings," he said.

Finally the engine coughed into life, began to purr, and they were off. Spiros had the tiller; Geoff and Gwen faced him from the prow, which now lifted up a little as they left the harbour and cut straight out to sea. It was then, for the first time, that Geoff noticed Spiros's furtiveness: the way he kept glancing back towards Achladi, as if anxious not to be observed. Unlikely that they would be, for the village seemed fast asleep. Or perhaps he was just checking landmarks, avoiding rocks or reefs or what have you. Geoff looked overboard. The water seemed deep enough to him. Indeed, it seemed much *too* deep! But at least there were no sharks . . .

Well out to sea, Spiros swung the boat south and followed the coastline for maybe two-and-a-half to three miles. The highest of Achladi's houses and apartments had slipped entirely from view by the time he turned in towards land again and sought a bight in the seemingly unbroken march of cliffs. The place was landmarked: a fang of rock had weathered free, shaping a stack that reared up from the water to form a narrow, deep channel between itself and the cliffs proper. In former times a second, greater stack had crashed oceanward and now lay like a reef just under the water across the entire frontage. In effect, this made the place a lagoon: a sandy beach to the rear, safe water, and the reef of shattered, softly matted rocks where the small waves broke.

There was only one way in. Spiros gentled his boat through the deep water between the crooked outcrop and the overhanging cliff. Clear of the channel, he nosed her into the beach and cut the motor with the keel grating on grit. Close to the beach, he stepped nimbly between his passengers, jumped ashore and dragged the boat a few inches up onto the sand. Geoff passed him the picnic things, then steadied the boat while Gwen took off her sandals and made to step down where the water met the sand. But Spiros was quick off the mark.

He stepped forward, caught her up, carried her two paces up the beach and set her down. His left arm had been under her thighs, his right under her back, cradling her. But when he set her down upon her own feet his right hand had momentarily cupped her breast, which he had quite deliberately squeezed.

Gwen opened her mouth, stood gasping her outrage, unable to give it words. Geoff had got out of the boat and was picking up their things to bring them higher up the sand. Spiros, slapping him on the back, stepped round him and shoved the boat off, splashed in shallow water a moment before leaping nimbly aboard. Gwen controlled herself, said nothing. She could feel the blood in her cheeks but hoped Geoff wouldn't notice. Not here, miles from anywhere. Not in this lonely place. No, there must be no trouble here.

For suddenly it had dawned on her just how very lonely it was. Beautiful, unspoiled, a lovers' idyll—but oh so very lonely...

"You alright, love?" said Geoff, taking her elbow. She was looking at Spiros standing silent in his boat. Their eyes seemed locked, it was as if she didn't see him but the mind behind the sunglasses, behind those disparate, dispassionate eyes. A message had passed between them. Geoff sensed it but couldn't fathom it. He had almost seemed to hear Spiros say "yes", and Gwen answer "no".

"Gwen?" he said again.

"I see you—later," Spiros called, grinning. It broke the spell. Gwen looked away, and Geoff called out:

"Six-thirty, right?"

Spiros waggled a hand this way and that palm-down, as if undecided. "Six, six-thirty—something," he said, shrugging. He started his motor, waved once, chugged out of the bay between the jutting sentinel rock and the cliffs. As he passed out of sight the boat's engine roared with life, its throaty growl rapidly fading into the distance . . .

Gwen said nothing about the incident; she felt sure that if she did, then Geoff would make something of it. Their entire holiday could so easily be spoiled. It was bad enough that for her the day had already been ruined. So she kept quiet, and perhaps a little too quiet. When Geoff asked her again if anything was wrong she told him she had a headache. Then, feeling a little unclean, she stripped herself quite naked and swam while he explored the beach.

Not that there was a great deal to explore. He walked the damp sand at the water's rim to the southern extreme and came up against the cliffs where they curved out into the sea. They were quite unscalable, towering maybe eighty or ninety feet to their jagged rim. Walking the hundred or so yards back the other way, the thought came to Geoff that if Spiros didn't come back for them—that is, if anything untoward should happen to him—they'd just have to sit it out until they were found. Which, since Spiros was the only one who knew they were here, might well be a long time. Having thought it, Geoff tried to shake the idea off but it wouldn't go away. The place was quite literally a trap. Even a decent swimmer would have to have at least a mile or more in him before considering swimming out of here.

Once lodged in Geoff's brain, the concept rapidly expanded itself. Before . . . he had looked at the faded yellow and bone-white façade of the cliffs against the incredible blue of the sky with admiration; the beach had been every man's dream of tranquillity, privacy, Eden with its own Eve; the softly lapping ocean had seemed like a warm, soothing bath reaching from horizon to horizon. But now...the place was so like Cape Greco. Except at Greco there had always been a way down to the sea—and up from it...

The northern end of the beach was much like the southern, the only difference being the great fang of rock protruding from the sea. Geoff stripped, swam out to it, was aware that the water here was a great deal deeper than back along the beach. But the distance was only thirty feet or so, nothing to worry about. And there were hand and footholds galore around the base of the pillar of upthrusting rock. He hauled himself up onto a tiny ledge, climbed higher (not too high), sat on a projecting fist of rock with his feet dangling and called to Gwen. His voice surprised him, for it seemed strangely small and panting. The cliffs took it up, however, amplified and passed it on. His shout reached Gwen where she splashed; she spotted him, stopped swimming and stood up. She waved, and he marvelled at her body, her tip-tilted breasts displayed where she stood like some lovely Mediterranean nymph, all unashamed. *Venus rising from the waves.* Except that here the waves were little more than ripples.

He glanced down at the water and was at once dizzy: the way it lapped at the rock and flowed so gently in the worn hollows of the stone, all fluid and glinting motion; and Geoff's stomach following the same routine, seeming to slosh loosely inside him. *Damn* this terror of his! What was he but eight, nine feet above the sea? God, he might as well feel sick standing on a thick carpet!

He stood up, shouted, jumped outward, towards Gwen.

Down he plunged into cool, liquid blue, and fought his way to the surface, and swam furiously to the beach. There he lay, half-in, half-out of the water, his heart and lungs hammering, blood coursing through his body. It had been such a little thing—something any ten-year-old child could have done—but to him it had been such an effort. And an achievement!

Elated, he stood up, sprinted down the beach, threw himself into the warm, shallow water just as Gwen was emerging. Carried back by him she laughed, splashed him, finally submitted to his hug. They rolled in twelve inches of water and her legs went round him; and there where the water met the sand they grew gentle, then fierce, and when it was done the sea laved their heat and rocked them gently, slowly dispersing their passion...

About four o'clock they ate, but very little. They weren't hungry; the sun was too hot; the silence, at first enchanting, had turned to a droning, sun-scorched monotony that beat on the ears worse than a city's roar. And there was a smell. When the light breeze off the sea swung in a certain direction, it brought something unpleasant with it. Drying seaweed, possibly.

To provide shade, Geoff had rigged up his shirt, slacks, and a large beach towel on a frame of drifted bamboo between the brittle, sandpapered branches of an old tree washed half-way up the sand. There in this tatty, makeshift teepee they'd spread their blanket, and retreated from the pounding sun. But as the smell came again Geoff crept out of the cramped shade, stood up and shielded his eyes to look along the wall of the cliffs. "It comes...from over there," he said, pointing.

Gwen joined him. "I thought you'd explored?" she said.

"Along the tide-line," he answered, nodding slowly. "Not along the base of the cliffs. Actually, they don't look too safe, and they overhang a fair bit in places. But if you'll look where I'm pointing—there, where the cliffs are cut back—is that water glinting?"

"A spring?" she looked at him. "A waterfall?"

"Hardly a waterfall," he said. "More a dribble. But what is it that's dribbling? I mean, springs don't stink, do they?"

Gwen wrinkled her nose. "Sewage, do you think?"

"*Yecchh!*" he said. "But at least it would explain why there's no one else here. I'm going to have a look."

She followed him to the place where the cliffs were notched in a V. Out of the sunlight, they both shivered a little. They'd put on swimwear for simple decency's sake, in case a boat should pass by, but now they hugged themselves as the chill of damp stone drew off their stored heat and brought goose-pimples to flesh which sun and sea had already roughened. And there, beneath the overhanging cliff, they found in the shingle a pool formed of a steady flow from on high. Without a shadow of a doubt, the pool was the source of the carrion stench; but here in the shade its water was dark, muddied, rippled, quite opaque. If there was anything in it, then it couldn't be seen.

As for the waterfall: it forked high up in the cliff, fell in twin streams, one of which was a trickle. Leaning out over the pool at its narrowest, shallowest point, Geoff cupped his hand to catch a few droplets. He held them to his nose, shook his head. "Just water," he said. "It's the pool itself that stinks."

"Or something back there?" Gwen looked beyond the pool, into the darkness of the cave formed of the V and the overhang.

Geoff took up a stone, hurled it into the darkness and silence. Clattering echoes sounded, and a moment later—

Flies! A swarm of them, disturbed where they'd been sitting on cool, damp ledges. They came in a cloud out of the cave, sent Geoff and Gwen yelping, fleeing for the sea. Geoff was bitten twice, Gwen escaped injury. The ocean was their refuge; it shielding them while the flies dispersed or returned to their vile-smelling breeding ground.

After the murky, poisonous pool the sea felt cool and refreshing. Muttering curses, Geoff stood in the shallows while Gwen squeezed the craters of the stings in his right shoulder and bathed them with salt water. When she was done he said, bitterly: "I've *had* it with this place! The sooner the Greek gets back the better."

His words were like an invocation. Towelling themselves dry, they heard the roar of Spiros's motor, heard it throttle back, and a moment later his boat came nosing in through the gap between the rock and the cliffs. But instead of landing he stood off in the shallow water. "Hallo," he called, in his totally unnecessary fashion.

"You're early," Geoff called back. And under his breath: *Thank God!*

"Early, yes," Spiros answered. "But I have thee troubles." He shrugged.

Gwen had pulled her dress on, packed the last of their things away. She walked down to the water's edge with Geoff. "Troubles?" she said, her voice a shade unsteady.

"Thee boat," he said, and pointed into the open, lolling belly of the craft, where they couldn't see. "I hitting thee rock when I leave Achladi. Is okay, but—" And he made his fifty-fifty sign, waggling his hand with the fingers open and the palm down. His face remained impassive, however.

Geoff looked at Gwen, then back to Spiros. "You mean it's unsafe?"

"For three peoples, unsafe—maybe." Again the Greek's shrug. "I thinks, I take thee lady first. Is okay, I come back. Is bad, I find other boat."

"You can't take both of us?" Geoff's face fell.

Spiros shook his head. "Maybe big problems," he said.

Geoff nodded. "Okay," he said to Gwen. "Go just as you are. Leave all this stuff here and keep the boat light." And to Spiros: "Can you come in a bit more?"

The Greek made a clicking sound with his tongue, shrugged apologetically. "Thee boat is broked. I not want thee more breakings. You swim?" He looked at Gwen, leaned over the side and held out his hand. Keeping her dress on, she waded into the water, made her way to the side of the boat. The water only came up to her breasts, but it turned her dress to a transparent, clinging film. She grasped the upper strake with one hand and made to drag herself aboard. Spiros, leaning backwards, took her free hand.

Watching, Geoff saw her come half-out of the water—then saw her freeze. She gasped loudly and twisted her wet hand in Spiros's grasp, tugged free of his grip, flopped back down into the water. And while the Greek regained his balance, she quickly swam back ashore. Geoff helped her from the sea. "Gwen?" he said.

Spiros worked his starter, got the motor going. He commenced a slow, deliberate circling of the small bay.

"Gwen?" Geoff said again. "What is it? What's wrong?" She was pale, shivering.

"He..." she finally started to speak. "He...had an erection! Geoff, I could see it bulging in his shorts, throbbing. My God—and I know it was for me! And the boat..."

"What about the boat?" Anger was building in Geoff's heart and head, starting to run cold in his blood.

"There was no damage—none that I could see, anyway. He...he just wanted to get me into that boat, on my own!"

Spiros could see them talking together. He came angling close into the beach, called out: "I bring thee better boat. Half an hour. Is safer. I see you." He headed for the channel between the sentinel rock and the cliff, and in another moment passed from sight . . .

"Geoff, we're in trouble," Gwen said, as soon as Spiros had left. "We're in serious trouble."

"I know it," he said. "I think I've known it ever since we got here. That bloke's as sinister as they come."

"And it's not just his eye, it's his mind," said Gwen. "He's sick." Finally, she told her husband about the incident when Spiros had carried her ashore from the boat.

"So that's what that was all about," he growled. "Well, something has to be done about him. We'll have to report him."

She clutched his arm. "We have to get back to Achladi before we can do that," she said quietly. "Geoff, I don't think he intends to let us get back!"

That thought had been in his mind, too, but he hadn't wanted her to know it. He felt suddenly helpless. The trap seemed sprung and they were in it. But what did Spiros intend, and how could he possibly hope to get away with it—whatever "it" was? Gwen broke into his thoughts:

"No one knows we're here, just Spiros."

"I know," said Geoff. "And what about that couple who . . . " He let it tail off. It had just slipped from his tongue. It was the last thing he'd wanted to say.

"Do you think I haven't thought of that?" Gwen hissed, gripping his arm more tightly yet. "He was the last one to see them, according to Petula—getting on a ferry, she said. But did they?" She stripped off her dress.

"What are you doing?" he asked, breathlessly.

"We came in from the north," she answered, wading out again into the water. "There were no beaches between here and Achladi. What about to the south? There are other beaches than this one, we know that. Maybe there's one just half a mile away. Maybe even less. If I can find one where there's a path up the cliffs . . . "

"Gwen," he said. "Gwen!" Panic was rising in him to match his impotence, his rage and terror.

She turned and looked at him, looked helpless in her skimpy bikini—and yet determined, too. And to think he'd considered her naïve! Well, maybe she had been. But no more. She managed a small smile, said, "I love you."

"What if you exhaust yourself?" He could think of nothing else to say.

"I'll know when to turn back," she said. Even in the hot sunlight he felt cold, and knew she must, too. He started towards her, but she was already into a controlled crawl, heading south, out across the submerged rocks. Watching her out of sight round the southern extreme of the jutting cliffs, he stood knotting and unknotting his fists at the edge of the sea . . .

For long moments Geoff stood there, cold inside and hot out. And at the same time cold all over. Then the sense of time fleeting by overcame him. He ground his teeth, felt his frustration overflow. He wanted to shout but feared Gwen would hear him and turn back. But there must be something he could do. With his bare hands? Like what? A weapon—he needed a weapon.

There was the knife they'd bought just for their picnic. He went to their things and found it. Only a three-inch blade, but sharp! Hand to hand it must give him something of an advantage. But what if Spiros had a bigger knife? He seemed to have a bigger or better everything else.

One of the drifted tree's branches was long, straight, slender. It pointed like a mocking, sandpapered wooden finger at the unscalable cliffs. Geoff applied his weight close to the main branch. As he lifted his feet from the ground the branch broke, sending him to his knees in the sand. Now he needed some binding material. Taking his unfinished spear with him, he ran to the base of the cliffs. Various odds and ends had been driven back there by past storms. Plastic Coke bottles, fragments of driftwood, pieces of cork . . . a nylon fishing net tangled round a broken barrel!

Geoff cut lengths of tough nylon line from the net, bound the knife in position at the end of his spear. Now he felt he had a *real* advantage! He looked around. The sun was sinking leisurely towards the sea, casting Geoff's long shadow on the sand. But how long since Spiros left? How much time remained till he got back? Geoff glanced at the frowning needle of the sentinel rock. A sentinel, yes. A watcher. Or a watchtower!

He put down his spear, ran to the northern point and sprang into the sea. Moments later he was clawing at the rock, dragging himself from the water, climbing. And scarcely a thought of danger; not from the sea or the climb; not from the deep water or the height. At thirty feet the rock narrowed down; he could lean to left or right and scan the sea to the north, in the direction of Achladi. Way out on the blue, sails gleamed white in the brilliant sunlight. On the far horizon, a smudge of smoke. Nothing else.

For a moment—the merest moment—Geoff's old nausea returned. He closed his eyes and flattened himself to the rock, gripped tightly where his fingers were bedded in cracks in the weathered stone. A mass of stone shifted slightly under the pressure of his right hand, almost causing him to lose his balance. He teetered for a second, remembered Gwen...the nausea passed, and with it all fear. He stepped a little lower, examined the great slab of rock which his hand had tugged loose. And suddenly an idea burned bright in his brain.

Which was when he heard Gwen's cry, thin as a keening wind, shrilling into his bones from along the beach. He jerked his head round, saw her there in the water inside the reef, wearily striking for the shore. She looked all in. His heart leaped into his mouth, and without pause he launched himself from the rock, striking the water feet first and sinking deep. No fear or effort to it this time; no time for any of that; surfacing, he struck for the shore. Then back along the beach, panting his heart out, flinging himself down in the small waves where she knelt, sobbing, her face covered by her hands.

"Gwen, are you all right? What is it, love? What's happened? I was sure you'd exhaust yourself!"

She tried to stand up, collapsed into his arms and shivered there; he cradled her where earlier they'd made love. And at last she could tell it.

"I...I stayed close to the shore," she gasped, gradually getting her breath. "Or rather, close to the cliffs. I was looking...looking for a way up. I'd gone about a third of a mile, I think. Then there was a spot where the water was very deep and the cliffs sheer. Something touched my legs and it was like an electric shock—I mean, it was so unexpected there in that deep water. To feel something slimy touching my legs like that. *Ugh!*" And she drew several gulping breaths before continuing:

"I thought: *God, sharks!* But then I remembered: there are no sharks in the Med. Still, I wanted to be sure. So...so I turned, made a shallow dive and looked to see what...what..." She broke down into sobbing again.

Geoff could do nothing but warm her, hug her tighter yet.

"Oh, but there *are* sharks in the Med, Geoff," she finally went on. "One shark, anyway. His name is Spiros! A spider? No, *he* is a shark! Under the sea there, I saw...a girl, naked, tethered to the bottom with a rope round her ankle. And down in the deeps, a stone holding her there."

"My God!" Geoff breathed.

"Her thighs, belly, were covered in those little green swimming crabs. She was all bloated, puffy, floating upright on her own internal gasses. Fish nibbled at her. Her nipples were gone..."

"The fish!" Geoff gasped. But Gwen shook her head.

"Not the fish," she rasped. "Her arms and breasts were black with bruises. Her nipples had been bitten through—*right* through! Oh, Geoff, Geoff!" She hugged him harder than ever, shivering hard enough to shake him. "I *know* what happened to her. It was him, Spiros." She paused, tried to control her shivering, which wasn't only the after-effect of the water.

And finally she went on: "After that I had no strength. But somehow I made it back."

"Get dressed," he told her then, his voice colder than she'd ever heard it. "Quickly! No, not your dress—my trousers, shirt. The slacks will be too long for you. Roll up the bottoms. But get dressed, get warm."

She did as he said. The sun, sinking, was still hot. Soon she was warm again, and calmer. Then Geoff gave her the spear he'd made and told her what he was going to do...

There were two of them, as like as peas in a pod. Geoff saw them, and the pieces fell into place. Spiros and his brother. The island's codes were tight. These two looked for loose women; loose in their narrow eyes, anyway. And from the passports of the honeymooners it had been plain that they weren't married. Which had made Gwen a whore, in their eyes. Like the Swedish girl, who'd met a man and gone to bed with him. As easy as that. So Spiros had tried it on, the easy way at first. By making it plain that he was on offer. Now that that hadn't worked, now it was time for the hard way.

Geoff saw them coming in the boat and stopped gouging at the rock. His fingernails were cracked and starting to bleed, but the job was as complete as he could wish. He ducked back out of sight, hugged the sentinel rock and thought only of Gwen. He had one chance and mustn't miss it.

He glanced back, over his shoulder. Gwen had heard the boat's engine. She stood half-way between the sea and the waterfall with its foul pool. Her spear was grasped tightly in her hands. *Like a young Amazon*, Geoff thought. But then he heard the boat's motor cut back and put every effort into concentrating on what he was doing.

The put-put-put of the boat's exhaust came closer. Geoff took a chance, glanced round the rim of the rock. Here they came, gentling into the channel between the rock and the cliffs. Spiros's brother wore slacks; both men were naked from the waist up; Spiros had the tiller. And his brother had a shotgun!

One chance. *Only one chance!*

The boat's nose came inching forward, began a slow pass directly below. Geoff gave a mad yell, heaved at the loose wedge of rock. For a moment he thought it would stick and put all his weight into it. And then it shifted, toppled.

Below, the brothers looked up, eyes huge in tanned, startled faces. The one with the shotgun was on his feet. He saw the falling rock in the instant before it smashed down on him and drove him through the bottom of the boat. His gun went off, both barrels, and the shimmering air near Geoff's head buzzed like a nest of wasps. Then, while all below was still in a turmoil, he aimed himself at Spiros and jumped.

Thrown about in the stern of his sinking boat, Spiros was making ready to dive overboard when Geoff's feet hit him. He was hurled into the water, Geoff narrowly missing the swamped boat as he, too, crashed down into the sea. Then a mad flurry of water as they both struck out for the shore.

Spiros was there first. Crying out, wild, outraged, frightened, he dragged himself from the sea. He looked round and saw Geoff coming through the water—saw his boat disappear with only ripples to mark its passing, and no sign of his brother—and started at a lop-sided run up the beach. Towards Gwen. Geoff swam for all he was worth, flew from the sea up onto the land.

Gwen was running, heading for the V in the cliff under the waterfall. Spiros was right behind her, arms reaching. Geoff came last, the air rasping in his lungs, Hell's fires blazing in his heart. He'd drawn blood and found it to his liking. But he stumbled, fell, and when he was up again he saw Spiros closing on his quarry. Gwen was backed up against the cliff, her feet in the water at the shallow end of the vile pool. The Greek made a low, apish lunge at her and she struck at him with her spear.

She gashed his face even as he grabbed her. His hand caught in the loose material of Geoff's shirt, tearing it from her so that her breasts lolled free. Then she stabbed at him again, slicing him across the neck. His hands flew to his face and neck; he staggered back from her, tripped, and sat down in chest-deep water; Geoff arrived panting at the pool and Gwen flew into his arms. He took the spear from her, turned it towards Spiros.

But the Greek was finished. He shrieked and splashed in the pool like the madman he was, seemed incapable of getting to his feet. His wounds weren't bad, but the blood was everywhere. That wasn't the worst of it: the thing he'd tripped on had floated to the surface. It was beginning to rot, but it was—or had been—a young man. Rubbery arms and legs tangled with Spiros's limbs; a ghastly, gaping face tossed with his frantic threshing; a great black hole showed where the bloated corpse had taken a shotgun blast to the chest, the shot that had killed him.

For a little while longer Spiros fought to be rid of the thing—screamed aloud as its gaping, accusing mouth screamed horribly, silently at him—then gave up and flopped back half-in, half-out of the water. One of the corpse's arms was draped across his heaving, shuddering chest. He lay there with his hands over his face and cried, and the flies came swarming like a black, hostile cloud from the cave to settle on him.

Geoff held Gwen close, guided her away from the horror down the beach to a sea which was a deeper blue now. "It's okay," he kept saying, as much to himself as to Gwen. "It's okay. They'll come looking for us. Sooner or later, they'll come."

As it happened, it was sooner...

"A starkly contemporary, scary anthology." —*Newsweek*

BEST NEW HORROR 2

Peter Straub, Jonathan Carroll, Harlan Ellison,
K.W. Jeter, Garry Kilworth, Thomas Ligotti,
David J. Schow, Ray Garton,
Karl Edward Wagner, F. Paul Wilson,
Gene Wolfe, and many more.

Edited by Stephen Jones
and Ramsey Campbell

[1990]

THE FIRST VOLUME of *Best New Horror* won both the British Fantasy Award and the World Fantasy Award. This helped establish the series amongst the readers and some publishers on both sides of the Atlantic, although it has always remained a struggle to convince people to submit material for consideration.

Back in the early days, Ramsey Campbell and I found ourselves spending quite considerable amounts of our own money acquiring books and magazines just so that we could read stories for the anthology. In fact, thirty years later I still have to do the same thing.

This time our Introduction had expanded to nine pages and the Necrology was up to thirteen. Ramsey and I were concerned about the much-hyped recessions in the movie and publishing industries (apparently some things never change), and we warned that the mid-list was under threat. Once again, we were scarily prophetic.

The publishers once again reused my Letraset logo, now embossed and with an added 2. This time the cover was an original piece by Spanish-Mexican illustrator Luis Rey, who lived in London. As with the first book, Robinson did it in trade paperback and Carroll & Graf went with a hardcover. However, a couple of years later I found an American paperback that neither Robinson nor I had been aware of. G&G claimed it was not a reprint, but a rebinding of their earlier edition, until I pointed out that it was, in fact, a *larger* format than the hardcover...!

For this second compilation we found ourselves working with some of the Big Names in genre publishing. Out of the twenty-eight stories in the book, we included work by such established authors as Peter Straub, Jonathan Carroll, Harlan Ellison, F. Paul Wilson, Gene Wolfe and Gahan Wilson.

However, the story I have chosen to represent this particular volume was from a relative newcomer. In fact, it was Michael Marshall Smith's first published story.

One of the most rewarding experiences about being an editor is discovering and nurturing new talent. I have always tried to leave slots for new or upcoming writers in *Best New Horror* and the other anthologies I have edited. Which is why it was such a thrill when David A. Sutton and I plucked 'The Man Who Drew Cats' out of the submission pile for *Dark Voices 2: The Pan Book of Horror*.

Rarely have I ever encountered a voice so assured or a writing style so effortless in a first tale. More than anyone else, it reminded me of the work of Stephen King, and given the accolades that both the tale and its author have subsequently received, I can only presume that I was not the only one...

MICHAEL MARSHALL SMITH

THE MAN WHO DREW CATS

MICHAEL MARSHALL SMITH is a novelist and screenwriter. Under this name he has published ninety short stories, and five novels—*Only Forward, Spares, One of Us, The Servants,* and *Hannah Green and her Unfeasibly Mundane Existence*—winning the Philip K. Dick, International Horror Guild, and August Derleth awards, along with the Prix Bob Morane in France. He has also won the British Fantasy Award for Best Short Fiction four times, more than any other author.

Writing as "Michael Marshall", he has published seven thrillers including *The Straw Men* series, *The Intruders*—adapted by BBC America into a TV series starring John Simm and Mira Sorvino—and *Killer Move.* His most recent novel under this name is *We Are Here.*

Now additionally writing as "Michael Rutger", he has published the adventure thriller *The Anomaly* and a sequel, *The Possession.*

Currently co-writing and executive producing development of *The Straw Men* for television, he is also Creative Consultant to The Blank Corporation, Neil Gaiman's production company in Los Angeles.

He lives in Santa Cruz, California, with his wife, son, and two cats.

"'The Man Who Drew Cats' was the first story I ever wrote," recalls the author. "I was on a three-month theatrical tour immediately after leaving university, and had just discovered Stephen King—so I was reading everything of his I could lay my hands on, hunting down his backlist in bookstores in every town we visited.

"One day I was wandering Edinburgh by myself, and stood watching a man doing a sidewalk chalk painting. From somewhere nearby I heard the sound of a child crying—and the idea for the story dropped straight into my head."

Smith transferred the action from Scotland to the American Midwest and wrote the story in a day. It was a stunning debut of a major talent...

TOM WAS A very tall man, so tall he didn't even have a nickname for it. Ned Black, who was at least a head shorter, had been "Tower Block" since the sixth grade, and Jack had a sign up over the door saying MIND YOUR HEAD, NED. But Tom was just Tom. It was like he was so tall it didn't bear mentioning even for a joke: be a bit like ragging someone for breathing.

Course there were other reasons too for not ragging Tom about his height or anything else. The guys you'll find perched on stools round Jack's bar watching the game and buying beers, they've known each other forever. Gone to Miss Stadler's school together, gotten under each other's mom's feet, double-dated right up to giving each other's best man's speech. Kingstown is a small place, you understand, and the old boys who come regular to Jack's mostly spent their childhoods in the same tree-house. Course they'd since gone their separate ways, up to a point: Pete was an accountant now, had a small office down Union Street just off the Square and did pretty good, whereas Ned was still pumping gas and changing oil and after forty years he did that pretty good too. Comes a time when men have known each other so long they forget what they do for a living most the time, because it just don't matter. When you talk there's a little bit of skimming stones down the quarry in second grade, a whisper of dolling up to go to that first dance, a tad of going to the housewarming when they moved ten years back. There's all that, so much more than you can say, and none of it's important except for having happened.

So we'll stop by and have a couple of beers and talk about the town and rag each other, and the pleasure's just in shooting the breeze and it don't really matter what's said, just the fact that we're all still there to say it.

But Tom, he was different. We all remember the first time we saw him. It was a long hot summer like we haven't seen in the ten years since, and we were lolling under the fans at Jack's and complaining about the tourists. Kingstown does get its share in the summer, even though it's not near the sea and we don't have a McDonald's and I'll be damned if I can figure out why folk'll go out of their way to see what's just a quiet little town near some mountains. It was as hot as Hell that afternoon and as much as a man could do to sit in his shirt-sleeves and drink the coolest beer he could find, and Jack's is the coolest for us, and always will be, I guess.

Then Tom walked in. His hair was already pretty white back then, and long, and his face was brown and tough with grey eyes like diamonds set in leather. He was dressed mainly in black with a long coat that made you hot just to look at it, but he looked comfortable like he carried his very own weather around with him and he was just fine.

He got a beer, and sat down at a table and read the town *Bugle*, and that was that.

It was special because there wasn't anything special about it. Jack's Bar isn't exactly exclusive and we don't all turn round and stare at anyone new if they come in, but that place is like a monument to shared times. If a tourist couple comes in out of the heat and sits down, nobody says anything—and maybe nobody even notices at the front of their mind—but it's like there's a little island of the alien in the water and the currents just don't ebb and flow the way they usually do, if you get what I mean. Tom just walked in and sat down and it was all right because it was like he was there just like we were, and could've been for thirty years. He sat and read his paper like part of the same river, and everyone just carried on downstream the way they were.

Pretty soon he goes up for another beer and a few of us got talking to him. We got his name and what he did—painting, he said—and after that it was just shooting the breeze. That quick. He came in that summer afternoon and just fell into the conversation like he'd been there all his life, and sometimes it was hard to imagine he hadn't been. Nobody knew where he came from, or where he'd been, and there was something real quiet about him. A stillness, a man in a slightly different world. But he showed enough to get along real well with us, and a bunch of old friends don't often let someone in like that.

Anyway, he stayed that whole summer. Rented himself a place just round the corner from the square, or so he said: I never saw it. I guess no one did. He was a private man, private like a steel door with four bars and a couple of six-inch padlocks, and when he left the square at the end of the day he could have vanished as soon as he turned the corner for all we knew. But he always came from that direction in the morning, with his easel on his back and paint-box under his arm, and he always wore that black coat like it was a part of him. But he always looked cool, and the funny thing was when you stood near him you could swear you felt cooler yourself. I remember Pete saying over a beer that it wouldn't surprise him none if, assuming it ever rained again, Tom would walk round in his own column of dryness. He was just joking, of course, but Tom made you think things like that.

Jack's bar looks right out onto the square, the kind of square towns don't have much anymore: big and dusty with old roads out each corner, tall shops and houses on all the sides and some stone paving in the middle round a fountain that ain't worked in living memory. Well in the summer that old square is just full of out-of-towners in pink towelling jump-suits and nasty jackets standing round saying "Wow" and taking pictures of our quaint old hall and our quaint old stores and even our quaint old selves if we stand still too long. Tom would sit out near the fountain and paint and those people would stand and watch for hours—but he didn't paint the houses or the square or the old Picture House. He painted animals, and painted them like you've never seen. Birds with huge blue speckled wings and cats with cutting green eyes; and whatever he painted it looked like it was just coiled up on the canvas ready to fly away. He didn't do them in their normal colours, they were all reds and purples and deep blues and greens— and yet they fair sparkled with life. It was a wonder to watch: he'd put up a fresh paper, sit looking at nothing in particular, then dip his brush into his paint and draw a line, maybe red, maybe blue. Then he'd add another, maybe the same colour, maybe not. Stroke by stroke you could see the animal build up in front of your eyes and yet when it was finished you couldn't believe it hadn't always been there. When he'd finished he'd spray it with some stuff to fix the paints and put a price on it and you can believe me those paintings were sold before they hit the ground. Spreading businessmen from New Jersey or somesuch and their bored wives would come alive for maybe the first time in years, and walk away with one of those paintings and their arms round each other, looking like they'd found a bit of something they'd forgotten they'd lost.

Come about six o'clock Tom would finish up and walk across to Jack's, looking like a sailing ship amongst rowing boats and saying yes he'd be back again tomorrow and yes, he'd be happy to do a painting for them. He'd get a beer and sit with us and watch the game and there'd be no paint on his fingers or his clothes, not a spot. I figured he'd got so much control over that paint it went where it was told and nowhere else.

I asked him once how he could bear to let those paintings go. I know if I'd been able to make anything that good in my whole life I couldn't let it out of my sight, I'd want to keep it to look at sometimes. He thought for a moment and then he said he believed it depends how much of yourself you've put into it. If you've gone deep down and pulled up what's inside and put it down, then you don't want to let it go: you want to keep it, so's you can check sometimes that it's still safely tied down. Comes a time when a painting's so right and so good that it's private, and no one'll understand it except the man who put it down. Only he is going to know what he's talking about. But the everyday paintings, well they were mainly just because he liked to paint animals, and liked for people to have them. He could only put a piece of himself into something he was going to sell, but they paid for the beers and I guess it's like us fellows in Jack's Bar: if you like talking, you don't always have to be saying something important.

Why animals? Well if you'd seen him with them I guess you wouldn't have to ask. He loved them, is all, and they loved him right back. The cats were always his favourites. My old Pa used to say that cats weren't nothing but sleeping machines put on the earth to do some of the humans' sleeping for them, and whenever Tom worked in the square there'd always be a couple curled up near his feet. And whenever he did a chalk drawing, he'd always do a cat.

Once in a while, you see, Tom seemed to get tired of painting on paper, and he'd get out some chalks and sit down on the baking flagstones and just do a drawing right there on the dusty rock. Now I've told you about his paintings, but these drawings were something else again. It was like because they couldn't be bought but would be washed away, he was putting more of himself into it, doing more than just shooting the breeze. They were just chalk on dusty stone and they were still in these weird colours, but I tell you children wouldn't walk near them because they looked so real, and they weren't the only ones, either. People would stand a few feet back and stare and you could see the wonder in their eyes. If they could've been bought there were people who would have sold their houses. I'm telling you. And it's a funny thing but a couple of times when I walked over to open the store up in the mornings I saw a dead bird or two on top of those drawings, almost like they had landed on it and been so terrified to find themselves right on top of a cat they'd dropped dead of fright. But they must have been dumped there by some real cat, of course, because some of those birds looked like they'd been mauled a bit. I used to throw them in the bushes to tidy up and some of them were pretty broken up.

Old Tom was a godsend to a lot of mothers that summer, who found they could leave their little ones by him, do their shopping in peace and have a soda with their friends and come back to find the kids still sitting quietly watching Tom paint. He didn't mind them at all and would talk to them and make them laugh, and kids of that age laughing is one of the best sounds there is. It's the kind of sound that makes the trees grow. They're young and curious and the world spins round them and when they laugh the world seems a brighter place because it takes you back to the time when you knew no evil and everything was good, or if it wasn't, it would be over by tomorrow.

And here I guess I've finally come down to it, because there was one little boy who didn't laugh much, but just sat quiet and watchful, and I guess he probably understands more of what happened that summer than any of us, though maybe not in words he could tell.

His name was Billy McNeill, and he was Jim Valentine's kid. Jim used to be a mechanic, worked with Ned up at the gas station and raced beat-up cars after hours. Which is why his kid is called McNeill now: one Sunday Jim took a corner a mite too fast and the car rolled and the gas tank caught and they never did find all the wheels. A year later his Mary married again. God alone knows why, her folks warned her, her friends warned her, but I guess love must just have been blind. Sam McNeill's work schedule was at best pretty empty, and mostly he just drank and hung out with friends who maybe weren't always this side of the law. I guess Mary had her own sad little miracle and got her sight back pretty soon, because it wasn't long before Sam got free with his fists when the evenings got too long and he'd had a lot too many. You didn't see Mary around much anymore. In these parts people tend to stare at black eyes on a woman, and a deaf man could hear the whisperings of "We Told Her So".

One morning Tom was sitting painting as usual, and little Billy was sitting watching him. Usually he just wandered off after a while but this morning Mary was at the doctor's and she came over to collect him, walking quickly with her face lowered. But not low enough. I was watching from the store, it was kind of a slow day. Tom's face never showed much. He was a man for a quiet smile and a raised eyebrow, but he looked shocked that morning. Mary's eyes were puffed and purple and there was a cut on her cheek an inch long. I guess we'd sort of gotten used to seeing her like that and if the truth be known some of the wives thought she'd got remarried a bit on the soon side and I suppose we may all have been a bit cold towards her, Jim Valentine having been so well-liked and all.

Tom looked from the little boy who never laughed much, to his mom with her tired unhappy eyes and her beat-up face, and his own face went from shocked to stony and I can't describe it any other way but that I felt a cold chill cross my heart from right across the square.

But then he smiled and ruffled Billy's hair and Mary took Billy's hand and they went off. They turned back once and Tom was still looking after them and he gave Billy a little wave and he waved back and mother and child smiled together.

That night in Jack's Tom put a quiet question about Mary and we told him the story. As he listened his face seemed to harden from within, his eyes growing flat and dead. We told him that old Lou Lachance, who lived next door to the McNeills, said that sometimes you could hear him shouting and her pleading till three in the morning and on still nights the sound of Billy crying for even longer than that. Told him it was a shame, but what could you do? Folks keep themselves out of other people's faces round here, and I guess Sam and his drinking buddies didn't have much to fear from nearly-retireders like us anyhow. Told him it was a terrible thing, and none of us liked it, but these things happened and what could you do.

Tom listened and didn't say a word. Just sat there in his black coat and listened to us pass the buck. After a while the talk sort of petered out and we all sat and watched the bubbles in our beers. I guess the bottom line was that none of us had really thought about it much except as another chapter of small-town gossip, and Jesus Christ did I feel ashamed about that by the time we'd finished telling it. Sitting there with Tom was no laughs at all. He had a real edge to him, and seemed more unknown than known that night. He stared at his laced fingers for a long time, and then he began, real slow, to talk.

He'd been married once, he said, a long time ago, and he'd lived in a place called Stevensburg with his wife Rachel. When he talked about her the air seemed to go softer and we all sat quiet and supped our beers and remembered how it had been way back when we first loved our own wives. He talked of her smile and the look in her eyes and when we went home that night I guess there were a few wives who were surprised at how tight they got hugged, and who went to sleep in their husband's arms feeling more loved and contented than they had in a long while.

He'd loved her and she him and for a few years they were the happiest people on earth. Then a third party had got involved. Tom didn't say his name, and he spoke real neutrally about him, but it was a gentleness like silk wrapped round a knife. Anyway his wife fell in love with him, or thought she had, or leastways she slept with him. In their bed, the bed they'd come to on their wedding night. As Tom spoke these words some of us looked up at him, startled, like we'd been slapped across the face.

Rachel did what so many do and live to regret till their dying day. She was so mixed up and getting so much pressure from the other guy that she decided to plough on with the one mistake and make it the biggest in the world.

She left Tom. He talked with her, pleaded even. It was almost impossible to imagine Tom ever doing that, but I guess the man we knew was a different guy from the one he was remembering. The pleading made no difference.

And so Tom had to carry on living in Stevensburg, walking the same tracks, seeing them around, wondering if she was as free and easy with him, if the light in her eyes was shining on him now. And each time the man saw Tom he'd look straight at him and crease a little smile, a grin that said he knew about the pleading and he and his cronies had had a good laugh over the wedding bed—and yes, I'm going home with your wife tonight and I know just how she likes it, you want to compare notes?

And then he'd turn and kiss Rachel on the mouth, his eyes on Tom, smiling. And she let him do it.

It had kept stupid old women in stories for weeks, the way Tom kept losing weight and his temper and the will to live. He took three months of it and then left without bothering to sell the house. Stevensburg was where he'd grown up and courted and loved and now wherever he turned the good times had rotted and hung like fly-blown corpses in all the cherished places. He'd never been back.

It took an hour to tell, and then he stopped talking a while and lit a hundredth cigarette and Pete got us all some more beers. We were sitting sad and thoughtful, tired like we'd lived it ourselves. And I guess most of us had, some little bit of it. But had we ever loved anyone the way he'd loved her? I doubt it, not all of us put together. Pete set the beers down and Ned asked Tom why he hadn't just beaten the living shit out of the guy. Now, no one else would have actually asked that, but Ned's a good guy, and I guess we were all with him in feeling a piece of that oldest and most crushing hatred in the world, the hate of a man who's lost the woman he loves to another, and we knew what Ned was saying. I'm not saying it's a good thing and I know you're not supposed to feel like that these days but show me a man who says he doesn't and I'll show you a liar. Love is the only feeling worth a tin shit but you've got to know that it comes from both sides of a man's character and the deeper it runs the darker the pools it draws from.

My guess is he just hated the man too much to hit him. Comes a time when that isn't enough, when nothing is ever going to be enough, and so you can't do anything at all. And as he talked the pain just flowed out like a river that wasn't ever going to be stopped, a river that had cut a channel through every corner of his soul. I learnt something that night that you can go your whole life without realising: that there are things that can be done that can mess someone up so badly, for so long, that they just cannot be allowed; that there are some kinds of pain that you cannot suffer to be brought into the world.

And then Tom was done telling and he raised a smile and said that in the end he hadn't done anything to the man except paint him a picture, which I didn't understand, but Tom looked like he'd talked all he was going to.

So we got some more beers and shot some quiet pool before going home. But I guess we all knew what he'd been talking about.

Billy McNeill was just a child. He should have been dancing through a world like a big funfair full of sunlight and sounds, and instead he went home at night and saw his mom being beaten up by a man with shit for brains who struck out at a good woman because he was too stupid to deal with the world. Most kids go to sleep thinking about bikes and climbing apple trees and skimming stones, and he was lying there hearing his mom get smashed in the stomach and then hit again as she threw up in the sink. Tom didn't say any of that, but he did. And we knew he was right.

The summer kept up bright and hot, and we all had our businesses to attend to. Jack sold a lot of beer and I sold a lot of ice cream (Sorry ma'am, just the three flavours, and no, Bubblegum Pistachio ain't one of them) and Ned fixed a whole bunch of cracked radiators. Tom sat right out there in the square with a couple of cats by his feet and a crowd around him, magicking up animals in the sun.

And I think that after that night Mary maybe got a few more smiles as she did her shopping, and maybe a few more wives stopped to talk to her. She looked a lot better too: Sam had a job by the sound of it and her face healed up pretty soon. You could often see her standing holding Billy's hand as they watched Tom paint for a while before they went home. I think she realised they had a friend in him. Sometimes Billy was there all afternoon, and he was happy there in the sun by Tom's feet and oftentimes he'd pick up a piece of chalk and sit scrawling on the pavement. Sometimes I'd see Tom lean over and say something to him and he'd look up and smile a simple child's smile that beamed in the sunlight. The tourists kept coming and the sun kept shining and it was one of those summers that go on for ever and stick in a child's mind, and tell you what summer should be like for the rest of your life. And I'm damn sure it sticks in Billy's mind, just like it does in all of ours.

Because one morning Mary didn't come into the store, which had gotten to being a regular sort of thing, and Billy wasn't out there in the square. After the way things had been the last few weeks that could only be bad news, and so I left the boy John in charge of the store and hurried over to have a word with Tom. I was kind of worried.

I was no more than halfway across to him when I saw Billy come running from the opposite corner of the square, going straight to Tom. He was crying fit to burst and just leapt up at Tom and clung to him, his arms wrapped tight round his neck. Then his mother came across from the same direction, running as best she could. She got to Tom and they just looked at each other. Mary's a real pretty girl but you wouldn't have believed it then. It looked like he'd actually broken her nose this time, and blood was streaming out of her lip. She started sobbing, saying Sam had lost his job because he was back on the drink and what could she do and then suddenly there was a roar and I was shoved aside and Sam was standing there, still wearing his slippers, weaving back and forth and radiating that aura of violence that keeps men like him safe. He started shouting at Mary to take the kid the fuck back home and she just flinched and cowered closer to Tom like she was huddling round a fire to keep out the cold. This just got Sam even wilder and he staggered forward and told Tom to get the fuck out of it if he knew what was good for him, and grabbed Mary's arm and tried to yank her towards him, his face terrible with rage.

Then Tom stood up. Now Tom was a tall man, but he wasn't a young man, and he was thin. Sam was thirty and built like the town hall. When he did work it usually involved moving heavy things from one place to another, and his strength was supercharged by a whole pile of drunken nastiness.

But at that moment the crowd stepped back as one and I suddenly felt very afraid for Sam McNeill. Tom looked like you could take anything you cared to him and it would just break, like he was a huge spike of granite wrapped in skin with two holes in the face where the rock showed through. And he was mad, not hot and blowing like Sam, but mad and *cold*.

There was a long pause. Then Sam weaved back a step and shouted: "You just come on home, you hear? Gonna be real trouble if you don't, Mary. Real trouble," and then stormed off across the square the way he came, knocking his way through the tourist vultures soaking up the spicy local colour.

Mary turned to Tom, so afraid it hurt to see, and said she guessed she'd better be going. Tom looked at her for a moment and then spoke for the first time.

"Do you love him?"

Even if you wanted to, you ain't going to lie to eyes like that, for fear something inside you will break.

Real quiet she said: "No," and began crying softly as she took Billy's hand and walked slowly back across the square.

Tom packed up his stuff and walked over to Jack's. I went with him and had a beer but I had to get back to the shop and Tom just sat there like a trigger, silent and strung up tight as a drum. Somewhere down near the bottom of those still waters something was stirring. Something I thought I didn't want to see.

About an hour later it was lunchtime and I'd just left the shop to have a break when suddenly something whacked into the back of my legs and nearly knocked me down. It was Billy. It was Billy and he had a bruise round his eye that was already closing it up.

I knew what the only thing to do was and I did it. I took his hand

and led him across to the Bar, feeling a hard anger pushing against my throat. When he saw Tom, Billy ran to him again and Tom took him in his arms and looked over Billy's shoulder at me, and I felt my own anger collapse utterly in the face of a fury I could never have generated. I tried to find a word to describe it but they all just seemed like they were in the wrong language. All I can say is I wanted to be somewhere else and it felt real cold standing there facing that stranger in a black coat.

Then the moment passed and Tom was holding the kid close, ruffling his hair and talking to him in a low voice, murmuring the words I thought only mothers knew. He dried Billy's tears and checked his eye and then he got off his stool, smiled down at him and said:

"I think it's time we did some drawing, what d'you say?" and, taking the kid's hand, he picked up his chalkbox and walked out into the square.

I don't know how many times I looked up and watched them that afternoon. They were sitting side by side on the stone, Billy's little hand wrapped round one of Tom's fingers, and Tom doing one of his chalk drawings. Every now and then Billy would reach across and add a little bit and Tom would smile and say something and Billy's gurgling laugh would float across the square. The store was real busy that afternoon and I was chained to that counter, but I could tell by the size of the crowd that a lot of Tom was going into that picture, and maybe a bit of Billy too.

It was about four o'clock before I could take a break. I walked across the crowded square in the mid-afternoon heat and shouldered my way through to where they sat with a couple of cold Cokes. And when I saw it my mouth just dropped open and took a five-minute vacation while I tried to take it in.

It was a cat all right, but not a normal cat. It was a life-size tiger. I'd never seen Tom do anything near that big before, and as I stood there in the beating sun trying to get my mind round it, it almost seemed to stand in three dimensions, a nearly living thing. Its stomach was very lean and thin, its tail seemed to twitch with colour, and as Tom worked on the eyes and jaws, his face set with a rigid concentration quite unlike his usual calm painting face, the snarling mask of the tiger came to life before my eyes. And I could see that he wasn't just putting a bit of himself in at all. This was a man at full stretch, giving all of himself and reaching down for more, pulling up bloody fistfuls and throwing them down. The tiger was all the rage I'd seen in his eyes, and more, and like his love for Rachel that rage just seemed bigger than any other man could comprehend. He was pouring it out and sculpting it into the lean and ravenous creature coming to pulsating life in front of us on the pavement, and the weird purples and blues and reds just made it seem more vibrant and alive.

I watched him working furiously on it, the boy sometimes helping, adding a tiny bit here and there that strangely seemed to add to it, and thought I understood what he'd meant that evening a few weeks back. He said he'd done a painting for the man who'd given him so much pain. Then, as now, he must have found what I guess you'd call something fancy like "catharsis" through his skill with chalks, had wrenched the pain up from within him and nailed it down onto something solid that he could walk away from. Now he was helping that little boy do the same, and the boy did look better, his bruised eye hardly showing with the wide smile on his face as he watched the big cat conjured up from nowhere in front of him.

We all just stood and watched, like something out of an old story, the simple folk and the magical stranger. It always feels like you're giving a bit of yourself away when you praise someone else's creation, and it's often done grudgingly, but you could feel the awe that day like a warm wind. Comes a time when you realise something special is happening, something you're never going to see again, and there isn't anything you can do but watch.

Well I had to go back to the store after a while. I hated to go but, well, John is a good boy, married now of course, but in those days his head was full of girls and it didn't do to leave him alone in a busy shop for too long.

And so the long hot day drew slowly to a close. I kept the store open till eight, when the light began to turn and the square emptied out with all the tourists going away to write postcards and see if we didn't have even just a *little* McDonald's hidden away someplace. I suppose Mary had troubles enough at home, realised where the boy would be and figured he was safer there than anywhere else, and I guess she was right.

Tom and Billy finished up drawing and then Tom sat and talked to him for some time. Then they got up and the kid walked slowly off to the corner of the square, looking back to wave at Tom a couple times. Tom stood and watched him go and when Billy had gone he stayed there a while, head down, like a huge black statue in the gathering dark. He looked kind of creepy out there and I don't mind telling you I was glad when he finally moved and started walking over towards Jack's. I ran out to catch up with him and drew level just as we passed the drawing. And then I had to stop. I just couldn't look at that and move at the same time.

Finished, the drawing was like nothing on earth, and I suppose that's exactly what it was. I can't hope to describe it to you, although I've seen it in my dreams many times in the last ten years. You had to be there, on that heavy summer night, had to know what was going on. Otherwise it's going to sound like it was just a drawing.

That tiger was out and out terrifying. It looked so mean and hungry, Christ I don't know what: it just looked like the darkest parts of mankind, the pain and the fury and the vengeful hate nailed down in front of you for you to see, and I just stood there and shivered in the humid evening air.

"We did him a picture," Tom said quietly.

"Yeah," I said, and nodded. Like I said, I know what "catharsis" means and I thought I understood what he was saying. But I really didn't want to look at it much longer. "Let's go have a beer, hey?"

The storm in Tom hadn't passed, I could tell, and he still seemed to thrum with crackling emotions looking for an earth, but I thought the clouds might be breaking and I was glad.

And so we walked slowly over to Jack's and had a few beers and watched some pool being played. Tom seemed pretty tired, but still alert, and I relaxed a little. Come eleven most of the guys started going on their way and I was surprised to see Tom get another beer. Pete, Ned and I stayed on, and Jack of course, though we knew our loving wives would have something to say about that. It just didn't seem time to go. Outside it had gotten pretty dark, though the moon was keeping the square in a kind of twilight and the lights in the bar threw a pool of warmth out of the front window.

Then, about twelve o'clock, it happened, and I don't suppose any of us will ever see the same world we grew up in again. I've told this whole thing like it was just me who was there, but we all were, and we remember it together.

Because suddenly there was a wailing sound outside, a thin cutting cry, getting closer. Tom immediately snapped to his feet and stared out the window like he'd been waiting for it. As we looked out across the square we saw little Billy come running and we could see the blood on his face from there. Some of us got to get up but Tom snarled at us to stay there and so I guess we just stayed put, sitting back down like we'd been pushed. He strode out the door and into the square and the boy saw him and ran to him and Tom folded him in his cloak and held him close and warm. But he didn't come back in. He just stood there, and he was waiting for something.

Now there's a lot of crap talked about silences. I read novels when I've the time and you see things like "Time stood still" and so on and you think bullshit it did. So I'll just say I don't think anyone in the world breathed in that next minute. There was no wind, no movement. The stillness and silence were there like you could touch them, but more than that: they were like that's all there was and all there ever had been.

We felt the slow red throb of violence from right across the square before we could even see the man. Then Sam came staggering into view waving a bottle like a flag and cursing his head off. At first he couldn't see Tom and the boy because they were the opposite side of the fountain, and he ground to a wavering halt, but then he started shouting, rough jags of sound that seemed to strike against the silence and die instead of breaking it, and he began charging across the square—and if ever there was a man with murder in his thoughts then it was Sam McNeill. He was like a man who'd given his soul the evening off. I wanted to shout to Tom to get the hell out of the way, to come inside, but the words wouldn't come out of my throat and we all just stood there, knuckles whitening as we clutched the bar and stared, our mouths open like we'd made a pact never to use them again. Tom just stood there, watching Sam come towards him, getting closer, almost as far as the spot where Tom usually painted. It felt like we were looking out of the window at a picture of something that happened long ago in another place and time, and the closer Sam got the more I began to feel very afraid for him.

It was at that moment that Sam stopped dead in his tracks, skidding forward like in some kid's cartoon, his shout dying off in his ragged throat. He was staring at the ground in front of him, his eyes wide and his mouth a stupid circle. Then he began to scream.

It was a high shrill noise like a woman, and coming out of that bull of a man it sent fear racking down my spine. He started making thrashing movements like he was trying to move backwards, but he just stayed where he was.

His movements became unmistakable at about the same time his screams turned from terror to agony. He was trying to get his leg away from something.

Suddenly he seemed to fall forward on one knee, his other leg stuck out behind him, and he raised his head and shrieked at the dark skies and we saw his face then and I'm not going to forget that face so long as I live. It was a face from before there were any words, the face behind our oldest fears and earliest nightmares, the face we're terrified of seeing on ourselves one night when we're alone in the dark and It finally comes out from under the bed to get us, like we always knew it would.

Then Sam fell on his face, his leg buckled up—and still he thrashed and screamed and clawed at the ground with his hands, blood running from his broken fingernails as he twitched and struggled. Maybe the light was playing tricks, and my eyes were sparkling anyway on account of being too paralysed with fear to even blink, but as he thrashed less and less it became harder and harder to see him at all, and as the breeze whipped up stronger his screams began to sound a lot like the wind. But still he writhed and moaned and then suddenly there was the most godawful crunching sound and then there was no movement or sound anymore.

Like they were on a string our heads all turned together and we saw Tom still standing there, his coat flapping in the wind. He had a hand on Billy's shoulder and as we looked we could see that Mary was there too now and he had one arm round her as she sobbed into his coat.

I don't know how long we just sat there staring but then we were ejected off our seats and out of the bar. Pete and Ned ran to Tom but Jack and I went to where Sam had fallen, and we stared down, and I tell you the rest of my life now seems like a build up to and a climb down from that moment.

We were standing in front of a chalk drawing of a tiger. Even now my scalp seems to tighten when I think of it, and my chest feels like someone punched a hole in it and tipped a gallon of ice water inside. I'll just tell you the facts: Jack was there and he knows what we saw and what we didn't see.

What we didn't see was Sam McNeill. He just wasn't there. We saw a drawing of a tiger in purples and greens, a little bit scuffed, and there was a lot more red round the mouth of that tiger than there had been that afternoon and I'm sure that if either of us could have dreamed of reaching out and touching it, it would have been warm too.

And the hardest part to tell is this. I'd seen that drawing in the afternoon, and Jack had too, and we knew that when it was done it was lean and thin.

I swear to God that tiger wasn't thin any more. What Jack and I were looking at was one fat tiger.

After a while I looked up and across at Tom. He was still standing with Mary and Billy, but they weren't crying anymore. Mary was hugging Billy so tight he squawked and Tom's face looked calm and alive and creased with a smile. And as we stood there the skies opened for the first time in months and a cool rain hammered down. At my feet colours began to run and lines became less distinct. Jack and I stood and watched till there was just pools of meaningless colours and then we walked slowly over to the others, not even looking at the bottle lying on the ground, and we all stayed there a long time in the rain, facing each other, not saying a word.

Well that was ten years ago, near enough. After a while Mary took Billy home and they turned to give us a little wave before they turned the corner. The cuts on Billy's face healed real quick, and he's a good looking boy now: he looks a lot like his dad and he's already fooling about in cars. Helps me in the store sometimes. His mom ain't aged a day and looks wonderful. She never married again, but she looks real happy the way she is.

The rest of us just said a simple goodnight. Goodnight was all we could muster and maybe that's all there was to say. Then we walked off home in the directions of our wives. Tom gave me a small smile before he turned and walked off alone. I almost followed him, I wanted to say something, but the end I just stayed where I was and watched him go. And that's how I'll always remember him best, because for a moment there was a spark in his eyes and I knew that some pain had been lifted deep down inside somewhere.

Then he walked and no one has seen him since, and like I said it's been about ten years now. He wasn't there in the square the next morning and he didn't come in for a beer. Like he'd never been, he just wasn't there. Except for the hole in our hearts: it's funny how much you can miss a quiet man.

We're all still here, of course, Jack, Ned, Pete and the boys, and all much the same, though even older and greyer. Pete lost his wife and Ned retired but things go on the same. The tourists come in the summer and we sit on the stools and drink our cold beers and shoot the breeze about ballgames and families and how the world's going to shit, and sometimes we'll draw close and talk about a night a long time ago, and about paintings and cats, and about the quietest man we ever knew, wondering where he is, and what he's doing. And we've had a six-pack in the back of the fridge for ten years now, and the minute he walks through that door and pulls up a stool, that's his.

BEST NEW HORROR

Robert R. McCammon

Thomas Ligotti

Nancy A. Collins

William F. Nolan

David F. Schow

Kim Newman

Karl Edward Wagner

and more

EDITED BY
STEPHEN
JONES
AND
RAMSEY
CAMPBELL

3

[1991]

*B*EST NEW HORROR 2 was the only book I have ever had censored by a publisher.

Ramsey and I had selected and contracted Roberta Lannes' disturbing serial-killer story 'Apostate in Denim' (from the first issue of *Iniquities* magazine) for the volume. However, when we delivered the book manuscript to Robinson, certain people in the company vehemently objected to the content of the story and refused to include it. Despite our protestations (how could a horror story be *too* horrific?), we were overruled. At least Roberta was very understanding about the whole matter, and she later included the tale in her 1997 collection *The Mirror of Night*.

For the third volume, Robinson once again used a cover painting by Luis Rey (of a werewolf-like monster crashing through a window) and added a "*3*" to the embossed Letraset logo. Carroll & Graf went a much classier route, completely re-designing the jacket for its hardcover and subsequent trade paperback editions.

This time our Introduction had crept up to eleven pages, while the Necrology had blossomed to fifteen. In our editorial summation, Ramsey and I took a reviewer for *Locus* magazine to task for his ill-informed assertion that the horror field was "limited in its relevance to anything".

The twenty-nine stories included return appearances by Robert R.

McCammon, Thomas Ligotti, Karl Edward Wagner and Kim Newman, amongst others. Rising star Michael Marshall Smith was represented with a second contribution (the British Fantasy Award-winning 'The Dark Land'), and we even featured a tale by award-winning Scottish comics writer Grant Morrison ('The Braille Encyclopedia').

However, the story I have chosen from this 1992 volume is by my co-editor, Ramsey Campbell. Over the years, Ramsey has been represented in *Best New Horror* more than any other author. In fact, he had stories in sixteen out of the first twenty editions (including two in Volume #17).

As anyone familiar with my Introductions knows, I usually frown upon editors including their own stories in their anthologies but, in the case of collaborative works, I think it is fine if it is the other editor who makes the selection. Over the five volumes I co-edited with Ramsey, he always disassociated himself when it came to his own work, and it was left up to me to make the final decision.

'The Same in Any Language' is another of those "fish out of water" travelogue tales that I love so dearly. The story was inspired by a visit Ramsey made to the Crete island of Spinalonga, the site of an abandoned leper colony, and the final paragraph is intended as a tribute to Stephen King...

RAMSEY CAMPBELL

THE SAME IN ANY LANGUAGE

R AMSEY CAMPBELL is described in the *Oxford Companion to English Literature* as "Britain's most respected living horror writer". He has been given more awards than any other writer in the field, including the Grand Master Award of the World Horror Convention, the Lifetime Achievement Award of the Horror Writers Association, the Living Legend Award of the International Horror Guild and the World Fantasy Lifetime Achievement Award. In 2015 he was made an Honorary Fellow of Liverpool John Moores University for outstanding services to literature.

Amongst his many novels are *The Face That Must Die, Incarnate, Midnight Sun, The Count of Eleven, Silent Children, The Darkest Part of the Woods, The Overnight, Secret Story, The Grin of the Dark, Thieving Fear, Creatures of the Pool, The Seven Days of Cain, Ghosts Know, The Kind Folk, Think Yourself Lucky* and *Thirteen Days by Sunset Beach.* He recently brought out his "Brichester Mythos" trilogy, consisting of *The Searching Dead, Born to the Dark* and *The Way of the Worm.*

Needing Ghosts, The Last Revelation of Gla'aki, The Pretence and *The Booking* are novellas, and his collections include *Waking Nightmares, Alone with the Horrors, Ghosts and Grisly Things, Told by the Dead, Just Behind You, Holes for Faces, Fearful Implications* and *By the Light of My Skull.* His non-fiction is collected as *Ramsey*

Campbell, Probably, while *Limericks of the Alarming and Phantasmal* is a history of horror fiction in the form of fifty limericks.

Campbell's novels *The Nameless*, *Pact of the Fathers* and *The Influence* have been filmed in Spain, and he is the President of the Society of Fantastic Films.

It has become something of a tradition over the years for me to include stories with a Mediterranean setting. Here's the second one in this volume—from my original co-editor—to chill our spines in a warmer climate.

"'The Same in Any Language' was a response to a request," reveals Campbell. "A resurrected *Weird Tales*, the legendary pulp magazine, was to publish an issue as a tribute to me, much to my delight. My first glimpse of a copy of *Weird Tales* in a shop window when I was six or seven years old started a yearning which only collecting the magazine could begin to satisfy.

"I'd wanted to use Spinalonga as a setting in any case, having forgotten that John Ware had already done so in the thirteenth volume of Herbert van Thal's increasingly pornographic *Pan Book of Horror Stories*. Ware's tale is an old-fashioned ghost story. How about mine?"

T HE DAY MY father is to take me where the lepers used to live is hotter than ever. Even the old women with black scarves wrapped around their heads sit inside the bus station instead of on the chairs outside the tavernas. Kate fans herself with her straw hat like a basket someone's sat on and gives my father one of those smiles they've made up between them. She's leaning forwards to see if that's our bus when he says "Why do you think they call them lepers, Hugh?"

I can hear what he's going to say, but I have to humour him. "I don't know."

"Because they never stop leaping up and down."

It takes him much longer to say the first four words than the rest of it. I groan because he expects me to, and Kate lets off one of her giggles I keep hearing whenever they stay in my father's and my room at the hotel and send me down for a swim. "If you can't give a grin, give a groan," my father says for about the millionth time, and Kate pokes him with her freckly elbow as if he's too funny for words. She annoys me so much that I say, "Lepers don't rhyme with creepers, Dad."

"I never thought they did, son. I was just having a laugh. If we can't laugh we might as well be dead, ain't that straight, Kate?" He winks at her thigh and slaps his own instead, and says to me, "Since you're so clever, why don't you find out when our bus is coming."

"That's it now."

"And I'm Hercules." He lifts up his fists to make his muscles bulge for Kate and says, "You're telling us that tripe spells A Flounder?"

"Elounda, dad. It does. The letter like a Y upside down is how they write an L."

"About time they learned how to write properly, then," he says, staring around to show he doesn't care who hears. "Well, there it is if you really want to trudge round another old ruin instead of having a swim."

"I expect he'll be able to do both once we get to the village," Kate says, but I can tell she's hoping I'll just swim. "Will you two gentlemen see me across the road?"

My mother used to link arms with me and my father when he was living with us. "I'd better make sure it's the right bus," I say and run out so fast I can pretend I didn't hear my father calling me back.

A man with skin like a boot is walking backwards in the dust behind the bus, shouting "Elounda" and waving his arms as if he's pulling the bus into the space in line. I sit on a seat opposite two Germans who block the aisle until they've taken off their rucksacks, but my father finds three seats together at the rear. "Aren't you with us, Hugh?" he shouts, and everyone on the bus looks at him.

When I see him getting ready to shout again I walk down the aisle. I'm hoping nobody notices me, but Kate says loudly, "It's a pity you ran off like that, Hugh. I was going to ask if you'd like an ice cream."

"No thank you," I say, trying to sound like my mother when she was only just speaking to my father, and step over Kate's legs. As the bus rumbles uphill I turn as much of my back on her as I can, and watch the streets.

Aghios Nikolaos looks as if they haven't finished building it. Some of the tavernas are on the bottom floors of blocks with no roofs, and sometimes there are more tables on the pavements outside than in. The bus goes downhill again as if it's hiccupping, and when it reaches the bottomless pool where young people with no children stay in the hotels with discos, it follows the edge of the bay. I watch the white boats on the blue water, but really I'm seeing the conductor coming down the aisle and feeling as if a lump is growing in my stomach from me wondering what my father will say to him.

The bus is climbing beside the sea when he reaches us. "Three for leper land," my father says.

The conductor stares at him and shrugs. "As far as you go," Kate says, and rubs herself against my father. "All the way."

When the conductor pushes his lips forwards out of his moustache and beard my father begins to get angry, unless he's pretending. "Where you kept your lepers. Spiny Lobster or whatever you call the damned place."

"It's Spinalonga, Dad, and it's off the coast from where we're going."

"I know that, and he should." My father is really angry now. "Did you get that?" he says to the conductor. "My ten-year-old can speak your lingo, so don't tell me you can't speak ours."

The conductor looks at me, and I'm afraid he wants me to talk Greek. My mother gave me a little computer that translates words into Greek when you type them, but I've left it at the hotel because my father said it sounded like a bird which only knew one note. "We're going to Elounda, please," I stammer.

"Elounda, boss," the conductor says to me. He takes the money from my father without looking at him and gives me the tickets and change. "Fish is good by the harbour in the evening," he says, and goes to sit next to the driver while the bus swings round the zigzags of the hill road.

My father laughs for the whole bus to hear. "They think you're so important, Hugh, you won't be wanting to go home to your mother."

Kate strokes his head as if he's her pet, then she turns to me. "What do you like most about Greece?"

She's trying to make friends with me like when she kept saying I could call her Kate, only now I see it's for my father's sake. All she's done is make me think how the magic places seemed to have lost their magic because my mother wasn't there with me, even Knossos where Theseus killed the Minotaur. There were just a few corridors left that might have been the maze he was supposed to find his way out of, and my father let me stay in them for a while, but then he lost his temper because all the guided tours were in foreign languages and nobody could tell him how to get back to the coach. We nearly got stuck overnight in Heraklion, when he'd promised to take Kate for dinner that night by the bottomless pool. "I don't know," I mumble, and gazes out the window.

"I like the sun, don't you? And the people when they're being nice, and the lovely clear sea."

It sounds to me as if she's getting ready to send me off swimming again. They met while I was, our second morning at the hotel. When I came out of the sea my father had moved his towel next to hers and she was giggling. I watch Spinalonga Island float over the horizon like a ship made of rock and grey towers, and hope she'll think I'm agreeing with her if that means she'll leave me alone. But she says, "I suppose most boys are morbid at your age. Let's hope you'll grow up to be like your father."

She's making it sound as if the leper colony is the only place I've wanted to visit, but it's just another old place I can tell my mother I've been. Kate doesn't want to go there because she doesn't like old places—she said if Knossos was a palace she was glad she's not a queen. I don't speak to her again until the bus has stopped by the harbour.

There aren't many tourists, even in the shops and tavernas lined up along the winding pavement. Greek people who look as if they were born in the sun sit drinking at tables under awnings like stalls in a market. Some priests who I think at first are wearing black hatboxes on their heads march by, and fishermen come up from their boats with octopuses on sticks like big kebabs. The bus turns round in a cloud of dust and petrol fumes while Kate hangs onto my father with one hand and flaps the front of her flowery dress with the other. A boatman stares at the tops of her boobs which make me think of spotted fish and shouts "Spinalonga" with both hands round his mouth.

"We've hours yet," Kate says. "Let's have a drink. Hugh may even get that ice cream if he's good."

If she's going to talk about me as though I'm not there I'll do my best not to be. She and my father sit under an awning and I kick dust on the pavement outside until she says, "Come under, Hugh. We don't want you with sunstroke."

I don't want her pretending she's my mother, but if I say so I'll only spoil the day more than she already has. I shuffle to the table next to the one she's sharing with my father and throw myself on a chair. "Well, Hugh," she says, "do you want one?"

"No thank you," I say, even though the thought of an ice cream or a drink starts my mouth trying to drool.

"You can have some of my lager if it ever arrives," my father says at the top of his voice, and stares hard at some Greeks sitting at a table. "Anyone here a waiter?" he says, lifting his hand to his mouth as if he's holding a glass.

When all the people at the table smile and raise their glasses and shout cheerily at him, Kate says, "I'll find someone and then I'm going to the little girls' room while you men have a talk."

My father watches her crossing the road and gazes at the doorway of the taverna once she's gone in. He's quiet for a while, then he says, "Are you going to be able to say you had a good time?"

I know he wants me to enjoy myself when I'm with him, but I also think what my mother stopped herself from saying to me is true—that he booked the holiday in Greece as a way of scoring off her by taking me somewhere she'd always wanted to go. He stares at the taverna as if he can't move until I let him, and I say, "I expect so, if we go to the island."

"That's my boy. Never give in too easily." He smiles at me with one side of his face. "You don't mind if I have some fun as well, do you?"

He's making it sound as though he wouldn't have had much fun if it had just been the two of us, and I think that was how he'd started to feel before he met Kate. "It's your holiday," I say.

He's opening his mouth after another long silence when Kate comes out of the taverna with a man carrying two lagers and a lemonade on a tray. "See that you thank her," my father tells me.

I didn't ask for lemonade. He said I could have some lager. I say, "Thank you very much," and feel my throat tightening as I gulp the lemonade, because her eyes are saying that she's won.

"That must have been welcome," she says when I put down the empty glass. "Another? Then I should find yourself something to do. Your father and I may be here for a while."

"Have a swim," my father suggests.

"I haven't brought my cossy."

"Neither have those boys," Kate says, pointing at the harbour. "Don't worry, I've seen boys wearing less."

My father smirks behind his hand, and I can't bear it. I run to the jetty the boys are diving off, and drop my T-shirt and shorts on it and my sandals on top of them, and dive in.

The water's cold, but not for long. It's full of little fish that nibble you if you only float, and it's clearer than tap water, so you can see down to the pebbles and the fish pretending to be them. I chase fish and swim underwater and almost catch an octopus before it squirms out to sea. Then three Greek boys about my age swim over, and we're pointing at ourselves and saying our names when I see Kate and my father kissing.

I know their tongues are in each other's mouths—getting some tongue, the kids at my school call it. I feel like swimming away as far as I can go and never coming back. But Stavros and Stathis and Costas are using their hands to tell me we should see who can swim fastest, so I do that instead. Soon I've forgotten my father and Kate, even when we sit on the jetty for a rest before we have more races. It must be hours later when I realise Kate is calling, "Come here a minute."

The sun isn't so hot now. It's reaching under the awning, but she and my father haven't moved back into the shadow. A boatman shouts "Spinalonga" and points at how low the sun is. I don't mind swimming with my new friends instead of going to the island, and I'm about to tell my father so when Kate says, "I've been telling your dad he should be proud of you. Come and see what I've got for you."

They've both had a lot to drink. She almost falls across the table as I go to her. Just as I get there I see what she's going to give me, but it's too late. She grabs my head with both hands and sticks a kiss on my mouth.

She tastes of old lager. Her mouth is wet and bigger than mine, and when it squirms it makes me think of an octopus. "Mmm-*mwa*," it says, and then I manage to duck out of her hands, leaving her blinking at me as if her eyes won't quite work. "Nothing wrong with a bit of loving," she says. "You'll find that out when you grow up."

My father knows I don't like to be kissed, but he's frowning at me as if I should have let her. Suddenly I want to get my own back on them in the only way I can think of. "We need to go to the island now."

"Better go to the loo first," my father says. "They wouldn't have one on the island when all their willies had dropped off." Kate hoots at that while I'm getting dressed, and I feel as if she's laughing at the way my ribs show through my skin however much I eat. I stop myself from shivering in case she or my father makes out that's a reason for us to go back to the hotel. I'm heading for the toilet when my father says, "Watch out you don't catch anything in there or we'll have to leave you on the island."

I know there are all sorts of reasons why my parents split up, but just now this is the only one I can think of—my mother not being able to stand his jokes and how the more she told him to finish the more he would do it, as if he couldn't stop himself. I run into the toilet, trying not to look at the pedal bin where you have to drop the used paper, and close my eyes once I've taken aim.

Is today going to be what I remember about Greece? My mother brought me up to believe that even the sunlight here had magic in it, and I expected to feel the ghosts of legends in all the old places. If there isn't any magic in the sunlight, I want there to be some in the dark. The thought seems to make the insides of my eyelids darker, and I can smell the drains. I pull the chain and zip myself up, and then I wonder if my father sent me in here so we'll miss the boat. I nearly break the hook on the door, I'm so desperate to be outside.

The boat is still tied to the harbour, but I can't see the boatman. Kate and my father are holding hands across the table, and my father's looking around as though he means to order another drink. I squeeze my eyes shut so hard that when I open them everything's gone black. The blackness fades along with whatever I wished, and I see the boatman kneeling on the jetty, talking to Stavros. "Spinalonga," I shout.

He looks at me, and I'm afraid he'll say it's too late. I feel tears building up behind my eyes. Then he stands up and holds out a hand towards my father and Kate. "One hour," he says.

Kate's gazing after a bus that has just begun to climb the hill. "We may as well go over as wait for the next bus," my father says, "and then it'll be back to the hotel for dinner."

Kate looks sideways at me. "And after all that he'll be ready for bed," she says like a question she isn't quite admitting to.

"Out like a light, I reckon."

"Fair enough," she says, and uses his arm to get herself up.

The boatman's name is Iannis, and he doesn't speak much English. My father seems to think he's charging too much for the trip until he realises it's that much for all three of us, and then he grins as if he thinks Iannis has cheated himself. "Heave ho then, Janice," he says with a wink at me and Kate.

The boat is about the size of a big rowboat. It has a cabin at the front and benches along the sides and a long box in the middle that shakes and smells of petrol. I watch the point of the boat sliding through the water like a knife and feel as if we're on our way to the Greece I've been dreaming of. The white buildings of Elounda shrink until they look like teeth in the mouth of the hills, and then Spinalonga floats up ahead.

It makes me think of an abandoned ship bigger than a liner, a ship so dead that it's standing still in the water without having to be anchored. The evening light seems to shine out of the steep rusty sides and the bony towers and walls high above the sea. I know it was a fort to begin with, but I think it might as well have been built for the lepers. I can imagine them trying to swim to Elounda and drowning because there wasn't enough left of them to swim with, if they didn't just throw themselves off the walls because they couldn't bear what they'd turned into. If I say these things to Kate I bet more than her mouth will squirm—but my father gets in first. "Look, there's the welcoming committee."

Kate gives a shiver that reminds me I'm trying not to feel cold. "Don't say things like that. They're just people like us, probably wishing they hadn't come."

I don't think she can see them any more clearly than I can. Their heads are poking over the wall at the top of the cliff above the little pebbly beach which is the only place a boat can land. There are five or six of them, only I'm not sure they're heads; they might be stones someone has balanced on the wall—they're almost the same colour. I'm wishing I had some binoculars when Kate grabs my father so hard the boat rocks and Iannis waves a finger at her, which doesn't please my father. "You keep your eye on your steering, Janice," he says.

Iannis is already taking the boat towards the beach. He didn't seem to notice the heads on the wall, and when I look again they aren't there. Maybe they belonged to some of the people who are coming down to a boat bigger than Iannis's. That boat chugs away as Iannis's bumps into the jetty. "One hour," he says. "Back here."

He helps Kate onto the jetty while my father glowers at him, then he lifts me out of the boat. As soon as my father steps onto the jetty, Iannis pushes the boat out again. "Aren't you staying?" Kate pleads.

He shakes his head and points hard at the beach. "Back here, one hour."

She looks as if she wants to run into the water and climb aboard the boat, but my father shoves his arm round her waist. "Don't worry, you've got two fellers to keep you safe, and neither of them with a girl's name."

The only way up to the fort is through a tunnel that bends in the middle so you can't see the end until you're nearly halfway in. I wonder how long it will take for the rest of the island to be as dark as the middle of the tunnel. When Kate sees the end she runs until she's in the open and stares at the sunlight, which is perched on top of the towers now. "Fancying a climb?" my father says.

She makes a face at him as I walk past her. We're in a kind of street of stone sheds that have mostly caved in. They must be where the lepers lived, but there are only shadows in them now, not even birds. "Don't go too far, Hugh," Kate says.

"I want to go all the way round, otherwise it wasn't worth coming."

"I don't, and I'm sure your father expects you to consider me."

"Now, now, children," my father says. "Hugh can do as he likes as long as he's careful and the same goes for us, eh, Kate?"

I can tell he's surprised when she doesn't laugh. He looks unsure of himself and angry about it, the way he did when he and my mother were getting ready to tell me they were splitting up. I run along the line of huts and think of hiding in one so I can jump out at Kate. Maybe they aren't empty after all; something rattles in one as if bones are crawling about in the dark. It could be a snake under part of the roof that's fallen. I keep running until I come to steps leading up from the street to the top of the island, where most of the light is, and I've started jogging up them when Kate shouts, "Stay where we can see you. We don't want you hurting yourself."

"It's all right, Kate, leave him be," my father says. "He's sensible."

"If I'm not allowed to speak to him I don't know why you invited me at all."

I can't help grinning as I sprint to the top of the steps and duck out of sight behind a grassy mound that makes me think of a grave. From up here I can see the whole island, and we aren't alone on it. The path I've run up from leads all round the island, past more huts and towers and a few bigger buildings, and then it goes down to the tunnel. Just before it does it passes the wall above the beach, and between the path and the wall there's a stone yard full of slabs. Some of the slabs have been moved away from holes like long boxes full of soil or darkness. They're by the wall where I thought I saw heads looking over at us. They aren't there now, but I can see heads bobbing down towards the tunnel. Before long they'll be behind Kate and my father.

Iannis is well on his way back to Elounda. His boat is passing one that's heading for the island. Soon the sun will touch the sea. If I went down to the huts I'd see it sink with me and drown. Instead I lie on the mound and look over the island, and see more of the boxy holes hiding behind some of the huts. If I went closer I could see how deep they are, but I quite like not knowing—if I was Greek I expect I'd think they lead to the underworld where all the dead live. Besides, I like being able to look down on my father and Kate and see them trying to see me.

I stay there until Iannis's boat is back at Elounda and the other one has almost reached Spinalonga, and the sun looks as if it's gone down to the sea for a drink. Kate and my father are having an argument. I expect it's about me, though I can't hear what they're saying; the darker it gets between the huts the more Kate waves her arms. I'm getting ready to let my father see me when she screams.

She's jumped back from a hut which has a hole behind it. "Come out, Hugh. I know it's you," she cries.

I can tell what my father's going to say, and I cringe. "Is that you, Hugh? Yoo-hoo," he shouts.

I won't show myself for a joke like that. He leans into the hut through the spiky stone window, then he turns to Kate. "It wasn't Hugh. There's nobody."

I can only just hear him, but I don't have to strain to hear Kate. "Don't tell me that," she cries. "You're both too fond of jokes."

She screams again, because someone's come running up the tunnel. "Everything all right?" this man shouts. "There's a boat about to leave if you've had enough."

"I don't know what you two are doing," Kate says like a duchess to my father, "but I'm going with this gentleman."

My father calls me twice. If I go to him I'll be letting Kate win. "I don't think our man will wait," the new one says.

"It doesn't matter," my father says, so fiercely that I know it does. "We've our own boat coming."

"If there's a bus before you get back I won't be hanging around," Kate warns him.

"Please yourself," my father says, so loud that his voice goes into the tunnel. He stares after her as she marches away; he must be hoping she'll change her mind. But I see her step off the jetty into the boat, and it moves out to sea as if the ripples are pushing it to Elounda.

My father puts a hand to his ear as the sound of the engine fades. "So every bugger's left me now, have they?" he says in a kind of shout at himself. "Well, good riddance."

He's waving his fists as if he wants to punch something, and he sounds as if he's suddenly got drunk. He must have been holding it back while Kate was there. I've never seen him like this. It frightens me, so I stay where I am.

It isn't only my father that frightens me. There's only a little bump of the sun left above the water now, and I'm afraid how dark the island may be once that goes. Bits of sunlight shiver on the water all the way to the island, and I think I see some heads above the wall of the yard full of slabs, against the light. Which side of the wall are they on? The light's too dazzling, it seems to pinch the sides of the heads so they look thinner than any heads I've ever seen. Then I notice a boat setting out from Elounda, and I squint at it until I'm sure it's Iannis's boat.

He's coming early to fetch us. Even that frightens me, because I wonder why he is. Doesn't he want us to be on the island now he realises how dark it's getting? I look at the wall, and the heads have gone. Then the sea puts the sun out, and it feels as if the island is buried in darkness.

I can still see my way down—the steps are paler than the dark—and I don't like being alone now I've started shivering. I back off from the mound, because I don't like to touch it, and almost back into a shape with bits of its head poking out and arms that look as if they've dropped off at the elbows. It's a cactus. I'm just standing up when my father says, "There you are, Hugh."

He can't see me yet. He must have heard me gasp. I go to the top of the steps, but I can't see him for the dark. Then his voice moves away. "Don't start hiding again. Looks like we've seen the last of Kate, but we've got each other, haven't we?"

He's still drunk. He sounds as if he's talking to somebody nearer to him than I am. "All right, we'll wait on the beach," he says, and his voice echoes. He's gone into the tunnel, and he thinks he's following me. "I'm here, Dad," I shout so loud that I squeak.

"I heard you, Hugh. Wait there. I'm coming." He's walking deeper into the tunnel. While he's in there my voice must seem to be coming from beyond the far end. I'm sucking in a breath that tastes dusty, so I can tell him where I am, when he says "Who's that?" with a laugh that almost shakes his words to pieces.

He's met whoever he thought was me when he was heading for the tunnel. I'm holding my breath—I can't breathe or swallow, and I don't know if I feel hot or frozen. "Let me past," he says as if he's trying to make his voice as big as the tunnel. "My son's waiting for me on the beach."

There are so many echoes in the tunnel I'm not sure what I'm hearing besides him. I think there's a lot of shuffling, and the other noise must be voices, because my father says, "What kind of language do you call that? You sound drunker than I am. I said my son's waiting."

He's talking even louder as if that'll make him understood. I'm embarrassed, but I'm more afraid for him. "Dad," I nearly scream, and run down the steps as fast as I can without falling.

"See, I told you. That's my son," he says as if he's talking to a crowd of idiots. The shuffling starts moving like a slow march, and he says, "All right, we'll all go to the beach together. What's the matter with your friends, too drunk to walk?"

I reach the bottom of the steps, hurting my ankles, and run along the ruined street because I can't stop myself. The shuffling sounds as though it's growing thinner, as if the people with my father are leaving bits of themselves behind, and the voices are changing too—they're looser. Maybe the mouths are getting bigger somehow. But my father's laughing, so loud that he might be trying to think of a joke. "That's what I call a hug. No harder, love, or I won't have any puff left," he says to someone. "Come on then, give us a kiss. They're the same in any language."

All the voices stop, but the shuffling doesn't. I hear it go out of the tunnel and onto the pebbles, and then my father tries to scream as if he's swallowed something that won't let him. I scream for him and dash into the tunnel, slipping on things that weren't on the floor when we first came through, and fall out onto the beach.

My father's in the sea. He's already so far out that the water is up to his neck. About six people who look stuck together and to him are walking him away as if they don't need to breathe when their heads start to sink. Bits of them float away on the waves my father makes as he throws his arms about and gurgles. I try to run after him, but I've got nowhere when his head goes underwater. The sea pushes me back on the beach, and I run crying up and down it until Iannis comes.

It doesn't take him long to find my father once he understands what I'm saying. Iannis wraps me in a blanket and hugs me all the way to Elounda and the police take me back to the hotel. Kate gets my mother's number and calls her, saying she's someone at the hotel who's looking after me because my father's drowned, and I don't care what she says, I just feel numb. I don't start screaming until I'm on the plane back to England, because then I dream that my father has come back to tell a joke. "That's what I call getting some tongue," he says, leaning his face close to mine and showing me what's in his mouth.

BEST NEW HORROR

Peter Atkins

Clive Barker

Les Daniels

Roberta Lannes

Kim Newman

EDITED BY
STEPHEN
JONES
AND
RAMSEY
CAMPBELL

4

Peter Straub

Karl Edward Wagner

and many more

[1992]

FOR THE FOURTH EDITION, Robinson Publishing foiled the now-familiar logo for the UK trade paperback. Thankfully, Carroll & Graf adapted the uncredited cover art for another classy-looking hardcover in the US.

Oddly, this time there was no American softcover edition (at least that I am aware of), although *Best New Horror 4* did become the first book in the series to get a foreign reprinting: *Horror: Il Meglio* (a phrase I've always wanted reproduced on a T-shirt) was published in Italy the following year in trade paperback with a dust-jacket painting by my old friend Les Edwards. Translation rights in other individual volumes have been sold to various countries over the years, although not nearly as often as I hoped.

At seventeen pages, the Introduction expanded for the first time beyond the eleven pages of the Necrology. Having had a go at a *Locus* reviewer the previous year, Ramsey and I strongly refuted comments made by Paul Brazier in the British SF magazine *Nexus*, in which he claimed that "the abattoir aspect of horror fiction has come to dominate the genre, until it seems we can expect blood to drip from every page..."

Roberta Lannes belatedly made it into the series with her tale "Dancing on a Blade of Dreams", and the twenty-four stories included *Hellraiser* alumni Clive Barker and Peter Atkins' first appearances in

Best New Horror. M. John Harrison was represented with two stories, including a collaboration with Simon Ings.

Ramsey and I have always agreed that humour can be a very important element in horror fiction and, when used well, has the ability to heighten the impact of the most gruesome tale. As an editor, I have also always felt that an anthology should comprise various different types of storytelling—to not only keep the reader off-balance, but to also offer differing moods and styles that hopefully compliment each other over the length of the book.

Norman Wisdom may not be all that familiar a name to American readers (he was something of an acquired taste in the UK as well), but for his debut in *Best New Horror*, Christopher Fowler used the British comedian as the inspiration for his tale of maniacal obsession.

Not only did the author watch every single Norman Wisdom movie before writing the story but—perhaps even more disturbingly—Chris admitted that he happened to find the comic really funny. It is unlikely that you will ever hear many people willing to admit to *that*...!

CHRISTOPHER FOWLER

NORMAN WISDOM AND
THE ANGEL OF DEATH

CHRISTOPHER FOWLER is the award-winning author of a number of short story collections and more than thirty novels, including the popular "Bryant & May" series of mysteries.

He has fulfilled several schoolboy fantasies—releasing a terrible Christmas pop single, becoming a male model, posing as the villain in a Batman graphic novel, running a night club, appearing in *The Pan Books of Horror Stories*, and standing in for James Bond.

His work divides into black comedy, horror, mystery, and tales unclassifiable enough to have publishers tearing their hair out.

His often hilarious and moving autobiography, *Paperboy*, was about growing up in London, while *The Book of Forgotten Authors*, featuring insightful mini-essays on ninety-nine forgotten authors and their forgotten books, was based on a series of columns he wrote for the *Independent on Sunday* newspaper.

Norman Wisdom (1915–2010) was a popular British comedian of the 1950s and '60s. His "little man" act, with him dressed in an ill-fitting suit and cloth cap, was often tinged with pathos.

"I watched every single Norman Wisdom film to write the following story," recalls Fowler, "and the idea came from reading about Asperger's Syndrome, the insidious disease that exists by degree in people who become obsessed with everything from train-spotting to *Star Trek*. If you've ever seen the home-video footage of mass-murderer Dennis Nilson and his victims, you'll know that far from being a Hannibal Lecter-type, he was a deeply boring man."

Diary Entry #1 Dated 2 July

THE PAST IS safe.

The future is unknown.

The present is a bit of a bastard.

Let me explain. I always think of the past as a haven of pleasant recollections. Long ago I perfected the method of siphoning off bad memories to leave only those images I still feel comfortable with. What survives in my mind is a seamless mosaic of faces and places that fill me with warmth when I choose to consider them. Of course, it's as inaccurate as those retouched Stalinist photographs in which comrades who have become an embarrassment have been imperfectly erased so that the corner of a picture still shows a boot or a hand. But it allows me to recall times spent with dear friends in the happy England that existed in the 1950s; the last era of innocence and dignity, when women offered no opinion on sexual matters and men still knew the value of a decent winter overcoat. It was a time that ended with the arrival of the Beatles, when youth replaced experience as a desirable national quality.

I am no fantasist. Quite the reverse; this process has a practical value. Remembering the things that once made me happy helps to keep me sane.

I mean that in *every* sense.

The future, however, is another kettle of fish. What can possibly be in store for us but something worse than the present? An acceleration of the ugly, tasteless, arrogant times in which we live. The Americans have already developed a lifestyle and a moral philosophy entirely modelled on the concept of shopping. What is left but to manufacture more things we don't need, more detritus to be thrown away, more vicarious thrills to be selfishly experienced? For a brief moment the national conscience flickered awake when it seemed that green politics was the only way to stop the planet from becoming a huge concrete turd. And what happened? Conversation was hijacked by the advertising industry and turned into a highly suspect sales concept.

No, it's the past that heals, not the future.

So what about the present? I mean right now.

At this moment, I'm standing in front of a full-length mirror reducing the knot of my tie and contemplating my frail, rather tired appearance. My name is Stanley Morrison, born March 1950 in East Finchley, North London. I'm a senior sales clerk for a large shoe firm, as they say on the quiz programmes. I live alone and have always done so, having never met the right girl. I have a fat cat called Hattie, named after Hattie Jacques, for whom I have a particular fondness in the role of Griselda Pugh in Series Five, Programmes One to Seven of *Hancock's Half Hour*, and a spacious but somewhat cluttered flat situated approximately 150 yards from the house in which I was born. My hobbies include collecting old radio shows and British films, of which I have an extensive collection, as well as a nigh-inexhaustible supply of amusing, detailed anecdotes about the forgotten British stars of the past. There's nothing I enjoy more than to recount these lengthy tales to one of my ailing, lonely patients and slowly destroy his will to live.

I call them my patients, but of course they aren't. I merely bring these poor unfortunates good cheer in my capacity as an official council HVF, that's a Hospital Visiting Friend. I am fully sanctioned by Haringey Council, an organisation filled with people of such astounding narrow-minded stupidity that they cannot see beyond their lesbian support groups to keeping the streets free of dog shit.

But back to the present.

I am rather tired at the moment because I was up half the night removing the remaining precious moments of life from a seventeen-year-old boy named David Banbury who had been in a severe motorcycle accident. Apparently he jumped the lights at the top of Shepherd's Hill and vanished under a truck conveying half-price personal stereos to the Asian shops in Tottenham Court Road. His legs were completely crushed, so much so that the doctor told me they couldn't separate his cycle leathers from his bones, and his spine was broken, but facial damage had been minimal, and the helmet he was wearing at the time of the collision had protected his skull from injury.

He hasn't had much of a life, by all accounts, having spent the last eight years in care, and has no family to visit him. Nurse Clarke informed me that he might well recover to lead a partially normal life, but would only be able to perform those activities involving a minimal amount of agonisingly slow movement, which would at least qualify him for a job in the Post Office.

Right now he could not talk, of course, but he could see and hear and feel, and I am reliably informed that he could understand every word I said, which was of great advantage as I was able to describe to him in enormous detail the entire plot of Norman Wisdom's 1965 masterpiece *The Early Bird*, his first colour film for the Rank Organisation, and I must say one of the finest examples of post-war British slapstick to be found on the face of this spinning planet we fondly call home.

On my second visit to the boy, my richly delineated account of the backstage problems involved in the production of an early Wisdom vehicle, *Trouble in Store*, in which the Little Comedian Who Won the Hearts of the Nation co-starred for the first time with his erstwhile partner and straight-man Jerry Desmonde, was rudely interrupted by a staff nurse who chose a crucial moment in my narration to empty a urine bag that seemed to be filling with blood. Luckily I was able to exact my revenge by punctuating my description of the film's highlights featuring Moira Lister and Margaret Rutherford with little twists of the boy's drip-feed to make sure that he was paying the fullest attention.

At half-past-seven yesterday evening I received a visit from the mentally disorientated liaison officer in charge of appointing visitors. Miss Chisholm is the kind of woman who has pencils in her hair and NUCLEAR WAR—NO THANKS stickers on her briefcase. She approaches her council tasks with the dispiriting grimness of a sailor attempting to plug leaks in a fast-sinking ship.

"Mr. Morrison," she said, trying to peer around the door of my flat, presumably in the vain hope that she might be invited in for a cup of tea, "you are one of our most experienced Hospital Helpers"—this part she had to check in her brimming folder to verify—"so I wonder if we could call upon you for an extracurricular visit at rather short notice."

She searched through her notes with the folder wedged under her chin and her case balanced on a raised knee. I did not offer any assistance. "The motorcycle boy..." She attempted to locate his name and failed.

"David Banbury," I said, helpfully supplying the information for her.

"He's apparently been telling the doctor that he no longer wishes to live. It's a common problem, but they think his case is particularly serious. He has no relatives." Miss Chisholm—if she has a Christian name I am certainly not privy to it—shifted her weight from one foot to the other as several loose sheets slid from her folder to the floor.

"I understand exactly what is needed," I said, watching as she struggled to reclaim her notes. "An immediate visit is in order."

As I made my way over to the hospital to comfort the poor lad, I thought of the ways in which I could free the boy from his morbid thoughts. First, I would recount all of the plot minutiae, technicalities and trivia I could muster surrounding the big-screen career and off-screen heartache of that Little Man Who Won All Our Hearts, Charlie Drake, climaxing with a detailed description of his 1966 magnum opus *The Cracksman*, in which he starred opposite a superbly erudite George Sanders, a man who had the good sense to kill himself when he grew bored with the world, and then I would encourage the boy to give up the fight, do the decent thing and die in his sleep.

As it happens, the evening turned out quite nicely.

By eleven-thirty I had concluded my description of the film, and detected a distinct lack of concentration on behalf of the boy, whose only response to my description of the frankly hysterical sewer-pipe scene was to blow bubbles of saliva from the corner of his mouth. In my frustration to command his attention, I applied rather more pressure to the sutures on his legs than I intended, causing the crimson blossom of a haemorrhage to appear through the blankets covering his pitifully mangled limbs.

I embarked upon a general plot outline of the classic 1962 Norman Wisdom vehicle *On the Beat*, never shifting my attention from the boy's eyes, which were now swivelling frantically in his waxen grey face, until the ruptured vessels of his leg could no longer be reasonably ignored. Then I summoned the night nurse. David Banbury died a few moments after she arrived at the bedside.

That makes eleven in four years.

Some didn't require any tampering with on my part, but simply gave up the ghost, losing the will to go on. I went home and made myself a cup of Horlicks, quietly rejoicing that another young man had gone to meet his maker with a full working knowledge of the later films of Norman Wisdom (not counting *What's Good for the Goose*, a prurient "adult" comedy directed by Menahem Golan which I regard as an offensive, embarrassing travesty unworthy of such a superb family performer).

Now, standing before the mirror attempting to comb the last straggling wisps of hair across my prematurely balding pate, I prepare to leave the house and catch the bus to work, and I do something I imagine most people have done from time to time when faced with their own reflection. I calm myself for the day ahead by remembering the Royal Variety Performance stars of 1952. The familiar faces of Naughton & Gold, Vic Oliver, Jewel & Warriss, Ted Ray, Winifred Atwell, Reg Dixon and the Tiller Girls crowd my mind as I steel myself to confront the self-centred young scum with whom I am forced to work. It is no secret that I have been passed over for promotion in my job on a number of occasions, but the most terrible slap-in-the-face yet performed by our new (foreign) management was administered last week, when a boy of just twenty-four was appointed as my superior! He likes people to call him Mick, walks around smiling like an idiot, travels to work wearing a Walkman, on which he plays percussive rubbish consisting of black men shouting at each other, and wears tight black jeans which seem specifically designed to reveal the contours of his genitalia. He shows precious little flair for the job, and has virtually no knowledge whatsoever of the pre-1960 British radio comedy scene.

Amazingly, everyone seems to like him.

Of course, he will have to go.

Diary Entry #2 Dated 23 August

Mick is a threat no more.

I simply waited until the appropriate opportunity arose, as I knew it eventually should. While I watched and listened, patiently enduring the oh-so-clever remarks he made to the office girls (most of whom resemble prostitutes from Michael Powell's excessively vulgar and unnecessary 1960 film *Peeping Tom*) about me, I comforted myself with memories of a happy, sunlit childhood, recalling a row of terraced houses patrolled by smiling policemen, uniformed milkmen and lollipop-ladies, a place in the past where Isobel Barnet was still guessing contestants' professions on *What's My Line*, Alma Cogan was singing 'Fly Me to the Moon' on the radio, cornflakes had red plastic guardsmen in their packets and everyone knew his place and damned well stayed in it. Even now when I hear the merry tinkle of 'Greensleeves' heralding the arrival of an ice-cream van beset by clamouring tots I get a painful, thrilling erection.

But I digress.

Last Tuesday, while shifting a wire-meshed crate in the basement workroom, Mick dislocated his little finger, cutting it rather nastily, so naturally I offered to accompany him to the casualty ward. As my flat is conveniently situated on the route to the hospital I was able to stop by for a moment, trotting out some absurd excuse for the detour. After waiting for over an hour to be seen, my nemesis was finally examined by Dr. MacGregor, an elderly physician of passing acquaintance whose name I only remember because it is also that of John Le Mesurier's character in *The Radio Ham*. My experience as an HVF had familiarised me with basic casualty procedures, and I knew that the doctor would most likely inject an antibiotic into the boy's hand to prevent infection. The needles for the syringes come in paper packets, and are sealed inside little plastic tubes that must be broken only by the attending physician. This is to prevent blood-carried infections from being transmitted.

It was hard to find a way around this, and indeed had taken dozens of attempts over the preceding months. The packets themselves were easy enough to open and reseal, but the tubes were a problem. After a great deal of practice, I found that I was able to melt the end of a tube closed without leaving any traces of tampering. To be on the safe side I had prepared three such needles in this fashion. (You must remember that, as well as having access to basic medical supplies—those items not actually locked away—I also possess an unlimited amount of patience, being willing to wait years if necessary to achieve my goals.)

While we waited for Dr. MacGregor to put in an appearance, the boy prattled on to me about work, saying how much he "truly valued my input". While he was thus distracted, it was a simple matter for me to replace the loose needles lying on the doctor's tray with my specially prepared ones.

A little while ago I throttled the life out of a very sick young man whose habit of nightly injecting drugs in the toilet of my local tube station had caused him to become ravaged with terminal disease. I would like to say that he died in order to make the world a safer, cleaner place, but the truth is that we went for a drink together and I killed him in a sudden fit of rage because he had not heard of Joyce Grenfell. How the Woman Who Won the Hearts of the Nation in her thrice-reprised role as Ruby Gates in the celebrated *St. Trinian's* films could have passed by him unnoticed is still a mystery to me. Anyway, I strangled the disgusting urchin with his own scarf and removed about a cupful of blood from his arm, into which I dropped a number of needles, filling their capillaries with the poisoned fluid. I then carefully wiped each one clean and inserted it into a tube, neatly resealing the plastic.

Dr. MacGregor was talking nineteen to the dozen as he inserted what he thought was a fresh needle into a vein on the back of Mick's hand. He barely even looked down to see what he was doing. Overwork and force of habit had won the day. Thank God for our decaying National Health Service, because I'd never have managed it if the boy had possessed private medical insurance. My unsuspecting adversary maintained an attitude of perky bravery as his finger was stitched up, and I laughed all the way home. Mick has been feeling unwell for several weeks now. A few days ago he failed to turn up for work. Apparently he has developed a complex and highly dangerous form of Hepatitis B. As they say, age and treachery will always overcome youth and enthusiasm.

Diary Entry #3 Dated 17 October

The hopeless liaison officer has returned with a new request.

Yesterday evening I opened the door of my flat to find her hovering on the landing uncertainly, as if she could not even decide where she felt comfortable standing.

"Can I help you?" I asked suddenly, knowing that my voice would make her jump. She had not caught me in a good mood. A month ago, Mick had been forced to resign through ill-health, but my promotion had still not been announced for consideration.

"Oh, Mr. Morrison, I didn't know if you were in," she said, her free hand rising to her flat chest.

"The best way to find out is by ringing the doorbell, Miss Chisholm." I opened the door wider. "Won't you come in?"

"Thank you." She edged gingerly past me with briefcase and folders, taking in the surroundings. Hattie took one look at her and shot off to her basket. "Oh, what an unusual room," she said, studying the walnut sideboard and armchairs, the matching butter-yellow standard lamps either side of the settee. "Do you collect Art Deco?"

"No," I said tersely. "This is my furniture. I suppose you'd like a cup of tea." I went to put the kettle on, leaving her hovering uncomfortably in the lounge. When I returned she was still standing, her head tilted on one side as she examined the spines of my post-war *Radio Times* collection.

"Please sit down, Miss Chisholm," I insisted. "I won't bite." And I really don't because teeth marks can be easily traced. At this instigation she perched herself on the edge of the armchair and nibbled at a bourbon. She had obviously rehearsed the speech that followed. "Mr. Morrison, I'm sure you've read in the papers that the health cuts are leaving hospitals in this area with an acute shortage of beds."

"I fear I haven't read a newspaper since they stopped printing *The Flutters* on the comic page of the *Daily Mirror*," I admitted, "but I have heard something of the sort."

"Well, it means that some people who are required to attend hospital for tests cannot be admitted as overnight patients any more. As you have been so very helpful in the past, we wondered if you could take in one of these patients."

"For how long?" I asked. "And what sort of patient?"

"It would be for two weeks at the most, and the patient I have in mind for you—" she churned up the contents of her disgusting briefcase trying to locate her poor victim's folder "—is a very nice young lady. She's a severe diabetic, and she's in a wheelchair. Apart from that, she's the same as you or I." She gave me a warm smile, then quickly looked away, sensing perhaps that I was not like other people. She handed me a dog-eared photograph of the patient, attached to a medical history that had more pages than an average weekly script of *The Clitheroe Kid*, a popular BBC radio show which for some reason has never been reissued on audio cassette.

"Her name is Saskia," said Miss Chisholm. "She has no family to speak of, and lives a long way from London. Ours is one of the few hospitals with the necessary equipment to handle complex drug and therapy trials for people like her. She desperately needs a place to stay. We can arrange to have her collected each day. We'd be terribly grateful if you could help. She really has nowhere else to go."

I studied the photograph carefully. The girl was pitifully small boned, with sallow, almost translucent skin. But she had attractive blonde hair, and well-defined features reminiscent of a young Suzy Kendall in Robert Hartford-Davis's patchy 1966 comedy portmanteau *The Sandwich Man*, in which Our Norman, playing an Irish priest, was not seen to his best advantage. What's more, she fitted in perfectly with my plans. A woman. That would certainly be different.

I returned the photograph with a smile. "I think we can work something out," I said.

Diary Entry #4 Dated 23 October

Saskia is here, and I must say that for someone so ill she is quite a tonic. The night she arrived, I watched as she struggled to negotiate her wheelchair around the flat without damaging the paintwork on the skirting boards, and despite many setbacks she managed it without a single protestation. Indeed, she has been here for two days now, and never seems to complain about anything or anyone. Apparently all of her life she has been prone to one kind of disease or another, and few doctors expected her to survive her childhood, so she is simply happy to be alive.

I have installed her in the spare room, which she insisted on filling with flowers purchased from the stall outside the hospital. Even Hattie, never the most amenable of cats, seems to have taken to her.

As my flat is on the second floor of a large Victorian house, she is a virtual prisoner within these walls during the hours outside her hospital visits. At those times the ambulance men carry her and the folded wheelchair up and down the stairs.

On her very first night here I entered the lounge to find her going through my catalogued boxes of BBC comedy archive tapes. I was just beginning to grow annoyed when she turned to me and asked if she could play some of them. No one had ever shown the least interest in my collection before. To test her, I asked which shows she would most enjoy hearing.

"I like Leslie Phillips in *The Navy Lark,* and the Fraser Hayes Four playing on *Round the Horne,*" she said, running a slim finger across the spines of the tape boxes. "And of course, *Hancock's Half Hour,* although I prefer the shows after Andrée Melly had been replaced by Hattie Jacques."

Suddenly I was suspicious.

This tiny girl could not be more than twenty-two years of age. How could she possibly be so familiar with radio programs that had scarcely been heard in thirty years? "My father was a great collector," she explained, as if she had just read my thoughts. "He used to play the old shows nearly every evening after dinner. It's one of the few lasting memories I have of my parents."

Well naturally, my heart went out to the poor girl. "I know exactly how you feel," I said. "I only have to hear Kenneth Williams say '*Good Evening*' and I'm reminded of home and hearth. They were such happy times for me."

For the next hour or so I sounded her out on other favourite film and radio memories of the past, but although there seemed no other common ground between us, she remained willing to listen to my happy tales and learn. At eleven o'clock she yawned and said that she would like to go to bed, and so I let her leave the lounge.

Last night Saskia was kept late at the hospital, and I was in bed by the time the heavy tread of the ambulance man was heard upon the stair. This morning she asked me if I would like her to cook an evening meal. After some initial concern with the hygiene problems involved in allowing one's meal to be cooked by someone else, I agreed. (In restaurants I assiduously question the waitresses about their sanitary arrangements.) Furthermore, I offered to buy produce for the projected feast, but she insisted on stopping by the shops on her way home from the hospital. Although she is frail, she demands independence. I will buy a bottle of wine. After being alone with my memories for so long, it is unnerving to have someone else in the apartment.

And yet it is rather wonderful.

Diary Entry #5 Dated 24 October

What an enthralling evening!

I feel as if I am truly alive for the first time in my life. Saskia returned early tonight—looking drawn and pale, but still vulnerably beautiful, with her blonde hair tied in a smart plait—and headed straight into the kitchen, where she stayed for several hours. I had arranged a ramp of planks by the cooker so that she could reach the hobs without having to rise from her chair.

Hattie, sensing that something tasty was being prepared, hung close to the base of the door, sniffing and licking her chops. To amuse Saskia while she cooked I played dialogue soundtracks which I had recorded in my local cinema as a child during performances of *Passport to Pimlico* and *The Lavender Hill Mob*, but the poor quality of the tapes (from a small reel-to-reel recorder I had smuggled into the auditorium) was such that I imagine the subtleties of these screenplays were rather lost to her, especially as she had the kitchen door shut and was banging saucepans about.

The meal was a complete delight. We had a delicious tomato and basil soup to start with, and a truly spectacular *salmon en croûte* as the main course, followed by cheese and biscuits.

Saskia told me about herself, explaining that her parents had been killed in a car crash when she was young. This tragedy had forced her to live with a succession of distant and ancient relatives. When the one she was staying with died, she was shunted into a foster home. No one was willing to take her, though, as the complications arising from her diabetes would have made enormous demands on any foster parent.

As she talked she ate very little, really only toying with her food. The diabetes prevents her from enjoying much of anything, but hopefully the tests she is undergoing will reveal new ways of coping with her restricted lifestyle.

The dining table is too low to comfortably incorporate Saskia's wheelchair, so I have promised to raise it for tomorrow's dinner, which I have insisted on cooking. I was rather nervous at the prospect, but then I thought: if a cripple can do it, so can I. Saskia is so kind and attentive, such a good listener. Perhaps it is time for me to introduce my pet topic into the dinner conversation.

Diary Entry #6 Dated 25 October

Disaster has struck!

Right from the start everything went wrong—and just as we were getting along so well. Let me set it out from the beginning.

The meal. I cooked a meal tonight that was not as elaborate as the one she had prepared, and nothing like as good. This was partly because I was forced to work late (still no news of my promotion), so most of the shops were shut, and partly because I have never cooked for a woman before. The result was a microwaved dinner that was still freezing cold in the centre of the dish, but if Saskia didn't like it she certainly didn't complain. Instead she gave a charming broad smile (one which she is using ever more frequently with me) and slowly chewed as she listened to my detailed description of the indignities daily heaped upon me at the office.

I had bought another bottle of wine, and perhaps had drunk a little too much of it by myself (Saskia being unable to drink for the rest of the week), because I found myself introducing the subject of him, Our Norman, the Little Man Who Won All Our Hearts, before we had even finished the main course. Wishing to present the topic in the correct context I chose to start with a basic chronology of Norman's film appearances, beginning with his thirteen-and-a-half-second appearance in *A Date with a Dream* in 1948. I had made an early decision to omit all but the most essential stage and television appearances of the Little Man for fear of tiring her, and in my description of the films stuck mainly to the classic set pieces, notably the marvellous "Learning to Walk" routine from *On the Beat* and the ten-minute "Tea-making" sequence from the opening of *The Early Bird*.

I was about to mention Norman's 1956 appearance with Ruby Murray at the Palladium in *Painting the Town* when I became distinctly aware of her interest waning. She was fidgeting about in her chair as if anxious to leave the table.

"Anyone would think you didn't like Norman Wisdom," I said, by way of a joke.

"Actually, I'm not much of a fan, no," she said suddenly, then added, "Forgive me, Stanley, but I've suddenly developed a headache." And with that she went to her room, without even offering to do the washing up. Before I went to bed I stood outside her door listening, but could hear nothing.

I have a bad feeling about this.

Diary Entry #7 Dated 27 October

She is avoiding me.

It sounds hard to believe, I know, but there can be no other explanation. Last night she returned to the flat and headed directly to her room. When I put my head around the door to see if she wanted a late-night cup of cocoa (I admit this was at three o'clock in the morning, but I could not sleep for worrying about her), it seemed that she could barely bring herself to be polite. As I stepped into the room, her eyes widened and she pulled the blankets around her in a defensive gesture, which seemed to suggest a fear of my presence. I must confess I am at a loss to understand her.

Could she have led me on, only pretending to share my interests for some secret purpose of her own?

Diary Entry #8 Dated 1 November

At work today we were informed that Mick had died. Complications from the hepatitis, annoyingly unspecified, but I gained the distinct impression that they were unpleasant. When one of the secretaries started crying I made a passing flippant remark that was, I fear, misconstrued, and the girl gave me a look of utter horror. She's a scruffy little tart who was sweet on Mick, and much given to conspiring with him about me. I felt like giving her something to be horrified about, and briefly wondered how she would look tied up with baling wire, hanging in a storm drain. The things we think about to get us through the day.

At home the situation has worsened. Saskia arrived tonight with a male friend, a doctor whom she had invited back for tea. While she was in the kitchen the two of us were left alone in the lounge, and I noticed that he seemed to be studying me from the corner of his eye. It was probably just an occupational habit, but it prompted me to wonder if Saskia had somehow voiced her suspicions to him (assuming she has any, which I consider unlikely).

After he had gone, I explained that it was not at all permissible for her to bring men into the house no matter how well she knew them, and she had the nerve to turn in her chair and accuse me of being old-fashioned!

"What on earth do you mean?" I asked her.

"It's not healthy, Stanley, surrounding yourself with all this," she explained, indicating the alphabetised film and tape cassettes that filled the shelves on the wall behind us. "Most of these people have been dead for years."

"Shakespeare has been dead for years," I replied, "and people still appreciate him."

"But he wrote plays and sonnets of lasting beauty," she persisted. "These people you listen to were just working comics. It's lovely to collect things, Stanley, but this stuff was never meant to be taken so seriously. You can't base your life around it." There was an irritating timbre in her voice that I had not noticed before. She sat smugly back in her wheelchair, and for a moment I wanted to smother her. I could feel my face growing steadily redder with the thought.

"Why shouldn't these people still be admired?" I cried, running to the shelves and pulling out several of my finest tapes. "Most of them had dreary lives filled with hardship and pain, but they made people laugh, right through the war and the years of austerity that followed. They carried on through poverty and ill-health and misery. Everyone turned on the radio to hear them. Everyone went to the pictures to see them. It was something to look forward to. They kept people alive. They gave the country happy memories. Why shouldn't someone remember them for what they did?"

"All right, Stanley. I'm sorry—I didn't mean to upset you," she said, reaching out her hand, but I pushed it away. It was then that I realised my cheeks were wet, and I turned aside in shame. To think that I had been brought to this state, forced to defend myself in my own home, by a woman, and a wheelchair-bound one at that.

"This is probably a bad time to mention it," said Saskia, "but I'm going to be leaving London earlier than I first anticipated. In fact, I'll be going home tomorrow. The tests haven't taken as long as the doctors thought."

"But what about the results?" I asked.

"They've already made arrangements to send them to my local GP. He'll decide whether further treatment is necessary."

I hastily pulled myself together and made appropriate polite sounds of disappointment at the idea of her departure, but inside a part of me was rejoicing. You see, I had been watching her hands as they rested on the arms of her wheelchair. They were trembling.

And she was lying.

Diary Entry #9 Dated 2 November

I have much to relate.

After our altercation last night, both of us knew that a new level in our relationship had been reached. The game had begun. Saskia refused my conciliatory offer of tea and went straight to her bedroom, quietly locking the door behind her. I know because I tried to open it at two o'clock this morning, and I heard her breath catch in the darkness as I twisted the knob from side to side.

I returned to my room and forced myself to stay there. The night passed slowly, with both of us remaining uncomfortably awake on our respective beds. In the morning, I left the house early so that I would not be forced to trade insincere pleasantries with her over breakfast. I knew she would be gone by the time I returned, and that, I think, suited both of us. I was under no illusions—she was a dangerous woman, too independent, too free-minded to ever become my friend. We could only be adversaries. And I was dangerous to her. I had enjoyed her company, but now she would only be safe far away from me. Luckily, I would never see her again. Or so I thought. For, fast as the future, everything changed between us.

Oh, how it changed.

This morning, I arrived at work to find a terse note summoning me to my supervisor's office. Naturally I assumed that I was finally being notified of my promotion. You may imagine my shock when, in the five-minute interview that followed, it emerged that far from receiving advancement within the company, I was being fired! I did not "fit in" with the new personnel, and as the department was being "stream-lined" they were "letting me go". Depending on my attitude to this news, they were prepared to make me a generous cash settlement if I left at once, so that they could immediately begin "implementing procedural changes".

I did not complain. This sort of thing has happened many times before. I do not fit in. I say this not to gain sympathy, but as a simple statement of fact. Intellect always impedes popularity. I accepted the cash offer. Disheartened, but also glad to be rid of my vile "colleagues", I returned home.

It was raining hard when I arrived at the front gate. I looked up through the dark sycamores and was surprised to find a light burning in the front room. Then I realised that Saskia was reliant on the council for arranging her transport, and as they were never able to specify an exact collection time, she was still in the house. I knew I would have to use every ounce of my control to continue behaving in a correct and civilised manner. As I turned the key in the lock I heard a sudden scuffle of movement inside the flat.

Throwing the door wide, I entered the lounge and found it empty. The sound was coming from my bedroom. A terrible deadness flooded through my chest as I tiptoed along the corridor, carefully avoiding the boards that squeaked.

Slowly, I moved into the doorway. She was on the other side of the room with her back to me. The panels of the wardrobe were folded open, and she had managed to pull one of the heavy-duty bin-liners out on the floor. Somehow she sensed that I was behind her, and the wheelchair spun around. The look on her face was one of profound disturbance.

"What have you done with the rest of them?" she said softly, her voice wavering. She had dislodged a number of air fresheners from the sacks, and the room stank of lavender.

"You're not supposed to be in here," I explained as reasonably as possible. "This is my private room."

I stepped inside and closed the door behind me. She looked up at the pinned pictures surrounding her. The bleak monochrome of a thousand celebrity photographs seemed to absorb the light within the room.

"Saskia. You're an intelligent girl. You're modern. But you have no respect for the past."

"The past?" Her lank hair was falling in her eyes, as she flicked it aside I could see she was close to tears. "What has the past to do with this?" She kicked out uselessly at the plastic sack and it fell to one side, spilling its rotting human contents onto the carpet.

"Everything," I replied, moving forward. I was not advancing on her, I just needed to get to the bedside cabinet. "The past is where everything has its rightful place."

"I know about your past, Stanley," she cried, pushing at the wheels of her chair, backing herself up against the wardrobe, turning her face from the stinking mess. "Nurse Clarke told me all about you."

"What did she say?" I asked, coming to a halt. I was genuinely curious. Nurse Clarke had hardly ever said more than two words to me.

"I know what happened to you. That's why I came here." She started to cry now, and wiped her nose with the back of her hand. Something plopped obscenely onto the floor as the sack settled. "She says you had the worst childhood a boy could ever have. Sexual abuse, violence. You lived in terror every day. Your father nearly killed you before the authorities took charge. Don't you see? That's why you're so obsessed with this stuff, this trivia, it's like a disease. You're just trying to make things all right again."

"That's a damn lie!" I shouted at her. "My childhood was perfect. You're making it up!"

"No," she said, shaking her head, snot flying from her nose. "I saw the marks when you were in the kitchen that first night. Cigarette burns on your arms. Cuts too deep to ever heal. I thought I knew how you must have felt. Like me, always shoved around, always towered over, always scared. I didn't expect anything like this. What were you thinking of?"

"Are you sure you don't know?" I asked, advancing towards the cabinet. "I'm the kind of person nobody notices. I'm invisible until I'm pointed out. I'm in a private world. I'm not even ordinary. I'm somewhere below that."

I had reached the cabinet, and now slowly pulled open the drawer, groping inside as she tried to conceal her panic, tried to find somewhere to wheel the chair.

"But I'm not alone," I explained. "There are many like me. I see them begging on the streets, soliciting in pubs, injecting themselves in alleyways. For them childhood is a scar that never heals, but still they try to stumble on. I end their stumbling, Saskia. Miss Chisholm says I'm an angel."

My fingers closed around the handle of the carving knife, but the point was stuck in the rear wall of the drawer. I gave it my attention and pulled it free, lowering the blade until it was flat against my leg. A sound from behind made me turn. With a dexterity that amazed me, the infuriating girl had opened the door and slipped through. I ran into the lounge to find her wheelchair poised before the tape archives and Saskia half-out of the seat, one hand pincering a stack of irreplaceable 78s featuring the vocal talents of Flanagan and Allen.

"Leave those alone!" I cried. "You don't understand."

She turned to me with what I felt as a look of deliberate malice on her face and raised the records high above her head. If I attacked her now, she would surely drop them.

"Why did you kill those people?" she asked simply. For a moment I was quite at a loss. She deserved an explanation. I ran my left thumb along the blade of the knife, drawing in my breath as the flesh slowly parted and the pain showed itself.

"I wanted to put their pasts right," I explained. "To give them the things that comfort. Tony Hancock. Sunday roast. Family favourites.

Smiling policemen. Norman Wisdom. To give them the freedom to remember."

I must have allowed the knife to come into view, because her grip on the records faltered and they slid from her hands to the floor. I don't think any smashed, but the wheels of her chair cracked several as she rolled forward.

"I can't give you back the past, Saskia," I said, walking towards her, smearing the knife blade with the blood from my stinging thumb. "I'm sorry, because I would have liked to."

She cried out in alarm, pulling stacks of records and tapes down upon herself, scattering them across the threadbare carpet. Then she grabbed the metal frame of the entire cabinet, as if trying to shake it loose from the wall. I stood and watched, fascinated by her fear.

When I heard the familiar heavy boots quickening on the stairs, I turned the knife over and pushed the blade hard into my chest. It was a reflex action, as if I had been planning to do this all along. Just as I had suspected, there was no pain. To those like us who suffered so long, there is no more pain.

Diary Entry #10 Dated 16 November

And now I am sitting here on a bench with a clean elastic bandage patching up my stomach, facing the bristling cameras and microphones, twenty enquiring faces before me, and the real probing questions have begun.

The bovine policewoman who interrogated me so unimaginatively during my initial detainment period bore an extraordinary resemblance to Shirley Abicair, the Australian zither player who performed superbly as Norman's love interest in Rank's 1954 hit comedy *One Good Turn*, although the *Evening News* critic found their sentimental scenes together an embarrassment.

I think I am going to enjoy my new role here. Newspapers are fighting for my story. They're already comparing me to Nilsen and Sutcliffe, although I would rather be compared to Christie or Crippen. Funny how everyone remembers the name of a murderer, but no one remembers the victim.

If they want to know, I will tell them everything. Just as long as I can tell them about my other pet interests.

My past is safe.

My future is known.

My present belongs to Norman.

THE

BEST NEW

HORROR

**THE YEAR'S BEST HORROR
STORIES BY SUCH MASTERS
OF DARK FANTASY AS:**

POPPY Z. BRITE
HARLAN ELLISON
DENNIS ETCHISON
KATHE KOJA
KIM NEWMAN
and many others

EDITED BY

STEPHEN JONES
AND
RAMSEY CAMPBELL

"The collection we'd
recommend if you have to
make a choice"
- *INTERZONE*

[1993]

BEING AN EDITOR is a tough job, but somebody's got to do it. Regrettably, as a full-time author, Ramsey decided that he could no longer devote so much of his time and energy ploughing through the piles of submissions, and so he reluctantly decided that *The Best New Horror Volume Five* would be his last as co-editor.

I certainly enjoyed our five years of collaboration and, generously, he has remained an unofficial advisor and sounding board for this series over the subsequent years.

With the fifth volume, Robinson decided to give the book a total re-design. And thank goodness that they did! With a new, improved, logo, a split cover design, and Luis Rey's superb artwork now highlighted in spot-varnish, the book finally achieved the impact I thought it deserved. It also resulted in Carroll & Graf dropping its alternative hardcover edition in favour of the new-look trade paperback, finally bringing a sense of cohesion back to the series.

With the book's total extent now more than 500 pages, the Introduction hit its stride at twenty-five pages, and the Necrology expanded to fourteen. For our final editorial together, Ramsey and I went on at some length about the current state of censorship on both sides of the Atlantic.

As we concluded: "So long as such controversy can be fanned by the cynical media, hypocritical politicians and misinformed public opinion, we should all be on our guard. It is all too easy to use horror fiction and films as a scapegoat for economic and social deprivation. As most intelligent people realise, fiction is only a reflection of life. The real problems exist elsewhere..."

Over the intervening years, nothing very much has happened for me to change that opinion.

Among the twenty-nine contributions was the first appearance in *Best New Horror* of the amazingly talented Terry Lamsley, along with Dennis Etchison's British Fantasy Award-winning story 'The Dog Park'. In fact, Ramsey and I dedicated the book to Dennis (who sadly died in 2019) in recognition of our first visit to Mexico with him some years earlier, when he acted as our intrepid guide.

However, choosing a representative story from this particular volume was easy.

Harlan Ellison had a reputation of sometimes being difficult to work with. Yet in all my dealings with him over the years, I never found him to be other than extremely pleasant and accommodating. In fact, when it came to publishing his work, he was the consummate professional— something an editor always appreciates.

At the time, the Bram Stoker Award-winning novella 'Mefisto in Onyx' was one of the longest pieces of fiction Harlan had written in some years. It was also, without any doubt, also one of the most powerful...

HARLAN ELLISON®

MEFISTO IN ONYX

H ARLAN ELLISON (1934–2018) won the Hugo Award eight-
and-a-half times, the Nebula Award four times, the Bram Stoker
Award five times (including Lifetime Achievement in 1996) and the
Mystery Writers of America Edgar Allan Poe Award twice.

He was also the recipient of the Silver Pen for Journalism by
International P.E.N., the World Fantasy Award, the Georges Méliès
fantasy film award, an unprecedented four Writers Guild of America
awards for Most Outstanding Teleplay and the International Horror
Guild's Living Legend Award. In 2006, he was made a Grand Master
by the Science Fiction and Fantasy Writers of America (SFWA).

Ellison moved to New York in his early twenties to pursue a writing
career, and over the next two years he published more than 100 stories
and articles. Relocating to California in 1962, he began selling to
Hollywood, co-scripting the 1966 movie *The Oscar* and contributing
two dozen scripts to such shows as *Star Trek, The Outer Limits, The
Man from U.N.C.L.E., The Alfred Hitchcock Hour, Cimarron Strip,
Route 66, Burke's Law* and *The Flying Nun.* His story 'A Boy and His
Dog' was filmed in 1975, starring Don Johnson, and he was a creative
consultant on the 1980s revival of *The Twilight Zone* TV series.

His books include *Rumble* (aka *Web of the City*), *Rockabilly* (aka
Spider Kiss), *All the Lies That Are My Life* and *Mefisto in Onyx*, while
some of his almost 2,000 short stories have been collected in *The*

119

Juvies (aka *Children of the Street*), *Ellison Wonderland, Paingod and Other Delusions, I Have No Mouth and I Must Scream, Love Ain't Nothing But Sex Misspelled, The Beast That Shouted Love at the Heart of the World, Deathbird Stories, Strange Wine, Shatterday, Stalking the Nightmare, Angry Candy, Slippage* and *The Essential Ellison: A 50-Year Retrospective* edited by Terry Dowling.

Ellison also edited the influential science fiction anthology *Dangerous Visions* in 1967, and followed it with a sequel, *Again Dangerous Visions*, in 1972.

More recently, he was the subject of Erik Nelson's revelatory feature-length documentary *Dreams with Sharp Teeth* (2008), chronicling the author's life and work, which was made over a period of twenty-seven years.

The powerful Bram Stoker Award-winning novella that follows (which the author referred to as a "toad-strangler") was originally written to be adapted into a movie starring Forrest Whitaker, which never happened.

As *The New York Times* said in its review: "It is a reminder that Ellison has not lost his capacity to convey stark, staring psychosis."

O NCE. I ONLY went to bed with her once. Friends for eleven years—before and since—but it was just one of those things, just one of those crazy flings: the two of us alone on a New Year's Eve, watching rented Marx Brothers videos so we wouldn't have to go out with a bunch of idiots and make noise and pretend we were having a good time when all we'd be doing was getting drunk, whooping like morons, vomiting on slow-moving strangers, and spending more money than we had to waste. And we drank a little too much cheap champagne; and we fell off the sofa laughing at Harpo a few times too many; and we wound up on the floor at the same time; and next thing we knew we had our faces plastered together, and my hand up her skirt, and her hand down in my pants...

But it was just the *once*, fer chrissakes! Talk about imposing on a cheap sexual liaison! She *knew* I went mixing in other peoples' minds only when I absolutely had no other way to make a buck. Or I forgot myself and did it in a moment of human weakness.

It was always foul.

Slip into the thoughts of the best person who ever lived, even Saint Thomas Aquinas, for instance, just to pick an absolutely terrific person you'd think had a mind so clean you could eat off it (to paraphrase my mother), and when you come out—take my word for it—you'd want to take a long, intense shower in Lysol.

Trust me on this: I go into somebody's landscape when there's *nothing else* I can do, no other possible solution... or I forget and do it in a moment of human weakness. Such as, say, the IRS holds my feet to the fire; or I'm about to get myself mugged and robbed and maybe murdered; or I need to find out if some specific she that I'm dating has been using somebody else's dirty needle or has been sleeping around without she's taking some extra-heavy-duty AIDS precautions; or a co-worker's got it in his head to set me up so I make a mistake and look bad to the boss and I find myself in the unemployment line again; or...

I'm a wreck for weeks after.

Go jaunting through a landscape trying to pick up a little insider arbitrage bric-a-brac, and come away no better heeled, but all muddy with the guy's infidelities, and I can't look a decent woman in the eye for days. Get told by a motel desk clerk that they're all full up and he's sorry as hell but I'll just have to drive on for about another thirty miles to find the next vacancy, jaunt into his landscape and find him lit up with neon signs that got a lot of the word *nigger* in them, and I wind up hitting the sonofabitch so hard his grandmother has a bloody nose, and usually have to hide out for three or four weeks after. Just about to miss a bus, jaunt into the head of the driver to find his name so I can yell for him to hold it a minute Tom or George or Willie, and I get smacked in the mind with all the garlic he's been eating for the past month because his doctor told him it was good for his system, and I start to dry-heave, and I wrench out of the landscape, and not only have I missed the bus, but I'm so sick to my stomach I have to sit down on the filthy curb to get my gorge submerged. Jaunt into a potential employer, to see if he's trying to lowball me, and I learn he's part of a massive cover-up of industrial malfeasance that's caused hundreds of people to die when this or that cheaply-made grommet or tappet or gimbal mounting under-performs and fails, sending the poor souls falling thousands of feet to shrieking destruction. Then just *try* to accept the job, even if you haven't paid your rent in a month. No way.

Absolutely: I listen in on the landscape *only* when my feet are being fried; when the shadow stalking me turns down alley after alley tracking me relentlessly; when the drywall guy I've hired to repair the damage done by my leaky shower presents me with a dopey smile and a bill three hundred and sixty bucks higher than the estimate. Or in a moment of human weakness.

But I'm a wreck for weeks after. For weeks.

Because you can't, you simply can't, you absolutely *cannot* know what people are truly and really like till you jaunt their landscape. If Aquinas had had my ability, he'd have very quickly gone off to be a hermit, only occasionally visiting the mind of a sheep or a hedgehog. In a moment of human weakness.

That's why in my whole life—and, as best I can remember back, I've been doing it since I was five- or six-years-old, maybe even younger—there have only been eleven, maybe twelve people, of all those who know that I can "read minds", that I've permitted myself to get close to. Three of them never used it against me, or tried to exploit me, or tried to kill me when I wasn't looking. Two of those three were my mother and father, a pair of sweet old black folks who'd adopted me, a late-in-life baby, and were now dead (but probably still worried about me, even on the Other Side), and whom I missed very very much, particularly in moments like this. The other eight, nine were either so turned off by the knowledge that they made sure I never came within a mile of them—one moved to another entire country just to be on the safe side, although her thoughts were a helluva lot more boring and innocent than she thought they were—or they tried to brain me with something heavy when I was distracted—I still have a shoulder separation that kills me for two days before it rains—or they tried to use me to make a buck for them. Not having the common sense to figure it out, that if I was *capable* of using the ability to make vast sums of money, why the hell was I living hand-to-mouth like some overaged grad student who was afraid to desert the university and go become an adult?

Now *they* was some dumb-ass muthuhfugguhs.

Of the three who never used it against me—my mom and dad—the last was Allison Roche. Who sat on the stool next to me, in the middle of May, in the middle of a Wednesday afternoon, in the middle of Clanton, Alabama, squeezing ketchup onto her All-American Burger, imposing on the memory of that one damned New Year's Eve sexual interlude, with Harpo and his sibs; the two of us all alone except for the fry-cook; and she waited for my reply.

"I'd sooner have a skunk spray my pants leg," I replied.

She pulled a napkin from the chrome dispenser and swabbed up the red that had overshot the sesame-seed bun and redecorated the Formica countertop. She looked at me from under thick, lustrous eyelashes; a look of impatience and violet eyes that must have been a killer when she unbottled it at some truculent witness for the defence. Allison Roche was a Chief Deputy District Attorney in and for Jefferson County, with her office in Birmingham. Alabama. Near where we sat, in Clanton, having a secret meeting, having All-American Burgers; three years after having had quite a bit of champagne, 1930s black-and-white video rental comedy, and black-and-white sex. One extremely stupid New Year's Eve.

Friends for eleven years. And once, just once; as a prime example of what happens in a moment of human weakness. Which is not to say that it wasn't terrific, because it was; absolutely terrific; but we never did it again; and we never brought it up again after the next morning when we opened our eyes and looked at each other the way you look at an exploding can of sardines, and both of us said *Oh Jeeezus* at the same time. Never brought it up again until this memorable afternoon at the greasy spoon where I'd joined Ally, driving up from Montgomery to meet her halfway, after her peculiar telephone invitation. Can't say the fry-cook, Mr. All-American, was particularly happy at the pigmentation arrangement at his counter. But I stayed out of his head and let him think what he wanted. Times change on the outside, but the inner landscape remains polluted.

"All I'm asking you to do is go have a chat with him," she said. She gave me that look. I have a hard time with that look. It isn't entirely honest, neither is it entirely disingenuous. It plays on my remembrance of that one night we spent in bed. And is just *dis*honest enough to play on the part of that night we spent on the floor, on the sofa, on the coffee counter between the dining room and the kitchenette, in the bathtub, and about nineteen minutes crammed among her endless pairs of shoes in a walk-in clothes closet that smelled strongly of cedar and virginity. She gave me that look, and wasted no part of the memory.

"I don't *want* to go have a chat with him. Apart from he's a piece of human shit, and I have better things to do with my time than to go on down to Atmore and take a jaunt through this crazy sonofabitch's diseased mind, may I remind you that of the hundred and sixty, seventy men who have died in that electric chair, including the original 'Yellow Mama' they scrapped in 1990, about a hundred and thirty of them were gentlemen of colour, and I do not mean you to picture any colour of a shade much lighter than that cuppa coffee you got sittin' by your left hand right this minute, which is to say that I, being an inordinately well-educated African-American who values the full measure of living negritude in his body, am not crazy enough to want to visit a racist '*co-*rectional centre' like Holman Prison, thank you very much."

"Are you finished?" she asked, wiping her mouth.

"Yeah. I'm finished. Case closed. Find somebody else."

She didn't like that. "There *isn't* anybody else."

"There has to be. Somewhere. Go check the research files at Duke University. Call the Fortean Society. Mensa. *Jeopardy*. Some 900 number astrology psychic hotline. Ain't there some semi-senile Senator with a full-time paid assistant who's been trying to get legislation through one of the statehouses for the last five years to fund this kind of bullshit research? What about the Russians . . . now that the Evil Empire's fallen, you ought to be able to get some word about their success with Kirlian auras or whatever those assholes were working at. Or you could—"

She screamed at the top of her lungs. "*Stop it, Rudy!*"

The fry-cook dropped the spatula he'd been using to scrape off the grill. He picked it up, looking at us, and his face (I didn't read his mind) said *If that white bitch makes one more noise I'm callin' the cops.*

I gave him a look he didn't want, and he went back to his chores, getting ready for the after-work crowd. But the stretch of his back and angle of his head told me he wasn't going to let this pass.

I leaned in towards her, got as serious as I could, and just this quietly, just this softly, I said, "Ally, good pal, listen to me. You've been one of the few friends I could count on, for a long time now. We have history between us, and you've *never*, not once, made me feel like a freak. So okay, I trust you. I trust you with something about me that causes immeasurable goddam pain. A thing about me that could get me killed. You've never betrayed me, and you've never tried to use me.

"Till now. This is the first time. And you've got to admit that it's not even as rational as you maybe saying to me that you've gambled away every cent you've got and you owe the mob a million bucks and would I mind taking a trip to Vegas or Atlantic City and taking a jaunt into the minds of some high-pocket poker players so I could win you enough to keep the goons from shooting you. Even *that*, as creepy as it would be if you said it to me, even *that* would be easier to understand than *this!*"

She looked forlorn. "There isn't anybody else, Rudy. *Please.*"

"What the hell is this all about? Come on, tell me. You're hiding something, or holding something back, or lying about—"

"*I'm not lying!*" For the second time she was suddenly, totally, extremely pissed at me. Her voice spattered off the white tile walls. The fry-cook spun around at the sound, took a step towards us, and I jaunted into his landscape, smoothed down the rippled Astro-Turf, drained away the storm clouds, and suggested in there that he go take a cigarette break out back. Fortunately, there were no other patrons at the elegant All-American Burger that late in the afternoon, and he went.

"Calm fer chrissakes down, will you?" I said.

She had squeezed the paper napkin into a ball.

She was lying, hiding, holding something back. Didn't have to be a telepath to figure *that* out. I waited, looking at her with a slow, careful distrust, and finally she sighed, and I thought, *Here it comes.*

"Are you reading my mind?" she asked.

"Don't insult me. We know each other too long."

She looked chagrined. The violet of her eyes deepened. "Sorry."

But she didn't go on. I wasn't going to be outflanked. I waited. After a while she said, softly, very softly, "I think I'm in love with him. I *know* I believe him when he says he's innocent."

I never expected that. I couldn't even reply.

It was unbelievable. Unfuckingbelievable. She was the Chief Deputy D.A. who had prosecuted Henry Lake Spanning for murder. Not just one murder, one random slaying, a heat of the moment Saturday night killing regretted deeply on Sunday morning but punishable by electrocution in the Sovereign State of Alabama nonetheless, but a string of the vilest, most sickening serial slaughters in Alabama history, in the history of the Glorious South, in the history of the United States. Maybe even in the history of the entire wretched human universe that went wading hip-deep in the wasted spilled blood of innocent men, women and children.

Henry Lake Spanning was a monster, an ambulatory disease, a killing machine without conscience or any discernible resemblance to a thing we might call decently human. Henry Lake Spanning had butchered his way across a half-dozen states; and they had caught up to him in Huntsville, in a garbage dumpster behind a supermarket, doing something so vile and inhuman to what was left of a sixty-five-year-old cleaning woman that not even the tabloids would get more explicit than *unspeakable*; and somehow he got away from the cops; and somehow he evaded their dragnet; and somehow he found out where the police lieutenant in charge of the manhunt lived; and somehow he slipped into that neighbourhood when the lieutenant was out creating roadblocks—and he gutted the man's wife and two kids. Also the family cat. And then he killed a couple of more times in Birmingham and Decatur, and by then had gone so completely out of his mind that they got him again, and the second time they hung onto him, and they brought him to trial. And Ally had prosecuted this bottom-feeding monstrosity.

And oh, what a circus it had been. Though he'd been *caught*, the second time, and this time for keeps, in Jefferson County, scene of three of his most sickening jobs, he'd murdered (with such a disgustingly similar m.o. that it was obvious he was the perp) in twenty-two of the sixty-seven counties; and every last one of them wanted him to stand trial in that venue. Then there were the other five states in which he had butchered, to a total body-count of fifty-six. Each of *them* wanted him extradited.

So, here's how smart and quick and smooth an attorney Ally is: she somehow managed to cosy up to the Attorney General, and somehow managed to unleash those violet eyes on him, and somehow managed to get and keep his ear long enough to con him into setting a legal precedent. Attorney General of the State of Alabama allowed Allison Roche to consolidate, to secure a multiple bill of indictment that forced Spanning to stand trial on all twenty-nine Alabama murder counts at once. She meticulously documented to the state's highest courts that Henry Lake Spanning presented such a clear and present danger to society that the prosecution was willing to take a chance (big chance!) of trying in a winner-take-all consolidation of venues. Then she managed to smooth the feathers of all those other vote-hungry prosecutors in those twenty-one other counties, and she put on a case that dazzled everyone, including Spanning's defence attorney, who had screamed about the legality of the multiple bill from the moment she'd suggested it.

And she won a fast jury verdict on all twenty-nine counts. Then she got *really* fancy in the penalty phase after the jury verdict, and proved up the *other* twenty-seven murders with their flagrantly identical trademarks, from those other five states, and there was nothing left but to sentence Spanning—essentially for all fifty-six—to the replacement for the "Yellow Mama".

Even as pols and power brokers throughout the state were murmuring Ally's name for higher office, Spanning was slated to sit in that new electric chair in Holman Prison, built by the Fred A. Leuchter Associates of Boston, Massachusetts, that delivers 2,640 volts of pure sparklin' death in 1/240th of a second, six times faster than the 1/40th of a second that it takes for the brain to sense it, which is—if you ask me—much too humane an exit line, more than three times the 700-volt jolt lethal dose that destroys a brain, for a pusbag like Henry Lake Spanning.

But if we were lucky—and the scheduled day of departure was very nearly upon us—if we were lucky, if there was a God and Justice and

Natural Order and all that good stuff, then Henry Lake Spanning, this foulness, this corruption, this thing that lived only to ruin... would end up as a pile of fucking ashes somebody might use to sprinkle over a flower garden, thereby providing this ghoul with his single opportunity to be of some use to the human race.

That was the guy that my pal Allison Roche wanted me to go and "chat" with, down to Holman Prison, in Atmore, Alabama. There, sitting on Death Row, waiting to get his demented head tonsured, his pants legs slit, his tongue fried black as the inside of a sheep's belly... down there at Holman my pal Allison wanted me to go "chat" with one of the most awful creatures made for killing this side of a hammerhead shark, which creature had an infinitely greater measure of human decency than Henry Lake Spanning had ever demonstrated. Go chit-chat, and enter his landscape, and read his mind, Mr. Telepath, and use the marvellous mythic power of extrasensory perception: this nifty swell ability that has made me a bum all my life, well, not *exactly* a bum: I do have a decent apartment, and I do earn a decent, if sporadic, living; and I try to follow Nelson Algren's warning never to get involved with a woman whose troubles are bigger than my own; and sometimes I even have a car of my own, even though at that moment such was not the case, the Camaro having been repo'd, and not by Harry Dean Stanton or Emilio Estevez, lemme tell you; but a bum in the sense of—how does Ally put it?—oh yeah—I don't "realise my full and forceful potential"—a bum in the sense that I can't hold a job, and I get rotten breaks, and all of this despite a Rhodes scholarly education so far above what a poor nigrahlad such as myself could expect that even Rhodes hisownself would've been chest-out proud as hell of me. A bum, mostly, despite an *outstanding* Rhodes scholar education and a pair of kind, smart, loving parents—even for foster-parents—shit, who died knowing the certain sadness that their only child would spend his life as a wandering freak unable to make a comfortable living or consummate a normal marriage or raise children without the fear of passing on this special personal horror... this astonishing ability fabled in song and story that I possess... that no one else seems to possess, though I know there must have been others, somewhere, sometime, somehow! Go, Mr. Wonder of Wonders, shining black Cagliostro of the modern world, go with this super nifty swell ability that gullible idiots and flying saucer assholes have been trying to prove exists for at least fifty years, that no one has been able to isolate the way I, me, the only one has been isolated, let me tell you about *isolation*, my brothers; and here I was, here was I, Rudy Pairis...just a guy, making a buck every now and then with nifty swell impossible ESP, resident of thirteen states and twice that many cities so far in his mere thirty years of landscape-jaunting life, here was I, Rudy Pairis, Mr. I-Can-Read- Your-Mind, being asked to go and walk through the mind of a killer who scared half the people in the world. Being asked by the only living person, probably, to whom I could not say no. And, oh, take me at my word here: I *wanted* to say no. *Was*, in fact, saying no at every breath. What's that? Will I do it? Sure, yeah sure, I'll go on down to Holman and jaunt through this sick bastard's mind landscape. Sure I will. You got two chances: slim, and none.

All of this was going on in the space of one greasy double cheeseburger and two cups of coffee.

The worst part of it was that Ally had somehow gotten involved with him. *Ally!* Not some bimbo bitch...but *Ally*. I couldn't believe it.

Not that it was unusual for women to become mixed up with guys in the joint, to fall under their "magic spell", and to start corresponding with them, visiting them, taking them candy and cigarettes, having conjugal visits, playing mule for them and smuggling in dope where the tampon never shine, writing them letters that got steadily more exotic, steadily more intimate, steamier and increasingly dependent emotionally. It wasn't that big a deal; there exist entire psychiatric treatises on the phenomenon; right alongside the papers about women who go stud-crazy for cops. No big deal indeed: hundreds of women every year find themselves writing to these guys, visiting these guys, building dream castles with these guys, fucking these guys, pretending that even the worst of these guys, rapists and woman-beaters and child molesters, repeat paedophiles of the lowest pustule sort, and murderers and stick-up punks who crush old ladies' skulls for food stamps, and terrorists and bunco barons...that one sunny might-be, gonna-happen pink cloud day these demented creeps will emerge from behind the walls, get back in the wind, become upstanding nine-to-five

Brooks Bros. Galahads. Every year hundreds of women marry these guys, finding themselves in a hot second snookered by the wily, duplicitous, motherfuckin' lying greaseball addictive behaviour of guys who had spent their sporadic years, their intermittent freedom on the outside, doing *just that*: roping people in, ripping people off, bleeding people dry, conning them into being tools, taking them for their every last cent, their happy home, their sanity, their ability to trust or love ever again.

But this wasn't some poor illiterate naïve woman-child. This was *Ally*. She had damned near pulled off a legal impossibility, come *that* close to Bizarro Jurisprudence by putting the Attorneys General of five other states in a maybe frame of mind where she'd have been able to consolidate a multiple bill of indictment *across state lines*! Never been done; and now, probably, never ever would be. But she could have possibly pulled off such a thing. Unless you're a stone court-bird, you can't know what a mountaintop that is! So, now, here's Ally, saying this shit to me. Ally, my best pal, stood up for me a hundred times; not some dip, but the steely-eyed Sheriff of Suicide Gulch, the over-forty, past the age of innocence, no-nonsense woman who had seen it all and come away tough but not cynical, hard but not mean.

"I think I'm in love with him," she had said.

"I *know* I believe him when he says he's innocent," she had said.

I looked at her. No time had passed. It was still the moment the universe decided to lie down and die. And I said, "So if you're certain this paragon of the virtues *isn't* responsible for fifty-six murders—that we *know* about—and who the hell knows how many more we *don't* know about, since he's apparently been at it since he was twelve years old—remember the couple of nights we sat up and you *told* me all this shit about him, and you said it with your skin crawling, *remember?*— then if you're so damned positive the guy you spent eleven weeks in court sending to the chair is innocent of butchering half the population of the planet—then why do you need me to go to Holman, drive all the way to Atmore, just to take a jaunt in this sweet peach of a guy?

"Doesn't your 'woman's intuition' tell you he's squeaky clean? Don't 'true love' walk yo' sweet young ass down the primrose path with sufficient surefootedness?"

"Don't be a smartass!" she said.

"Say again?" I replied, with disfuckingbelief.

"I said: don't be such a high-verbal goddamned smart aleck!"

Now *I* was steamed. "No, I shouldn't be a smartass: I should be your pony, your show dog, your little trick bag mind-reader freak! Take a drive over to Holman, Pairis; go right on into Rednecks from Hell; sit your ass down on Death Row with the rest of the niggers and have a chat with the one white boy who's been in a cell up there for the past three years or so; sit down nicely with the king of the fucking vampires, and slide inside his garbage dump of a brain—and what a joy *that's* gonna be, I can't believe you'd ask me to do this—and read whatever piece of boiled shit in there he calls a brain, and see if he's jerking you around. *That's* what I ought to do, am I correct? Instead of being a smartass. Have I got it right? Do I properly pierce your meaning, pal?"

She stood up. She didn't even say *Screw you, Pairis!*

She just slapped me as hard as she could.

She hit me a good one straight across the mouth.

I felt my upper teeth bite my lower lip. I tasted the blood. My head rang like a church bell. I thought I'd fall off the goddam stool. When I could focus, she was just standing there, looking ashamed of herself, and disappointed, and mad as hell, and worried that she'd brained me. All of that, all at the same time. Plus, she looked as if I'd broken her.

"Okay," I said wearily, and ended the word with a sigh that reached all the way back into my hip pocket. "Okay, calm down. I'll see him. I'll do it. Take it easy."

She didn't sit down. "Did I hurt you?"

"No, of course not," I said, unable to form the smile I was trying to put on my face. "How could you possibly hurt someone by knocking his brains into his lap?"

She stood over me as I clung precariously to the counter, turned halfway around on the stool by the blow. Stood over me, the balled-up paper napkin in her fist, a look on her face that said she was nobody's fool, that we'd known each other a long time, that she hadn't asked this kind of favour before, that if we were buddies and I loved her, that I would see she was in deep pain, that she was conflicted, that she needed to know, *really* needed to know without a doubt, and in the name of God—in which she believed, though I didn't, but either way what the hell—that I do this thing for her, that I just *do it* and not give her any more crap about it.

So I shrugged, and spread my hands like a man with no place to go, and I said, "How'd you get into this?"

She told me the first fifteen minutes of her tragic, heartwarming, never-to-be- ridiculed story still standing. After fifteen minutes I said, "Fer chrissakes, Ally, at least *sit down*! You look like a damned fool standing there with a greasy napkin in your mitt." A couple of teenagers had come in. The four-star chef had finished his cigarette out back and was reassuringly in place, walking the duckboards and dishing up All-American arterial cloggage.

She picked up her elegant attaché case and without a word, with only a nod that said let's get as far from them as we can, she and I moved to a double against the window to resume our discussion of the varieties of social suicide available to an unwary and foolhardy gentleman of the coloured persuasion if he allowed himself to be swayed by a cagey and cogent, clever and concupiscent female of another colour entirely.

See, what it is, is this:

Look at that attaché case. You want to know what kind of an Ally this Allison Roche is? Pay heed, now.

In New York, when some wannabe junior ad exec has smooched enough butt to get tossed a bone account, and he wants to walk his colours, has a need to signify, has got to demonstrate to everyone that he's got the juice, first thing he does, he hies his ass downtown to Barney's, West 17th and 7th, buys hisself a Burberry, loops the belt casually *behind*, leaving the coat open to suh*wing*, and he circumnavigates the office.

In Dallas, when the wife of the CEO has those six or eight upper-management husbands and wives over for an *intime, faux* casual dinner, *sans* place-cards, *sans entrée* fork, *sans cérémonie*, and we're talking the kind of woman who flies Virgin Air instead of the Concorde, she's so in charge she don't got to use the Orrefors, she can put out the Kosta Boda and say *give a fuck*.

What it is, kind of person so in charge, so easy with they own self, they don't *have* to laugh at your poor dumb struttin' Armani suit, or your bedroom done in Laura Ashley, or that you got a gig writing articles of person Ally Roche is, you take a look at that attaché case, and it'll tell you everything you need to know about how strong she is, because it's an Atlas. Not a Hartmann. Understand: she could *afford* a Hartmann, that gorgeous imported Canadian belting leather, top of the line, somewhere around nine-hundred-and-fifty bucks maybe, equivalent of Orrefors, a Burberry, breast of guinea hen and Mouton Rothschild 1492 or 1066 or whatever year is the most expensive, drive a Rolls instead of a Bentley and the only difference is the grille... but she doesn't *need* to signify, doesn't *need* to suh*wing*, so she gets herself this Atlas. Not some dumb chickenshit Louis Vuitton or Mark Cross all the divorcée real estate ladies carry, but an Atlas. Irish hand-leather. Custom tanned cowhide. Hand-tanned in Ireland by out-of-work IRA bombers. Very classy. Just a state understated. See that attaché case? That tell you why I said I'd do it?

She picked it up from where she'd stashed it, right up against the counter wall by her feet, and we went to the double over by the window, away from the chef and the teenagers, and she stared at me till she was sure I was in a right frame of mind, and she picked up where she'd left off.

The next twenty-three minutes by the big greasy clock on the wall she related from a sitting position. Actually, a series of sitting positions. She kept shifting in her chair like someone who didn't appreciate the view of the world from that window, someone hoping for a sweeter horizon. The story started with a gang-rape at the age of thirteen, and moved right along: two broken foster-home families, a little casual fondling by surrogate poppas, intense studying for perfect school grades as a substitute for happiness, working her way through John Jay College of Law, a truncated attempt at wedded bliss in her late twenties, and the long miserable road of legal success that had brought her to Alabama. There could have been worse places.

I'd known Ally for a long time, and we'd spent totals of weeks and months in each other's company. Not to mention the New Year's Eve of the Marx Brothers. But I hadn't heard much of this. Not much at all.

Funny how that goes. Eleven years. You'd think I'd've guessed or suspected or *some*thing. What the hell makes us think we're friends with *any*body, when we don't know the first thing about them, not really?

What are we, walking around in a dream? That is to say: what the fuck are we *thinking*!?!

And there might never have been a reason to hear *any* of it, all this Ally that was the real Ally, but now she was asking me to go somewhere I didn't want to go, to do something that scared the shit out of me; and she wanted me to be as fully informed as possible.

It dawned on me that those same eleven years between us hadn't really given her a full, laser-clean insight into the why and wherefore of Rudy Pairis, either. I hated myself for it. The concealing, the holding-back, the giving up only fragments, the evil misuse of charm when honesty would have hurt. I was facile, and a very quick study; and I had buried all the equivalents to Ally's pains and travails. I could've matched her, in spades; or blacks, or just plain nigras. But I remained frightened of losing her friendship. I've never been able to believe in the myth of unqualified friendship. Too much like standing hip-high in a fast-running, freezing river. Standing on slippery stones.

Her story came forward to the point at which she had prosecuted Spanning; had amassed and winnowed and categorised the evidence so thoroughly, so deliberately, so flawlessly; had orchestrated the case so brilliantly; that the jury had come in with guilty on all twenty-nine, soon—in the penalty phase—fifty-six. Murder in the first. Premeditated murder in the first. Premeditated murder with special ugly circumstances in the first. On each and every of the twenty-nine. Less than an hour it took them. There wasn't even time for a lunch break. Fifty-one minutes it took them to come back with the verdict guilty on all charges. Less than a minute per killing. Ally had done that.

His attorney had argued that no direct link had been established between the fifty-sixth killing (actually, only his twenty-ninth in Alabama) and Henry Lake Spanning. No, they had not caught him down on his knees eviscerating the shredded body of his final victim— ten-year-old Gunilla Ascher, a parochial school girl who had missed her bus and been picked-up by Spanning just about a mile from her home in Decatur—no, not down on his knees with the can opener still in his sticky red hands, but the m.o. was the same, and he was there in Decatur, on the run from what he had done in Huntsville, what they had *caught* him doing in Huntsville, in that dumpster, to that old woman. So they *couldn't* place him with his smooth, slim hands inside dead Gunilla Ascher's still-steaming body. So what? They could not have been surer he was the serial killer, the monster, the ravaging nightmare whose methods were so vile the newspapers hadn't even *tried* to cobble up some smart-aleck name for him like The Strangler or The Backyard Butcher. The jury had come back in fifty-one minutes, looking sick, looking as if they'd try and try to get everything they'd seen and heard out of their minds, but knew they never would, and wishing to God they could've managed to get out of their civic duty on this one.

They came shuffling back in and told the numbed court: hey, put this slimy excuse for a maggot in the chair and cook his ass till he's fit only to be served for breakfast on cinnamon toast. This was the guy my friend Ally told me she had fallen in love with. The guy she now believed to be innocent.

This was seriously crazy stuff.

"So how did you get, er, uh, how did you...?"

"How did I fall in love with him?"

"Yeah. That."

She closed her eyes for a moment, and pursed her lips as if she had lost a flock of wayward words and didn't know where to find them. I'd always known she was a private person, kept the really important history to herself—hell, until now I'd never known about the rape, the ice mountain between her mother and father, the specifics of the seven-month marriage—I'd known there'd been a husband briefly; but not what had happened; and I'd known about the foster homes; but again, not how lousy it had been for her—even so, getting *this* slice of steaming craziness out of her was like using your teeth to pry the spikes out of Jesus' wrists.

Finally, she said, "I took over the case when Charlie Whilborg had his stroke..."

"I remember."

"He was the best litigator in the office, and if he hadn't gone down two days before they caught..." she paused, had trouble with the name, went on, "...before they caught Spanning in Decatur, and if Morgan County hadn't been so worried about a case this size, and bound Spanning over to us in Birmingham...all of it so fast nobody really had a chance to talk to him...I was the first one even got *near* him, everyone was so damned scared of him, of what they *thought* he was..."

"Hallucinating, were they?" I said, being a smartass.

"Shut up. The office did most of the donkeywork after that first interview I had with him. It was a big break for me in the office; and I got obsessed by it. So after the first interview, I never spent much actual time with Spanky, never got too close, to see what kind of a man he really..."

I said: "Spanky? Who the hell's 'Spanky'?"

She blushed. It started from the sides of her nostrils and went out both ways toward her ears, then climbed to the hairline. I'd seen that happen only a couple of times in eleven years, and one of those times had been when she'd farted at the opera. *Lucia di Lammermoor.*

I said it again: "Spanky? You're putting me on, right? You call him *Spanky?*" The blush deepened. "Like the fat kid in *The Little Rascals*... c'mon, I don't fuckin' be*lieve* this!"

She just glared at me.

I felt the laughter coming. My face started twitching.

She stood up again. "Forget it. Just forget it, okay?" She took two steps away from the table, towards the street exit. I grabbed her hand and pulled her back, trying not to fall apart with laughter, and I said, "Okay okay okay...I'm *sorry*...I'm really and truly, honest to goodness, may I be struck by a falling space lab no kidding 100 per cent absolutely sorry...but you gotta admit...catching me unawares like that...I mean, come *on*, Ally...*Spanky!?!* You call this guy who murdered at least fifty-six people Spanky? Why not Mickey, or Froggy, or Alfalfa...? I can understand not calling him Buckwheat, you can save that one for me, but *Spanky*???"

And in a moment *her* face started to twitch; and in another moment she was starting to smile, fighting it every micron of the way; and in another moment she was laughing and swatting at me with her free hand; and then she pulled her hand loose and stood there falling apart with laughter; and in about a minute she was sitting down again. She threw the balled-up napkin at me.

"It's from when he was a kid," she said. "He was a fat kid, and they made fun of him. You know the way kids are…they corrupted Spanning into 'Spanky' because *The Little Rascals* were on television and…oh, shut *up*, Rudy!" She watched me with an exasperated wariness till she was sure I wasn't going to run any more dumb gags on her, and then she resumed. "After Judge Fay sentenced him, I handled Spa…*Henry's* case from our office, all the way up to the appeals stage. I was the one who did the pleading against clemency when Henry's lawyers took their appeal to the Eleventh Circuit in Atlanta.

"When he was denied a stay by the appellate, three-to-nothing, I helped prepare the brief when Henry's counsel went to the Alabama Supreme Court; then when the Supreme Court refused to hear his appeal, I thought it was all over. I knew they'd run out of moves for him, except maybe the Governor; but that wasn't ever going to happen. So I thought: *that's that*.

"When the Supreme Court wouldn't hear it three weeks ago, I got a letter from him. He'd been set for execution next Saturday, and I couldn't figure out why he wanted to see *me*."

I asked, "The letter…it got to you how?"

"One of his attorneys."

"I thought they'd given up on him."

"So did I. The evidence was so overwhelming; half-a-dozen counsellors found ways to get themselves excused; it wasn't the kind of case that would bring any litigator good publicity. Just the number of eyewitnesses in the parking lot of that Winn-Dixie in Huntsville… must have been fifty of them, Rudy. And they all saw the same thing, and they all identified Henry in line-up after line-up, twenty, thirty, could have been fifty of them if we'd needed that long a parade. And all the rest of it…"

I held up a hand. *I know*, the flat hand against the air said. She had told me all of this. Every grisly detail, till I wanted to puke. It was as if I'd done it all myself, she was so vivid in her telling. Made my jaunting nausea pleasurable by comparison. Made me so sick I couldn't even think about it. Not even in a moment of human weakness.

"So the letter comes to you from the attorney..."

"I think you know this lawyer. Larry Borlan; used to be with the ACLU; before that he was senior counsel for the Alabama Legislature down to Montgomery; stood up, what was it, twice, three times, before the Supreme Court? Excellent guy. And not easily fooled."

"And what's *he* think about all this?"

"He thinks Henry's absolutely innocent."

"Of all of it?"

"Of everything."

"But there were fifty disinterested random eyewitnesses at one of those slaughters. Fifty, you just said it. Fifty, you could've had a parade. All of them nailed him cold, without a doubt. Same kind of kill as all the other fifty-five, including that school-kid in Decatur when they finally got him. And Larry Borlan thinks he's not the guy, right?"

She nodded. Made one of those sort of comic pursings of the lips, shrugged, and nodded. "Not the guy."

"So the killer's still out there?"

"That's what Borlan thinks."

"And what do *you* think?"

"I agree with him."

"Oh, jeezus, Ally, my aching boots and saddle! You got to be workin' some kind of off-time! The killer is still out here in the mix, but there hasn't been a killing like those Spanning slaughters for the three years that he's been in the joint. Now *what* do that say to you?"

"It says whoever the guy *is*, the one who killed all those people, he's *days* smarter than all the rest of us, and he set up the perfect free-floater to take the fall for him, and he's either long far gone in some other state, working his way, or he's sitting quietly right here in Alabama, waiting and watching. And smiling." Her face seemed to sag with misery. She started to tear up, and said, "In four days he can stop smiling."

Saturday night.

"Okay, take it easy. Go on, tell me the rest of it. Borlan comes to you, and he begs you to read Spanning's letter and...?"

"He didn't beg. He just gave me the letter, told me he had no idea what Henry had written, but he said he'd known me a long time, that he thought I was a decent, fair-minded person, and he'd appreciate it in the name of our friendship if I'd read it."

"So you read it."

"I read it."

"Friendship. Sounds like you an' him was *good* friends. Like maybe you and I were good friends?"

She looked at me with astonishment.

I think *I* looked at me with astonishment. "Where the hell did *that* come from?" I said.

"Yeah, really," she said, right back at me, "where the hell *did* that come from?" My ears were hot, and I almost started to say something about how if it was okay for *her* to use our Marx Brothers indiscretion for a lever, why wasn't it okay for me to get cranky about it? But I kept my mouth shut; and for once knew enough to move along. "Must've been *some* letter," I said.

There was a long moment of silence during which she weighed the degree of shit she'd put me through for my stupid remark, after all this was settled; and having struck a balance in her head, she told me about the letter.

It was perfect. It was the only sort of come-on that could lure the avenger who'd put you in the chair to pay attention. The letter had said that fifty-six was not the magic number of death. That there were many, *many* more unsolved cases, in many, *many* different states; lost children, runaways, unexplained disappearances, old people, college students hitchhiking to Sarasota for Spring Break, shopkeepers who'd carried their day's take to the night deposit drawer and never gone home for dinner, hookers left in pieces in Hefty bags all over town, and death death death unnumbered and unnamed. Fifty-six, the letter had said, was just the start. And if she, her, no one else, Allison Roche, my pal Ally, would come on down to Holman, and talk to him, Henry Lake Spanning would help her close all those open files. National rep. Avenger of the unsolved. Big time mysteries revealed. "So you read the letter, and you went . . ."

"Not at first. Not immediately. I was sure he was guilty, and I was pretty certain at that moment, three years and more, dealing with the case, I was pretty sure if he said he could fill in all the blank spaces, that he could do it. But I just didn't like the idea. In court, I was always twitchy when I got near him at the defence table. His eyes, he never took them off me. They're blue, Rudy, did I tell you that...?"

"Maybe. I don't remember. Go on."

"Bluest blue you've ever seen...well, to tell the truth, he just plain *scared* me. I wanted to win that case so badly, Rudy, you can never know...not just for me or the career or for the idea of justice or to avenge all those people he'd killed, but just the thought of him out there on the street, with those blue eyes, so blue, never stopped looking at me from the moment the trial began...the *thought* of him on the loose drove me to whip that case like a howling dog. I *had* to put him away!"

"But you overcame your fear."

She didn't like the edge of ridicule on the blade of that remark. "That's right. I finally 'overcame my fear' and I agreed to go see him."

"And you saw him."

"Yes."

"And he didn't know shit about no other killings, right?"

"Yes."

"But he talked a good talk. And his eyes was blue, so blue."

"Yes, you asshole."

I chuckled. Everybody is somebody's fool.

"Now let me ask you this—very carefully—so you don't hit me again: the moment you discovered he'd been shuckin' you, lyin', that he *didn't* have this long, unsolved crime roster to tick off, why didn't you get up, load your attaché case, and hit the bricks?"

Her answer was simple. "He begged me to stay a while."

"That's it? He *begged* you?"

"Rudy, he has no one. He's *never* had anyone." She looked at me as if I were made of stone, some basalt thing, an onyx statue, a figure carved out of melanite, soot and ashes fused into a monolith. She feared she could not, in no way, no matter how piteously or bravely she phrased it, penetrate my rocky surface.

Then she said a thing that I never wanted to hear.

"Rudy..."

Then she said a thing I could never have imagined she'd say. Never in a million years.

"Rudy…"

Then she said the most awful thing she could say to me, even more awful than that she was in love with a serial killer.

"Rudy… go inside… read my mind… I need you to know, I need you to understand… Rudy…"

The look on her face killed my heart.

I tried to say no, oh god no, not that, please, no, not that, don't ask me to do that, please *please* I don't want to go inside, we mean so much to each other, I don't *want* to know your landscape. Don't make me feel filthy, I'm no peeping-tom, I've *never* spied on you, never stolen a look when you were coming out of the shower, or undressing, or when you were being sexy… I never invaded your privacy, I wouldn't *do* a thing like that… we're friends, I don't need to know it all, I don't *want* to go in there. I can go inside anyone, and it's always awful… please don't make me see things in there I might not like, you're my friend, please don't steal that from me…

"Rudy, *please*. Do it."

Oh jeezusjeezusjeezus, again, she said it again!

We sat there. And we sat there. And we sat there longer. I said, hoarsely, in fear, "Can't you just… just *tell* me?"

Her eyes looked at stone. A man of stone. And she tempted me to do what I could do casually, tempted me the way Faust was tempted by Mefisto, Mephistopheles, Mefistofele, Mephostopilis. Black rock Dr. Faustus, possessor of magical mind-reading powers, tempted by thick, lustrous eyelashes and violet eyes and a break in the voice and an imploring movement of hand to face and a tilt of the head that was pitiable and the begging word *please* and all the guilt that lay between us that was mine alone. The seven chief demons. Of whom Mefisto was the one "not loving the light".

I knew it was the end of our friendship. But she left me nowhere to run. Mefisto in onyx.

So I jaunted into her landscape.

I stayed in there less than ten seconds. I didn't want to know everything

I could know; and I definitely wanted to know *nothing* about how she really thought of me. I couldn't have borne seeing a caricature of a bug-eyed, shuffling, thick-lipped darkie in there. Mandingo man. Steppin Porchmonkey Rudy Pair...

Oh god, what was I thinking!

Nothing in there like that. Nothing! Ally wouldn't *have* anything like that in there. I was going nuts, going absolutely fucking crazy, in there, back out in less than ten seconds. I want to block it, kill it, void it, waste it, empty it, reject it, squeeze it, darken it, obscure it, wipe it, do away with it like it never happened. Like the moment you walk in on your momma and poppa and catch them fucking, and you want never to have known that.

But at least I understood.

In there, in Allison Roche's landscape, I saw how her heart had responded to this man she called Spanky, not Henry Lake Spanning. She did not call him, in there, by the name of a monster; she called him a honey's name. I didn't know if he was innocent or not, but *she* knew he was innocent. At first she had responded to just talking with him, about being brought up in an orphanage, and she was able to relate to his stories of being used and treated like chattel, and how they had stripped him of his dignity, and made him afraid all the time. She knew what that was like. And how he'd always been on his own. The running-away. The being captured like a wild thing, and put in this home or that lock-up or the orphanage "for his own good". Washing stone steps with a tin bucket full of grey water, with a horsehair brush and a bar of lye soap, till the tender folds of skin between the fingers were furiously red and hurt so much you couldn't make a fist.

She tried to tell me how her heart had responded, with a language that has never been invented to do the job. I saw as much as I needed, there in that secret landscape, to know that Spanning had led a miserable life, but that somehow he'd managed to become a decent human being. And it showed through enough when she was face to face with him, talking to him without the witness box between them, without the adversarial thing, without the tension of the courtroom and the gallery and those parasite creeps from the tabloids sneaking around taking pictures of him, that she identified with his pain. Hers had been not the same, but similar; of a kind, if not of identical intensity.

She came to know him a little.

And came back to see him again. Human compassion. In a moment of human weakness.

Until, finally, she began examining everything she had worked up as evidence, trying to see it from *his* point of view, using *his* explanations of circumstantiality. And there were inconsistencies. Now she saw them. Now she did not turn her prosecuting attorney's mind from them, recasting them in a way that would railroad Spanning; now she gave him just the barest possibility of truth. And the case did not seem as incontestable.

By that time, she had to admit to herself, she had fallen in love with him. The gentle quality could not be faked; she'd known fraudulent kindness in her time.

I left her mind gratefully. But at least I understood. "Now?" she asked.

Yes, now. Now I understood. And the fractured glass in her voice told me. Her face told me. The way she parted her lips in expectation, waiting for me to reveal what my magic journey had conveyed by way of truth. Her palm against her cheek. All that told me. And I said, "Yes."

Then, silence, between us.

After a while she said, "I didn't feel anything."

I shrugged. "Nothing to feel. I was in for a few seconds, that's all."

"You didn't see everything?"

"No."

"Because you didn't want to?"

"Because..."

She smiled. "I understand, Rudy."

Oh, do you? Do you really? That's just fine. And I heard me say, "You made it with him yet?"

I could have torn off her arm; it would've hurt less.

"That's the second time today you've asked me that kind of question. I didn't like it much the first time, and I like it less *this* time."

"You're the one wanted me to go into your head. I didn't buy no ticket for the trip."

"Well, you were in there. Didn't you look around enough to find out?"

"I didn't look for that."

"What a chickenshit, wheedling, lousy and *cowardly* . . ."

"I haven't heard an answer, Counsellor. Kindly restrict your answers to a simple yes or no."

"Don't be ridiculous! He's on Death Row!"

"There are ways."

"How would *you* know?"

"I had a friend. Up at San Rafael. What they call Tamal. Across the bridge from Richmond, a little north of San Francisco."

"That's San Quentin."

"That's what it is, all right."

"I thought that *friend* of yours was at Pelican Bay?"

"Different friend."

"You seem to have a lot of old chums in the joint in California."

"It's a racist nation."

"I've heard that."

"But Q ain't Pelican Bay. Two different states of being. As hard time as they pull at Tamal, it's worse up to Crescent City. In the Shoe."

"You never mentioned 'a friend' at San Quentin."

"I never mentioned a lotta shit. That don't mean I don't know it. I am large, I contain multitudes."

We sat silently, the three of us: me, her, and Walt Whitman. *We're fighting*, I thought. Not make-believe, dissin' some movie we'd seen and disagreed about; this was nasty. Bone nasty and memorable. No one ever forgets this kind of fight. Can turn dirty in a second, say some trash you can never take back, never forgive, put a canker on the rose of friendship for all time, never be the same look again.

I waited. She didn't say anything more; and I got no straight answer; but I was pretty sure Henry Lake Spanning had gone all the way with her. I felt a twinge of emotion I didn't even want to look at, much less analyse, dissect, and name. *Let it be*, I thought. Eleven years. Once, just once. *Let it just lie there and get old and withered and die a proper death like all ugly thoughts.*

"Okay. So I go on down to Atmore," I said. "I suppose you mean in the very near future, since he's supposed to bake in four days. Sometime very soon: like today."

She nodded.

I said, "And how do I get in? Law student? Reporter? Tag along as Larry Borlan's new law clerk? Or do I go in with you? What am I, friend of the family, representative of the Alabama State Department of Corrections; maybe you could set me up as an inmate's rep from 'Project Hope.'"

"I can do better than that," she said. The smile. "Much."

"Yeah, I'll just bet you can. Why does that worry me?"

Still with the smile, she hoisted the Atlas onto her lap. She unlocked it, took out a small manila envelope, unsealed but clasped, and slid it across the table to me. I pried open the clasp and shook out the contents.

Clever. Very clever. And already made up, with my photo where necessary, admission dates stamped for tomorrow morning, Thursday, absolutely authentic and foolproof.

"Let me guess," I said, "Thursday mornings, the inmates of Death Row have access to their attorneys?"

"On Death Row, family visitation Monday and Friday. Henry has no family. Attorney visitations Wednesdays and Thursdays, but I couldn't count on today. It took me a couple of days to get through to you..."

"I've been busy."

"...but inmates consult with their counsel on Wednesday and Thursday mornings."

I tapped the papers and plastic cards. "This is very sharp. I notice my name and my handsome visage already here, already sealed in plastic. How long have you had these ready?"

"Couple of days."

"What if I'd continued to say no?"

She didn't answer. She just got that look again.

"One last thing," I said. And I leaned in very close, so she would make no mistake that I was dead serious. "Time grows short. Today's Wednesday. Tomorrow's Thursday. They throw those computer-controlled twin switches Saturday night midnight. What if I jaunt into him and find out you're right, that he's absolutely innocent? What then? They going to listen to me? Fiercely high-verbal black boy with the magic mind-read power?

"I don't think so. Then what happens, Ally?"

"Leave that to me." Her face was hard. "As you said: there are ways. There are roads and routes and even lightning bolts, if you know where to shop. The power of the judiciary. An election year coming up. Favours to be called in."

I said, "And secrets to be wafted under sensitive noses?"

"You just come back and tell me Spanky's telling the truth," and she smiled as I started to laugh, "and I'll worry about the world one minute after midnight Sunday morning."

I got up and slid the papers back into the envelope, and put the envelope under my arm. I looked down at her and I smiled as gently as I could, and I said, "Assure me that you haven't stacked the deck by telling Spanning I can read minds."

"I wouldn't do that."

"Tell me."

"I haven't told him you can read minds."

"You're lying."

"Did you...?"

"Didn't have to. I can see it in your face, Ally."

"Would it matter if he knew?"

"Not a bit. I can read the sonofabitch cold or hot, with or without. Three seconds inside and I'll know if he did it all, if he did part of it, if he did none of it."

"I think I love him, Rudy."

"You told me that."

"But I wouldn't set you up. I need to know... that's why I'm asking you to do it."

I didn't answer. I just smiled at her. She'd told him. He'd know I was coming. But that was terrific. If she hadn't alerted him, I'd have asked her to call and let him know. The more aware he'd be, the easier to scorch his landscape.

I'm a fast study, king of the quick learners: vulgate Latin in a week; standard apothecary's pharmacopoeia in three days; Fender bass on a weekend; Atlanta Falcons' play book in an hour; and, in a moment of human weakness, what it feels like to have a very crampy, heavy-flow menstrual period, two minutes flat.

So fast, in fact, that the more somebody tries to hide the boiling pits of guilt and the crucified bodies of shame, the faster I adapt to their landscape. Like a man taking a polygraph test gets nervous, starts to sweat, ups the galvanic skin response, tries to duck and dodge, gets himself hinky and more hinky and hinkier till his upper lip could water a truck garden, the more he tries to hide from me... the more he reveals... the deeper inside I can go.

There is an African saying: *Death comes without the thumping of drums*. I have no idea why that one came back to me just then.

Last thing you expect from a prison administration is a fine sense of humour. But they got one at the Holman facility.

They had the bloody monster dressed like a virgin.

White duck pants, white short sleeve shirt buttoned up to the neck, white socks. Pair of brown ankle-high brogans with crepe soles, probably neoprene, but they didn't clash with the pale, virginal apparition that came through the security door with a large, black brother in Alabama Prison Authority uniform holding onto his right elbow.

Didn't clash, those work shoes, and didn't make much of a tap on the white tile floor. It was as if he floated. Oh yes, I said to myself, oh yes indeed: I could see how this messianic figure could wow even as tough a cookie as Ally. *Oh my, yes.*

Fortunately, it was raining outside.

Otherwise, sunlight streaming through the glass, he'd no doubt have a halo. I'd have lost it. Right there, a laughing jag would *not* have ceased. Fortunately, it was raining like a sonofabitch.

Which hadn't made the drive down from Clanton a possible entry on any deathbed list of Greatest Terrific Moments in My Life. Sheets of aluminium water, thick as misery, like a never-ending shower curtain that I could drive through for an eternity and never really penetrate. I went into the ditch off the I-65 half-a-dozen times. Why I never ploughed down and buried myself up to the axles in the sucking goo running those furrows, never be something I'll understand.

But each time I skidded off the Interstate, even the twice I did a complete three-sixty and nearly rolled the old Fairlane I'd borrowed from John the C Hepworth, even then I just kept digging, slewed like an epileptic seizure, went sideways and climbed right up the slippery grass and weeds and running, sucking red Alabama goo, right back onto that long black anvil pounded by rain as hard as roofing nails. I took it then, as I take it now, to be a sign that Destiny was determined the mere heavens and earth would not be permitted to fuck me around. I had a date to keep, and Destiny was on top of things.

Even so, even living charmed, which was clear to me, even so: when I got about five miles north of Atmore, I took the 57 exit off the I-65 and a left onto 21, and pulled in at the Best Western. It wasn't my intention to stay overnight that far south—though I knew a young woman with excellent teeth down in Mobile—but the rain was just hammering and all I wanted was to get this thing done and go fall asleep. A drive that long, humping something as lame as that Fairlane, hunched forward to scope the rain...with Spanning in front of me...all I desired was surcease. A touch of the old oblivion.

I checked in, stood under the shower for half an hour, changed into the three-piece suit I'd brought along, and phoned the front desk for directions to the Holman facility.

Driving there, a sweet moment happened for me. It was the last sweet moment for a long time thereafter, and I remember it now as if it were still happening. I cling to it.

In May, and on into early June, the Yellow Lady's Slipper blossoms. In the forests and the woodland bogs, and often on some otherwise undistinguished slope or hillside, the yellow and purple orchids suddenly appear.

I was driving. There was a brief stop in the rain. Like the eye of the hurricane. One moment sheets of water, and the next, absolute silence before the crickets and frogs and birds started complaining; and darkness on all sides, just the idiot staring beams of my headlights poking into nothingness; and cool as a well between the drops of rain; and I was driving. And suddenly, the window rolled down so I wouldn't fall asleep, so I could stick my head out when my eyes started to close, suddenly I smelled the delicate perfume of the sweet May-blossoming Lady's Slipper. Off to my left, off in the dark somewhere on a patch of hilly ground, or deep in a stand of invisible trees, *Cypripedium calceolus* was making the night world beautiful with its fragrance.

I neither slowed, nor tried to hold back the tears.

I just drove, feeling sorry for myself; for no good reason I could name.

Way, way down—almost to the corner of the Florida Panhandle, about three hours south of the last truly imperial barbecue in that part of the world, in Birmingham—I made my way to Holman. If you've never been inside the joint, what I'm about to say will resonate about as clearly as Chaucer to one of the gentle Tasaday.

The stones call out.

That institution for the betterment of the human race, the Organised Church, has a name for it. From the fine folks at Catholicism, Lutheranism, Baptism, Judaism, Islamism, Druidism...Ismism...the ones who brought you Torquemada, several spicy varieties of Inquisition, original sin, holy war, sectarian violence, and something called "pro-lifers" who bomb and maim and kill...comes the catchy phrase Damned Places.

Rolls off the tongue like *God's On Our Side*, don't it? Damned Places.

As we say in Latin, the *situs* of malevolent shit. The *venue* of evil happenings. *Locations* forever existing under a black cloud, like residing in a rooming house run by Jesse Helms or Strom Thurmond. The big slams are like that. Joliet, Dannemora, Attica, Rahway State in Jersey, that hellhole down in Louisiana called Angola, old Folsom—not the new one, the old Folsom—Q, and Ossining. Only people who read about it call it "Sing Sing". Inside, the cons call it Ossining. The Ohio State pen in Columbus. Leavenworth, Kansas. The ones they talk about among themselves when they talk about doing hard time. The Shoe at Pelican Bay State Prison. In there, in those ancient structures mortared with guilt and depravity and no respect for human life and just plain meanness on both sides, cons and screws, in there where the walls and floors have absorbed all the pain and loneliness of a million men and women for decades...in there, the stones call out.

Damned places. You can feel it when you walk through the gates and go through the metal detectors and empty your pockets on counters and open your briefcase so that thick fingers can rumple the papers. You feel it. The moaning and thrashing, and men biting holes in their own wrists so they'll bleed to death.

And I felt it worse than anyone else.

I blocked out as much as I could. I tried to hold on to the memory of the scent of orchids in the night. The last thing I wanted was to jaunt into somebody's landscape at random. Go inside and find out what he had done, what had *really* put him here, not just what they'd got him for. And I'm not talking about Spanning; I'm talking about every one of them. Every guy who had kicked to death his girlfriend because she brought him Bratwurst instead of spicy Cajun sausage. Every pale, wormy Bible-reciting psycho who had stolen, buttfucked, and sliced up an altar boy in the name of secret voices that "tole him to g'wan *do* it!" Every amoral druggie who'd shot a pensioner for her food stamps. If I let down for a second, if I didn't keep that shield up, I'd be tempted to send out a scintilla and touch one of them. In a moment of human weakness.

So I followed the trusty to the Warden's office, where his secretary checked my papers, and the little plastic cards with my face encased in them, and she kept looking down at the face, and up at my face, and down at my face, and up at the face in front of her, and when she couldn't restrain herself a second longer she said, "We've been expecting you, Mr. Pairis. Uh. Do you *really* work for the President of the United States?"

I smiled at her. "We go bowling together."

She took that highly, and offered to walk me to the conference room where I'd meet Henry Lake Spanning. I thanked her the way a well-mannered gentleman of colour thanks a Civil Servant who can make life easier or more difficult, and I followed her along corridors and in and out of guarded steel-riveted doorways, through Administration and the segregation room and the main hall to the brown-panelled, stained walnut, white tile over cement floored, rollout security-windowed, white-draperied, drop-ceiling with two-inch acoustical Celotex squared conference room, where a Security Officer met us.

She bid me fond adieu, not yet fully satisfied that such a one as I had come, that morning, on Air Force One, straight from a 7–10 split with the President of the United States.

It was a big room.

I sat down at the conference table; about twelve feet long and four feet wide; highly polished walnut, maybe oak. Straight-back chairs: metal tubing with a light yellow upholstered cushion. Everything quiet, except for the sound of matrimonial rice being dumped on a connubial tin roof. The rain had not slacked off. Out there on the I-65 some luck-lost bastard was being sucked down into red death.

"He'll be here," the Security Officer said.

"That's good," I replied. I had no idea why he'd tell me that, seeing as how it was the reason I was there in the first place. I imagined him to be the kind of guy you dread sitting in front of, at the movies, because he always explains everything to his date. Like a *bracero* labourer with a valid green card interpreting a Woody Allen movie line-by-line to his illegal-alien cousin Humberto, three weeks under the wire from Matamoros. Like one of a pair of Beltone-wearing octogenarians on the loose from a rest home for a wild Saturday afternoon at the mall, plonked down in the third level multiplex, one of them describing whose ass Clint Eastwood is about to kick, and why. All at the top of her voice.

"Seen any good movies lately?" I asked him.

He didn't get a chance to answer, and I didn't jaunt inside to find out, because at that moment the steel door at the far end of the conference room opened, and another Security Officer poked his head in, and called across to Officer Let-Me-State-the-Obvious, "Dead man walking!"

Officer Self-Evident nodded to him, the other head poked back out, the door slammed, and my companion said, "When we bring one down from Death Row, he's gotta walk through the Ad Building and Segregation and the Main Hall. So everything's locked down. Every man's inside. It takes some time, y'know."

I thanked him.

"Is it true you work for the President, yeah?"

He asked it so politely, I decided to give him a straight answer; and to hell with all the phoney credentials Ally had worked up. "Yeah," I said, "we're on the same *bocce* ball team."

"Izzat so?" he said, fascinated by sports stats.

I was on the verge of explaining that the President was, in actuality, of Italian descent, when I heard the sound of the key turning in the security door, and it opened outwards, and in came this messianic apparition in white, being led by a guard who was seven feet in any direction.

Henry Lake Spanning, *sans* halo, hands and feet shackled, with the chains cold-welded into a wide anodised steel belt, shuffled toward me; and his neoprene soles made no disturbing cacophony on the white tiles.

I watched him come the long way across the room, and he watched me right back. I thought to myself, *Yeah, she told him I can read minds. Well, let's see which method you use to try and keep me out of the landscape.* But I couldn't tell from the outside of him, not just by the way he shuffled and looked, if he had fucked Ally. But I knew it had to've been. Somehow. Even in the big lockup. Even here.

He stopped right across from me, with his hands on the back of the chair, and he didn't say a word, just gave me the nicest smile I'd ever gotten from anyone, even my momma. *Oh, yes,* I thought, *oh my goodness, yes.* Henry Lake Spanning was either the most masterfully charismatic person I'd ever met, or so good at the charm con that he could sell a slashed throat to a stranger.

"You can leave him," I said to the great black behemoth brother.

"Can't do that, sir."

"I'll take full responsibility."

"Sorry, sir; I was told someone had to be right here in the room with you and him, all the time."

I looked at the one who had waited with me. "That mean you, too?"

He shook his head. "Just one of us, I guess."

I frowned. "I need absolute privacy. What would happen if I were this man's attorney of record? Wouldn't you have to leave us alone? Privileged communication, right?"

They looked at each other, this pair of Security Officers, and they looked back at me, and they said nothing. All of sudden Mr. Plain-as-the-Nose-on-Your-Face had nothing valuable to offer; and the sequoia with biceps "had his orders".

"They tell you who I work for? They tell you who it was sent me here to talk to this man?" Recourse to authority often works. They mumbled yessir yessir a couple of times each, but their faces stayed right on the mark of *sorry, sir, but we're not supposed to leave anybody alone with this man*. It wouldn't have mattered if they'd believed I'd flown in on Jehovah One.

So I said to myself *fuckit* I said to myself, and I slipped into their thoughts, and it didn't take much rearranging to get the phone wires re-strung and the underground cables re-routed and the pressure on their bladders something fierce.

"On the other hand..." the first one said.

"I suppose we could..." the giant said.

And in a matter of maybe a minute-and-a-half one of them was entirely gone, and the great one was standing outside the steel door, his back filling the double-pane chickenwire-imbedded security window. He effectively sealed off the one entrance or exit to or from the conference room; like the three hundred Spartans facing the tens of thousands of Xerxes's army at the Hot Gates.

Henry Lake Spanning stood silently watching me. "Sit down," I said. "Make yourself comfortable."

He pulled out the chair, came around, and sat down.

"Pull it closer to the table," I said.

He had some difficulty, hands shackled that way, but he grabbed the leading edge of the seat and scraped forward till his stomach was touching the table.

He was a handsome guy, even for a white man. Nice nose, strong cheekbones, eyes the colour of that water in your toilet when you toss in a tablet of 2000 Flushes. Very nice looking man. He gave me the creeps.

If Dracula had looked like Shirley Temple, no one would've driven a stake through his heart. If Harry Truman had looked like Freddy Krueger, he would never have beaten Tom Dewey at the polls. Joe Stalin and Saddam Hussein looked like sweet, avuncular friends of the family, really nice looking, kindly guys—who just incidentally happened to slaughter millions of men, women, and children. Abe Lincoln looked like an axe murderer, but he had a heart as big as Guatemala.

Henry Lake Spanning had the sort of face you'd trust immediately if you saw it in a TV commercial. Men would like to go fishing with him; women would like to squeeze his buns. Grannies would hug him on sight; kids would follow him straight into the mouth of an open oven. If he could play the piccolo, rats would gavotte around his shoes. What saps we are. Beauty is only skin deep. You can't judge a book by its cover.

Cleanliness is next to godliness. Dress for success. What saps we are. So what did that make my pal, Allison Roche?

And why the hell didn't I just slip into his thoughts and check out the landscape?

Why was I stalling?

Because I was scared of him.

This was fifty-six verified, gruesome, disgusting murders sitting forty-eight inches away from me, looking straight at me with blue eyes and soft, gently blond hair. Neither Harry nor Dewey would've had a prayer.

So why was I scared of him? Because; that's why.

This was damned foolishness. I had all the weaponry, he was shackled, and I didn't for a second believe he was what Ally *thought* he was: innocent. Hell, they'd caught him, literally, red-handed. Bloody to the armpits, fer chrissakes. Innocent, my ass! *Okay, Rudy*, I thought, *get in there and take a look around.* But I didn't. I waited for him to say something.

He smiled tentatively, a gentle and nervous little smile, and he said, "Ally asked me to see you. Thank you for coming."

I looked *at* him, but not *into* him.

He seemed upset that he'd inconvenienced me. "But I don't think you can do me any good, not in just three days."

"You scared, Spanning?"

His lips trembled. "Yes I am, Mr. Pairis. I'm about as scared as a man can be." His eyes were moist.

"Probably gives you some insight into how your victims felt, whaddaya think?" He didn't answer. His eyes were moist.

After a moment just looking at me, he scraped back his chair and stood up. "Thank you for coming, sir. I'm sorry Ally imposed on your time." He turned and started to walk away. I jaunted into his landscape.

Oh my god, I thought. He was innocent.

Never done any of it. None of it. Absolutely no doubt, not a shadow of a doubt. Ally had been right. I saw every bit of that landscape in there, every fold and crease; every bolt hole and rat run; every gully and arroyo; all of his past, back and back and back to his birth in Lewistown, Montana, near Great Falls, thirty-six years ago; every day of his life right up to the minute they arrested him leaning over that disembowelled cleaning woman the real killer had tossed into the dumpster.

I saw every second of his landscape; and I saw him coming out of the Winn-Dixie in Huntsville; pushing a cart filled with grocery bags of food for the weekend. And I saw him wheeling it around the parking lot toward the dumpster area overflowing with broken-down cardboard boxes and fruit crates. And I heard the cry for help from one of those dumpsters; and I saw Henry Lake Spanning stop and look around, not sure he'd heard anything at all. Then I saw him start to go to his car, parked right there at the edge of the lot beside the wall because it was a Friday evening and everyone was stocking up for the weekend, and there weren't any spaces out front; and the cry for help, weaker this time, as pathetic as a crippled kitten; and Henry Lake Spanning stopped cold, and he looked around; and we *both* saw the bloody hand raise itself above the level of the open dumpster's filthy green steel side. And I saw him desert his groceries without a thought to their cost, or that someone might run off with them if he left them unattended, or that he only had eleven dollars left in his checking account, so if those groceries were snagged by someone he wouldn't be eating for the next few days... and I watched him rush to the dumpster and look into the crap filling it... and I felt his nausea at the sight of that poor old woman, what was left of her... and I was with him as he crawled up onto the dumpster and dropped inside to do what he could for that mass of shredded and pulped flesh.

And I cried with him as she gasped, with a bubble of blood that burst in the open ruin of her throat, and she died. But though *I* heard the scream of someone coming around the corner, Spanning did not;

and so he was still there, holding the poor mass of stripped skin and black bloody clothing, when the cops screeched into the parking lot. And only *then*, innocent of anything but decency and rare human compassion, did Henry Lake Spanning begin to understand what it must look like to middle-aged *hausfraus*, sneaking around dumpsters to pilfer cardboard boxes, who see what they think is a man murdering an old woman.

I was with him, there in that landscape within his mind, as he ran and ran and dodged and dodged. Until they caught him in Decatur, seven miles from the body of Gunilla Ascher. But they had him, and they had positive identification, from the dumpster in Huntsville; and all the rest of it was circumstantial, gussied up by bed-ridden, recovering Charlie Whilborg and the staff in Ally's office. It looked good on paper—so good that Ally had brought him down on twenty-nine-*cum*-fifty-six counts of murder in the vilest extreme.

But it was all bullshit.

The killer was still out there.

Henry Lake Spanning, who looked like a nice, decent guy, was exactly that. A nice, decent, good-hearted, but most of all *innocent* guy.

You could fool juries and polygraphs and judges and social workers and psychiatrists and your mommy and your daddy, but you could *not* fool Rudy Pairis, who travels regularly to the place of dark where you can go but not return.

They were going to burn an innocent man in three days. I had to do something about it.

Not just for Ally, though that was reason enough; but for this man who thought he was doomed, and was frightened, but didn't have to take no shit from a wiseguy like me.

"Mr. Spanning," I called after him. He didn't stop. "Please," I said. He stopped shuffling, the chains making their little charm bracelet sounds, but he didn't turn around.

"I believe Ally is right, sir," I said. "I believe they caught the wrong man; and I believe all the time you've served is wrong; and I believe you ought not die."

Then he turned slowly, and stared at me with the look of a dog that has been taunted with a bone. His voice was barely a whisper. "And why is that, Mr. Pairis? Why is it that you believe me when nobody else but Ally and my attorney believed me?"

I didn't say what I was thinking. What I was thinking was that I'd been *in* there, and I *knew* he was innocent. And more than that, I knew that he truly loved my pal Allison Roche.

And there wasn't much I wouldn't do for Ally.

So what I said was: "I know you're innocent, because I know who's guilty."

His lips parted. It wasn't one of those big moves where someone's mouth flops open in astonishment; it was just a parting of the lips. But he was startled; I knew that as I knew the poor sonofabitch had suffered too long already.

He came shuffling back to me, and sat down.

"Don't make fun, Mr. Pairis. Please. I'm what you said, I'm scared. I don't want to die, and I surely don't want to die with the world thinking I did those…those things."

"Makin' no fun, captain. I know who ought to burn for all those murders. Not six states, but eleven. Not fifty-six dead, but an even seventy. Three of them little girls in a day nursery, and the woman watching them, too."

He stared at me. There was horror on his face. I know that look real good. I've seen it at least seventy times.

"I know you're innocent, Cap'n because *I'm* the man they want. *I'm* the guy who put your ass in here."

In a moment of human weakness. I saw it all. What I had packed off to live in that place of dark where you can go but not return. The wall-safe in my drawing-room. The four-foot-thick walled crypt encased in concrete and sunk a mile deep into solid granite.

The vault whose composite laminate walls of judiciously sloped extremely thick blends of steel and plastic, the equivalent of six hundred to seven hundred mm of homogenous depth protection approached the maximum toughness and hardness of crystaliron, that iron grown with perfect crystal structure and carefully controlled quantities of impurities that in a modern combat tank can shrug off a hollow charge warhead like a spaniel shaking himself dry. The Chinese puzzle box. The hidden chamber. The labyrinth. The maze of the mind where I'd sent all seventy to die, over and over and over, so I wouldn't hear their screams, or see the ropes of bloody tendon, or stare into the pulped sockets where their pleading eyes had been.

When I had walked into that prison, I'd been buttoned up totally. I was safe and secure, I knew nothing, remembered nothing, suspected nothing.

But when I walked into Henry Lake Spanning's landscape, and I could not lie to myself that he was the one, I felt the earth crack. I felt the tremors and the upheavals, and the fissures started at my feet and ran to the horizon; and the lava boiled up and began to flow. And the steel walls melted, and the concrete turned to dust, and the barriers dissolved; and I looked at the face of the monster.

No wonder I had such nausea when Ally had told me about this or that slaughter ostensibly perpetrated by Henry Lake Spanning, the man she was prosecuting on twenty-nine counts of murders I had committed. No wonder I could picture all the details when she would talk to me about the barest description of the murder site. No wonder I fought so hard against coming to Holman.

In there, in his mind, his landscape open to me, I saw the love he had for Allison Roche, for my pal and buddy with whom I had once, just once...

Don't try tellin' me that the Power of Love can open the fissures. I don't want to hear that shit. I'm telling *you* that it was a combination, a buncha things that split me open, and possibly maybe one of those things was what I saw between them.

I don't know that much. I'm a quick study, but this was in an instant. A crack of fate. A moment of human weakness. That's what I told myself in the part of me that ventured to the place of dark: that I'd done what I'd done in moments of human weakness.

And it was those moments, not my "gift", and not my blackness, that had made me the loser, the monster, the liar that I am.

In the first moment of realisation, I couldn't believe it. Not me, not good old Rudy. Not likeable Rudy Pairis never done no one but hisself wrong his whole life.

In the next second I went wild with anger, furious at the disgusting thing that lived on one side of my split brain. Wanted to tear a hole through my face and yank the killing thing out, wet and putrescent, and squeeze it into pulp.

In the next second I was nauseated, actually wanted to fall down and puke, seeing every moment of what I had done, unshaded, unhidden, naked to this Rudy Pairis who was decent and reasonable and law-abiding, even if such a Rudy was little better than a well-educated fuc-up. But not a killer... I wanted to puke.

Then, finally, I accepted what I could not deny.

For me, never again, would I slide through the night with the scent of the blossoming Yellow Lady's Slipper. I recognised that perfume now.

It was the odour that rises from a human body cut wide open, like a mouth making a big, dark yawn.

The other Rudy Pairis had come home at last.

They didn't have half-a-minute's worry. I sat down at a little wooden writing table in an interrogation room in the Jefferson County D.A.'s offices, and I made up a graph with the names and dates and locations. Names of as many of the seventy as I actually knew. (A lot of them had just been on the road, or in a men's toilet, or taking a bath, or lounging in the back row of a movie, or getting some cash from an ATM, or just sitting around doing nothing but waiting for me to come along and open them up, and maybe have a drink off them, or maybe just something to snack on... down the road.) Dates were easy, because I've got a good memory for dates. And the places where they'd find the ones they didn't know about, the fourteen with exactly the same m.o. as the other fifty-six, not to mention the old-style rip-and-pull can opener I'd used on that little Catholic bead-counter Gunilla Whatsername, who did Hail Mary this and Sweet Blessed Jesus that all the time I was opening her up, even at the last, when I held up parts of her insides for her to look at, and tried to get her to lick them, but she died first. Not half-a-minute's worry for the State of Alabama. All in one swell foop they corrected a tragic miscarriage of justice, nobbled a maniac killer, solved fourteen more murders than they'd counted on (in five additional states, which made the police departments of those five additional states extremely pleased with the law enforcement agencies of the Sovereign State of Alabama), and made first spot on the evening news on all three major networks, not to mention CNN, for the better part of a week. Knocked the Middle East right out of the box. Neither Harry Truman nor Tom Dewey would've had a prayer.

Ally went into seclusion, of course. Took off and went somewhere down on the Florida coast, I heard. But after the trial, and the verdict, and Spanning being released, and me going inside, and all like that, well, oo-poppadow as they used to say, it was all reordered properly. *Sat cito si sat bene*, in Latin: "It is done quickly enough if it is done well." A favourite saying of Cato. The Elder Cato.

And all I asked, all I begged for, was that Ally and Henry Lake Spanning, who loved each other and deserved each other, and whom I had almost fucked up royally, that the two of them would be there when they jammed my weary black butt into that new electric chair at Holman.

Please come, I begged them.

Don't let me die alone. Not even a shit like me. Don't make me cross over into that place of dark, where you can go, but not return—without the face of a friend. Even a former friend. And as for you, Captain, well, hell didn't I save your life so you could enjoy the company of the woman you love? Least you can do. Come on now; be there or be square!

I don't know if Spanning talked her into accepting the invite, or if it was the other way around; but one day about a week prior to the event of cooking up a mess of fried Rudy Pairis, the Warden stopped by my commodious accommodations on Death Row and gave me to understand that it would be SRO for the barbecue, which meant Ally my pal, and her boyfriend, the former resident of the Row where now I dwelt in durance vile.

The things a guy'll do for love.

Yeah, that was the key. Why would a very smart operator who had gotten away with it, all the way free and clear, why would such a smart operator suddenly pull one of those hokey courtroom "I did it, I did it!" routines, and as good as strap himself into the electric chair?

Once. I only went to bed with her once. The things a guy'll do for love.

When they brought me into the death chamber from the holding cell where I'd spent the night before and all that day, where I'd had my last meal (which had been a hot roast beef sandwich, double meat, on white toast, with very crisp french fries, and hot brown country gravy poured over the whole thing, apple sauce, and a bowl of Concord grapes), where a representative of the Holy Roman Empire had tried to make amends for destroying most of the gods, beliefs, and cultures of my black forebears, they held me between Security Officers, neither one of whom had been in attendance when I'd visited Henry Lake Spanning at this very same correctional facility slightly more than a year before.

It hadn't been a bad year. Lots of rest; caught up on my reading, finally got around to Proust and Langston Hughes, I'm ashamed to admit, so late in the game; lost some weight; worked out regularly; gave up cheese and dropped my cholesterol count. Ain't nothin' to it, just to do it.

Even took a jaunt or two or ten, every now and awhile. It didn't matter none. I wasn't going anywhere, neither were they. I'd done worse than the worst of them; hadn't I confessed to it? So there wasn't a lot that could ice me, after I'd copped to it and released all seventy of them out of my unconscious, where they'd been rotting in shallow graves for years. No big thang, Cuz.

Brought me in, strapped me in, plugged me in. I looked through the glass at the witnesses.

There sat Ally and Spanning, front row centre. Best seats in the house. All eyes and crying, watching, not believing everything had come to this, trying to figure out when and how and in what way it had all gone down without her knowing anything at all about it. And Henry Lake Spanning sitting close beside her, their hands locked in her lap. True love.

I locked eyes with Spanning. I jaunted into his landscape.

No, I *didn't*.

I *tried* to, and couldn't squirm through. Thirty years, or less, since I was five or six, I'd been doing it; without hindrance, all alone in the world the only person who could do this listen in on the landscape trick; and for the first time I was stopped. Absolutely no fuckin' entrance. I went wild! I tried running at it full-tilt, and hit something khaki-coloured, like beach sand, and only slightly giving, not hard, but resilient. Exactly like being inside a ten-foot-high, fifty-foot diameter paper bag, like a big shopping bag from a supermarket, that stiff butcher's paper kind of bag, and that colour, like being inside a bag that size, running straight at it, thinking you're going to bust through . . . and being thrown back. Not hard, not like bouncing on a trampoline, just shunted aside like the fuzz from a dandelion hitting a glass door. Unimportant. Khaki-coloured and not particularly bothered.

I tried hitting it with a bolt of pure blue lightning mental power, like someone out of a Marvel comic, but that wasn't how mixing in other people's minds works. You don't think yourself in with a psychic battering-ram. That's the kind of arrant foolishness you hear spouted by unattractive people on public access cable channels, talking about The Power of Love and The Power of the Mind and the ever-popular toe-tapping Power of a Positive Thought. Bullshit; I don't be home to *that* folly!

I tried picturing myself in there, but that didn't work, either. I tried blanking my mind and drifting across, but it was pointless. And at that moment it occurred to me that I didn't really know *how* I jaunted. I just . . . did it. One moment I was snug in the privacy of my own head, and the next I was over there in someone else's landscape. It was instantaneous, like teleportation, which also is an impossibility, like telepathy.

But now, strapped into the chair, and them getting ready to put the leather mask over my face so the witnesses wouldn't have to see the smoke coming out of my eye-sockets and the little sparks as my nose hairs burned, when it was urgent that I get into the thoughts and landscape of Henry Lake Spanning, I was shut out completely. And right *then*, that moment, I was scared!

Presto, without my even opening up to him, there he was: inside my head. He had jaunted into *my* landscape.

"You had a nice roast beef sandwich, I see."

His voice was a lot stronger than it had been when I'd come down to see him a year ago. A *lot* stronger inside my mind.

"Yes, Rudy, I'm what you knew probably existed somewhere. Another one. A shrike." He paused. "I see you call it 'jaunting in the landscape'. I just called myself a shrike. A butcherbird. One name's as good as another. Strange, isn't it; all these years; and we never met anyone else? There *must* be others, but I think—now I can't prove this, I have no real data, it's just a wild idea I've had for years and years—I think they don't know they can do it."

He stared at me across the landscape, those wonderful blue eyes of his, the ones Ally had fallen in love with, hardly blinking.

"Why didn't you let me know before this?"

He smiled sadly. "Ah, Rudy. Rudy, Rudy, Rudy; you poor benighted pickaninny. Because I needed to suck you in, kid. I needed to put out a bear trap, and let it snap closed on your scrawny leg, and send you over. Here, let me clear the atmosphere in here..." And he wiped away all the manipulation he had worked on me, way back a year ago, when he had so easily covered his own true thoughts his past, his life, the real panorama of what went on inside his landscape—like bypassing a surveillance camera with a continuous-loop tape that continues to show a placid scene while the joint is being actively burgled—and when he convinced me not only that he was innocent, but that the real killer was someone who had blocked the hideous slaughters from his conscious mind and had lived an otherwise exemplary life. He wandered around my landscape—and all of this in a second or two, because time has no duration in the landscape, like the hours you can spend in a dream that are just thirty-seconds long in the real world, just before you wake up—and he swept away all the false memories and suggestions, the logical structure of sequential events that he had planted that would dovetail with my actual existence, my true memories, altered and warped and rearranged so I would believe that I had done all seventy of those ghastly murders...so that I'd believe, in a moment of horrible realisation, that I was the demented psychopath who had ranged state to state to state, leaving piles of ripped flesh at every stop. Blocked it all, submerged it all, sublimated it all, me. Good old Rudy Pairis, who never killed anybody. I'd been the patsy he was waiting for.

"There, now, kiddo. See what it's really like? "You didn't do a thing.

"Pure as the driven snow, nigger. That's the truth. And what a find you were. Never even suspected there was another like me, till Ally came to interview me after Decatur. But there you were, big and black as a Great White Hope, right there in her mind. Isn't she fine, Pairis? Isn't she something to take a knife to? Something to split open like a nice piece of fruit warmed in a summer sunshine field, let all the steam rise off her... maybe have a picnic..."

He stopped.

"I wanted her right from the first moment I saw her.

"Now, you know, I could've done it sloppy, just been a shrike to Ally, that first time she came to the holding cell to interview me; just jump into her, that was my plan. But what a noise that Spanning in the cell would've made, yelling it wasn't a man, it was a woman, not Spanning, but Deputy D.A. Allison Roche...too much noise, too many complications. But I *could* have done it, jumped into her. Or a guard, and then slice her at my leisure, stalk her, find her, let her steam...

"You look distressed, Mr. Rudy Pairis. Why's that? Because you're going to die in my place? Because I could have taken you over at any time, and didn't? Because after all this time of your miserable, wasted, lousy life you finally find someone like you, and we don't even have the convenience of a chat? Well, that's sad, that's really sad, kiddo. But you didn't have a chance."

"You're stronger than me; you kept me out," I said.

He chuckled.

"Stronger? Is that all you think it is? Stronger? You still don't get it, do you?" His face, then, grew terrible. "You don't even understand now, right now that I've cleaned it all away and you can *see* what I did to you, do you?

"Do you think I stayed in a jail cell, and went through that trial, all of that, because I couldn't do anything about it? You poor jig slob. I could have jumped like a shrike any time I wanted to. But the first time I met your Ally I saw *you*."

I cringed. "And you waited...? For me, you spent all that time in prison, just to get to me...?"

"At the moment when you couldn't do anything about it, at the moment you couldn't shout 'I've been taken over by someone else, I'm Rudy Pairis here inside this Henry Lake Spanning body, help me, help me!' Why stir up noise when all I had to do was bide my time, wait a bit, wait for Ally, and let Ally go for you."

I felt like a drowning turkey, standing idiotically in the rain, head tilted up, mouth open, water pouring in. "You can...leave the mind... leave the body...go out...jaunt, jump permanently..."

Spanning sniggered like a schoolyard bully.

"You stayed in jail three years just to get *me?*"

He smirked. Smarter than thou.

"Three years? You think that's some big deal to me? You don't think I could have someone like you running around, do you? Someone who can 'jaunt' as I do? The only other shrike I've ever encountered. You think I wouldn't sit in here and wait for you to come to me?"

"But three *years*..."

"You're what, Rudy...thirty-one, is it? Yes, I can see that. Thirty-one. You've never jumped like a shrike. You've just entered, jaunted, gone into the landscapes, and never understood that it's more than reading minds. You can change domiciles, black boy. You can move out of a house in a bad neighbourhood—such as strapped into the electric chair—and take up residence in a brand, spanking, new housing complex of million-and-a-half-buck condos, like Ally."

"But you have to have a place for the other one to go, don't you?" I said it just flat, no tone, no colour to it at all. I didn't even think of the place of dark, where you can go...

"Who do you think I am, Rudy? Just who the hell do you think I was when I started, when I learned to shrike, how to jaunt, what I'm telling you now about changing residences? You wouldn't know my first address. I go a long way back.

"But I can give you a few of my more famous addresses. Gilles de Rais, France, 1440; Vlad Tepes, Romania, 1462; Elizabeth Bathory, Hungary, 1611; Catherine DeShayes, France, 1680; Jack the Ripper, London, 1888; Henri Désiré Landru, France, 1915; Albert Fish, New York City, 1934; Ed Gein, Plainfield, Wisconsin, 1954; Myra Hindley, Manchester, 1963; Albert DeSalvo, Boston, 1964; Charles Manson, Los Angeles, 1969; John Wayne Gacy, Norwood Park Township, Illinois, 1977.

"Oh, but how I do go on. And on. And on and on and on, Rudy, my little porch monkey. That's what I do. I go on. And on and on. Shrike will nest where it chooses. If not in your beloved Allison Roche, then in the cheesy fucked-up black boy, Rudy Pairis. But don't you think that's a waste, kiddo? Spending however much time I might have to spend in your socially unacceptable body, when Henry Lake Spanning is such a handsome devil? Why should I have just switched with you when Ally lured you to me, because all it would've done is get you screeching and howling that you weren't Spanning, you were this nigger son who'd had his head stolen...and then you might have manipulated some guards or the Warden...

"Well, you see what I mean, don't you?

"But now that the mask is securely in place, and now that the electrodes are attached to your head and your left leg, and now that the Warden has his hand on the switch, well, you'd better get ready to do a lot of drooling."

And he turned around to jaunt back out of me, and I closed the perimeter. He tried to jaunt, tried to leap back to his own mind, but I had him in a fist. Just that easy. Materialised a fist, and turned him to face me.

"Fuck you, Jack the Ripper. And fuck you twice, Bluebeard. And on and on and on fuck you Manson and Boston Strangler and any other dipshit warped piece of sick crap you been in your years. You sure got some muddy-shoes credentials there, boy.

"What I care about all those names, Spanky my brother? You really think I don't know those names? I'm an educated fellah, Mistuh Rippuh, Mistuh Mad Bomber. You missed a few. Were you also, did you inhabit, hast thou possessed Winnie Ruth Judd and Charlie Starkweather and Mad Dog Coll and Richard Speck and Sirhan Sirhan and Jeffrey Dahmer? You the boogieman responsible for *every* bad number the human race ever played? You ruined Sodom and Gomorrah, burned the Great Library of Alexandria, orchestrated the Reign of Terror *dans Paree*, set up the Inquisition, stoned and drowned the Salem witches, slaughtered unarmed women and kids at Wounded Knee, bumped off John Kennedy?

"I don't think so.

"I don't even think you got so close as to share a pint with Jack the Ripper. And even if you did, even if you *were* all those maniacs, you were small potatoes, Spanky. The least of us human beings outdoes you, three times a day. How many lynch ropes you pulled tight, M'sieur Landru?

"What colossal egotism you got, makes you blind, makes you think you're the only one, even when you find out there's someone else, you can't get past it. What makes you think I didn't know what you can do? What makes you think I didn't let you do it, and sit here waiting for you like you sat there waiting for me, till this moment when you can't do shit about it?

"You so goddam stuck on yourself, Spankyhead, you never give it the barest that someone else is a faster draw than you.

"Know what your trouble is, Captain? You're old, you're *real* old, maybe hundreds of years who gives a damn old. That don't count for shit, old man. You're old, but you never got smart. You're just mediocre at what you do.

"You moved from address to address. You didn't have to be Son of Sam or Cain slayin' Abel, or whoever the fuck you been . . . you could've been Moses or Galileo or George Washington Carver or Harriet Tubman or Sojourner Truth or Mark Twain or Joe Louis. You could've been Alexander Hamilton and helped found the Manumission Society in New York. You could've discovered radium, carved Mount Rushmore, carried a baby out of a burning building. But you got old real fast, and you never got any smarter. You didn't need to, did you, Spanky? You had it all to yourself, all this 'shrike' shit, just jaunt here and jaunt there, and bite off someone's hand or face like the old, tired, boring, repetitious, no-imagination stupid shit that you are.

"Yeah, you got me good when I came here to see your landscape. You got Ally wired up good. And she suckered me in, probably not even knowing she was doing it . . . you must've looked in her head and found just the right technique to get her to make me come within reach. Good, m'man; you were excellent. But I had a year to torture myself. A year to sit here and think about it. About how many people I'd killed, and how sick it made me, and little by little I found my way through it.

"Because ... and here's the big difference 'tween us, dummy:

"I unravelled what was going on ... it took time, but I learned. Understand, asshole? *I* learn! *You* don't.

"There's an old Japanese saying—I got lots of these, Henry m'man—I read a whole lot—and what it says is, 'Do not fall into the error of the artisan who boasts of twenty years' experience in his craft while in fact he has had only one year of experience—twenty times.'" Then I grinned back at him.

"Fuck you, sucker," I said, just as the Warden threw the switch and I jaunted out of there and into the landscape and mind of Henry Lake Spanning.

I sat there getting oriented for a second; it was the first time I'd done more than a jaunt ... this was ... *shrike*; but then Ally beside me gave a little sob for her old pal, Rudy Pairis, who was baking like a Maine lobster, smoke coming out from under the black cloth that covered my, his, face; and I heard the vestigial scream of what had been Henry Lake Spanning and thousands of other monsters, all of them burning, out there on the far horizon of my new landscape; and I put my arm around her, and drew her close, and put my face into her shoulder and hugged her to me; and I heard the scream go on and on for the longest time, I think it was a long time, and finally it was just wind ... and then gone ... and I came up from Ally's shoulder, and I could barely speak.

"Shhh, honey, it's okay," I murmured. "He's gone where he can make right for his mistakes. No pain. Quiet, a real quiet place; and all alone forever. And cool there. And dark."

I was ready to stop failing at everything, and blaming everything. Having fessed up to love, having decided it was time to grow up and be an adult—not just a very quick study who learned fast, extremely fast, a lot faster than anybody could imagine an orphan like me could learn, than *any*body could imagine—I hugged her with the intention that Henry Lake Spanning would love Allison Roche more powerfully, more responsibly, than anyone had ever loved anyone in the history of the world. I was ready to stop failing at everything.

And it would be just a whole lot easier as a white boy with great big blue eyes.

Because—get on this now—all my wasted years didn't have as much to do with blackness or racism or being overqualified or being unlucky or being high-verbal or even the curse of my "gift" of jaunting, as they did with one single truth I learned waiting in there, inside my own landscape, waiting for Spanning to come and gloat:

I have always been one of those miserable guys who *couldn't get out of his own way.* Which meant I could, at last, stop feeling sorry for that poor nigger, Rudy Pairis.

Except, maybe, in a moment of human weakness.

This story, for Bob Bloch, because I promised.

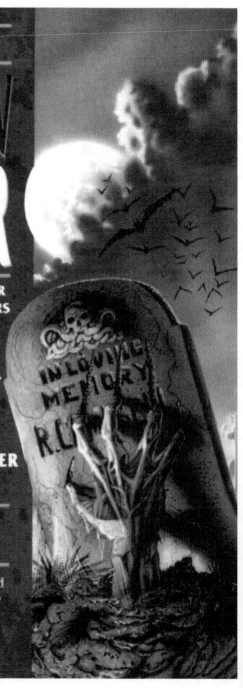

THE
BEST NEW
HORROR

**THE YEAR'S BEST HORROR
STORIES BY SUCH MASTERS
OF DARK FANTASY AS:**

ROBERT BLOCH
RAMSEY CAMPBELL
HARLAN ELLISON
CHARLES GRANT
KIM NEWMAN
KARL EDWARD WAGNER
and many others

EDITED BY
STEPHEN JONES

"Captures best the range and
breadth of the horror genre"
- *LOCUS*

[1994]

A S A TRIBUTE to Ramsey's inestimable contribution to the series, for the 1995 edition I asked artist Luis Rey to add a little joke into his atmospheric cover painting.

At a launch party (those were the days!) for the book at the annual British Fantasy Convention, the publisher recreated the cover as, literally, the icing on the cake.

The sixth edition of *The Best New Horror* won the International Horror Guild Award and was the first of two volumes to appear under the Raven Books imprint in the UK. This was a new genre list that I launched and edited for Robinson for a couple of years, until I was reluctantly forced to come to the conclusion—thanks to corporate interference from within the company—that it was not worth all the hard work.

For my first volume as solo editor, the Introduction grew to thirty-one pages and the Necrology was now up to eighteen. In my editorial I warned against the law of diminishing returns as the genre was swamped with "...sequels, inferior copies, share-cropped worlds, media novelisations and role-playing tie-ins, most of them written and published with little or no thought given to their intrinsic value of lasting worth."

It was advice that many authors and publishers would do well to still heed today...

The twenty-two contributions included the welcome return of Harlan Ellison and Terry Lamsley, along with such "regulars" as Charles L. Grant, Joel Lane, Ramsey Campbell, Nicholas Royle, Michael Marshall Smith and Kim Newman (with a marvellous contemporary re-imagining of the Zorro mythology that was nominated for a World Fantasy Award).

Esther M. Friesner also contributed a rare piece of verse, but this sixth compilation was touched with personal sadness.

In this edition were stories by two old friends and colleagues—Karl Edward Wagner's hallucinatory 'In the Middle of a Snow Dream' and Robert Bloch's Bram Stoker Award-winning 'The Scent of Vinegar'. Both authors had died within a month of each other the previous year, and the book was dedicated to their memory.

Paul McAuley is another old friend and also one of the UK's most respected science fiction writers. His award-winning story 'The Temptation of Dr. Stein' may have been set in the same alternate history as his novel *Pasquale's Angel*, but it involved a certain mad scientist memorably portrayed by eccentric English actor Ernest Thesiger in James Whale's classic movie *Bride of Frankenstein*.

In fact, Paul returned to the character with 'The True History of Doctor Pretorius', which I selected for the following year's *Best New Horror*, and 'Dr. Pretorius and the Lost Temple', which appeared in Volume #14.

PAUL J. McAULEY

THE TEMPTATION OF DR. STEIN

PAUL J. McAULEY is a former researcher and lecturer on botany turned full-time writer who lives in North London. He has published more than twenty crime and science fiction novels, including *Fairyland* (which won the Arthur C. Clarke and John W. Campbell Awards), *The Quiet War*, *Gardens of the Sun* and *Evening's Empires*. More recent titles include *Something Coming Through*, *Into Everywhere* and *Austral*.

McAuley also edited the anthology *In Dreams* with Kim Newman, wrote the Doctor Who novella *The Eye of the Tyger* and a BFI Film Classic on Terry Gilliam's film *Brazil*. He has also published more than eighty short stories, winning the British Fantasy Award for the one that follows.

As the author recalls: "Long ago and in another country I wrote a novel, *Pasquale's Angel*, set in a history different from ours, in which Renaissance Florence had blossomed into a world super-power thanks to the infernal devices of its Great Engineer, Leonardo Da Vinci.

"As the hero of the story—a hapless apprentice painter—plunged ever deeper into a tangle of murder and state secrets, he briefly encountered one Dr. Pretorious, an alternate version of the gin-loving necromancer immortalised by the great English eccentric Ernest Thesiger in James Whale's 1935 movie *Bride of Frankenstein*.

"Dr. Pretorious lived on after the novel in a clutch of stories that were mostly set in the 19th and 20th centuries of our own history, but this one, written for *The Mammoth Book of Frankenstein*, is a kind of prequel to *Pasquale's Angel*, recounting the events which led to Dr. Pretorious quitting Venice for the Great Engineer's Florence some ten years earlier…"

D R. STEIN PRIDED himself on being a rational man. When, in the months following his arrival in Venice, it became his habit to spend his free time wandering the city, he could not admit that it was because he believed that his daughter might still live, and that he might see her amongst the cosmopolitan throng. For he harboured the small, secret hope that when *Landsknechts* had pillaged the houses of the Jews of Lodz, perhaps his daughter had not been carried off to be despoiled and murdered, but had instead been forced to become a servant of some Prussian family. It was no more impossible that she had been brought here, for the Council of Ten had hired many *Landsknechts* to defend the city and the *terraferma* hinterlands of its empire.

Dr. Stein's wife would no longer talk to him about it. Indeed, they hardly talked about anything these days. She had pleaded that the memory of their daughter should be laid to rest in a week of mourning, just as if they had interred her body. They were living in rooms rented from a cousin of Dr. Stein's wife, a banker called Abraham Soncino, and Dr. Stein was convinced that she had been put up to this by the women of Soncino's family. Who knew what the women talked about when locked in the bathhouse overnight, while they were being purified of their menses? No good, Dr. Stein was certain. Even Soncino, a genial, uxorious man, had urged that Dr. Stein mourn his daughter. Soncino had said that his family would bring the requisite food to begin the mourning; after a week all the community would commiserate with Dr. Stein and his wife before the main Sabbath service, and with God's help this terrible wound would be healed. It had taken all of Dr. Stein's powers to refuse this generous offer courteously. Soncino was a good man, but this was none of his business.

As winter came on, driven out by his wife's silent recriminations, or so he told himself, Dr. Stein walked the crowded streets almost every afternoon. Sometimes he was accompanied by an English captain of the Night Guard, Henry Gorrall, to whom Dr. Stein had become an unofficial assistant, helping identify the cause of death of one or another of the bodies found floating in the backwaters of the city.

There had been more murders than usual that summer, and several well-bred young women had disappeared. Dr. Stein had been urged to help Gorrall by the Elders of the *Beth Din*; already there were rumours that the Jews were murdering Christian virgins and using their blood to animate a Golem. It was good that a Jew—moreover, a Jew who worked at the city hospital, and taught new surgical techniques at the school of medicine—was involved in attempting to solve this mystery.

Besides, Dr. Stein enjoyed Gorrall's company. He was sympathetic to Gorrall's belief that everything, no matter how unlikely, had at base a rational explanation. Gorrall was a humanist, and did not mind being seen in the company of a man who must wear a yellow star on his coat. On their walks through the city, they often talked on the new philosophies of nature compounded in the University of Florence's Great Engineer, Leonardo da Vinci, quite oblivious to the brawling bustle all around them.

Ships from twenty nations crowded the quay in the long shadow of the Campanile, and their sailors washed through the streets. Hawkers cried their wares from flotillas of small boats that rocked on the wakes of barges or galleys. Gondoliers shouted vivid curses as skiffs crossing from one side of the Grand Canal to the other got in the way of their long, swift craft. Sometimes a screw-driven Florentine ship made its way up the Grand Canal, its Hero's engine laying a trail of black smoke, and everyone stopped to watch this marvel. Bankers in fur coats and tall felt hats conducted the business of the world in the piazza before San Giacometto, amid the rattle of the new clockwork abacuses and the subdued murmur of transactions.

Gorrall, a bluff muscular man with a bristling black beard and a habit of spitting sideways and often, because of the plug of tobacco he habitually chewed, seemed to know most of the bankers by name, and most of the merchants, too—the silk and cloth-of-gold mercers and sellers of fustian and velvet along the Mercerie, the druggists, gold-smiths and silversmiths, the makers of white wax, the iron-mongers, coopers and perfumers who had stalls and shops in the crowded little streets off the Rialto. He knew the names of many of the yellow-scarfed prostitutes, too, although Dr. Stein wasn't surprised at this, since he had first met Gorrall when the captain had come to the hospital for mercury treatment of his syphilis. Gorrall even knew, or pretended to know, the names of the cats which stalked between the feet of the crowds or lazed on cold stone in the brittle winter sunshine, the true rulers of Venice.

It was outside the cabinet of one of the perfumers of the Mercerie that Dr. Stein for a moment thought he saw his daughter. A grey-haired man was standing in the doorway of the shop, shouting at a younger man who was backing away and protesting that there was no blame that could be fixed to his name.

"You are his friend!"

"Sir, I did not know what it was he wrote, and I do not know and I do not care why your daughter cries so!"

The young man had his hand on his long knife, and Gorrall pushed through the gathering crowd and told both men to calm down. The wronged father dashed inside and came out again, dragging a girl of about fourteen, with the same long black hair, the same white, high forehead, as Dr. Stein's daughter.

"Hannah," Dr. Stein said helplessly, but then she turned, and it was not her. Not his daughter. The girl was crying, and clasped a sheet of paper to her bosom—wronged by a suitor, Dr. Stein supposed, and Gorrall said that it was precisely that. The young man had run off to sea, something so common these days that the Council of Ten had decreed that convicted criminals might be used on the galleys of the navy because of the shortage of free oarsman. Soon the whole city might be scattered between Corfu and Crete, or even further, now that Florence had destroyed the fleet of Cortés, and opened the American shore.

Dr. Stein did not tell his wife what he had seen. He sat in the kitchen long into the evening, and was still there, warmed by the embers of the fire and reading Leonardo's *Treatise on the Replication of Motion* by the poor light of a tallow candle, when the knock at the door came. It was just after midnight. Dr. Stein picked up the candle and went out, and saw his wife standing in the doorway to the bedroom.

"Don't answer it," she said. With one hand she clutched her shift to her throat; with the other she held a candle. Her long black hair, streaked with grey, was down to her shoulders.

"This isn't Lodz, Belita," Dr. Stein said, perhaps with unnecessary sharpness. "Go back to bed. I will deal with this."

"There are plenty of Prussians here, even so. One spat at me the other day. Abraham says that they blame us for the body-snatching, and it's the doctors they'll come for first."

The knocking started again. Husband and wife both looked at the door. "It may be a patient," Dr. Stein said, and pulled back the bolts.

The rooms were on the ground floor of a rambling house that faced onto a narrow canal. An icy wind was blowing along the canal, and it blew out Dr. Stein's candle when he opened the heavy door. Two city guards stood there, flanking their captain, Henry Gorrall.

"There's been a body found," Gorrall said in his blunt, direct manner. "A woman we both saw this very day, as it happens. You'll come along and tell me if it's murder."

The woman's body had been found floating in the Rio di Noale. "An hour later," Gorrall said, as they were rowed through the dark city, "and the tide would have turned and taken her out to sea, and neither you or I would have to chill our bones."

It was a cold night indeed, just after St. Agnes' Eve. An insistent wind off the land blew a dusting of snow above the roofs and prickly spires of Venice. Fresh ice crackled as the gondola broke through it, and larger pieces knocked against its planking. The few lights showing in the façades of the *palazzi* that lined the Grand Canal seemed bleary and dim. Dr. Stein wrapped his ragged loden cloak around himself and asked, "Do you think it murder?"

Gorrall spat into the black, icy water. "She died for love. That part is easy, as we witnessed the quarrel this very afternoon. She wasn't in the water long, and still reeks of booze. Drank to get her courage up, jumped. But we have to be sure. It could be a bungled kidnapping, or some cruel sport gone from bad to worse. There are too many soldiers with nothing to do but patrol the defences and wait for a posting in Cyprus."

The drowned girl had been laid out on the pavement by the canal, and covered with a blanket. Even at this late hour, a small crowd had gathered, and when a guard twitched the blanket aside at Dr. Stein's request, some of the watchers gasped.

It was the girl he had seen that afternoon, the perfumer's daughter. The soaked dress which clung to her body was white against the wet flags of the pavement. Her long black hair twisted in ropes about her face. There was a little froth at her mouth, and blue touched her lips. Dead, there was nothing about her that reminded Dr. Stein of his daughter.

Dr. Stein manipulated the skin over the bones of her hand, pressed one of her fingernails, closed her eyelids with thumb and forefinger. Tenderly, he covered her with the blanket again. "She's been dead less than an hour," he told Gorrall. "There's no sign of a struggle, and from the flux at her mouth I'd say it's clear she drowned."

"Killed herself most likely, unless someone pushed her in. The usual reason, I'd guess, which is why her boyfriend ran off to sea. Care to make a wager?"

"We both know her story. I can find out if she was with child, but not here."

Gorrall smiled. "I forget that you people don't bet."

"On the contrary. But in this case I fear you're right."

Gorrall ordered his men to take the body to the city hospital. As they lifted it into the gondola, he said to Dr. Stein, "She drank to get courage, then gave herself to the water, but not in this little canal. Suicides favour places where their last sight is a view, often of a place they love. We'll search the bridge at the Rialto—it is the only bridge crossing the Grand Canal, and the tide is running from that direction—but all the world crosses there, and if we're not quick, some beggar will have carried away her bottle and any note she may have left. Come on, doctor. We need to find out how she died before her parents turn up and start asking questions. I must have something to tell them, or they will go out looking for revenge."

If the girl had jumped from the Rialto bridge, she had left no note there—or it had been stolen, as Gorrall had predicted. Gorrall and Dr. Stein hurried on to the city hospital, but the body had not arrived. Nor did it. An hour later, a patrol found the gondola tied up in a backwater. One guard was dead from a single sword-cut to his neck. The other was stunned, and remembered nothing. The drowned girl was gone.

Gorrall was furious, and sent out every man he had to look for the body-snatchers. They had balls to attack two guards of the night watch, he said, but when he had finished with them they'd sing falsetto under the lash on the galleys. Nothing came of his enquiries. The weather turned colder, and an outbreak of pleurisy meant that Dr. Stein had much work in the hospital. He thought no more about it until a week later, when Gorrall came to see him.

"She's alive," Gorrall said. "I've seen her."

"A girl like her, perhaps." For a moment, Dr. Stein saw his daughter, running towards him, arms widespread. He said, "I don't make mistakes. There was no pulse, her lungs were congested with fluid, and she was as cold as the stones on which she lay."

Gorrall spat. "She's walking around dead, then. Do you remember what she looked like?"

"Vividly."

"She was the daughter of a perfumer, one Filippo Rompiasi. A member of the Great Council, although of the two thousand five hundred who have that honour, I'd say he has about the least influence. A noble family so long fallen on hard times that they have had to learn a trade."

Gorrall had little time for the numerous aristocracy of Venice, who, in his opinion, spent more time scheming to obtain support from the Republic than playing their part in governing it.

"Still," he said, scratching at his beard and looking sidelong at Dr. Stein, "it'll look very bad that the daughter of a patrician family walks around after having been pronounced dead by the doctor in charge of her case."

"I don't recall being paid," Dr. Stein said.

Gorrall spat again. "Would I pay someone who can't tell the quick from the dead? Come and prove me wrong and I'll pay you from my own pocket. With a distinguished surgeon as witness, I can draw up a docket to end this matter."

The girl was under the spell of a mountebank who called himself Dr. Pretorious, although Gorrall was certain that it wasn't the man's real name. "He was thrown out of Padua last year for practising medicine without a license, and was in jail in Milan before that. I've had my eye on him since he came ashore on a Prussian coal barge this summer. He vanished a month ago, and I thought he'd become some other city's problem. Instead, he went to ground. Now he proclaims this girl to be a miraculous example of a new kind of treatment."

There were many mountebanks in Venice. Every morning and afternoon there were five or six stages erected in the Piazza San Marco for their performances and convoluted orations, in which they praised the virtues of their peculiar instruments, powders, elixirs and other concoctions. Venice tolerated these madmen, in Dr. Stein's opinion, because the miasma of the nearby marshes befuddled the minds of her citizens, who besides were the most vain people he had ever met, eager to believe any promise of enhanced beauty and longer life.

Unlike the other mountebanks, Dr. Pretorious was holding a secret court. He had rented a disused wine store at the edge of the Prussian *Fondaco*, a quarter of Venice where ships were packed tightly in the narrow canals and every other building was a merchant's warehouse. Even walking beside a captain of the city guard, Dr. Stein was deeply uneasy there, feeling that all eyes were drawn to the yellow star he must by law wear, pinned to the breast of his surcoat. There had been an attack on the synagogue just the other day, and pig-shit had been smeared on the mezuzah fixed to the door-post of a prominent Jewish banker. Sooner or later, if the body-snatchers were not caught, a mob would sack the houses of the wealthiest Jews on the excuse of searching out and destroying the fabled Golem which existed nowhere but in their inflamed imaginations.

Along with some fifty others, mostly rich old women and their servants, Gorrall and Dr. Stein crossed a high arched bridge over a dark, silently running canal, and, after paying a ruffian a soldo each for the privilege, entered through a gate into a courtyard lit by smoky torches. Once the ruffian had closed and locked the gate, two figures appeared at a tall open door that was framed with swags of red cloth.

One was a man dressed all in black, with a mop of white hair. Behind him a woman in white lay half-submerged in a kind of tub packed full of broken ice. Her head was bowed, and her face hidden by a fall of black hair. Gorrall nudged Dr. Stein and said that this was the girl.

"She looks dead to me. Anyone who could sit in a tub of ice and not burst to bits through shivering must be dead."

"Let's watch and see," Gorrall said, and lit a foul-smelling cigarillo.

The white-haired man, Dr. Pretorious, welcomed his audience, and began a long rambling speech. Dr. Stein paid only a little attention, being more interested in the speaker. Dr. Pretorious was a gaunt, bird-like man with a clever, lined face and dark eyes under shaggy brows which knitted together when he made a point. He had a habit of stabbing a finger at his audience, of shrugging and laughing immodestly at his own boasts. He did not, Dr. Stein was convinced, much believe his speech, a curious failing for a mountebank.

Dr. Pretorious had the honour, it appeared, of introducing the true Bride of the Sea, one recently dead but now animated by an ancient Egyptian science. There was much on the long quest he had made in search of the secret of this ancient science, and the dangers he had faced in bringing it here, and in perfecting it. He assured his audience that as it had conquered death, the science he had perfected would also conquer old age, for was that not the slow victory of death over life? He snapped his fingers, and, as the tub seemed to slide forward of its own accord into the torchlight, invited his audience to see for themselves that this Bride of the Sea was not alive.

Strands of kelp had been woven into the drowned girl's thick black hair. Necklaces layered at her breast were of seashells of the kind that anyone could pick from the beach at the mouth of the lagoon.

Dr. Pretorious pointed to Dr. Stein, called him out. "I see we have here a physician. I recognise you, sir. I know the good work that you do at the Pietà, and the wonderful new surgical techniques you have brought to the city. As a man of science, would you do me the honour of certifying that this poor girl is at present not living?"

"Go on," Gorrall said, and Dr. Stein stepped forward, feeling both foolish and eager.

"Please, your opinion," Dr. Pretorious said with an ingratiating bow. He added, *sotto voce*, "This is a true marvel, doctor. Believe in me." He held a little mirror before the girl's red lips, and asked Dr. Stein if he saw any evidence of breath.

Dr. Stein was aware of an intense sweet, cloying odour: a mixture of brandy and attar of roses. He said, "I see none."

"Louder, for the good people here."

Dr. Stein repeated his answer.

"A good answer. Now, hold her wrist. Does her heart beat?"

The girl's hand was as cold as the ice from which Dr. Pretorious lifted it. If there was a pulse, it was so slow and faint that Dr. Stein was not allowed enough time to find it. He was dismissed, and Dr. Pretorious held up the girl's arm by the wrist and, with a grimace of effort, pushed a long nail though her hand.

"You see," he said with indecent excitement, giving the wrist a little shake so that the pierced hand flopped to and fro. "You see! No blood! No blood! Eh? What living person could endure such a cruel mutilation?"

He seemed excited by his demonstration. He dashed inside the doorway, and brought forward a curious device, a glass bowl inverted on a stalk of glass almost as tall as he, with a band of red silk twisted inside the bowl and around a spindle at the bottom of the stalk. He began to work a treadle, and the band of silk spun around and around.

"A moment," Dr. Pretorious said, as the crowd began to murmur. He glared at them from beneath his shaggy eyebrows as his foot pumped the treadle. "A moment, if you please. The apparatus must receive a sufficient charge."

He sounded flustered and out of breath. Any mountebank worth his salt would have had a naked boy painted in gilt and adorned with cherub wings to work the treadle, Dr. Stein reflected, and a drum roll besides. Yet the curious amateurism of this performance was more compelling than the polished theatricality of the mountebanks of the Piazza San Marco.

Gold threads trailed from the top of the glass bowl to a big glass jar half-filled with water and sealed with a cork. At last, Dr. Pretorious finished working the treadle, sketched a bow to the audience—his face shiny with sweat—and used a stave to sweep the gold threads from the top of the glass bowl onto the girl's face.

There was a faint snap, as of an old glass broken underfoot at a wedding. The girl's eyes opened and she looked about her, seeming dazed and confused.

"She lives, but only for a few precious minutes," Dr. Pretorious said. "Speak to me, my darling. You are a willing bride to the sea, perhaps?"

Gorrall whispered to Dr. Stein, "That's definitely the girl who drowned herself?" and Dr. Stein nodded. Gorrall drew out a long silver whistle and blew on it, three quick blasts. At once, a full squad of men-at-arms swarmed over the high walls. Some of the old women in the audience started to scream. The ruffian in charge of the gate charged at Gorrall, who drew a repeating pistol with a notched wheel over its stock. He shot three times, the wheel ratcheting around as it delivered fresh charges of powder and shot to the chamber. The ruffian was thrown onto his back, already dead as the noise of the shots echoed in the courtyard. Gorrall turned and levelled the pistol at the red-cloaked doorway, but it was on fire, and Dr. Pretorious and the dead girl in her tub of ice were gone.

Gorrall and his troops put out the fire and ransacked the empty wine store. It was Dr. Stein who found the only clue, a single broken seashell by a hatch that, when lifted, showed black water a few *braccia* below, a passage that Gorrall soon determined led out into the canal.

Dr. Stein could not forget the dead girl, the icy touch of her skin, her sudden start into life, the confusion in her eyes. Gorrall thought that she only seemed alive, that her body had been preserved perhaps by tanning, that the shine in her eyes was glycerine, the bloom on her lips pigment of the kind the apothecaries made of powdered beetles.

"The audience wanted to believe it would see a living woman, and the flickering candles would make her seem to move. You'll be a witness, I hope."

"I touched her," Dr. Stein said. "She was not preserved. The process hardens the skin."

"We keep meat by packing it in snow, in winter," Gorrall said. "Also, I have heard that there are magicians in the far Indies who can fall into so deep a trance that they do not need to breathe."

"We know she is not from the Indies. I would ask why so much fuss was made of the apparatus. It was so clumsy that it seemed to me to be real."

"I'll find him," Gorrall said, "and we will have answers to all these questions."

But when Dr. Stein saw Gorrall two days later, and asked about his enquiries into the Pretorious affair, the English captain shook his head and said, "I have been told not to pursue the matter. It seems the girl's father wrote too many begging letters to the Great Council, and he has no friends there. Further than that, I'm not allowed to say." Gorrall spat and said with sudden bitterness, "You can work here twenty-five years, Stein, and perhaps they'll make you a citizen, but they will never make you privy to their secrets."

"Someone in power believes Dr. Pretorious's claims, then."

"I wish I could say. Do you believe him?"

"Of course not."

But it was not true, and Dr. Stein immediately made his own enquiries. He wanted to know the truth, and not, he told himself, because he had mistaken the girl for his daughter. His interest was that of a doctor, for if death could be reversed, then surely that was the greatest gift a doctor could possess. He was not thinking of his daughter at all.

His enquiries were first made amongst his colleagues at the city hospital, and then in the guild hospitals and the new hospital of the Arsenal. Only the director of the last was willing to say anything, and warned Dr. Stein that the man he was seeking had powerful allies.

"So I have heard," Dr. Stein said. He added recklessly, "I wish I knew who they were."

The director was a pompous man, placed in his position through politics rather than merit. Dr. Stein could see that he was tempted to divulge what he knew, but in the end he merely said, "Knowledge is a dangerous thing. If you would know anything, start from a low rather than a high place. Don't overreach yourself, doctor."

Dr. Stein bridled at this, but said nothing. He sat up through the night, thinking the matter over. This was a city of secrets, and he was a stranger, and a Jew from Prussia to boot. His actions could easily be mistaken for those of a spy, and he was not sure that Gorrall could help him if he was accused. Gorrall's precipitate attempt to arrest Dr. Pretorious had not endeared him to his superiors, after all.

Yet Dr. Stein could not get the drowned girl's face from his mind, the way she had given a little start and her eyes had opened under the tangle of gold threads. Tormented by fantasies in which he found his daughter's grave and raised her up, he paced the kitchen, and in the small hours of the night it came to him that the director of the Arsenal hospital had spoken the truth even if he had not known it.

In the morning, Dr. Stein set out again, saying nothing to his wife of what he was doing. He had realised that Dr. Pretorious must need simples and other necessaries for his trade, and now he went from apothecary to apothecary with the mountebank's description. Dr. Stein found his man late in the afternoon, in a mean little shop in a *calle* that led off a square dominated by the brightly painted façade of the new church of Santa Maria de Miracoli.

The apothecary was a young man with a handsome face but small, greedy eyes. He peered at Dr. Stein from beneath a fringe of greasy black hair, and denied knowing Dr. Pretorious with such vehemence that Dr. Stein did not doubt he was lying.

A soldo soon loosened his tongue. He admitted that he might have such a customer as Dr. Stein described, and Dr. Stein asked at once, "Does he buy alum and oil?"

The apothecary expressed surprise. "He is a physician, not a tanner."

"Of course," Dr. Stein said, hope rising in him. A second soldo bought Dr. Stein the privilege of delivering the mountebank's latest order, a jar of sulphuric acid nested in a straw cradle.

The directions given by the apothecary led Dr. Stein through an intricate maze of *calli* and squares, ending in a courtyard no bigger than a closet, with tall buildings soaring on either side, and no way out but the narrow passage by which he had entered. Dr. Stein knew he was lost, but before he could turn to begin to retrace his steps, someone seized him from behind. An arm clamped across his throat. He struggled and dropped the jar of acid, which by great good luck, and the straw padding, did not break. Then he was on his back, looking up at a patch of grey sky which seemed to rush away from him at great speed, dwindling to a speck no bigger than a star.

Dr. Stein was woken by the solemn tolling of the curfew bells. He was lying on a mouldering bed in a room muffled by dusty tapestries and lit by a tall tallow candle. His throat hurt and his head ached. There was a tender swelling above his right ear, but he had no double vision or dizziness. Whoever had hit him had known what they were about.

The door was locked, and the windows were closed by wooden shutters nailed tightly shut. Dr. Stein was prying at the shutters when the door was unlocked and an old man came in. He was a shrivelled gnome in a velvet tunic and doublet more suited to a young gallant. His creviced face was drenched with powder, and there were hectic spots of rouge on his sunken cheeks.

"My master will talk with you," this ridiculous creature said.

Dr. Stein asked where he was, and the old man said that it was his master's house. "Once it was mine, but I gave it to him. It was his fee."

"Ah. You were sick, and he cured you."

"I was cured of life. He killed me and brought me back, so that I will live forever in the life beyond death. He's a great man."

"What's your name?"

The old man laughed. He had only one tooth in his head, and that a blackened stump. "I've yet to be christened in this new life. Come with me."

Dr. Stein followed the old man up a wide marble stair that wound through the middle of what must be a great *palazzo*. Two stories below was a floor tiled black and white like a chessboard; they climbed past two more floors to the top.

The long room had once been a library, but the shelves of the dark bays set off the main passage were empty now; only the chains which had secured the books were left. It was lit by a scattering of candles whose restless flames cast a confusion of flickering light that hid more than it revealed. One bay was penned off with a hurdle, and a pig moved in the shadows there. Dr. Stein had enough of a glimpse of it to see that there was something on the pig's back, but it was too dark to be sure quite what it was. Then something the size of a mouse scuttled straight in front of him—Dr. Stein saw with a shock that it ran on its hind legs, with a stumbling, crooked gait.

"One of my children," Dr. Pretorious said.

He was seated at a plain table scattered with books and papers. Bits of glassware and jars of acids and salts cluttered the shelves that rose behind him. The drowned girl sat beside him in a high-backed chair. Her head was held up by a leather band around her forehead; her eyes were closed and seemed bruised and sunken. Behind the chair was the same apparatus that Dr. Stein had seen used in the wine store. The smell of attar of roses was very strong.

Dr. Stein said, "It was only a mouse, or a small rat."

"You believe what you must, doctor," Dr. Pretorious said, "but I hope to open your eyes to the wonders I have performed." He told the old man, "Fetch food."

The old man started to complain that he wanted to stay, and Dr. Pretorious immediately jumped up in a sudden fit of anger and threw a pot of ink at his servant. The old man sputtered, smearing the black ink across his powdered face, and at once Dr. Pretorious burst into laughter. "You're a poor book," he said. "Fetch our guest meat and wine. It's the least I can do," he told Dr. Stein. "Did you come here of your own will, by the way?"

"I suppose the apothecary told you that I asked for you. That is, if he was an apothecary."

Dr. Pretorious said, with a quick smile, "You wanted to see the girl, I suppose, and here she is. I saw the tender look you gave her, before we were interrupted, and see that same look again."

"I knew nothing of my colleague's plans."

Dr. Pretorious made a steeple with his hands, touched the tip of the steeple to his bloodless lips. His fingers were long and white, and seemed to have an extra joint in them. He said, "Don't hope he'll find you."

"I'm not afraid. You brought me here because you wanted me here."

"But you should be afraid. I have power of life and death here."

"The old man said you gave him life everlasting."

Dr. Pretorious said carelessly, "Oh, so he believes. Perhaps that's enough."

"Did he die? Did you bring him back to life?"

Dr. Pretorious said, "That depends what you mean by life. The trick is not raising the dead, but making sure that death does not reclaim them."

Dr. Stein had seen a panther two days after he had arrived in Venice, brought from the Friendly Isles along with a great number of parrots. So starved that the bones of its shoulders and pelvis were clearly visible under its sleek black pelt, the panther ceaselessly padded back and forth inside its little cage, its eyes like green lamps. It had been driven mad by the voyage, and Dr. Stein thought that Dr. Pretorious was as mad as that panther, his sensibility quite lost on the long voyage into the unknown regions which he claimed to have conquered. In truth, they had conquered him.

"I have kept her on ice for much of the time," Dr. Pretorious said. "Even so, she is beginning to deteriorate." He twitched the hem of the girl's gown, and Dr. Stein saw on her right foot a black mark as big as his hand, like a sunken bruise. Despite the attar of roses, the reek of gangrene was suddenly overpowering.

He said, "The girl is dead. I saw it for myself, when she was pulled from the canal. No wonder she rots."

"It depends what you mean by death. Have you ever seen fish in a pond, under ice? They can become so sluggish that they no longer move. And yet they live, and when warmed will move again. I was once in Gotland. In winter, the nights last all day, and your breath freezes in your beard. A man was found alive after two days lying in a drift of snow. He had drunk too much, and had passed out; the liquor had saved him from freezing to death, although he lost his ears and his fingers and toes. This girl was dead when she was pulled from the icy water, but she had drunk enough to prevent death from placing an irreversible claim on her body. I returned her to life. Would you like to see how it is done?"

"Master?"

It was the old man. With cringing deference, he offered a tray bearing a tarnished silver wine decanter, a plate of beef, heavily salted and greenish at the edges, and a loaf of black bread.

Dr. Pretorious was on him in an instant. The food and wine flew into the air; Dr. Pretorious lifted the old man by his neck, dropped him to the floor. "We are busy," he said, quite calmly.

Dr. Stein started to help the old man to gather the food together, but Dr. Pretorious aimed a kick at the old man, who scuttled away on all fours.

"No need for that," Dr. Pretorious said impatiently. "I shall show you, doctor, that she lives." The glass bowl sang under his long fingernails; he smoothed the belt of frayed red silk with tender care. He looked sidelong at Dr. Stein and said, "There is a tribe in the far south of Egypt who have been metalworkers for three thousand years. They apply a fine coat of silver to ornaments of base metal by immersing the ornaments in a solution of nitrate of silver and connecting them to tanks containing plates of lead and zinc in salt water. Split by the two metals, the opposing essences of the salt-water flow in different directions, and when they join in the ornaments draw the silver from solution. I have experimented with that process, and will experiment more, but even when I substitute salt water with acid, the flow of essences is as yet too weak for my purpose. This—" he rapped the glass bowl, which rang like a bell "—is based on a toy that their children played with, harnessing that same essence to give each other little frights. I have greatly enlarged it, and developed a way of storing the essence it generates. For this essence lives within us, too, and is sympathetic to the flow from this apparatus. By its passage through the glass the silk generates that essence, which is stored here, in this jar. Look closely if you will. It is only ordinary glass, and ordinary water, sealed by a cork, but it contains the essence of life."

"What do you want of me?"

"I have done much alone. But, doctor, we can do so much more together. Your reputation is great."

"I have the good fortune to be allowed to teach the physicians here some of the techniques I learned in Prussia. But no surgeon would operate on a corpse."

"You are too modest. I have heard the stories of the man of clay your people can make to defend themselves. I know it is based on truth. Clay cannot live, even if bathed in blood, but a champion buried in the clay of the earth might be made to live again, might he not?"

Dr. Stein understood that the mountebank believed his own legerdemain. He said, "I see that you have great need of money. A man of learning would only sell books in the most desperate circumstances, but all the books in this library have gone. Perhaps your sponsors are disappointed, and do not pay what they have promised, but it is no business of mine."

Dr. Pretorious said sharply, "The fancies in those books were a thousand years old. I have no need of them. And it might be said that you owe me money. Interruption of my little demonstration cost me at least twenty soldi, for there were at least that many dowagers eager to taste the revitalising essence of life. So I think that you are obliged to help me, eh? Now watch, and wonder."

Dr. Pretorious began to work the treadles of his apparatus. The sound of his laboured breathing and the soft tearing sound made by the silk belt as it revolved around and around filled the long room. At last, Dr. Pretorious twitched the gold wires from the top of the glass bowl so that they fell across the girl's face. In the dim light, Dr. Stein saw the snap of a fat blue flame that for a moment jumped amongst the ends of the wires. The girl's whole body shuddered. Her eyes opened.

"A marvel!" Dr. Pretorious said, panting from his exercise. "Each day she dies. Each night I bring her to life."

The girl looked around at his voice. The pupils of her eyes were of different sizes. Dr. Pretorious slapped her face until a faint bloom appeared on her cheeks.

"You see! She lives! Ask her a question. Anything. She has returned from death, and there is more in her head than in yours or mine. Ask!"

"I have nothing to ask," Dr. Stein said.

"She knows the future. Tell him about the future," he hissed into the girl's ear.

The girl's mouth worked. Her chest heaved as if she was pumping up something inside herself, then she said in a low whisper, "It is the Jews that will be blamed."

Dr. Stein said, "That's always been true."

"But that's why you're here, isn't it?"

Dr. Stein met Dr. Pretorious's black gaze. "How many have you killed, in your studies?"

"Oh, most of them were already dead. They gave themselves for science, just as in the ancient days young girls were sacrificed for the pagan gods."

"Those days are gone."

"Greater days are to come. You will help. I know you will. Let me show you how we will save her. You will save her, won't you?"

The girl's head was beside Dr. Pretorious'. They were both looking at Dr. Stein. The girl's lips moved, mumbling over two words. A cold mantle crept across Dr. Stein's skin. He had picked up a knife when he had stooped to help the old man, and now, if he could, he had a use for it.

Dr. Pretorious led Dr. Stein to the pen where the pig snuffled in its straw. He held up a candle, and Dr. Stein saw clearly, for an instant, the hand on the pig's back. Then the creature bolted into shadow.

It was a human hand, severed at the wrist and poking out of the pink skin of the pig's back as if from a sleeve. It looked alive: the nails were suffused, and the skin was as pink as the pig's skin.

"They don't last long," Dr. Pretorious said. He seemed pleased by Dr. Stein's shock. "Either the pig dies, or the limb begins to rot. There is some incompatibility between the two kinds of blood. I have tried giving pigs human blood before the operation, but they die even more quickly. Perhaps with your help I can perfect the process. I will perform the operation on the girl, replace her rotten foot with a healthy one. I will not have her imperfect. I will do better. I will improve her, piece by piece. I will make her a true Bride of the Sea, a wonder that all the world will worship. Will you help me, doctor? It is difficult to get bodies. Your friend is causing me a great deal of nuisance...but you can bring me bodies, why, almost every day. So many die in winter. A piece here, a piece there. I do not need the whole corpse. What could be simpler?"

He jumped back as Dr. Stein grabbed his arm, but Dr. Stein was quicker, and knocked the candle into the pen. The straw was aflame in an instant, and the pig charged out as soon as Dr. Stein pulled back the hurdle. It barged at Dr. Pretorious as if it remembered the torments he had inflicted upon it, and knocked him down. The hand flopped to and fro on its back, as if waving.

The girl could have been asleep, but her eyes opened as soon as Dr. Stein touched her cold brow. She tried to speak, but she had very little strength now, and Dr. Stein had to lay his head on her cold breast to hear her mumble the two words she had mouthed to him earlier.

"*Kill me.*"

Behind them, the fire had taken hold in the shelving and floor, casting a lurid light down the length of the room. Dr. Pretorious ran to and fro, pursued by the pig. He was trying to capture the scampering mice-things which had been driven from their hiding places by the fire, but even with their staggering bipedal gait they were faster than he was. The old man ran into the room, and Dr. Pretorious shouted, "Help me, you fool!"

But the old man ran past him, ran through the wall of flames that now divided the room, and jumped onto Dr. Stein as he bent over the drowned girl. He was as weak as a child, but when Dr. Stein tried to push him away he bit into Dr. Stein's wrist and the knife fell to the floor. They reeled backwards and knocked over a jar of acid. Instantly, acrid white fumes rose up as the acid burnt into the wood floor. The old man rolled on the floor, beating at his smoking, acid-drenched costume.

Dr. Stein found the knife and drew its sharp point down the length of the blue veins of the drowned girl's forearms. The blood flowed surprisingly quickly. Dr. Stein stroked the girl's hair, and her eyes focused on his. For a moment it seemed as if she might say something, but with the heat of the fire beating at his back he could not stay any longer.

Dr. Stein knocked out a shutter with a bench, hauled himself onto the window-ledge. As he had hoped, there was black water directly below: like all *palazzi*, this one rose straight up from the Grand Canal. Smoke rolled around him. He heard Dr. Pretorious shout at him and he let himself go, and gave himself to air, and then water.

Dr. Pretorious was caught at dawn the next day, as he tried to leave the city in a hired skiff. The fire set by Dr. Stein had burnt out the top floor of the *palazzo*, no more, but the old man had died there. He had been the last in the line of a patrician family that had fallen on hard times: the *palazzo* and an entry in the *Libro d'Oro* was all that was left of their wealth and fame.

Henry Gorrall told Dr. Stein that no mention need be made of his part in this tragedy. "Let the dead lay as they will. There's no need to disturb them with fantastic stories."

"Yes," Dr. Stein said, "the dead should stay dead."

He was lying in his own bed, recovering from a rheumatic fever brought about by the cold waters into which he had plunged on his escape. Winter sunlight pried at the shutters of the white bedroom, streaked the fresh rushes on the floor.

"It seems that Pretorious has influential friends," Gorrall said. "There won't be a trial and an execution, much as he deserves both. He's going straight to the galleys, and no doubt after a little while he will contrive, with some help, to escape. That's the way of things here. His name wasn't really Pretorious, of course. I doubt if we'll ever know where he came from. Unless he told you something of himself."

Outside the bedroom there was a clamour of voices as Dr. Stein's wife welcomed in Abraham Soncino and his family, and the omelettes and other egg dishes they had brought to begin the week of mourning.

Dr. Stein said, "Pretorious claimed that he was in Egypt, before he came here."

"Yes, but what adventurer was not, after the Florentines conquered it and let it go? Besides, I understand that he stole the apparatus not from any savage tribe, but from the Great Engineer of Florence himself. What else did he say? I'd know all, not for the official report, but my peace of mind."

"There aren't always answers to mysteries," Dr. Stein told his friend. The dead should stay dead. Yes. He knew now that his daughter had died. He had released her memory when he had released the poor girl that Dr. Pretorious had called back from the dead. Tears stood in his eyes, and Gorrall clumsily tried to comfort him, mistaking them for tears of grief.

BEST NEW HORROR

THE YEAR'S BEST HORROR
STORIES BY SUCH MASTERS
OF DARK FANTASY AS:

**RAMSEY CAMPBELL
NEIL GAIMAN
STEPHEN GALLAGHER
GRAHAM MASTERTON
PAUL J. McAULEY
MICHAEL MARSHALL SMITH**
and many others

EDITED BY
STEPHEN JONES

"A must for all horror fans...
a collector's collection"
- *KIRKUS*

[1995]

FOR THE SEVENTH volume of *The Best New Horror*, Luis Rey contributed, in my opinion, his finest cover to the series, ably showcased by Robinson's classy design.

Once again issued under the soon-to-be-defunct Raven Books imprint, the Introduction leapt to forty-three pages while the Necrology crept up to nineteen. Although both sections were now taking me a huge amount of time each year to research and compile, I also added a section of 'Useful Addresses' which I thought might function as a helpful reference source for readers and authors alike.

At almost 600 pages, this was one of the biggest volumes ever published in the series.

This time I got to sound off about a personal irritation at avaricious writers and others who actively solicit awards in our genre. Not only is it debasing to them and their work, but it also dilutes the worth of any prize that is cynically canvassed for in this way.

Unfortunately, many of today's awards in the field continue to be diminished by active campaigning and manipulation by those desperate to win them at any price.

Volume #7 contained twenty-six stories, including a posthumously published tale by the great pulp writer Manly Wade Wellman (who died in 1986), and another belated contribution by writer Jane Rice, who regularly appeared in John W. Campbell's pulp magazine *Unknown* in the 1940s.

Brian Stableford's genre-bending novella 'The Hunger and Ecstasy of Vampires' was certainly the longest contribution in the book, but this time I've selected one of the shortest—Neil Gaiman's 'Queen of Knives'.

Neil has never been scared to take chances with his fiction, and this creepy prose poem is another example of one of our most creative writers once again pushing the boundaries of the genre; and like Christopher Fowler's story earlier in this volume, it also stands as a tribute to another almost-forgotten British comedian of the 1960s.

NEIL GAIMAN

QUEEN OF KNIVES

NEIL GAIMAN's *Norse Mythology*—the author's retelling of the ancient stories—topped the best-sellers lists on both sides of the Atlantic.

His novel *The Ocean at the End of the Lane* was a best-selling "Book of the Year", and his other titles include *American Gods* (now in its third season as a TV series), *The Graveyard Book, Coraline, Neverwhere,* the essay collection *The View from the Cheap Seats,* and *The Sandman* series of graphic novels, amongst many other notable works.

His fiction has received numerous awards, including the Carnegie and Newbery medals, along with the Hugo, Nebula, World Fantasy and Eisner awards.

Originally from England, he now divides his time between the UK, where he recently turned *Good Omens*—originally a novel he wrote with Terry Pratchett—into another television series, and the US, where he is professor in the arts at Bard College.

"'Queen of Knives' is the third of a set of three story-poems about men and women and violence," explains Gaiman. "The other two are 'The White Road', which was reprinted in *The Year's Best Fantasy and Horror,* and 'Eaten (Scenes from a Moving Picture)', which appeared in Ellen Datlow's *Off Limits: Tales of Alien Sex* anthology. However, due to the vagaries of publishing, 'Queen of Knives' was the first to appear.

"It was written for the interestingly-designed *Tombs* anthology. I see it as a companion piece to the graphic novel I did with Dave McKean, *Mr. Punch*, with its view of the adult world from a child's perspective. It is, of course, true in every detail. The comedian is the now almost completely forgotten Harry Worth (1917–89)."

"The re-appearance of the lady is a matter of individual taste."
—Will Goldston, *Tricks and Illusions*.

WHEN I WAS a boy, from time to time,
I stayed with my grandparents
(old people: I knew they were old—
chocolates in their house
remained uneaten until I came to stay,
this, then, was ageing).
My grandfather always made breakfast at sun-up:
A pot of tea, for her and him and me,
some toast and marmalade
(the Silver Shred and the Gold). Lunch and dinner,
those were my grandmother's to make, the kitchen
was again her domain, all the pans and spoons,
the mincer, all the whisks and knives, her loyal subjects.
She would prepare the food with them, singing her little songs:
Daisy Daisy give me your answer do,
or sometimes,
You made me love you, I didn't want to do it,
I didn't want to do it.
She had no voice, not one to speak of.

Business was very slow.
My grandfather spent his days at the top of the house,
in his tiny darkroom where I was not permitted to go,
bringing out paper faces from the darkness,

the cheerless smiles of other people's holidays.
My grandmother would take me for grey walks along the
    promenade.
Mostly I would explore
the small wet grassy space behind the house,
the blackberry brambles and the garden shed.

It was a hard week for my grandparents
forced to entertain a wide-eyed boy-child, so
one night they took me to the King's Theatre. The King's...

Variety!

The lights went down, red curtains rose.
A popular comedian of the day,
came on, stammered out his name (his catchphrase),
pulled out a sheet of glass, and stood half-behind it,
raising the arm and leg that we could see;
reflected he seemed to fly—it was his trademark,
so we all laughed and cheered. He told a joke or two,
quite badly. His haplessness, his awkwardness,
these were what we had come to see.
Bemused and balding and bespectacled,
he reminded me a little of my grandfather.
And then the comedian was done.
Some ladies danced all legs across the stage.
A singer sang a song I didn't know.

The audience were old people,
like my grandparents, tired and retired,
all of them laughing and applauding.

In the interval my grandfather
queued for a choc-ice and a couple of tubs.
We ate our ices as the lights went down.
The "SAFETY CURTAIN" rose, and then the real curtain.

The ladies danced across the stage again,
and then the thunder rolled, the smoke went puff,
a conjurer appeared and bowed. We clapped.

The lady walked on, smiling from the wings:
glittered. Shimmered. Smiled.
We looked at her, and in that moment flowers grew,
and silks and pennants tumbled from his fingertips.

The flags of all nations, said my grandfather, nudging me.
They were up his sleeve.
Since he was a young man,
(I could not imagine him as a child)
my grandfather had been, by his own admission,
one of the people who knew how things worked.
He had built his own television,
my grandmother told me, when they were first married,
it was enormous, though the screen was small.
This was in the days before television programmes;
they watched it, though,
unsure whether it was people or ghosts they were seeing.
He had a patent, too, for something he invented,
but it was never manufactured.
Stood for the local council, but he came in third.
He could repair a shaver or a wireless,
develop your film, or build a house for dolls.
(The doll's house was my mother's. We still had it at my house,
shabby and old it sat out in the grass, all rained-on and forgot.)

The glitter lady wheeled on a box.
The box was tall: grown-up-person-sized, and black.
She opened up the front.
They turned it round and banged upon the back.
The lady stepped inside, still smiling,
The magician closed the door on her.

When it was opened she had gone.
He bowed.

Mirrors, explained my grandfather. *She's really still inside.*
At a gesture, the box collapsed to matchwood.
A trapdoor, assured my grandfather;
Grandma hissed him silent.

The magician smiled, his teeth were small and crowded;
he walked, slowly, out into the audience.
He pointed to my grandmother, he bowed,
a Middle-European bow,
and invited her to join him on the stage.
The other people clapped and cheered.
My grandmother demurred. I was so close
to the magician, that I could smell his aftershave,
and whispered "Me, oh, me..." But still,
he reached his long fingers for my grandmother.

Pearl, go on up, said my grandfather. *Go with the man.*

My grandmother must have been, what? Sixty, then?
She had just stopped smoking,
was trying to lose some weight. She was proudest
of her teeth, which, though tobacco-stained were all her own.
My grandfather had lost his, as a youth,
riding his bicycle; he had the bright idea
to hold on to a bus to pick up speed.
The bus had turned,
and Grandpa kissed the road.
She chewed hard liquorice, watching TV at night,
or sucked hard caramels, perhaps to make him wrong.
She stood up, then, a little slowly.
Put down the paper tub half-full of ice cream,
the little wooden spoon—

went down the aisle, and up the steps.
And on the stage.

The conjurer applauded her once more—
A good sport. That was what she was. A sport.
Another glittering woman came from the wings,
bringing another box—
this one was red.

That's her, nodded my grandfather, *the one
who vanished off before. You see? That's her.*
Perhaps it was. All I could see
was a woman who sparkled, standing next to my grandmother,
(who fiddled with her pearls, and looked embarrassed.)
The lady smiled and faced us, then she froze,
a statue, or a window mannequin,
The magician pulled the box, with ease,
down to the front of stage, where my grandmother waited.
A moment or so of chitchat:
where she was from, her name, that kind of thing.
They'd never met before? She shook her head.

The magician opened the door,
my grandmother stepped in.

Perhaps it's not the same one, admitted my grandfather,
on reflection,
I think she had darker hair, the other girl.
I didn't know.
I was proud of my grandmother, but also embarrassed,
hoping she'd do nothing to make me squirm,
that she wouldn't sing one of her songs.

She walked into the box. They shut the door.
He opened a compartment at the top, a little door. We saw

my grandmother's face. *Pearl? Are you all right Pearl?*
My grandmother smiled and nodded.
The magician closed the door.

The lady gave him a long thin case,
so he opened it. Took out a sword
and rammed it through the box.

And then another, and another
And my grandfather chuckled and explained
The blade slides in the hilt, and then a fake
slides out the other side.

Then he produced a sheet of metal, which
he slid into the box half the way up.
It cut the thing in half. The two of them,
the woman and the man, lifted the top
half of the box up and off, and put it on the stage,
with half my grandma in.

The top half.

He opened up the little door again, for a moment,
My grandmother's face beamed at us, trustingly.
When he closed the door before,
she went down a trapdoor,
And now she's standing half-way up,
my grandfather confided.
She'll tell us how it's done, when it's all over.
I wanted him to stop talking: I needed the magic.

Two knives now, through the half-a-box,
at neck-height.
Are you there, Pearl? asked the magician. *Let us know*
—do you know any songs?

My grandmother sang *Daisy Daisy*.
He picked up the part of the box,
with the little door in it—the head part—
and he walked about, and she sang
Daisy Daisy first at one side of the stage,
and at the other.

That's him, said my grandfather, *and he's throwing his voice.*
It sounds like Grandma, I said.
Of course it does, he said. *Of course it does.*
He's good, he said. *He's good. He's very good.*

The conjuror opened up the box again,
now hatbox-sized. My grandmother had finished *Daisy Daisy*,
and was on a song which went
My my here we go the driver's drunk and the horse won't go
now we're going back now we're going back
back back back to London Town.

She had been born in London. Told me ominous tales
from time to time to time
of her childhood. Of the children who ran into her father's shop
shouting *shonky shonky sheeny*, running away;
she would not let me wear a black shirt because,
she said, she remembered the marches through the East End.
Moseley's black-shirts. Her sister got an eye blackened.

The conjurer took a kitchen knife,
pushed it slowly through the red hatbox.
And then the singing stopped.
He put the boxes back together,
pulled out the knives and swords, one by one by one.
He opened the compartment in the top: my grandmother smiled,
embarrassed, at us, displaying her own old teeth.
He closed the compartment, hiding her from view.
Pulled out the last knife.

Opened the main door again,
and she was gone.
A gesture, and the red box vanished too.
It's up his sleeve, my grandfather explained, but seemed unsure.

The conjurer made two doves fly from a burning plate.
A puff of smoke, and he was gone as well.

She'll be under the stage now, or back-stage,
said my grandfather,
having a cup of tea. She'll come back to us with flowers,
or with chocolates. I hoped for chocolates.

The dancing girls again.
The comedian, for the last time.
And all of them came on together at the end.
The grand finale, said my grandfather. *Look sharp,*
perhaps she'll be back on now.

But no. They sang
when you're riding along
on the crest of the wave
and the sun is in the sky.

The curtain went down, and we shuffled out into the lobby.
We loitered for a while.
Then we went down to the stage door,
and waited for my grandmother to come out.
The conjurer came out in street clothes;
the glitter woman looked so different in a mac.

My grandfather went to speak to him. He shrugged,
told us he spoke no English and produced
a half-a-crown from behind my ear,
and vanished off into the dark and rain.
I never saw my grandmother again.

We went back to their house, and carried on.
My grandfather now had to cook for us.
And so for breakfast, dinner, lunch and tea
we had golden toast, and silver marmalade
and cups of tea.
Till I went home.

He got so old after that night
as if the years took him all in a rush.
Daisy Daisy, he'd sing, *give me your answer do.*
If you were the only girl in the world and I were the only boy.
My old man said follow the van.
My grandfather had the voice in the family,
they said he could have been a cantor,
but there were snapshots to develop,
radios and razors to repair...
his brothers were a singing duo: the Nightingales,
had been on television in the early days.

He bore it well. Although, quite late one night,
I woke, remembering the liquorice sticks in the pantry,
I walked downstairs:
my grandfather stood there in his bare feet.

And, in the kitchen, all alone,
I saw him stab a knife into a box.
You made me love you.
I didn't want to do it.

THE
MAMMOTH BOOK OF
BEST NEW
HORROR

THE YEAR'S BEST HORROR
STORIES BY SUCH MASTERS
OF DARK FANTASY AS:

POPPY Z. BRITE
STORM CONSTANTINE
CHRISTOPHER FOWLER
IAIN SINCLAIR
MICHAEL MARSHALL SMITH
KARL EDWARD WAGNER
and many others

EDITED BY
STEPHEN JONES

"The best single horror
collection of the year."
– KIRKUS

[1996]

L UIS REY'S "EYEBALLS" painting may not have been quite as effective as his previous three contributions, but it ended his association with the series and rounded out a run of four covers that, so far as I am concerned, represented the indisputable high point of *Best New Horror's* design and packaging up to that time.

With an Introduction now running to forty-eight pages and a twenty-one page Necrology, the non-fiction elements of the book were finally becoming as important as the fiction. This time I looked at the decline in horror publishing during the second half of the 1990s, and predicted a resurgence in the genre with the new millennium.

In retrospect, horror never did return to the dizzy heights of popularity it achieved in the 1980s, but after the boom-and-bust years it did finally re-establish itself again as a viable publishing niche before the next cycle began to decay again.

The twenty-four stories included a final contribution by the late Karl Edward Wagner ('Final Cut') and marked the first of two appearances to date of literary writer Iain Sinclair ('Hardball'). Volume #8 was one of those rare occasions in the series where I didn't use a story by Ramsey Campbell, so the book was—belatedly—dedicated to him instead.

Up until then I had succeeded in limiting the contributions (except for collaborations) to one story per author in each volume. However, the publication of Terry Lamsley's second remarkable collection of short stories, *Conference with the Dead: Tales of Supernatural Terror*, forced me to break my own rule and finally accept two stories by a single author. His darkly humorous 'Walking the Dog' opened the book, while the even more disturbing story that follows memorably closed the eighth edition of *The Best New Horror*...

TERRY LAMSLEY

THE BREAK

TERRY LAMSLEY was born in the south of England but lived in
the north for most of his life. He currently resides in Amsterdam,
Holland.

His first collection of supernatural stories, *Under the Crust*, was
initially published in a small paperback edition in 1993. Originally
intended to only appeal to local readers and the tourist market in
Lamsley's home town of Buxton, Derbyshire, in the heart of England's
Peak District (the volume's six tales are all set in or around the area),
its reputation quickly grew, helped when *Under the Crust* reached the
hands of the late Karl Edward Wagner, editor of *The Year's Best Horror
Stories* series.

Wagner was instrumental in the book being nominated for three
World Fantasy Awards in 1994, and ultimately winning the Best
Novella award for the title story of the collection. Ramsey Campbell
accepted it on the author's behalf, and Lamsley's reputation as a writer
of supernatural fiction was assured.

In 1997, Canada's Ash-Tree Press reissued *Under the Crust* as a
handsome hardcover, limited to just 500 copies and now as sought-
after as the long out-of-print first edition. A year earlier, Ash-Tree
had published a second collection of Lamsley's short stories,
Conference with the Dead: Tales of Supernatural Terror, and it was
followed in 2000 by a third collection, *Dark Matters*. Night Shade

Books reprinted the International Horror Guild Award-winning *Conference with the Dead* in 2005, with the limited edition containing a previously uncollected story.

Made Ready & Cupboard Love (2006) is a collection of two original novellas from Subterranean Press, while *R.I.P.* (2009) is another novella from PS Publishing.

"'The Break' grew out of my memories of childhood holidays and of later experiences as a vagrant doing menial jobs in vast, strange, seedy hotels in various seaside resorts when I was in my teens," recalls Lamsley. "Happy days!"

You might not agree after you've read this...

INSTEAD OF GETTING undressed straight away, as Gran had told him to, Danny pulled aside one of the curtains she had drawn together and peered out again at the jetty, on the edge of the harbour to the right of him, to see what the men on the boat were doing. The little craft, a fishing smack, had docked five minutes earlier, and he had watched with admiration as the men aboard had manoeuvred it into place as easily as if they were parking a car. The sky was getting darker and the sea was flat, black and shiny, except for the white lace of tiny waves tacked along the edge of the beach. He could no longer make out the shape of the hull of the vessel, but the jetty was built of pale, slightly yellow stone against which he could see, in silhouette, the top of the boat and the activities of the two sailors on board.

They had pulled a cumbersome object, a box of some kind, up from the deck with a winch operated by a third man, above them on the jetty. He had been waiting for them, staring out to sea, for some time before they had arrived. Danny had asked his Gran to open the top window because it was an oppressively warm evening and the hotel room had a flat, earthy smell, like the inside of a greenhouse in winter. Through it he could hear the rattle of the hoist's cranking chain as the box lurched into the air, and the barking shouts of the man operating it. He was a very big man, dressed in heavy, unseasonable garments that made him look like a bear. He moved like a bear as well, Danny thought, with rolling, lunging motions, and seemed to have trouble keeping his balance.

When the box rose to the level of his shoulders the man pulled it around with a rope attached to the top of the hoist, then slowly lowered it onto the jetty. It must have slipped its chains at the last moment because Danny saw it suddenly drop a few inches, and heard it land with a sound that made him think it was very heavy, and made of wood. The bear-like man walked around it quickly, inspecting it, then shouted sharply down to the others on the boat. At once, a light came on in the cabin at the front of the smack. The engine started clunking, the third man cast off the ropes, and the vessel curved away out into the bay beyond, leaving a widening ark of crumpled tin-foil foam in its wake.

"Danny—please. It's *so* late, and you've not even got into your pyjamas!"

Gran didn't seem at all cross, as his mother would have been, but she sounded strained and disappointed in him. Danny hadn't heard her come in, but she always moved like that—so quietly and carefully, like a phantom. He dropped the edge of the curtain and, feeling slightly ashamed of himself, took the tray bearing a mug of chocolate and some toast she had brought him for supper, and set it down on the table beside his bed.

"I'm not tired, Gran," he lied, then yawned hugely, giving the game away. "I was watching the sea," he explained, somewhat inaccurately.

"You've got all week for that," Gran said, folding a triangle of quilt tidily back away from his pillow to display how temptingly comfortable the bed beneath it looked.

Danny said, "I like the boats. There's hundreds in the harbour. Will we be able to go for a trip on one?"

"I can't take Grandad, and I mustn't leave him behind, but perhaps you could go on your own, if I think it's safe."

"Is Grandad ill?" Danny asked, plugging the sink and twisting the taps to run water for his evening wash. When Gran didn't answer he turned back to her and added, "He looks all right. I can't *see* anything wrong with him."

"He's not exactly ill, like you were last winter, with your chest. It's just that, recently, he's got a bit . . . forgetful."

"Yes," Danny agreed, "I've noticed that," and saw his Gran's face darken. "I mean, sometimes, he looks at me as though he doesn't know who I am. When I met you both at the station, and you left me with him and went to get a magazine, he asked me what my name was."

"Oh dear," said Gran, poking nervously at the grey curl that dangled down over her right eye, "did he really?"

"Then, when I told him, he just shook his head, as though he'd never heard of me."

"I'm sorry."

"It's not your fault," Danny said generously. "He got my name right later." He began to brush his teeth.

Pleased to be presented with this enforced curtailment of the conversation, when she had been thinking how she could change the subject without arousing in Danny an alarming suspicion that her husband was worse than he really was, Gran decided to make an exit.

"Breakfast is at eight-thirty," she said, after kissing Danny goodnight on the top of his head.

"Can I go on my own, or must I wait for you?"

"No, you're big enough now to make your own way down, I think."

"Of course I am," Danny agreed. "I was last year, when we went to Brighton, but you wouldn't believe me."

Gran smiled, but she didn't seem to agree with him. "Into bed now, Danny," she insisted. "I'll look in soon to make sure you're asleep."

When she had gone Danny sipped the chocolate and pulled a face. It didn't taste anything like it did at home, when his mother made it.

He poured the drink down the sink, ate the toast quickly, got into his pyjamas, then could not resist taking one more peep out the window before getting into bed.

The man on the jetty was still there. He was pushing the big heavy box towards the shore with great difficulty. He was bending behind it, almost on all fours, looking more than ever like a fat black bear. Although obviously pushing with all his strength, he was only managing to move it inches at a time. After two or three strenuous efforts he stopped, leaned against the box as though exhausted, then strained to shove it a couple of times more. It made a harsh crunching sound as it moved, as if it was sliding across a surface scattered with broken glass. The box was still only a few feet from where it had landed. At that rate, Danny thought, it would take the man all night to reach the end of the jetty!

He could hear the box sliding and grinding along every now and then as he lay in bed, but it didn't sound as if it was getting any nearer. He felt sorry for the man. Why didn't he get someone to help him? He had looked somehow very lonely out there, and the way he had spoken to the men on the fishing boat, and they to him, had not sounded at all friendly. It occurred to Danny that it was likely that the man was not nice to know, and had no friends.

When Gran peeped in, twenty minutes later, she could tell from his breathing that he was asleep. She was closing the door again when she heard the sound of the huge box being moved outside, and went to the window. By mistake, she had only brought her reading glasses on holiday with her, but was just able to see what Danny had seen and, like him, watched and speculated about the man on the jetty. At that moment he was leaning on the far edge of the box and his white blob of a face was looking up towards the hotel, or seemed to be. He remained in this pose for only a few moments, then suddenly bent down, shuffled his legs back a little, and began to push. His body appeared to compress as he increased his effort then, though Gran's faulty vision could detect no movement, the box grated on the stone surface of the jetty as it jerked a few inches closer, and the figure behind it elongated. This happened three times, then the man stood up, stretched his back, arced his arms above his head, and glanced up towards the hotel again.

Gran stepped away from the window and closed her eyes for a moment as a harsh, cold light shone in on her. She realised it was the headlights of a car turning off the promenade, up into the town. She suddenly felt an unexpected evening breeze from somewhere, that made the edges of the curtains flutter, and caused her to twitch and clench her teeth and shudder.

Because of that, and because she didn't want Danny woken up by any noise, she shut the window before she left the room.

∞

Someone knocked on the door. Danny opened his eyes, registered the dim daylight beyond the curtains, and waited. Gran never needed inviting. When, after a static silence, whoever it was knocked again, Danny sat up and called, "Come in." A young woman in a pale blue overall stepped sideways into the room. Still holding the door handle she showed him a sketch of a smile and said, "G'morning. Tea or coffee?"

Danny had not been expecting this. Hotels he had stayed in in the past had provided equipment for guests to make their own refreshments. He asked for tea and, while the girl was busy at a trolley he could see parked on the corridor outside, hauled himself up out of the last few yards of sleep, feeling obscurely embarrassed and slightly irritated.

The girl placed the tea by his bed and gave it an extra stir. She said, "Sleep well?" in a distant sort of way.

"Mmm, yes. Very, thank you."

"Good," the girl acknowledged, and bent down over him and began fussing with his pillow. Danny made some effort to sit up. The girl must have thought he was having difficulty doing so, as she reached behind his head with her right hand and supported the upper part of his back. It was a gentle, helpful movement, but Danny didn't like it. The girl's fingers were thin and hard against his spine and there was something investigative about the way she touched him that made him uneasy, as though she was literally weighing him up, and testing the quality of the flesh beneath his pyjamas.

He reared up away from her hand and shook his shoulders. The girls' thumb and fingers rested for a moment on the top of his arm, almost squeezing, before she turned away to open the curtains with a flourish, revealing rain spotted windows and, beyond, the grimy grey sky of the disappointing day outside.

"They say it will clear up later," the girl assured him, and the edgy smile shifted briefly across her face again. Danny couldn't understand why he didn't like her. There was nothing about her looks to upset him. She had a sharp, but almost pretty face, and she was obviously trying to be nice. She couldn't help having hard, bony fingers.

After she had gone Danny snuggled down into the bed again until he remembered the man on the jetty the night before. He played a game in his mind, laying bets with himself about how far the man had moved the box. In the end he decided there would be no sign of it. Someone would have been to collect it, and taken it away.

He hopped out of bed to check, and saw the box still on the jetty, not far from where he had last seen it. A large sheet of dark green tarpaulin, tied in place with a strand of rope, had been draped over it. A puddle of rain had formed on top of it. There was no sign of the man. The jetty was otherwise empty.

Danny found that if he stood on tiptoe he could just see over the roofs of the hotels on the street below him onto the beach to the left of the jetty. It too was deserted now, except for piles of deckchairs and a solitary dog, jumping and jerking in the foam at the water's edge, tugging savagely at something, probably a strand of black seaweed, that glistened like a hank of wet, soapy human hair. From time to time the dog dropped the weed, held up its head, and snapped its jaws open and shut.

Realising his window had been closed, because he couldn't hear the creature barking, Danny climbed onto the sill and opened it. Cold damp air straight off the sea surged into the room. He could hear the sloshing breakers of the turning tide, slightly baffled by the veils of wind-blown rain that were sweeping across the town, and the urgent, worried yapping of the dog, sounding much further off than it really was.

He washed, dressed quickly in a new T-shirt and jeans, and set out to find the dining room. The hotel was full of the smell of breakfast, and he hoped he could find his food by following his nose. He soon took a wrong turning, however, and wandered into a half-lit, grey painted room full of wheelchairs and pale-blue, uncomfortable looking furniture.

There was a large mural on the wall depicting, in faded primary colours, what he thought must be Heaven, with naked sexless angels leading stooping elderly humans, in white togas, through an English rural landscape, drawn in such a way as to suggest a vast perspective.

At the top of the picture other angels, with tiny golden wings, flew through the sky, pulling strings of smiling old people along behind them. Yet more of the Heavenly hosts, playing musical instruments, rested on cotton wool clouds beneath a beneficent, smirking sun, while a multitude of ancient mortals hovered around them, listening to their concert with obvious gratitude and appreciation.

At first Danny thought he was alone in the room, then he noticed, scattered along the walls, a number of elderly people, seemingly asleep in their seats and wheelchairs. They were lolling sideways, backwards, or forward, like inanimate puppets. One old man, his liver-spotted head quite bald on top, with an aura of pearly curls of unbrushed hair stretching up from the back of his neck to above his ears like coral or fungus, lay stretched out face down on the table in front of him.

Danny, chilled by the atmosphere of the room, froze on the spot for a few moments. Nobody moved, or showed in any way they were aware he was there, until a voice to his left called out, "Nurse! Is it you? Can you prop me up? My cushion slipped. I've lost it."

Danny turned towards the sound and saw an incredibly thin old lady leaning at a sharp angle out of a wheelchair. She was resting on one arm, with her elbow in her lap, and stretching so far forward, she seemed to defy gravity. Her other arm dangled, limp as a bell rope, by her side. She had had to lift her head right back to see him, and her toothless mouth hung open wide, as dark inside as a railway tunnel. A pair of red-rimmed glasses rested slightly askew on her nose. Behind them, it seemed, her eyes were shut.

At the sound of her voice some of the other old people began to stir. A man's tremulous voice called out insistently, "I'm hungry." Someone started to cough and spit, another to moan, as though suddenly in pain, and a woman protested tiredly, "Mrs. Grange has wet herself again. *When* are you going to do something about her?"

Danny stared at the floor below the person closest to the old lady who had spoken last, and saw, under her chair, a dark stain on the carpet.

The woman who had complained that she had lost her cushion repeated her plea for help, now sounding cross. Danny moved towards her and must have stepped into her line of vision because she said fiercely, "Who are you? You're just a boy! Are they sending children, now, to look after us?"

Danny snatched up the cushion and thrust it towards the woman, who whined, "That's no good to me, unless you pick me up and pull me back. Can't you see that if it wasn't for the strap, I'd have fallen on my face? You can't leave me like this...I can hardly breathe..." and her voice died away, as though she were indeed expiring.

Danny saw she was held in place by a thick white belt tied tight around her waist and the back of her chair. She was so thin, the belt buckle on her stomach was only a couple of inches from the fabric of the chair against her spine.

Danny placed his hand on the top of her chest, that felt like a bird cage under his palms, and tried to push her upright, but he was not tall enough, and must have done something painful, because she gave a shriek and shouted, "What are you doing, child? What are you doing? Let go, for God's sake...you're *hurting* me."

Some of the other old people started to shout abuse at him then, and he felt his eyes flood and his throat constrict, and knew he was going to cry.

A man's voice, coming from just behind Danny, said, "What's the matter Betty? You *are* making a fuss. The young gentleman is only trying to help."

The scrawny woman said, "Where have you been Kelvin? Where's our breakfast? You're ever so late."

"No I'm not," the man said. "I'm just on time."

"You're a bloody liar," the woman suggested peevishly. "What do you mean by sending bits of kids to look after us?"

"He's not on the staff, Betty, he's a guest," the man explained, easily hauling the woman upright and adjusting her limbs so she sat in a comfortable, balanced position.

"Then why is he here? This is no place for kids."

"I don't know." The man, who was dressed in a white jacket, like the Chinese who worked in Danny's local chip shop wore, gave him a curious, slightly angry look that was only partly disguised by the shadow of a smile he managed to force across his face. He had a bony, narrow head, with dark hair brushed back tight against his scalp, and a large nose under which sprouted a pencil moustache. His smile reminded Danny of the girl who had brought him tea half an hour earlier, who had also seemed to find it hard to form her features into a good humoured expression for more than a second.

"I expect he's got lost," the man continued. "Is that right, young man?"

Danny, choking back tears, wiped his fingers under his nose and nodded.

"I expect you were looking for the dining room?"

Danny didn't stop nodding.

"This is the Twilight Lounge. The room you want is on the floor below. You should have kept on walking, down another flight of stairs."

The man clasped Danny's shoulder unnecessarily hard and steered him out of the door. Two or three of the old people shouted, "Nurse, *nurse!*" in protest at being left alone again.

"Back in a tick," the man yelled, with an edge of irritation. His voice was so loud, Danny looked up at him, startled. Noticing this the man explained, in a more moderate tone, "They're deaf, sonny. Most of them are deaf," and led Danny to the top of the stairs and pointed the way to the dining room.

Danny, no longer crying, and bursting with curiosity now, said, "Those old people back there . . . they thought you were a nurse, didn't they?"

"That's what I am."

"But this is a hotel, not a hospital!"

"It's a bit of both," the man said, after a short pause.

"Oh," Danny said, totally confused.

Back in the lounge the old people were cackling and calling for Kelvin, who gave Danny a horrible wink, that briefly distorted the whole of one side of his face, then retreated to join them.

A portly woman pushed a heated trolley reeking of bacon out of the lift and across the corridor into the Twilight Lounge. She was greeted with a tiny, ironic ovation from the residents.

Danny ran down to the dining room, which was almost empty. He had left his room at exactly eight-thirty, and the incident in the lounge had only lasted two or three minutes.

He sat alone at a table close to a rain-flecked window that looked out to sea. He could see the box on the jetty and, through a gap between two of the buildings below, a slice of the promenade and the beach beyond. The box looked bigger and somehow heavier from the lower level. The wind blew up under the tarpaulin draped across it, causing the hanging sides of the covering to flap mournfully. It looked as though someone inside the box was reaching about through holes in the sides with their hands, trying to find some way out.

When, fifteen minutes later, Gran and Grandad came to join him, Danny had almost finished breakfast. He wondered if he should have waited and eaten with them, but Gran said nothing about that. Perhaps she hadn't noticed. She had a preoccupied, anxious look on her face that Danny was getting used to seeing there. She kept half an eye on Grandad all the time, was aware of every move he made, and turned to give him her full attention whenever he spoke. Something about the way she treated her husband made Danny feel quite grown up, as though he and Grandad had changed places.

The room filled up with old people. Danny looked out for anyone his age, but there was only one girl, a couple of years older and four inches taller than him, who pulled a tight face when he smiled at her, and didn't look up from her plate again.

When Grandad had finished eating he asked Gran what day it was. She told him Sunday, but a little later he asked the same question and, when she tried to get him to remember the answer she had given him earlier, he said he hadn't asked her before, and if she didn't know what day it was, why didn't she just admit it?

Gran put her hand on his arm and, very quietly, said she had told him, and not long ago. Grandad insisted she hadn't, in a high, strange voice, and Danny thought he looked worried, even frightened.

A waitress came to clear the table and Grandad said to her, "My wife has forgotten what day it is. Perhaps you can enlighten her?"

The girl arched her eyebrows, looked from Grandad to Gran and back, and tried to smile.

Why is it nobody at this place can smile for more than a second? Danny thought, and for the first time began to wonder if he was going to enjoy the holiday.

The girl looked unsure of how to respond to Grandad's request for such basic information, hoping, but doubting, it was a joke. To avoid her embarrassment, Danny looked out of the window, towards the box on the jetty.

A big bird was standing on top of it. As Danny, watched the bird started strutting backwards and forwards, half-opening and closing its long, slender wings. It was just some kind of gull, Danny supposed. It was that sort of shape, but he had no idea they could grow so big and he had never seen one that dark before. Perhaps it had been caught in an oil slick? Suddenly, it launched itself off the edge of the box and soared into the sky.

Danny turned back to the table when the waitress said, "It's Sunday, of course. All day."

Grandad said, "Thank you very much, and gave Gran a silly, mocking shake of his head.

Anger, embarrassment, and some other indefinable pain registered on Gran's face. She got to her feet. As she did so, Grandad automatically rose from his chair, only more slowly, with less agility.

Danny jumped up to help him. "What are we going to do today?" he said. "It's raining. Do we have to stay in?"

"*We* will," Gran said, "for now. But you can go for a walk, to explore, if you want to."

"Definitely," Danny said. "It's dead boring here."

Gran gave him the first real smile he had received all day. "Don't catch cold though, and ruin your holiday."

"No problem. I'll be alright."

As Danny moved around the table to follow his grandparents, something moved out of the grey clouds beyond the window next to him, and descended towards him. The oversized gull he had seen landed on the balcony a yard from the window. It folded its wings with an air of deliberation and craned its neck. It turned sideways on awkward, stumbling feet, cocked its head at an angle, and stared at Danny down one side of its beak.

The beak was grimy yellow, like a heavy smoker's teeth. The bird stretched forward and screamed, as though announcing its presence, then stood motionless, watching him. It was at least four times as big as any gull Danny had seen before, and he thought he had been right about the oil slick, because its inky plumage had a glossy sheen, like the wet tarpaulin on the box it had been standing on when he had first noticed it.

"Danny!"

Gran's voice. She and Grandad were waiting for him at the door. Everyone in the room turned towards him.

They're all so old, he thought.

He knew Todley Bay was popular with elderly people, and owed its reputation to what it had to offer that age group. His mother had told him all that weeks ago, and explained that the holiday was intended as a break for Gran and Grandad, and that he had to be on his best behaviour all the time, and not give them any worries.

So he knew the resort would be *their* sort of place, with probably not much going for kids, but he had not expected to see so *many* old people. Most of them looked really ancient. There was hardly anyone in the room under—what? He wildly guessed...seventy? Eighty?

Except for the waitresses, and the girl he had noticed, he was the only young person present. He looked for the girl again, and saw she was watching him, like the others. She gave him a withering look that actually made him shudder. There was something about her, he decided, which set her among the old people. She looked used up, done in, worn out. Then he realised she was probably very ill, and felt sorry for her at once.

He hurried to the door, but looked back before stepping out. The gull hadn't moved. It was still there, glaring in through the window.

Danny was keen to get spending. He'd been saving up his pocket money for weeks and couldn't wait to drop some of it into slot-machines, or buy sticks of his favourite pineapple rock and things to play with on the beach.

But the shops were disappointing. They were dingy and dark, with a lot of old stock that no one would ever buy, and the proprietors watched him all the time, as though they thought he were a thief. In one store down near the beach the rock and other sweets were covered in grey dust, and looked shrivelled-up inside their wrappers. Danny bought a stick, because he had to buy something, but it tasted worse than the pencils he was in the habit of chewing at school, so he threw it in a bin.

He wandered into the town, that sprawled almost perpendicularly up the hill behind the bay, in search of anything interesting, but soon got bored with endless rows of cream painted houses advertising BED & BREAKFAST or offering themselves as RESIDENTIAL HOMES FOR THE AGED. He passed a church that was open, with the bell ringing, but nobody went in or out. A gaunt and gloomy vicar with a lead-grey face was standing at the door, stiff as a waxwork, waiting to shake someone's hand.

It got tiring, climbing up the steep streets, so Danny turned back. His feet wanted to run down the sharp incline towards the beach, so he let them. The soles of his trainers slapped like clapping hands on the wet, empty streets, and he began to feel exhilarated, the way you should feel on holiday.

The tide was on its way out and he ran without stopping right down the beach to the water's edge. It was cold down there, and a wind driving off the sea carried a miserable, almost invisible mist with it, but Danny tried not to let that bother him. He threw some pebbles at a jellyfish, played tag with the waves, then trotted along until he was suddenly brought up short by the jetty, half of which still stretched out into the sea. It was about ten feet high, but there were steps up the side, which he climbed without thinking.

As he reached the top, and looked across the harbour beyond, something called out to his right, towards the town. It sounded like the voice of a demented woman screeching his name. He turned and saw, five yards away, the box, and, hovering above it, with its feet stretching down, about to land, the enormous gull. It called again, almost dancing on the tarpaulin with the tips of its claws as it carved at the air with it wings to keep itself just in flight, then settled and became motionless and silent, like a stuffed bird in a museum.

It was staring straight at Danny. There was something threatening about the creature's posture—it looked tense, as though it was ready to burst into furious action any second. Cautiously, Danny took a few paces towards it. It side-stepped once, adjusting its position slightly in a gust of buffeting wind, but showed no fear of him, or any sign that it was about to fly away. Its position on the box put it slightly higher than Danny's head, so its beak was just above his eyes.

The beak resembled a scaled-down sword from a fantasy film. It was at least eight inches long, and the upper section curved sharply down in a cruel, hard, hooked point. Danny thought the bird would have no trouble opening up his skull with a weapon like that on its head.

When he was a few feet away, and still beyond the gull's reach, Danny stopped, worried about his eyes, that suddenly seemed very vulnerable. He saw that the bird had a cold and crazy look in its eyes, which reminded him of snakes and alligators.

Danny blew air out through his pursed lips, and shook his head. He realised he was afraid, and not just of the gull. There was more to it than that. The air around him felt charged and dangerous. Beyond the jetty, the town itself seemed to be watching him, poised and ready to tumble forward on top of him in a huge avalanche if he did the wrong thing. Something, he sensed, was in the balance.

For the first time he took a close look at the box. It was made of wood, bound with strips of greenish metal that could have been brass, and its unpainted surface was mottled with patches of dank, dark-emerald growth. Probably some kind of marine weed. It stood in a puddle of its own making. The wood was waterlogged, which partly explained why the man he had seen pushing it had found the task such heavy going. The lid, if it had a lid, was under the flapping tarpaulin cover, but something about the box gave Danny the impression it was locked up very tight. It looked impenetrable! Briefly he wondered what, if anything, was inside it, then hastily closed his mind to the ugly images that were trying to crawl up out of his imagination.

All at once, Danny wanted to get back into the town. The jetty was narrow, but the box took up less than half its width. He could slip past it easily, but in doing so, he would put himself well within the reach of the gull. If it attacked him, he might fall off the jetty. It was a long way down to the beach, and there were flint rocks sticking out of the sand below. He took another look at the creature's beak. The gull glared back and nodded curtly once, as if to confirm his apprehensions.

"Look," Danny said, without having any idea why, "I don't want anything to do with this. I'm just here on holiday." Then he added, "I'm sorry," in a tone more of confusion than apology, and turned and fled back down the steps.

He didn't stop running when he felt the sand of the beach under his feet, but continued right up to the hotel. When he had almost reached it, just as he was trotting up the drive, the sun slid out from behind the clouds above him and its light blazed down on all the town like a laser beam.

The rest of the day was showery, so the three of them didn't stray far from the TV in the Hotel lounge. When he went to bed Danny thought he could hear the box being pushed along the jetty again, but he was so tired, even though he had done nothing much all day, he fell asleep almost at once.

Next morning, when the girl came into his room, threw back the curtains to reveal a blue, cloudless sky, and came towards him with a cup of tea, he jumped up in bed at once, so she wouldn't have any excuse to touch him. Even so, she put one hand on his head and poked about in his hair while he sipped his drink, as though she was gently feeling for lumps.

It seemed to Danny that her finger-tips were like cold, hard marbles rolling about on his scalp. He assumed it was a gesture of affection—he couldn't think what else it could be, and resisted the urge to duck away. But, when she sat down next to him, he jumped out of bed, ran to the sink, and started washing.

In the morning he spent an hour in a drab little seafront café with his grandparents drinking banana milkshakes. After lunch the three of them went down to the beach. Grandad, in a boyish mood, led the way. He looked as though he was wearing someone else's clothes, because he had lost so much weight in the last year, but Danny recognised the fawn trousers the old man had worn on the last three of their previous holidays together.

Gran, Danny noticed, seemed more anxious than ever about Grandad when he was at all boisterous, as though she was scared his behaviour might get out of hand. As soon as Grandad had put his cap on backwards, and his face had taken on the now all-too-familiar clown's witless smile that had come to haunt it recently, Gran's features had responded by setting into a rigid, pained expression. She looked as though she had a bad headache.

Grandad had wandered away from her twice, and the second time it had taken her half an hour to locate him. He had been with two men who were leading him away, or seemed to be. They had not spoken to her when she had reclaimed her husband, and she hadn't liked the look of them. They looked like muggers, she said.

Danny, feeling sympathy for both his grandparents, took care to be on his best behaviour when he was with them, but he wished they'd loosen up. He was now definitely beginning to wonder what kind of holiday it was going to be!

Gran decided it was too windy to sit on the beach, so she steered Grandad into a shelter on the promenade from where they could watch Danny doing the things children do on such occasions. He made a cake-like sandcastle without much enthusiasm, because he was beginning to wonder if he was too old for such activities, then stripped down to his trunks and sped towards the sea, now quite a long way out.

In places the surface of the sand had been formed into hard ridges by the action of the out-going tide. They ran along the whole length of the beach. They hurt the soles of his bare feet if he ran, and forced him to slow down and walk carefully. To Danny, it looked as though hundreds of endless fat worms lay paralysed just below the surface.

Old Man Sand's got wrinkles, he said to himself, and laughed at the thought, though there was something not-very-nice about the idea that he found alarming and tried to shove to the back of his mind.

After paddling for a while in the shallow sea, that was starting to warm in the sun, and taking a short, leisurely swim, he noticed he felt constrained and uneasy. Something was missing! Except for the sound of waves breaking on the shore, and the occasional scream of gulls (ordinary sized gulls, that was), the beach was strangely quiet. Conspicuous by its absence, he realised, was hubbub, pandemonium. He missed the voices of children yelling and shouting in excitement to each other, and telling their parents about what they were up to at the tops of their voices. The whole beach, the entire Bay even, though now more populated, was muffled, silent, and somehow static. Like a painting. Danny looked about him at his fellow bathers.

There were not many. Within twenty yards of him half a dozen elderly people, their trousers and skirts rolled or hitched up, wandered about ankle-deep at the water's edge.

A beefy man with bulging eyes and purple skin, looking as though his whole body had been beaten into one huge bruise, occasionally hurled himself into deeper water further out and swam a few stiff, furious strokes.

A woman in a lime-green costume, standing in the sea close to Danny, suddenly stooped, lowered herself to her knees, sat on her heels and bowed her head in a praying attitude. Her flesh oozed out around the edges of her costume like viscous liquid when she moved. Her skin was crinkled, like the monkey's brain in a bottle in the biology lab at Danny's school. She seemed uncomfortable in the position she had adopted and wriggled around so she could lay back on the sand.

A wave breaking over her created the illusion that she was sliding feet first into the sea. Seconds later, when it withdrew, Danny imagined he saw something in the water, clasped around her ankles, tugging her away from the beach.

This impression was so strong he walked closer to get a better look at her. The next wave was bigger, however, and submerged her completely. She did not, as Danny expected, start up when the water covered her face, but her body yawed slightly in the drag of the tide. Her eyes were shut and her mouth was open wide. She could have been shouting, laughing or even yawning.

Baffled and alarmed, Danny thought he ought to try to help the woman, though she gave no indication that she was at all distressed. He wondered if he should ask one of the other old people for their assessment of the situation, then saw that two of them were now also kneeling down. The red-skinned man who had been swimming had vanished, but Danny was sure he had not passed him on his way back to the beach. The last time he had seen him, the man had been in the act of lunging forward in a clumsy dive.

Out in the area where the man had been standing, Danny noticed, for the first time, what looked like dark shadows under the waves. They appeared to be moving. He thought they must be weed-covered rocks, just visible at the bottom of the grey-green water.

One of the two people who were kneeling lay back in the water.

Danny suddenly looked down at his feet. He thought something had touched his right ankle. The sand next to it was disturbed, as though some fast-moving object had hurriedly dug down into it. He turned and ran a few yards out of the water, stood on the nearly dry sand, and looked back. The tide must be coming in fast, he thought, as there was no sign of the woman in the green costume. He could no longer see some of the other people who had been paddling, but a handful more had stumbled forward off the beach into the sea. He realised that none of them had nodded to him, or given him so much as a glance.

He shrugged, and jogged back to where Gran and Grandad were sitting in the shelter. Gran looked more relaxed, perhaps because Grandad was asleep. She held a finger to her lips to warn Danny to keep his voice down, and asked him if he was enjoying himself. Danny didn't want to upset her by telling the truth about how he did feel at that moment, which in any case would be difficult to explain, so he just nodded. He asked for money for an ice cream.

As Gran fumbled in her purse, Danny noticed a man sitting on the bench on the other side of Grandad was watching him. He was heavily built, with a bald head and heavy jowls and was dressed in old, dark, working clothes. He could have been a fisherman. He had one arm along the bench behind Grandad's head. Two fingers of his hand rested on Grandad's shoulder. As Danny looked back at him, he lifted the fingers and curled them back towards his palm.

Danny got ice creams for himself and Gran, and hurried back. The bald man had gone, so Danny sat in the vacant place.

"Who was that man, Gran?" he asked.

"Which man?"

"The one who had his arm around Grandad."

"Danny, what do you mean? I'm sure he wasn't doing anything of the kind."

"He was," Danny insisted. "I think he wanted Grandad to go with him."

Gran, hearing the conviction in his voice, leaned forward and turned to look at him.

"This is a funny place, isn't it?" Danny continued.

"Todley Bay? Don't you like it here?"

"Not as much as Brighton."

"I think it's very nice."

"There's no kids."

Gran smiled. "There must be some."

"I can't see any."

Gran pushed her glasses up her nose and looked around. "Not here, at the moment, perhaps," she conceded, "but on the beach..."

Danny swallowed the last of his ice cream and wiped his mouth. "No. It's all old people, everywhere."

"You're exaggerating. What about that girl who's staying at our hotel. She's about your age. Why don't you try to get to know her?"

"She's sick. I bet she never leaves the hotel."

"Um," Gran agreed thoughtfully, "she doesn't look well. I expect she's convalescing."

"I think she's dying," Danny said, matter-of-factly.

"Danny!" Gran said loudly, causing Grandad to twitch out of his doze, "I'm sure that's not true. What *has* got into you?"

"What's the trouble?" Grandad demanded. "What's got into who?"

"Danny, Harry. I don't think he's enjoying himself. He's in a very strange mood."

"Danny?" said Grandad, looking at his grandson as though he were a total stranger.

The grim look returned to Gran's face. She glanced at her watch. "Good heavens, look at the time. We'd better start back for the evening meal," she said, rising from her seat. Grandad rose up with her, like a Siamese twin joined to her at the shoulder.

Danny was surprised how easy it was to get lost in the hotel. The corridors and public rooms were decorated uniformly throughout, which made it hard to get your bearings, but even so, it didn't explain why he lost his way quite so often. He kept finding himself on the wrong floor! He'd carefully count the turns in the flights of stairs, so he was sure he knew exactly where he was, only to discover he was one, or even two, floors out.

He noticed quite a few of the old people wandering around in even deeper bafflement than usual from time to time, which made him feel better, because it suggested he wasn't the only one experiencing this peculiar disorientation.

A couple of times Danny bumped into Kelvin, the nurse with the thin pencil moustache, who told him how to get to where he wanted to go. He wasn't exactly unfriendly, but he must have been a very busy man, because he hardly stopped long enough to give the necessary directions before he blustered off again.

On the third night of the holiday, after leaving his grandparents in the TV Lounge, Danny searched about down wrong corridors for ten minutes before he found his room. He complimented himself—he was getting better. The night before it had taken twice that long to get his bearings.

As he was putting on his pyjamas, he heard the big box being shoved along the jetty. A shining mist that had crawled up off the sea with the onset of darkness had vanished when he looked out of the window. The air was clear, and he could see the man had nearly got the box to the end of the jetty. Danny was very interested to see what would happen next, because he knew there were two steps up from the jetty to the promenade and the street beyond, and he couldn't see how one man could possibly get the box up them without help.

He got into bed and pretended to be asleep when Gran came, so she only stayed a moment. (He felt bad about it, but he had become fed-up with her company that evening, because she was wearing herself out fussing over Grandad, who was definitely going ga-ga. They were both getting visibly worse daily. A lot of the time it was a *pain* being with them.)

When Gran had gone, Danny got up again and looked out the window. The box was about a foot from the steps, and the man had gone. He watched for a while, but nothing happened, so he slid back between the sheets, feeling let-down and disappointed, and fell asleep. Later, something woke him up. Noises, coming from the direction of the jetty. Different noises! He trotted to the window and looked out.

The man was back. He had set a lantern on the edge of the top step, and had placed a long metal tube or roller, four or five inches in diameter, at the base of the box, on the side closest to the steps. He was lifting the box with a jack.

When it was the right height he kicked the roller under it on one side, let the box drop, then went around to the far side to repeat the process. When the roller was under the full length of the leading edge of the box, he went behind it and began to push. After a struggle, it moved a short distance towards the steps, and the side of the box above the roller rose a little higher. After giving three huge shoves the man got another, thicker roller from somewhere and laid it in front of the first one he had positioned. Then he went behind the box, and pushed and pushed.

The front edge of the thing was soon higher than the bottom step and, in twenty minutes, after the man had put more rollers in place and done a lot more heaving, it was hovering a good distance above and beyond the top of the second. Then the man hit a problem. Because it was inclined at an angle, he was finding it increasingly difficult to move the box. He was having to push it up, as well as forward. He seemed to give up then, and went and sat on the top step and stared down at the box.

Danny watched the slumped figure for a while until he got bored. He thought the man might have gone to sleep. He was just about ready to return to bed when he saw movements on the beach below him. The tide was almost in, and a man was walking off the narrow strip of sand, diagonally out into the sea.

The small, thin, stooping figure, dressed in dark clothes, was just visible against the inky water, moving slowly and regularly, as though setting out for a stroll on the ocean bed. When the sea was in up to his waist he stopped, sank back into the water and disappeared from sight. Danny thought—no, he knew—the person, whoever he was, had stretched out on the sand, like the woman in the green costume he had seen the day before.

There were a few deckchairs left out on the beach, Danny noticed, spread about near where the now presumably drowning man had been when he'd first sighted him. To his amazement he could see shapes, that could only be people, sprawling in some of the chairs. Danny peered at his watch. It was almost midnight—it had been dark for almost two hours!

They're moon-bathing, he thought, and smiled uneasily in the dark, aware that the people didn't look at all funny.

As he looked back out the window he saw something scuttle up out of the sea, across the beach, in among the parked deckchairs. It moved like a spider. It clung close to the sand, had no definite shape, and at first Danny thought it was dead seaweed, broken loose from its roots, washed ashore, dried in the sun, and blowing in the wind. Until he realised there was no wind to speak of, certainly not enough to set in motion anything more substantial than a scrap of paper.

What he could see was moving of its own volition, and soon demonstrated that it had considerable strength! A section of its edge blended with the outline of one of the occupied chairs, which lifted and tumbled over on its side, tipping the person seated on it onto the sand. The figure lay motionless for as long as it took the mobile shape to dart around and attach itself to an outstretched arm, the part of the body closest to the sea. The body twitched once, then slid smoothly to the tide line and into the waves beyond, where it, and the thing pulling it, sank out of sight. Then, for a time, nothing moved on the beach that Danny could see, though his eyes were alert for the slightest motion.

It was a sound from the end of the jetty that grabbed his attention next—a loud grunt of pain or effort, or both. He turned just in time to see the bear-like man heave the box almost into the air and up onto the edge of the promenade. The action seemed to have spent the last of his energy. He flopped around picking up the rollers and tucking them under his arm like a man at the last extreme of exhaustion, then staggered off towards the harbour. Danny watched him shrink away into the darkness, then realised he was stiff with standing still, and crawled into bed.

He fell asleep wondering what the man, who was awake most nights, did in the daytime.

It was very hot next day. So much so that Gran and Grandad sat on the beach for the first time. They couldn't walk far in the sand, because of

Gran's feet, so Danny put up deckchairs for them at the bottom of the steps that led to the promenade. He sat with them for a while, watching the beach fill with elderly holidaymakers then, for something to say, because the old pair were not inclined to talk in the heat, he mentioned that he had seen people on the sands late at night.

"I expect they were workmen tidying up all the litter," Gran said.

"The tide does that," Danny said, "when it goes in and out. No, they were sitting in chairs, like we are, or walking into the sea."

"Danny, you were dreaming. They'd have caught their deaths of cold."

Danny wanted to say he thought they were dead, or looked it, but knew that Gran would say he was talking nonsense and get cross with him.

Even so, he couldn't help saying, "I wish we *had* gone to Brighton. This place is *weird.*"

"I think it's very pleasant," Gran said, "and restful. There's none of the noise and fuss you get at so many holiday places nowadays. And people are so nice and polite."

"You didn't like those men who tried to walk off with Grandad," Danny observed.

"You were probably wrong about them. Perhaps they thought Grandad was lost and they were taking him to a policeman."

Danny didn't answer, because he had just spotted, not far away along the beach, one of the deckchairs he had seen someone slumped in last night. He knew it was the same one, because it was in exactly the same position in relation to a stack of chairs next to it as it had been when he had seen it from his bedroom window.

It was facing away from him but he could tell it was occupied because the canvas seat was bulging down and back. He was about to go and take a look at it and its occupant when something made him change his mind. There was a cloud of flies swarming above the chair, dozens of them, big black ones, he thought he could almost hear them buzzing. No one else had set up their deckchairs for a good distance all around that particular one, Danny noticed.

"Look at all those flies, Gran," he said.

"What?"

"Over there—look." He pointed. "Above that chair."

"I can't see *flies*, Danny, if they land on me. My eyes aren't good enough. I can only just see the chair."

For some reason this remark made Danny rather anxious. He felt suddenly isolated and vulnerable. Looking around he discovered he was, as far as he could see, the only child on the beach.

He shut his eyes then, and pretended to sunbathe, but he couldn't settle. His mind was swirling with vague apprehensions.

For the first time all week he found he was missing his parents. At first, he had been relieved to get away from them. They had been so grumpy and depressing recently, though they had continued to treat him as kindly as they had always done. Nevertheless, life at home had been different since his father had received the letter telling him his job would no longer exist in ten weeks, and his parents had taken to endless grinding arguments about money. Danny heard them late at night in the room below his, their voices rasping on like two blunt saws taking turns to cut through a particularly thick, hard log.

They were worried about Gran and Grandad too, and Danny could understand why now. He realised that the whole family had problems. He had problems! Suddenly he wanted to talk to his parents very badly, but he knew he wouldn't see them until the end of the week.

After half-an-hour he went and got some drinks. Grandad insisted on coming with him, somewhat to Danny's relief. He tried not to listen to Grandad's talk, because he seemed to think Danny was someone he had worked with years ago in Canada. That was unnerving, but he felt glad he was not walking alone.

The way to the café took them past the huge, brass-bound box parked on the promenade. Even in bright sunlight it looked sinister Danny thought, though other passers-by seemed unawed by it. The wood had dried out a lot, and was beginning to crack, and the mossy weed clinging to it had turned grey and ash-like. A heat-haze shimmered over the tarpaulin.

There was no sign of the great gull but, when Danny looked up into the sky, he saw, very high up, a black dot that was growing larger as it descended fast towards the ground. Danny grabbed Grandad's hand to hurry him along. He had a vision of what the bird could do with its beak if it hit someone after descending at that speed from that height.

He made sure, when they returned to Gran with their drinks, they went by a roundabout way along the beach, keeping well clear of the box. The route took them past the deckchair that had been shrouded with flies. It was empty now. Danny got the impression that a small group of youngish men in overalls, moving down the beach towards the sea, were carrying something they had lifted from the chair but, in the confusion of people, it was hard to be sure. He went quite near the chair and saw there were still a few flies on duty there, hovering over a wet, red-brown stain on the canvas seat.

It seemed to be a bad day for insects. Early in the afternoon millions of tiny silver and brown flies with thin bodies and long legs appeared from nowhere on the beach. They hopped rather than flew, and got all over Danny's bare legs and arms. They were strangely dry and weightless, like the congregations of corpses that gather on window ledges in empty houses in the summer, and seemed almost without substance. They didn't bite or sting. They were just disgusting. Danny had soon had enough of them. He asked Gran if he could go for a boat trip around the bay.

"You said I could, and if I don't go soon, the holiday will be over," he pleaded.

"There's still three more whole days," Gran said, but she agreed he could do as he had asked. They left their beach-bag and Danny's towels on their chairs because Gran said she was sure there were no thieves about, and the three of them made their way to the harbour.

One of the two boats that did trips was out beyond the headland, just visible in the distance, and the second was almost full and ready to go. It was a big, wide boat that Gran declared quite safe, so she gave Danny some money and told him to get on board. He found a seat at the front and waved at his grandparents with his handkerchief for a joke. Gran waved back, and Grandad copied her movements exactly, a sight that made Danny laugh aloud.

A teenage boy in sun-bleached denim jumped onto the boat and began collecting money and handing out tickets, then a man stepped quickly down from the harbour, started the engine, and grasped hold of the wheel.

It was the bear-like man who Danny had seen moving the box. There was no mistaking his rolling movements, and he was wearing the same clothes as he had been the night before. Danny could tell by the shape of him. The only difference was that at night the man wore a cap and now had nothing on his bald head. Danny got a good look at his face, and not for the first time. He was sure the man had been sitting next to Grandad the day before, with his arm around the back of Grandad's chair and his fingers on the old man's shoulder.

Danny jumped up to get off the boat just as, with a grinding growl of the engine that echoed off the hill behind the town, it cut away from the harbour wall. The man glanced sharply at him and the teenager asked him to get back in his seat. Danny did so at once, and tried to make himself small and inconspicuous.

The man, at the front of the boat, was facing away from Danny. He made an announcement about safety procedures as he steered the vessel out through the maze of moored pleasure-craft to the harbour mouth, then handed the wheel over to his young mate when they reached the open sea. He turned around, sat down, and lit a little cigar. As he blew out smoke he raised his head and glanced quickly around at his passengers. When he saw Danny, he took another sharp drag at his cigar and seemed to shake his head slightly. The gesture had no clear meaning that Danny could interpret, but it frightened him because he felt he had been singled out, perhaps even recognised.

He remembered when he had been watching the man pushing the box along the jetty he had got the impression that the fellow had looked back up at him on a number of occasions, though there was no chance he could really have seen a small boy standing some considerable distance away in the dark, half-hidden behind a curtain. Unless he had remarkable eyesight! He certainly had remarkable eyes, which stared through Danny as though they were focused on a point a million miles behind his head.

Danny thought of the huge black seagull then, that had been so high in the sky above the box when he had passed close to it with Grandad just a couple of hours earlier. The bird must have good eyesight too—

it had dropped down at once when it had seen him approach, or so it had appeared to Danny.

Why? Did it think he was going to do some harm to the box, that it seemed to be guarding? Danny couldn't believe that. He hadn't the means or strength to damage it, even if, for some crazy reason, he'd had the inclination to do so. He wasn't bothered about the box—he wanted nothing to do with it, as he had told the bird when he had come close to it on the jetty two days ago. At the time it he had felt foolish talking to a seagull, but not so now. He just wished he had said more. He was afraid he had not made himself understood.

When, after a quarter-of-an-hour, the boat turned its prow into the Bay again for the return trip, Danny was glad the ride was half-over. He'd been too confused and anxious to enjoy himself and imagined he was seasick, his stomach felt so queasy. He was very glad when the man, whose hard, unfriendly gaze had returned to him every few minutes, got up to take over the wheel again as they approached the harbour.

Gran was waiting for him on the promenade, holding onto a railing at the very edge of the harbour. Danny waved, but he knew she wouldn't see him. He doubted if she could even see the boat, but she knew what time he was due to return, and was just being there for him.

Grandad sat on a bench a few feet behind her, talking to a man seated next to him. His conversation was animated—he waved his arms and at one point stood up and made a gesture, incomprehensible to Danny, to illustrate some point he was making. Danny guessed he thought his companion was someone from years back in his past, when his life had been exciting, and that they were sharing some adventure together.

As Grandad, in his enthusiasm, took a few steps away from the bench, another man, who Danny had not noticed, but who must have been standing near by, screwed up some paper he had been eating out of and tossed it into a bin. Then he sidled closer to Grandad as though he were on wheels, in a sliding, gliding movement that arrested Danny's attention completely, and totally altered his understanding of the scene he was witnessing.

The man on the bench got up, stood next to Grandad, and pointed inland to somewhere in the town. When Grandad turned to look, the man took his arm, and began, with a certain amount of force, Danny thought, to lead him away. The second man, moving as though he were sliding on ice, fell in behind them.

Gran, still peering myopically out to sea, was obviously unaware of what was going on behind her. The boat was coming in to dock now, and Danny could see her bland, smiling face staring out at the blur of the world in front of her.

He half-stood up and shouted at her, and made jerking movements with his hand intended to make her look behind. As he rose to his feet some of the other passengers thought he was getting ready to disembark and also started to get up off their seats. Perceiving this, the man who was steering the boat turned and yelled something to his mate, who jumped onto a chair and called to everyone to be seated. In the confusion of people bobbing up and down Danny lost sight of Gran, but he was careful to keep an eye on Grandad, who was being led slowly uphill into the town.

Not a purposeful walker at the best of times, Grandad liked to stop and start when the urge took him, and the two men were plainly having trouble getting him to go where they wanted him to, and were making slow progress.

The boat bumped against the harbour wall and the teenager skipped ashore to fasten the ropes. The bear-like man took his place next to the couple of steps up the side of the vessel and helped his frail, nervous passengers onto dry land by steering them across the short gangplank, whether they wanted him to or not.

Danny tried to squeeze forward in the queue, getting a few sharp comments from some old ladies as he did so. When his turn to disembark came he tried to avoid the hands of the man by almost running off the boat, but without success. He felt fingers like tentacles curl around his upper arm to stop him in mid-stride.

The man lifted him effortlessly and half-turned him so they were face to face. Danny could smell cigar smoke on his breath, and other more strange odours that he had never come across before. There was a scrap of tobacco on the man's lip that must have irritated him, as he flicked it with his tongue, and spat it out over Danny's shoulder with a toss of his head. The action reminded Danny of squirrels he had seen in the park at home, standing on their hind legs and spitting out indigestible fragments of nuts they were eating.

Not that there was anything cute or squirrel-like about the man's appearance. His heavily-featured face with its sharp, down-curving nose, and receding, almost horizontal forehead was set hard in an ambiguous mask of contempt and vague curiosity, as though Danny were a not-very-fine example of something that, had it been of better or different quality, would perhaps have interested him. Either his head was unusually small, or it seemed so in proportion to the bulk of his vast, barrel-like body. His little gimlet eyes bore in on Danny's like nails. In the irises of each of them Danny could see tiny reflections of his own frightened face.

The man loosened his grip on Danny's arms and ran his hands down them to the wrists, pressing with his finger tips, feeling for the bones beneath the flesh. He held the joints of Danny's wrists between his thumbs and fingers and lifted them to the height of his shoulders, so the boy's hands hung in front of him like a half-animated puppet's.

Danny squirmed and looked back over his shoulder. Gran was just behind him on the promenade. He could tell from the confusion and apprehension on her face that she was close enough to see what was happening to him.

He tried to get away from the man's grasp, and yelled out, "Grandad's gone. They've taken him away again. Get after him. He's gone up into the town."

The man moved then, and held Danny out so he was hanging by his wrists over the side of the boat next to the little gangplank. The vessel was about twelve inches from the harbour wall and rocking slightly, up and down and from side to side, in the wake of other boats passing beyond. Danny thought if the man let go and he fell he might be crushed between the wall and the side of the boat.

The water below his feet, the colour of boiled cabbage, and marbled with rainbow-tinted whorls of diesel fuel, looked deep, thick and viscous, like glue. Darker shapes moved below its surface. It somehow looked hungry too. Danny imagined his broken body being sucked down into it, dragged under the keel, and pulled out to sea by swirling undercurrents.

He was only suspended thus for a few seconds before the man stretched out over the side of the boat and lowered him slowly onto the edge of the harbour and released him, but they were long seconds, and terrible while they lasted. Some of the elderly people waiting their turn to go ashore thought the man had played an amusing joke on Danny, and squawked with laughter as he ran shouting to his grandmother.

By this time she had discovered her husband's absence, and, as soon as Danny's toes touched the ground, went stumbling away on her arthritic feet to look for him.

"Up the hill," Danny yelled, "they've taken him up the hill."

Gran turned to him with a hopeless look, already out of breath and concerned about her hammering heart.

"Don't worry," Danny said as he overtook her. "Wait here. I'll get him back."

The streets were full of old people drifting back and forth from the beach. They reacted too slowly to get out of Danny's way so he had to run a zig-zag course around them. He lost sight of Grandad from time to time but knew he must soon catch up with him because the trio had come to a stop half way up the hill.

They seemed to be arguing. They were standing just inside an alleyway between two decrepit looking red-brick Victorian hotels. The man who had been seated on the bench next to Grandad had had hold of his sleeve. He wasn't actually tugging at it, but was making it impossible for the old man to retreat.

The other would-be abductor, with the smooth, oily movements, was gliding around the pair of them, talking all the while, and making calming gestures with his outstretched hands. Danny could hear Grandad's voice. He was bellowing at the two men that had had enough of their nonsense. He was going to arrest them. Didn't they know he was a member of the Mounted Police? He was back in the past in Canada again. His face looked more worried than he sounded, but brightened when he saw Danny, who assumed he had been recognised for once.

The two men, following the old man's gaze, turned to see Danny running towards them. The one with peculiar movements detached himself from the tableau and slid towards Danny like a skater. He was dressed in a tight black jacket and shiny trousers, like a waiter's. Danny couldn't be sure, but it seemed that the man's feet, encased in narrow patent-leather shoes, hardly moved, and never quite touched the floor—as though he were suspended a fraction of an inch above the pavement. Perhaps because he was, nevertheless, coming at Danny fast, his form seemed slightly blurred, his features indistinct. When they were almost touching they both side-stepped to avoid each other in the same direction, and collided.

Danny expected to get hurt. He heard himself shout to Grandad to get away as he made contact, then automatically shut his eyes to protect them. He felt a sensation as though he had run into a large, soft mattress that gave to the slightest pressure. There was no indication that what he had hit was anything like a human body that contained flesh and bones, and whatever it was gave way on contact and spread out alarmingly, as though it had come apart. Danny thought he had run right through it and somehow come out the other side.

He opened his eyes and saw what looked like a two dimensional drawing of a bloated human figure expanding above and in front of him. It was floating away, and waving its flattened arms and legs slowly, like someone drowning in a dream, and clawing desperately at the air with its hands. Almost at once its fingertips appeared to grasp onto something nvisible—a hard thin edge of reality, perhaps—and dug in and held on. Then, with an obviously painful effort, it pulled itself back together, contracted, shrunk into itself, and reformed.

All this happened very quickly and, almost before Danny had time to think, the man was hovering in front of him again, with a mildly expectant look on his bland, undistinguished face, exactly like a waiter lingering at a table in expectation of an order. It was as though he were silently challenging Danny to believe that the astonishing metamorphosis he had just observed had indeed happened, and was trying to suggest, by his unconcerned expression and the shear ordinariness of his appearance, that it could not have done.

But Danny *knew*. He knew what he had seen. He knew a great deal all of a sudden, and what he didn't know he guessed.

He flung himself at Grandad, latched onto his arm, and pulled the old man sideways down the hill with all his strength. They tottered along like the contestants in a three-legged race, barging into a number of ancient holidaymakers who they were not able to brush aside, and stumbling and almost falling on the steep incline.

Gran was waiting for them on the promenade. She looked as though she was going to cry when she saw Grandad's face. It was blank and empty, like a paper mask before the features have been painted on it.

Gran said, "Where were they taking him, Danny? What did they want him for?"

Danny couldn't bring himself to say what he thought he knew. He pretended to be more out of breath than he was, and stammered something about muggers. He could see Gran was terribly distraught, but knew this was because of the state her husband was in, and because he had nearly been stolen from her. Thankfully, she could not have seen what occurred when he, Danny, collided with the man in the waiter's outfit, so he wouldn't be called upon to give an explanation of that. On the other hand, he realised, if she had seen, she would at least be more aware of what they were up against.

He looked back up the hill to see if the men had followed him, but there was no sign of them. Suddenly his stomach lurched, and he felt a surge of dizzying nausea, a return of the sea-sickness that had started half an hour earlier when he had been on the boat, now exacerbated by his recent experiences.

"Gran," he said, "I'm ill. Let's get away from here. This is a terrible place."

Misunderstanding him, thinking he merely wanted to return to the hotel, Gran nodded emphatically. She put her arm around her husband's shoulder and steered him away. The old man walked like an automaton, staring down at the pavement just in front of his dragging feet and saying nothing. Danny dawdled behind all the way to the hotel, to keep the couple in his sight.

Danny looked even worse than he felt when the three of them got together in the dining room for their evening meal. Gran led Grandad in by the elbow. His walk had developed an aimless, twisting tendency that had to be corrected every few steps, and his eyes looked empty and uncomprehending, like a blind man's, or someone concussed. The old man would eat nothing, and Danny couldn't.

Gran stuffed some meat into her mouth and made a show of chewing it to encourage him to do the same, but the smell and appearance of what was on his plate convulsed his stomach and he had to get up and away. Gran's face took on an even more concerned expression when he explained how sick he was. He hated to put this extra burden on her, but he had no alternative. She dug in her bag for some pills, instructed him on the dosage, and told him to get to bed. Danny said "Good night" to Grandad, who made no response at all.

"He's lost his tongue," Gran said, trying to make a half-angry, desperate joke of it, but sounding instead, strangely, much younger than her years, and on the edge of tears again.

Danny dragged himself up the wide blue-carpeted stairs feeling dizzy and disorientated. The spaces around him seemed much wider than he knew they were, as though the hotel had expanded in all directions—a process that appeared to be obscurely continuing out at the edge of his vision. He counted flights from floor to floor grimly, passing hand-over-hand on the stair rail like a man hauling himself along a rope to safety. It occurred to him to take the lift, but he knew his stomach wouldn't stand for that.

On the second floor corridor he heard a confusion of hushed sounds behind him, and somebody called out sharply for him to step aside.

Two men in white jackets were approaching him, pushing a grey painted metal stretcher-bearer. On it was a slender human form half-wrapped in a loose-knit white blanket. The lower part of the face of this person was encased in a plastic mask attached by a tube to a cylinder slung below the stretcher. A pink tube curled up from the blanket to what looked like a brown bladder on a stick one of the men was holding above his head.

Danny realised the figure on the stretcher was the young girl he had seen in the dining room a few times. She was lying on her side with her eyes wide open. The transparent mask had a black rim that underlined and isolated her eyes. They looked like two shiny purple holes drilled into her almost bald head. Her little white ears stuck out like toadstools from the sides of her scalp that looked as though it was made of scrubbed white wood. Danny realised that normally she must wear some kind of wig.

She stared at him hard as she passed, giving him an even worse version of the withering look he was used to seeing on her face, and rose up and turned as she passed to keep him in view. Danny found he was pressing his back against the wall to get away from her.

The power of her gaze had a negative force strong enough to repel him physically. It felt like a protracted bomb blast.

She struggled to keep her eyes on him, to keep up the pressure, and tried to sit up. As she did so the blanket slid down from her shoulders to her waist and Danny saw what looked like black shadows, just beneath the skin, sliding down over the ribs of her flat white chest to take shelter under the blanket over her belly. It was as though they were afraid of the light.

The shapes moved hastily, but with purposeful, controlled caution, like fish seeking the safety of deeper, darker waters. The girl kept her purple-black eyes on Danny until one of the men pressed her back down and pulled the blanket up to her chin. They stopped the stretcher at the service lift and Danny, released from the repulsive attraction of the girl, turned his back on them and staggered away.

He found his room at last, wriggled clumsily out of his clothes, pulled the curtains across the open window to hold back the early evening sunlight, clambered into bed and fell, sweating and squirming, into feverish sleep.

Suddenly, Danny was staring into the dark. His eyes had clicked open with a snap that was almost audible. His whole body was rigid with tension. His senses were as alert as a hunter's and, when at last he moved, he moved stealthily. He peeled the quilt smoothly back off the bed and stood up. As he did so the sound that had woken him was repeated somewhere out beyond his window. It was a sliding sound similar to the noises he had heard earlier in the week, but not quite the same. It was a lighter, easier sound. The box was moving faster.

Danny crept to the window and edged the curtain to one side just far enough to give him a view of the section of the street visible between two hotels at the lower level. The sound seemed to be coming from down there.

Seconds later he heard it again, as a long corner of shadow stretched out to his left along the street below. It was followed by the blunt black end of the box, which slid swiftly into full view and came to rest at a point halfway between the hotels. But only for a moment—the bear-like man behind it hardly paused for rest before pushing it on out of sight. The box was only briefly visible, but Danny noticed that the tarpaulin had been removed from the top, and that an upper section seemed to be slightly askew, as though the lid had been lifted and not properly replaced.

Something has been taken out, or has come out, Danny thought. Either that or the box has been opened in preparation for something that was going to be put into it. Or was going to get into it...For a second Danny had a dim vision of something huge and dark clambering out to make way for something frail and white that was desperate to clamber in. He shut his eyes and shook his head to shatter the fantasy, and went and sat on his bed.

He almost went back to the window to take a look at what, if anything, was going on on the beach, but decided against it. He was still feeling ill. He was weak and cold, though his skin was damp with sweat. The pills Gran had given him had helped, but their effect had worn off. But he knew she had more in her bag.

He went into the corridor, and tapped on the door of his grandparents' room. No answer. He tapped again, louder, then tried the handle. The door wouldn't move when he pushed it. It must be earlier than he thought, he decided, if it is locked. Gran and Grandad always went to bed at ten. They must be somewhere downstairs, probably in the television lounge.

He set off at a trot along the corridor and ran down the stairs. It wasn't so easy to get lost going down into the hotel because you just kept on going until you reached the bottom, then you stopped. Or so he had assumed. It had worked before.

Nevertheless, he misjudged where he was, and found he had wandered into the Twilight Lounge. It was pitch-dark in there, but he knew where he was, because of the sharp, faint smell of urine. He stood for a moment just inside the door and heard a rustling noise, like paper being slowly crumpled, then someone sighed, and he thought he heard liquid dripping. A wheelchair creaked. *They're waking up!* Danny thought, and hurtled off without bothering to shut the door behind him.

When he found the Television Lounge it was unoccupied. The big set in the corner was still on, filling the room with jumpy silver light and swirls of romantic music from the ancient black and white costume drama that was showing. Danny noticed the clock on the video player below the TV said 01:47. In the morning, that was. He'd never been awake at that time before, that he could remember. It wasn't surprising there was nobody about, but why weren't his grandparents in their room? In the past Danny had often had a feeling that grownups did things after their children had gone to bed that they never talked about. It had only ever been a vague suspicion before, but now the idea played on his mind. Where were the adults . . . what were they up to? He would have to find out.

Whenever he had gone in and out of the hotel before there had always been someone at the reception desk, but now even that post was deserted. It seemed that the only people other than himself in the building were the ancient residents in the Twilight Lounge and, young as he was, Danny knew he couldn't expect help or advice from them. They had their own problems.

His only hope of finding his Gran and her medication was to contact a member of staff, and ask them to take him to her. Then he remember-ed he had seen a big sign that said

STAFF QUARTERS
STAFF ONLY BEYOND THIS POINT
PLEASE

on a door at the rear of the hotel. Surely, he would find assistance there!

He ran down the silent corridor towards the kitchens, found the door, and saw with relief that it was half-open. Beyond it, grey carpeted stairs led down to the basement. He could her music thumping somewhere below, so someone must be awake down there. He glanced again at the off-putting sign on the door, then ventured cautiously onto the stairs. He felt that what he was doing was probably wrong, but guessed that if people were cross with him for venturing where he should not go, they wouldn't do him any harm, and would take him to his grandparents just to get rid of him.

Everything in the staff quarters was smaller and shabbier than on the floors above. The corridors were narrow, illuminated by dim, unshaded yellow bulbs, and the drab carpets were worn and hard. He passed lots of numbered doors, some of them split and cracked, as though the locks had been forced, or they had been punched or kicked. He kept walking, without trying to rouse anyone who might be beyond them, because he could tell, from the increasing volume of the music, he was getting closer to its source. In fact, when he turned the first corner, he walked right into it. Two doors, one marked STAFF and the other RECREATION, stood open wide and he found he had gate-crashed a party in full swing.

There were about two dozen people in the long, low-ceilinged room, and most of them were sitting at a couple of trestle tables covered by white paper tablecloths. The air was murky with what at first he thought was smoke, then realised was a thin damp mist, like fog.

A couple were dancing, away to one side, and a girl in a black, tight, silky outfit twirled somewhat awkwardly to the music, alone in the centre of the available space. She stopped when she saw Danny, and stared at him as though he were an apparition. He recognised her as the girl who had brought him tea in bed each morning, and at once began to feel uneasy.

The girl came and crouched down in front of him, on tip-toes, with her knees bent. She stayed like that for a while, without speaking or moving, weighing him up with her eyes. The calculating quality of her gaze chilled Danny's blood. He wanted to speak, but his lips had gone stiff and his tongue felt like leather. He was aware that other people in the room beyond had become aware of his presence, and were also watching him. Someone with an old man's voice gave a creaky laugh that was echoed by a woman's shrill, mirthless cackle. A man, shouting over the music, said something he didn't catch, then most of them laughed. Danny was just thinking of running off when the girl reached out and took his left elbow in her hand. Then she said sharply, "What are *you* doing here?"

As she waited for his answer her thin fingers massaged the bones of his elbow and her thumb pressed painfully into his inner arm. He mumbled something about his grandparents that was inaudible to the girl, who shook her head to indicate she could not hear him.

Then, desperately, he shouted, "I've lost my Gran. I want someone to help me find her."

As he did so, the rock music tape that had been playing ended abruptly, and he found himself shouting into total silence. His voice sounded like a scream. It frightened him.

The girl moved her head back slightly under the impact of it. She rose up again, still holding Danny's arm, and pulled him further into the room towards the tables. A man on a bench moved to one side to make way for him. The girl, by manipulating his arm, forced him to sit in the vacant space. The man next to him gave him a toothy smile. It was Kelvin, the moustachioed nurse who had rescued him from the people in the Twilight Lounge at the start of the holiday. He still looked reasonably friendly.

Danny recognised a few of the faces of the people seated around him. To his horror, he saw, opposite him across the table, the man in a waiter's uniform—the one with the strange, sliding locomotion, who had tried to lure his grandfather away, and who Danny had run literally right into. The man looked very solid now however, and seemed amused to find Danny in his present predicament.

Danny licked his dry lips and tried to avoid looking anyone in the eye by looking down at the paper cloth on the table in front of him. It was bare except for dishes of nuts and crisps, a couple of big cut-glass decanters almost full of what looked like tomato juice, and a quantity of glasses containing drinks of this liquid. The people around him lifted these glasses to their mouths from time to take a sip, then their eyes would roll and they pursed and smacked their lips with almost ecstatic satisfaction. It was obvious they relished their refreshments.

Danny liked tomato juice himself, but he couldn't understand why anyone should make such a fuss about it. It was nothing special. Last Christmas his father had drunk lots of it with vodka, and there had been a row between his parents when his dad had fallen from his chair when they had guests round, but there was no sign of any vodka on the tables now. Yet the people at the party, if that was what it was, seemed to think tomato juice was the finest drink in the world!

The man opposite him, the one dressed like a waiter, poured a fresh glass of the liquid and handed it to Danny. The drink had a funny smell, not a bit like tomato juice, that Danny detected as soon as he had taken the glass, and he looked at it suspiciously. He raised it to his lips and sniffed. As he did so, the girl, who still had hold of his arm, increased the pressure of her grasp on his elbow.

Danny saw, out of the corner of his eye, that the girl's face was flushed and excited and...hungry looking. The tip of her tongue appeared briefly against her upper lip, and her brow arched up as her eyes stretched wide. He could tell she wanted him to try the drink. She wanted him to try it very much. And so did all the other people. They were all watching him with sharp, intense anticipation.

Danny held the glass a couple of inches from his mouth. His hand was not quite steady.

"What is this?" he asked. "It's not tomato juice, is it?"

"Did we say it was?" someone said. "Did *anyone* say it was?"

Everybody shook their heads.

"It's a fine drink," the girl said softly. "A rare old vintage. Something you won't have tasted before. But once you've tried it, you'll want more of it. There's no doubt about that."

"I don't like the smell," Danny said nervously.

"Never mind that. It's not the taste or the smell that matters, it's what it does for you," the girl insisted.

Danny said nothing.

"It won't harm you," someone said. "We drink it all the time, and look at us. We're lucky here, we get plenty of it."

"The fine old stuff," the girl repeated, almost singing, as though she was quoting a popular song, "the rare old vintage."

Danny lowered his mouth to the glass and took a sip. The drink was thick and flat and metallic and slightly warm. It was neither good nor bad. He drank some more, and found he was suddenly thirsty. He emptied the glass slowly and put it down.

"Well?" asked the girl.

"It's okay," Danny said, unenthusiastically.

"Would you like some more?"

Danny was a polite boy. "Not at the moment, thank you," he said, and for some reason most of the people seated around him started to laugh. It was relaxed, good-humoured laughter. Danny noticed the girl had released her hold on his arm at last and, when the laughter had subsided, he repeated his request to be taken to his gran. Someone made a joke that made no sense, about taking Gran to Danny, then Kelvin got up and told Danny it was too late to disturb Gran now, but he would take him back up to his room in the service lift. Danny would have to sort his other problems out in the morning.

To Danny's surprise, the entrance to the lift was at the back of the room they were in. Kelvin went and leaned on the button and, high up in the hotel, the lift lurched and groaned as it begun unsteadily to descend. When it arrived Kelvin had trouble pulling the slightly rusty, cage-like bars of the metal outer door open, then cursed as he bent to tug up the inner door that rose and slid back somewhere at the top of the lift. A cloud of the cold, steamy looking mist Danny had noticed earlier wafted out of the lift shaft, surged across the floor, then floated up towards the ceiling on a cushion of warm air.

Danny saw at once that the lift was not empty. The huge brass-bound box he had seen so many times before was in there, taking up most of the space.

It had been pushed up tight against one wall and there was just a narrow gap vacant to one side of it. Kelvin motioned to Danny to get in beside it. Danny shook his head and backed off a little way. He saw that the lid of the box was now in place, but could tell it was loose, unsealed. The dry wooden structure had finger wide splits in it, and its sides were warped and slightly concave. In places, the wood had sunk away from the brass to reveal sections of the ancient, primitive nails that held it together. The seaweed that had been growing on it had shrunk, withered and turned colourless, like old wreathes in a graveyard.

Kelvin gave Danny a look that the boy recognised as the expression Todley Bay people sometimes put on their faces when they wanted to smile. It was probably meant to be encouraging, but Danny thought it had an impatient edge to it. Kelvin was in a hurry. Probably he wanted to get back for more of the red juice before the others drank it all.

Kelvin said, "What's the matter? Get in. I'll get you to your room in no time."

Danny pointed to the box. "What's that?"

"This?" Kelvin stepped forward and thumped the lid of the box with his fist. "Nothing for you to worry about, anyway. Not for a long time, I shouldn't think. You needn't trouble yourself about that."

"Is it empty?"

"I expect so." To placate Danny, Kelvin lifted the lid slightly, and peered inside. He took a long, hard look.

"Are you sure," Danny insisted nervously.

"Well," Kevin said, lowering the lid, "it's not quite empty, but don't go bothering yourself about that."

"What's in there?"

"If you really want to know, sonny, I'll show you. I'll lift you up so you can take a look inside, if you think it'll make you happy. But I wouldn't recommend it."

"I don't want to see inside. I don't want to go near it. I don't want anything to do with it."

"You don't have to like it, son," Kevin said, now definitely irritable, "but if you want me to show you to your room, you're going to have to ride up with it. So get in."

Danny waited for a long moment, and stared at the box. Something could be hiding in there, observing him, staring back at him through the cracks in the sides. But, if there was, he didn't feel it was necessarily out to harm him, it could be that it was just...curious about him. If there *was* anything in there, it wasn't him, Danny, it was after – or so, for no clear reason, he began to believe.

He decided to test his theory, since he could see no other option, and stepped quickly into the lift before he could think about his situation any more. He suddenly wanted to get to bed more than anything else he could think of.

Kelvin followed Danny onto the floor of the lift, shut the outer gates, pulled down the inner door, squeezed in along the side of the box beside the boy, and pushed a button. A stump of fluorescent tube set in the roof flickered and almost died. Something high in the building squealed as it took the strain. The sheet metal panels on the walls creaked all around them, and the lift juddered—hesitated—lurched—then began to rise slowly, swinging slightly from side to side because it was out of balance.

Danny kept as far away from the box as he could in yellow-green gloom that was almost darkness, and gulped to relieve his dry throat and mouth, that now seemed to be full of imaginary dust.

Kelvin saw him swallowing air, and said, "What's the trouble?"

"I'm very thirsty," Danny admitted.

"Well, yes, you will be. It's only to be expected. But you'll get used to it. That's the way it is."

"I don't understand," Danny complained.

The lift shuddered to a halt.

"You will," Kelvin said, and stooped to pull up the door. He said something else as he tugged aside the doors of the metal cage, but Danny couldn't hear him over the clanging of the iron bars. Kelvin stepped onto the corridor and pointed to a door a little way away that Danny recognised at once as his own, leading to his room.

"You get to bed now," Kelvin ordered, "and don't go looking for your gran any more tonight."

In his room Danny drank at least a pint of water out of the tap at the washbasin. It was warm, and tasted slightly ferric, like the drink he had been given in the basement. He realised then that he hadn't felt at all ill since he had taken that crimson drink. In fact, it had made him feel very good – he was almost glowing with health inside. But he was tired out.

He flung himself into bed and slept at once.

Someone was moving quietly about in his room. Danny knew from the quality of the light it was early morning, so assumed the girl had let herself in to deliver his tea. Good, because he still had a thirst like an ache in the back of his throat. He didn't want to talk to her, however, for obvious reasons, so kept his face under the quilt.

Then, whoever was in the room sat down on his bed. Someone big and heavy. He knew this, because the whole bed sank in the middle, whereas it had only dipped slightly when the girl had perched on it on previous occasions.

A big person had come into his room, uninvited, and was sitting on his bed! An image of the bear-like man carved into his mind and filled him with fear. *He's come for me, or he's come for the box, or he's come for both*, Danny thought, and he nearly stopped breathing.

Then the someone cleared his throat and said, "Danny, I know you're awake. It's me, don't worry." It was his father's voice.

Danny sat up with a jerk. "Dad! What are you doing here? What's wrong?"

His father's face was crumpled and tired, and his usually immaculately combed hair stuck up in bristles in a dozen places. His eyes looked sore and the flesh below them was flaky and grey. He was wearing his best suit over a white shirt that looked grimy at the collar, as though he'd worn it one day too many, and his tie was loose and askew.

"Danny, I'm sorry, but the holiday's over. Something's happened, so your mother and I came down here overnight. The car broke down. It's been very difficult, but were here now, so..."

"Has something happened to Grandad?" Danny asked, thinking he could see the light. "Have they got him then? Has he disappeared?" He jumped out of bed, went to the sink, and drank more warm washing water from his tooth-mug.

His father looked confused. "No, he's okay. Your mother is with him now. It's Gran, I'm afraid. You're going to have to know... I'm sorry Danny, but she passed away, during the night."

"Passed away?"

Realising the euphemism was above and beyond Danny, his father explained that Gran was dead.

Three hours later Danny, his parents, and Grandad were waiting in the hotel foyer for a taxi to take them to the station. The manager of the establishment, a razor thin, crop-haired woman in a black and white check blouse and grey suit, was commiserating with his mother, who was crying softly all the time that she was speaking. Danny heard part of the conversation, but didn't understand much of what was said.

"—terribly sad time—everything done that could be done—first-rate staff who are used to dealing with death—see it all the time—we've taken care of the body—leave everything to us—unfortunately, another guest *in extremis*, even now, as I speak—and so young, just a girl—but of course, we prefer to deal with older people—the more mature person—ripe old age is our speciality—you understand?"

The manageress sounded as though she had been reading from a publicity handout and had suddenly discovered that the last page was missing. She took a dive into sudden silence. Her sympathetic expression, set in stone, seemed only to affect her face below her eyes, which were empty and uninvolved. She and Danny's mother were seated on two gold-painted chairs, facing each other almost knee to knee.

"It was meant to be a break for them both," Danny's mother said, glad of a silence to break. She pushed her nose into her handkerchief and wiped her eyes. "She only had six months to live. That's what they told her, and she was so worried about leaving my father behind. He has Alzheimer's disease, so she was hoping to find somewhere here in Todley Bay where he could spend what time he has left in comfort. He could last years. She wanted to leave him in good hands."

The manageress nodded and clucked her tongue.

"She insisted on bringing the boy, because it would be their last chance of a holiday together, though I didn't think it was right. But you can't argue with someone who's going to die soon, can you? Especially if it's your own mother, so I let him come."

The manageress nodded and looked about her for some excuse to get away. No obvious opportunity presented itself.

"It's so terribly sad, that she should be denied those last few months they promised her," Danny's mother said, and hid her face in her hands.

Danny was keeping an eye on Grandad. The old man was quite oblivious to his wife's death. He had a loopy half-smile on his face, and was rubbing his hands together a lot, as though they were cold, or he were washing them. He kept strolling off, and Danny kept leading him back to his parents.

Danny used these opportunities to buy soft drinks from a machine in the bar. He could feel them all sloshing about in his stomach, but he still wanted more. Or perhaps he wanted something else. It was a funny kind of thirst he had, that would not be quenched, and there didn't seem to be anything he could do about it.

He had tried to explain his other worry to his father and mother, about the people who had attempted to lure Grandad away, but his mother had started to get angry with him, and told him that this was no time for him to talk rubbish.

It was obvious his father thought he was fantasising too. He had shaken his head at Danny when the boy had mentioned the man who travelled across the ground without moving his feet, like a skater. So Danny shut up. He realised there was no point in trying to get through to his parents, who were both up to their ears in troubles of their own, so he gave himself the job of protecting Grandad. He was delighted when his father told him the four of them were returning home by train at once, that very morning.

When the taxi came Danny sat in the back with Grandad and his mother, who was now overwhelmed with grief. He held her hand, but got the impression she was unaware that he was there. Strangely, he had no feelings at all about Gran's death. It meant nothing to him yet. He was more concerned with the torrent of weeping beside him, and alarmed at his mother's inconsolable condition. He felt Grandad was safe now.

As the taxi drove along the seafront Danny saw the great bulk of the box ahead of them on the edge of the promenade. Someone had started to push it back towards the jetty, but hadn't got very far. The oily-black, overgrown gull was perched on top of it, standing in perfect balance on one leg. Its head was set at an angle. It seemed to be carefully scrutinising the traffic moving towards it.

The taxi, travelling slowly because a number of elderly people were dawdling and doddering across the road to get to the beach, came almost to a stop less than ten feet from the box. Danny slid down in his seat and turned away, trying to make himself invisible, just as the driver saw a gap ahead and accelerated into it, taking the vehicle some way beyond the box and the bird. Danny, thinking and hoping he had got by unobserved, couldn't resist turning around and sticking his head up over the top of the back seat to take one last look out the rear window at the gull.

The bird was riding the air a few inches above the boot of the taxi. Its beak dipped down towards the glass of the rear window, and it stared with one dead-reptile-eye straight into both of Danny's. It retained this pose for a moment, then broke away from the taxi with a single tug of its wings that took it soaring into the air.

Danny expected it to follow the vehicle, but it didn't. It climbed up to a vast height at incredible speed, as though it had seen a hole in the sky it was afraid was due to close. Then it seemed to change its mind. It plummeted back towards the town and disappeared behind the roofs to the right, ahead of the taxi.

Danny's father, sitting next to the driver, looked at his watch and remarked that they might miss the train. The driver shrugged, indicated towards the clutter of old people crossing the road ahead, and said he was doing his best.

When they got to the station there was no queue at the ticket office. Even so, Danny's father had to write a cheque, and seemed to take an age doing so.

Danny bought a tin of Coke, gulped it down, then stood with the other two and a little heap of luggage at the ticket barrier, ready to assault the platform to get to the train the instant they were free to do so.

When his father emerged running with the tickets Danny grabbed some of the baggage and shot past the ticket inspector right behind him. His father, with one arm around his still distraught wife, scuttled awkwardly alongside the train looking for an empty compartment. They were halfway along the platform before Danny thought to look back to see where Grandad was. There was no sign of him.

Danny stopped and looked all around. Except for himself and his parents, the platform was empty. He shouted to his father, and felt the eyes of dozens of passengers on the train turn to stare at him curiously from behind the dusty carriage windows. His father understood what had happened at once.

"We've got to find him Danny. Go back. You take the right and I'll go left. He can't be far."

Danny shed his baggage and pelted back through the barrier again. He saw Grandad almost at once, standing by a newspaper kiosk, talking to the man in waiter's uniform. The man was half-hidden in a doorway. His face was just visible, and only his arms protruded. They undulated in beckoning, luring movements, like the tentacles of an octopus. Grandad, shifting from foot to foot, was rubbing his hands and smacking his forehead in gestures of wild indecision. He also seemed to be laughing anxiously, like a donkey, with his mouth wide open. The man in the doorway slid back a few inches, like a man on roller skates, and Danny could see his feet were definitely not touching the ground. His body even seemed to float up a little way as he receded, and Danny remembered that he had no bones, no *substance*.

Danny shouted wordlessly at Grandad, who froze. The man in the doorway glanced at Danny, sneered, and vanished. He went out in an instant, like a fused light.

Danny grabbed Grandad's arm and yanked him away, almost pulling the old man off his feet. He seemed to get the idea for once, however, and, to Danny's surprise, started running quite fast. So fast in fact, the boy found it hard to steer him. He urged him in the right direction by pushing and pulling, a procedure that constantly threatened to entangle their legs and trip them both.

The man at the barrier, who had watched the whole performance with some amusement, let them through and signalled to the guard at the far end of the station that the train could go.

It started moving almost at once, sending Danny into a panic. There was no sign of his parents or the luggage, so he assumed that they had got on board. One of the doors of the nearest carriage was hanging invitingly open. Danny urged Grandad towards it, then trotted alongside as the old man climbed up the step to the corridor. As he did so he glanced back and saw his mother struggling towards him clutching the luggage. Behind her, running desperately through the ticket barrier, was his father, his face purple with unaccustomed effort. Both his parents looked very angry.

For a moment Danny thought he was going to start to scream and cry in protest against the waves of confusion and frustration that were sweeping over him.

He turned to pull Grandad back. It was obvious that his parents would not reach the train in time to get aboard, since the carriage next to him was now moving at running speed. He shouted to Grandad to get down, then realised that it would be very dangerous if he did try to disembark. Nevertheless, the old man turned and appeared to make some confident attempt to get back off the step.

As he did so an arm reached out from the carriage door and the big hand at the end of it took firm hold of Grandad's shoulder and started to pull him in. A second hand emerged to take a grip on the other shoulder and Grandad was lifted up off his feet altogether and hauled into the darkness beyond the door. Then a figure leaned out for the handle of the door and quickly pulled it shut. Danny saw the hawk-like nose and receding forehead of the bear-like man for just a second, peering out at him from behind the window at the upper part of the door, then the train gathered speed, retreated along the line, and snaked away out of the platform.

Then Danny did begin to scream and cry. He cried even louder when his mother caught up with him and started to blame him for what had occurred. Her face was a damp, white puffy blotch of grief and anger. His father, when he joined them, tried to calm things down.

"We can phone ahead, down the line, and get someone to go on the train at the next stop and bring him off," he said, but his wife didn't seem to hear him.

"He's senile," she protested. "He doesn't know where he is or what he's doing. He might just open a door and walk out while the train is moving. Anything could happen."

"It's not just that," Danny yelled, now quite beside himself. "One of those men was in the carriage. They've got him now. They've been trying to get him all week."

"What men, Danny?" his father said, trying to conceal his impatience.

"The ones I told you about," Danny said, "but you wouldn't listen."

On the very edge of anger, his father said, "And why would these men want an old man like Grandad, for God's sake?"

"For his blood," said Danny, "and some of them want his bones."

Then his mother dropped all the luggage that she was carrying and stepped very close to Danny. "How could you talk such rubbish?" she yelled. "At a time like this...on the day of my mother's death?"

She spluttered to a halt, overwhelmed with indignation and rage.

A surge of intense and actually painful thirst, a craving for a drink that was not available, a liquid he could not obtain, cut into Danny, and made him gag. He put his fingers into his mouth to touch his tongue to see if it was as dry as it seemed to be. It was.

His father, alarmed by the expression on Danny's face, asked him what was wrong.

"I'm drying up inside Dad," Danny said, suddenly afraid to hear his own words. "I've got a terrible..." his tongue clicked against his pallet, "...a terrible, awful thirst."

His mother regained her voice then. Her face was wet, wild, and dangerous, like a storm at sea. She howled at Danny wordlessly, and held her shaking hands, half-clenched like claws, in front of her face. "What are you trying to do to me?" she screamed at last. "How can you stand there and...*talk*...*such*...*nonsense*? After all that's happened, at a time like this, *you stand there whining about your thirst!*"

Danny, shattered, feeling quite alone, stood grey-faced and devastated by the injustice of it all. Something in his expression must have pushed his mother over the edge of her patience at that moment, because, for the first time in her life, she slapped Danny hard across the face. Her ring cut the flesh of his cheek.

Danny broke away and ran. His mouth gaped open in a scream that only he could hear. Warm blood trickled down his cheek and into his mouth. The taste of it was at once familiar. It was like, but not quite the same as, what he was seeking. What he needed to quench his thirst.

Thinking about the dying girl back at the hotel, Danny ran right out of the station into the slowly moving holiday crowds passing back and forth along the front of Todley Bay. He darted through them like a wraith. Nobody seemed to notice him. He moved so fast, he thought he might be invisible.

He hoped the staff back at the hotel would understand, and be kind to him.

❦

When he got there he found they were only too happy to receive him. They took him in, concealed him, and urged him to be patient.

The feast, they told him, though not of the rare old vintage of the night before, was almost ready. It would soon be served.

So, for the present, Danny had to content himself with that.

THE
MAMMOTH BOOK OF
BEST NEW
HORROR

**THE YEAR'S BEST HORROR
STORIES BY SUCH MASTERS
OF DARK FANTASY AS:**

**RAMSEY CAMPBELL
DENNIS ETCHISON
CHRISTOPHER FOWLER
DAVID J. SCHOW
MICHAEL MARSHALL SMITH
KIM NEWMAN**

and many others

EDITED BY
STEPHEN JONES

"A superb range of
mature, challenging tales."
– TIME OUT

[1997]

WITH VOLUME #9 the publisher again decided that *Best New Horror* needed a new look. Unfortunately, it got one.

At least the trite photo-shopped image that finally appeared on the cover was not as garish as the version they originally wanted to use.

They also decided that, in the UK at least, *Best New Horror* should be folded into Robinson's very successful series of "Mammoth Book" titles, which they (not unreasonably) believed would give the volume a higher profile amongst booksellers and readers.

Carroll & Graf obviously needed a bit more persuading and, as a result, only the British edition of this edition was re-titled *The Mammoth Book of Best New Horror*.

By now the Introduction had reached sixty-two pages and the Necrology was hovering around twenty-eight. For the ninth volume I concentrated my ire on those practitioners of so-called "extreme horror".

I find most literary "movements" slightly incestuous and cliquey anyway, but this loosely connected band of misogynistic and gratuitous horror writers belonged to a club that I certainly had no interest in joining. Like the "Splatterpunks" a decade before them, I predicted that they were destined to end up as a marginal footnote in the history of the genre. I may not have been entirely correct in that assessment, as the trend continues to this day.

Champions of the equally pointless "New Weird" movement should also take note...

The book featured just nineteen stories—the lowest number since the series began. However, this was partially due to the inclusion of Douglas E. Winter's satirical novella 'The Zombies of Madison County'.

Veteran 1960s author John Burke was also represented, as was David Langford, a former contributor to the Fontana and Armada horror anthologies who is better known for his multiple Hugo Award-winning non-fiction these days.

Every year I read countless vampire or Cthulhu Mythos stories for possible inclusion in *Best New Horror*. Rarely do they achieve anything new or different within their respective sub-genres (this statement obviously excludes Kim Newman's ongoing *Anno Dracula* series, about which more later). There usually has to be something very special about such stories for me to even consider including them in the anthology.

With Caitlín R. Kiernan it is all about the language and atmosphere. 'Emptiness Spoke Eloquent' is a sequel to Bram Stoker's *Dracula* (or, as the author readily admits, Francis Ford Coppola's uneven 1992 movie adaptation). "Eloquent" is the right word to describe Caitlín's first contribution to *Best New Horror*, which supplies an answer for those readers who—like the author—ever wondered what happened next to Mina Harker...

CAITLÍN R. KIERNAN

EMPTINESS SPOKE ELOQUENT

CAITLÍN R. KIERNAN is the author of the novels *Silk, Threshold, Low Red Moon, Murder of Angels, Daughter of Hounds, The Red Tree* and *The Drowning Girl: A Memoir*. She also wrote the movie novelisation of *Beowulf* and, more recently, she has published the "Siobhan Quinn" series of urban fantasies (*Blood Oranges, Red Delicious and Cherry Bomb*) under the pseudonym "Kathleen Tierney".

Her shorter tales of the weird, fantastic and macabre have been collected in a number of volumes, including *Tales of Pain and Wonder, From Weird and Distant Shores, To Charles Fort with Love, Alabaster, A is for Alien, The Ammonite Violin & Others, Two Worlds and In Between: The Best of Caitlín R. Kiernan (Volume One), Confessions of a Five-Chambered Heart, The Ape's Wife and Other Tales, Beneath an Oil-Dark Sea: The Best of Caitlín R. Kiernan (Volume Two), Dear Sweet Filthy World, Houses Under the Sea: Mythos Stories* and *The Dinosaur Tourist.*

Kiernan is a multiple recipient of the World Fantasy Award, the Bram Stoker Award, the International Horror Guild Award and the Shirley Jackson Award, as well as a winner of the Nebula Award, the British Fantasy Award and the Mythopoeic Award.

"I started working on this piece in November 1993," reveals the author. "It was my third short story, and it would remain unfinished until May 1997. November 1993 also saw the release of Francis Ford

Coppola's *Bram Stoker's Dracula* and, regardless of whether or not it was the most faithful screen adaptation of Stoker's novel, it certainly affected me more deeply than any other ever has. But it did leave me with a nagging question that I often have at the end of good films and books, especially good horror and dark fantasy: 'What happens next?'

"It isn't that Coppola didn't find a wonderful place to close the film, just that I couldn't possibly imagine the woman that Mina Harker had become returning to her previous life as a meek typist, going back to her middle-class existence as Jonathan Harker's wife. So I started asking myself questions, and 'Emptiness Spoke Eloquent' was the eventual outcome."

L UCY HAS BEEN at the window again, her sharp nails tap-tapping on the glass, scratching out there in the rain like an animal begging to be let in. Poor Lucy, alone in the storm. Mina reaches to ring for the nurse, but stops halfway, forcing herself to believe all she's hearing is the rasping limbs of the crape myrtle, whipped by the wind, winter-bare twigs scritching like fingernails on the rain-slick glass. She forces her hand back down onto the warm blanket. And, she knows well enough, that this simple action says so much. Retreat, pulling back from the cold risks; windows kept shut against night and chill and the thunder.

There was so much of windows.

On the colour television bolted high to the wall, tanks and soldiers in the Asian jungle and that bastard Nixon, soundless.

Electric-white flash and almost at once, a thunderclap that rattles the sky, and sends a shudder through the concrete and steel skeleton of the hospital and the windows and old Mina, safe and warm, in her blanket.

Old Mina.

She keeps her eyes open, avoiding sleep, and memories of other storms.

And Lucy at her window.

Again she considers the nurse, that pale angel to bring pills to grant her mercy, blackness and nothingness, the dreamless space between hurtful wakings. Oh, if dear Dr. Jack, with his pitiful morphine, his chloral and laudanum, could see the marvels that men have devised to unleash numbness, the flat calm of mind and body and soul. And she *is* reaching then, for the call button and for Jonathan's hand, that he should call Seward, anything against the dreams and the scritching at the window.

This time she won't look, eyes safe on the evening news, and the buzzer makes no sound in her room. This time she will wait for the soft rubber-soled footsteps, she will wait for the door to open and Andrea or Neufield or whoever is on duty to bring oblivion in a tiny paper cup.

But after a minute, a minute-and-a-half, and no response, Mina turns her head, giving in by turtle-slow degrees, and she watches the rain streaking the dark glass, the restless shadows of the crape myrtle.

June 1904

The survivors of the Company of Light stood in the rubble at the base of the castle on the Arges and looked past iron and vines, at the empty, soulless casements. It seemed very little changed, framed now in the green froth of the Carpathian summer instead of snow, ice, and bare grey stone.

The trip had been Jonathan's idea, had become an obsession, despite her protests and Arthur's and in the end, seeing how much the journey would cost her, even Van Helsing's. Jack Seward, whose moods had grown increasingly black since their steamer had docked in Varna, had refused to enter the castle grounds and stood alone outside the gates. Mina held little Quincey's hand perhaps too tightly and stared silently up at the moss-chewed battlements.

There was a storm building in the east, over the mountains. Thunder rumbled like far-off cannon, and the warm air smelled of rain and ozone and the heavy purplish blooms hanging from the creepers. Mina closed her eyes and listened, or *tried* to listen the way she had that November day years before. Quincey squirmed, restless six, by her side. The gurgle and splash of the swollen river, rushing unseen below them, and the raucous calls of birds, birds she didn't recognise. But nothing else.

And Van Helsing arguing with Jonathan.

"...now, Jonathan, now you are satisfied?"

"Shut up. Just shut the bloody hell up."

What are you listening for, Mina?

Lord Godalming lit his pipe, some Turkish blend, exotic spice and smoke, sulphur from his match. He broke into the argument, something about the approaching storm, about turning back.

What do you expect you'll hear?

The thunder answered her, much closer this time, and a sudden, cold gust was blown out before the storm.

He's not here, Mina. He's not here.

Off in the mountains, drifting down through passes and trees, a wild animal cried out, just once, in pain or fear or maybe anger. And Mina opened her eyes, blinked, waiting for the cry to come again, but then the thunder cracked like green wood overhead and the first drops of rain, fat and cold, began to fall. The Professor took her arm, leading her away, mumbling Dutch under his breath, and they left Jonathan standing there, staring blankly up at the castle. Lord Godalming waited, helpless, at his side.

And in the falling rain, her tears lost themselves, and no one saw them.

November 1919

Fleeing garish victory, Mina had come back to Whitby hardly two weeks after the armistice. Weary homecomings for the living and maimed and flag-draped caskets. She'd left Quincey behind to settle up his father's affairs.

From the train, the lorry from the station, her bags carried off to a room she hadn't seen yet; she would not sleep at the Westenra house at the Crescent, although it was among the portion of the Godalming estate left to her after Arthur Holmwood's death. She took her tea in the inn's tiny dining room, sitting before the bay windows. From there she could see down the valley, past red roofs and whitewash to the harbour pilings and the sea. The water glittered, sullen under the low sky. She shivered and pulled her coat tighter, sipped at the Earl Grey and lemon in cracked china, the cup glazed as dark as the brooding sky. And if she looked back the other way, towards East Cliff, she might glimpse the ruined abbey, the parish church, and the old graveyard.

Mina refilled her cup from the mismatched teapot on the table, stirred at the peat-coloured water, watching the bits of lemon pulp swirl in the little maelstrom.

She'd go to the graveyard later, maybe tomorrow.

And again the fact, the cold candour of her situation, washed over and through her; she had begun to feel like a lump of gravel polished smooth by a brook. That they were all dead now, and she'd not attended even a single funeral. Arthur first, almost four years back now, and then Jack Seward, lost at Suvla Bay. The news about Jonathan hadn't reached her until two days after the drunken cacophony of victory had erupted in Trafalgar Square and had finally seemed to engulf the whole of London. He'd died in some unnamed village along the Belgian border, a little east of Valenciennes, a senseless German ambush only hours before the cease-fire.

She laid her spoon aside, watched the spreading stain it made on her napkin. The sky was ugly, bruised.

A man named MacDonnell, a grey-bearded Scotsman, had come to her house, bearing Jonathan's personal things—his pipe, the brass-framed daguerreotype of her, an unfinished letter. The silver crucifix he'd worn like a scar the last twenty years. The man had tried to comfort her, offering half-heard reassurances that her husband had been as fine a corporal as any on the Front. She thought sometimes that she might have been more grateful to him for his trouble.

She still had the unfinished letter, carried with her from London, and she might look at it again later, though she knew it almost by heart now. Scribblings she could hardly recognise as his, mad and rambling words about something trailing his battalion through the fields and muddy trenches.

Mina sipped her tea, barely noticing that it had gone cold, and watched the clouds outside as they swept in from the sea and rushed across the rocky headland.

⁓

A soupy fog in the morning, misty ghosts of ships and men torn apart on the reef, and Mina Harker followed the curve of stairs up from the town, past the ruined Abbey, and into the old East Cliff churchyard. It seemed that even more of the tombstones had tumbled over, and she remembered the elderly sailors and fishermen and whalers that had come here before, Mr. Swales and the others, and wondered if anyone ever came here now. She found a bench and sat, looking back down to where Whitby lay hidden from view. The yellow lantern eyes of the lighthouses winked in the distance, bookending the invisible town below.

She unfolded Jonathan's letter and the chilling breeze fingered the edges of the paper.

The foghorns sounded, that throaty bellow, perplexed and lonesome.

Before leaving London, she'd taken all the papers, the typed pages and old notebooks, the impossible testament of the Company, from the wall safe where Jonathan had kept them. Now they were tucked carefully inside the brocade canvas satchel resting on the sandy cobbles at her feet.

. . . and burn them, Mina, burn every trace of what we have seen, scrawled in that handwriting that was Jonathan's, and also surely no one's she'd ever met.

And so she had sat at the hearth, these records in her lap, watching the flames, feeling the heat on her face. Had lifted a letter to Lucy from the stack, held the envelope a moment, teasing the fire as a child might tease a cat with table scraps.

"No," she whispered, closing her eyes against the hungry orange glow, and putting the letter back with the rest. *It's all I have left, and I'm not that strong.*

Far out at sea, she thought she heard bells, and down near Tate Hill Pier, a dog barking. But the fog made a game of sound and she couldn't be sure she'd heard anything but the surf and her own breathing. Mina lifted the satchel and set it on the bench beside her.

Earlier that morning she'd stood before the looking glass in her room at the inn, staring into the soft eyes of a young woman, not someone who had seen almost forty-two years and the horrors of her twentieth. As she had so often done before her own mirrors, she'd looked for the age that should have begun to crease and ruin her face and found only the faintest crow's feet.

... every trace, Mina, if we are ever to be truly free of this terrible damnation.

She opened the satchel and laid Jonathan's letter inside, pressed it between the pages of his old diary, then snapped the clasp shut again. *Now*, she thought, filled suddenly with the old anger, black and acid, *I might fling it into the sea, lose these memories here, where it started.*

Instead, she hugged the bag tightly to her and watched the lighthouses as the day began to burn the mist away.

Before dusk, the high clouds had stacked themselves out beyond Kettleness, filling the eastern sky with thunderheads, their bruise-black underbellies already dumping sheets of rain on a foamy white sea. Before midnight, the storm had reared above Whitby Harbour and made landfall. In her narrow room above the kitchen, framed in wood and plaster and faded gingham wallpaper haunted by a hundred thousand boiled cabbages, Mina dreamed.

She was sitting at the small window, shutters thrown back, watching the storm walk the streets, feeling the icy salt spray and rain on her face. Jonathan's gold pocket watch lay open on the writing desk, ticking loud above the crash and boom outside. MacDonnell had not brought the watch back from Belgium, and she'd not asked him about it.

Quick and palsied fingers of lightning forked above the rooftops and washed the world in an instant of daylight.

On the bed behind her, Lucy said something about Churchill and the cold wind and laughed. Chandelier diamond tinkling and asylum snigger between velvet and gossamer and rust-scabbed iron bars.

And still laughing, "Bitch... apostate, Wilhelmina coward."

Mina looked down, watching the hands, hour, minute, second, racing themselves around the dial. The fob was twisted and crusted with something dark.

"Lucy, please..." and her voice came from very far away, and it sounded like a child asking to be allowed up past her bedtime.

Groan and bedspring creak, linen rustle and a sound wetter than the pounding rain. Lucy Westenra's footsteps moved across the bare floor, her heels clocking, ticking off the shortening distance.

Mina looked back down, and Drawbridge Road was absurdly crowded with bleating sheep, soppy wool in the downpour, and the gangling shepherd, a scarecrow blown from the wheat fields west of Whitby. Twiggy fingers beneath his burlap sleeve, driving his flock towards the harbour.

Lucy was standing very close now. Stronger than the rain and the old cabbage stink, anger that smelled like blood and garlic bulbs and dust. Mina watched the sheep and the storm.

"Turn *around*, Mina. Turn around and look at me and tell me that you even loved Jonathan."

Turn around Mina and tell

"Please, Lucy, don't leave me here."

and tell me that you even loved

And the sheep were turning, their short necks craning upwards and she saw they had red little rat eyes, and then the scarecrow howled.

Lucy's hands were cool silk on Mina's fevered shoulders.

"Don't leave, not yet..."

And Lucy's fingers, like hairless spider legs, had crawled around Mina's cheeks, and seized her jaw. Something brittle and dry, something crackling papery against her teeth, was forced past her lips.

On the street, the sheep were coming apart in the storm, reduced to yellowed fleece and fat-marbled mutton; a river of crimson sluicing between paving stones. Grinning skulls and polished white ribs, and the scarecrow had turned away, and broken up in the gale.

Lucy's fingers pushed the first clove of garlic over Mina's tongue, then shoved another into her mouth.

And she felt the cold steel at her throat.

We loved you, Mina, loved you as much as the blood and the night and even as much as

Mina Harker woke up in the hollow space between lightning and thunderclap.

Until dawn, when the storm tapered off to gentle drizzle and distant echoes, she sat alone on the edge of the bed, shaking uncontrollably and tasting bile and remembered garlic.

January 1922

Mina held the soup to the Professor's lips, chicken steam curling in the cold air. Abraham Van Helsing, eighty-seven and so much more dead than alive, tried to accept a little of the thin, piss-yellow broth. He took a clumsy sip, and the soup spilled from his mouth, dribbling down his chin into his beard. Mina wiped his lips with the stained napkin lying across her lap.

He closed his grey-lashed eyes and she set the bowl aside. Outside, the snow was falling again, and the wind yowled wolf noises around the corners of his old house. She shivered, trying to listen, instead, to the warm crackle from the fireplace, and the Professor's laboured breath. In a moment, he was coughing again, and she was helping him sit up, holding his handkerchief.

"Tonight, Madam Mina, tonight . . . " and he smiled, wan smile, and his words collapsing into another fit, the wet consumptive rattle. When it passed, she eased him back into the pillows, and noticed a little more blood on the ruined handkerchief.

Yes, she thought, *perhaps*. And once she would have tried to assure him that he would live to see spring and his damned tulips and another spring after that, but she only wiped the sweaty strands of hair from his forehead, and pulled the moth-gnawed quilt back around his bony shoulders.

Because there was no one else and nothing to keep her in England, she'd made the crossing to Amsterdam the week before Christmas; Quincey had been taken away by the influenza epidemic after the war. Just Mina now, and this daft old bastard. And soon enough, there would be only her.

"Shall I read for a bit, Professor?" They were almost halfway through Mr. Conrad's *The Arrow of Gold*. She was reaching for the book on the nightstand (and saw that she'd set the soup bowl on it) when his hand, dry and hot, closed softly around her wrist.

"Madam Mina," and already he was releasing her, his parchment touch withdrawn and there was something in his eyes now besides cataracts and the glassy fever flatness. His breath wheezed in, then forced itself harshly out again.

"I am *afraid*," he said, his voice barely a rasping whisper slipped into and between the weave of the night.

"You should rest now, Professor," she told him, wishing against anything he might say.

"So much a fraud I was, Madam Mina."

Did you ever even love?

"It was *my* hand that sent her, by my *hand*."

"Please, Professor. Let me call for a priest. I cannot..."

The glare that flashed then behind his eyes—something wild and bitter, a vicious humour—made her look away, scissoring her fraying resolve.

"Ah," he sighed, and "Yes," and something strangled that might have been laughter. "So, I confess my guilt. So, I scrub the blood from my hands with that other blood?"

The wind banged and clattered at the shuttered windows, looking for a way inside. And for a moment, the empty space filled with mantel-clock ticking and the wind and his ragged breathing, there was nothing more.

Then he said, "Please, Madam Mina, I am thirsty."

She reached for the pitcher and the chipped drinking glass.

"Forgive me, sweet Mina..."

The glass was spotty, and she wiped roughly at its rim with her blue skirt.

"...had it been hers to choose..." and he coughed again, once, a harsh and broken sound, and Mina wiped at the glass harder.

Abraham Van Helsing sighed gently, and she was alone.

When she was done, Mina carefully returned the glass to the table with the crystal pitcher, the unfinished book, and the cold soup. When she turned to the bed, she caught her reflection in the tall dressing mirror across the room. The woman staring back could easily have passed for a young thirty. Only her eyes, hollow, bottomless things, betrayed her.

∽

May 1930

As twilight faded from the narrow rue de l'Odéon, Mina Murray sipped her glass of Chardonnay and roamed the busy shelves of Shakespeare and Company. The reading would begin soon, some passages from Colette's new novel. Mina's fingers absently traced the spines of the assembled works of Hemingway and Glenway Wescott and D.H. Lawrence, titles and authors gold or crimson or flat-black pressed into cloth. Someone she half-recognised from a café or party or some other reading passed close, whispering a greeting, and she smiled in response, then went back to the books.

And then Mlle. Beach was asking everyone to please take their seats, a few straight-backed chairs scattered among the shelves and bins. Mina found a place close to the door and watched as the others took their time, quietly talking among themselves, laughing at unheard jokes. Most of them she knew by sight, a few by name and casual conversation, one or two by reputation only. Messieurs Pound and Joyce, and Radclyffe Hall in her tailored English suit and sapphire cuff links. There was an unruly handful of minor Surrealists she recognised from the rue Jacob bistro where she often took her evening meals. And at first unnoticed, a tallish young woman, unaccompanied, choosing a chair off to one side.

Mina's hands trembled, and she spilled a few drops of the wine on her blouse.

The woman sat down, turning her back to Mina. Beneath the yellowish glow of the bookstore's lamps, the woman's long hair blazed red-gold. The murmuring pack of Surrealists seated themselves in the crooked row directly in front of Mina, and she quickly looked away. Sudden sweat and her mouth gone dry, a dull undercurrent of nausea, and she hastily, clumsily, set her wine glass on the floor.

That name, held so long at bay, spoken in a voice she thought she'd forgotten.

Lucy.

Mina's heart, an arrhythmic drum, raced inside her chest like a frightened child's.

Sylvia Beach was speaking again, gently hushing the murmuring crowd, introducing Colette. There was measured applause as the writer stepped forward, and something sarcastic mumbled by one of the Surrealists. Mina closed her eyes tightly, cold and breathing much too fast, sweaty fingers gripping at the edges of her chair. Someone touched her arm and she jumped, almost cried out, gasping loud enough to draw attention.

"Mademoiselle Murray, *êtes-vous bon?*"

She blinked, dazed, recognising the boy's unshaven face as one of the shop's clerks, but unable to negotiate his name.

"*Oui, je vais bien.*" And she tried to smile, blinking back sucking in vertigo and dismay. "*Merci . . . je suis désolé.*"

He nodded, doubtful, reluctantly returning to his windowsill behind her.

At the front of the gathering, Colette had begun to read, softly relinquishing her words. Mina glanced to where the red-haired woman had sat down, half expecting to find the chair empty, or occupied by someone else entirely. She whispered a faithless prayer that she'd merely hallucinated, or suffered some trick of light and shadow. But the woman was still there, though turned slightly in her seat so that Mina could now see her profile, her full lips and familiar cheekbones. The smallest sound, a bated moan, escaped from Mina's pale lips, and she saw an image of herself, rising, pushing past bodies and through the bookstore's doors, fleeing headlong through the dark Paris streets to her tiny flat on Saint-Germain.

Instead, Mina Murray sat perfectly still, watching, in turn, the reader's restless lips and the delicate features of the nameless red-haired woman wearing Lucy Westenra's face.

After the reading, as the others milled and mingled, spinning respectful pretensions about *Sido* (and Madame Colette in general), Mina inched towards the door. The crowd seemed to have doubled during the half-hour, and she squeezed, abruptly claustrophobic, between shoulders and cigarette smoke. But four or five of the rue Jacob Surrealists were planted solidly—typically confrontational—in the shop's doorway, muttering loudly among themselves, the novelist already forgotten in their own banter.

"*Pardon*," she said, speaking just loudly enough to be heard above their conversation. "*Puis-je...*" Mina pointed past the men, to the door.

The one closest her, gaunt and unwashed, almost pale enough to pass for an albino, turned towards her. Mina remembered his face, its crooked nose. She'd once seen him spit at a nun outside the Deux Magots. He gave no sign that he intended to let her pass, and she thought that even his eyes looked unclean. *Carrion eyes,* she thought.

"Mademoiselle Murray. Please, one moment."

Mina matched the man's glare a second longer, and then, slowly, turned, recognising Adrienne Monnier; her own shop, the Maison des Amis des Livres, stood, dark-windowed tonight, across the street. It was generally acknowledged that Mlle. Monnier shared considerable responsibility for the success of Shakespeare and Company.

"I have here someone who would very much like to meet you." The red-haired woman was standing at Adrienne's side, sipping dark wine. She smiled, and Mina saw that she had hazel-green eyes.

"This is Mademoiselle Carmicheal from New York. She says that she is a great admirer of your work, Mina. I was just telling her that you've recently placed another story with the *Little Review*."

"*Anna* Carmicheal," the woman said, eager and silken-voiced, offering Mina her hand. Detached, drifting, Mina watched herself accept it.

Anna Carmicheal, from New York. Not Lucy.

"Thank you," Mina said, her voice gone the same dead calm as the sea before a squall.

"Oh, Christ no, thank *you*, Miss Murray."

Not Lucy, not Lucy at all, and Mina noticed how much taller than Lucy Westenra this woman was, her hands more slender, and there was a small mole at the corner of her rouged lips.

Then Adrienne Monnier was gone, pulled back into the crowd by a fat woman in an ugly ostrich-plumed hat, leaving Mina alone with Anna Carmichael. Behind her, the divided Surrealists argued, a threadbare quarrel and wearisome zeal.

"I've been reading you since 'The White Angel of Carfax', and last year, my God, last year I read 'Canto Babel' in *Harper's*. In America,

Miss Murray, they're saying that you're the new Poe, that you make Le Fanu and all those silly Victorians look—"

"Yes, well," Mina began, uncertain what she meant to say, only meaning to interrupt. The dizziness, sharpening unreality, was rushing back, and she leaned against a shelf for support.

"Miss Murray?" And a move, then, as if to catch someone who had stumbled, long fingers alert. Anna Carmichael took a cautious step forward, closing the space between them.

"Mina, please. Just Mina."

"Are you—?"

"Yes," but she was sweating again. "Forgive me, Anna. Just a little too much wine on an empty stomach."

"Then please, let me take you to dinner."

Lips pursed, Mina bit the tip of her tongue, biting hard enough to bring a salted hint of blood, and the world began to tilt back into focus, the syrupy blackness at the edges of her vision withdrawing by degrees.

"Oh, no. I couldn't," she managed. "Really, it's not . . ."

But the woman was taking her by the arm, her crescent-moon smile baring teeth like perfectly spaced pearls, every bit the forceful American. She thought of Quincey Morris, and wondered if this woman had ever been to Texas.

"But I insist, Mina. It'll be an honour, and in return, well, I won't feel so guilty if I talk too much."

Together, arm in arm, they elbowed their way through the Surrealist blockade, the men choosing to ignore them. Except her gaunt albino, and Mina imagined something passing between him and Anna Carmichael, unspoken, or simply unspeakable.

"I hate those idiot bastards," Anna whispered, as the door jangled shut behind them. She held Mina's hand tightly, squeezing warmth into her clammy palm, and surprising herself, Mina squeezed back.

Out on the gaslit rue de l'Odéon, a warm spring breeze was blowing, and the night air smelled like coming rain.

The meal had been good, though Mina had hardly tasted the little she'd eaten. Cold chicken and bread, salad with wild thyme and goat cheese, chewed and swallowed indifferently. And more than her share from a large carafe of some anonymous red Bordeaux. She'd listened to the woman who was not Lucy talk, endless talk of Anna Carmichael's copious ideas on the macabre and of Mina's writing.

"I actually went to the Carfax estate," she'd said, and then paused, as if she had expected some particular reaction. "Just last summer. There's some restoration underway now, you know."

"No," Mina answered, sipping her wine, and picking apart a strip of breast meat with her fork. "No, I wasn't aware of that."

Finally, the waitress had brought their bill, and Anna had grudgingly allowed Mina to leave the tip. While they'd eaten, the shower had come and gone, leaving the night dank and chilly and unusually quiet. Their heels sounded like passing time on the wet cobblestones. Anna Carmichael had a room in one of the less expensive Left Bank hotels, but they walked together back to Mina's flat.

When Mina woke, it was raining again, and for a few uncounted minutes she lay still, listening, smelling the sweat and incense, a hint of rose and lilac in the sheets. Finally, there was only a steady drip, falling perhaps from the leaky gutters of the old building, and maybe from the eaves, striking the flagstones in the little garden. She could still smell Anna Carmichael on her skin. Mina closed her eyes, and thought about going back to sleep, realising only very slowly that she was now alone in the bed.

The rain was over and the drip—the minute and measured splash of water on water, that clockwork cadence—*wasn't* coming from outside. She opened her eyes and rolled over, into the cold and hollow place made by Anna's absence. The lavatory light was burning; Mina blinked and called out her name, calling

Lucy

"Anna?"

drip and drip and drip and

"Anna?" and her throat tightened, whatever peace she'd awakened with suddenly leached away by fear and adrenaline. "Anna, are you all right?"

did you call for Lucy, at first, did I

drip and drip and

The floor was cold against her feet. Mina stepped past the chiffonier, bare floorboards giving way to a time- and mildew- and foot-dulled mosaic of ceramic polygons. Some of the tiles were missing, leaving dirty liver-coloured cavities in the design. The big tub, chipped alabaster enamel and the black cast iron showing through, lion's feet claws frozen in moulded rictus, grappling for some hold on the slick tiles.

Lucy Westenra lay, empty again, in the tub filled almost to over-flowing. Each drop of water swelled like an abscess until its own weight tore it free of the brass faucet, and so it fell, losing itself in the crimson water. The suicide's wrists hung limply over the sides, hands open; her head tilted back at a broken angle. And there were three bright smiles carved into her flesh, all of them offered to Heaven, or only to Mina.

The straight razor lay, wet and its blade glinting sticky scarlet, on the floor where it had fallen from Lucy's hand. And, like the dripping water, Mina stood until gravity pulled her free, and she fell.

October 1946

After the war and the ammonia antiseptic rooms where electrodes bridged the writhing space between her eyes with their deadening quick sizzle, after the long years that she was kept safe from herself and the suicidal world kept safe from her, Mina Murray came back to London.

A new city to embrace the mop-water grey Thames, changed utterly, scarred by the Luftwaffe's firestorms and aged by the twenty-four years of her absence. She spent three days walking the streets, destruction like a maze for her to solve or discard in frustration. At Aldermanbury, she stood before the ruins of St. Mary's and imagined—no, *wished*— her hands around Van Helsing's neck. His brittle, old bones to break apart like charred timbers and shattered pews. *Is this it, you old bastard? Is this what we saved England for?*

And the question, recognising its own intrinsic senselessness, its inherent futility, had hung nowhere, like all those blown-out windows framing the autumn-blue sky, the hallways ending only in rubble. Or her reflection, the woman a year from seventy looking back from a windowpane that seemed to have somehow escaped destruction especially for this purpose, for this moment. Mina Murray was a year from seventy, and she almost looked it.

The boy sitting on the wall watched the woman get out of the taxi, an old woman in black stockings and a black dress with a high collar, her eyes hidden behind dark spectacles. He absently released the small brown lizard he'd been tormenting, and it skittered gratefully away into some crack or crevice in the tumbledown masonry. The boy thought the woman looked like a widow, but better to pretend she was a spy for the Gerrys on a clandestine rendezvous, secrets to be exchanged for better secrets. She walked in short steps that seemed like maybe she was counting off the distance between them. In the cool, bright morning, her shoes clicked, a coded signal click, possibly, Morse-code click, and he thought perhaps he should quickly hide himself behind the crumbling wall, but then she saw him, and it was too late. She paused, then waved hesitantly as the taxi pulled away. Too late, so he waved back, and, there. She was just an old woman again.

"Hello," she said, fishing about for something in her handbag. She took out a cigarette out, and when he asked, the widow gave him one, also. She lit it for him with a silver lighter and turned to stare at the gutted ruins of Carfax Abbey, at the broken, precarious walls braced against their inevitable collapse. Noisy larks and sparrows sang to themselves in the limbs of the blasted trees, and further on, the duck pond glinted in the sun.

The woman leaned against the wall and sighed out smoke. "They didn't leave much, did they?" she asked him.

"No, Ma'am," he said. "It was one of them doodlebugs last year that got it," and he rocket-whistled for her, descending octaves and sticking a big rumbling boom stuck on the end. The woman nodded and crushed her cigarette out against a raw edge of mortar, ground it back and forth, the black ash smear against oatmeal grey, and she dropped the butt at her feet.

"It's haunted, you know," the boy told her, "Mostly at night, though," and she smiled, and he glimpsed her nicotine-stained teeth past the lipstick bruise of her lips. She nodded again.

"Yes," she said. "Yes. I guess that it is, isn't it?"

Mina killed the boy well back from the road, the straight razor she'd bought in Cheapside slipped out of her purse while he was digging about for bits of shrapnel to show her, jagged souvenirs of a pleasant fall afternoon in Purfleet. One gloved hand fast over his mouth and only the smallest muffled sound of surprise before she drew the blade quick across his throat, and the boy's life sprayed out dark and wet against the flagstones. He was the first murder she'd done since returning to England, and so she sat with him a while in the chilly shade of the tilted wall, his blood drying to a crust around her mouth.

Once, she heard a dog barking excitedly off towards the wreck that had been Jack Seward's asylum such a long time ago. There was a shiver of adrenaline, and her heart skipped a beat and raced for a moment because she thought maybe someone was coming, that she'd been discovered. But no one came, and so she sat with the boy and wondered at the winding knot of emptiness still inside her, unchanged and, evidently, unchangeable.

An hour later, she'd left the boy beneath a scraggly hedgerow and went to wash her hands and face in the sparkling pool. If there *were* ghosts at Carfax, they kept their distance.

August 1955

The cramped and cluttered office on West Houston was even hotter than usual, the Venetian blinds drawn shut to keep the sun out, so only the soft glow from Audry Cavanaugh's brass desk lamp, gentle incandescence through the green glass shade. But the dimness went unheeded by the sticky, resolute Manhattan summer. The office was sweltering, and Mina had to piss again. Her bladder ached, and she sweated and wrinkled her nose at the stale, heavy smell of the expensive English cigarettes the psychoanalyst chain-smoked. A framed and faded photograph of Carl Jung dangled on its hook behind the desk, and Mina felt his grey and knowing eyes, wanting inside her, wanting to see and know and draw reason from insanity.

"You're looking well today, Wilhelmina," Dr. Cavanaugh said, then offered a terse smile. She lit another cigarette, and exhaled a great cloud into the torpid air of the office. The smoke settled about her head like a shroud. "Sleeping any better?"

"No," Mina told her, which was true. "Not really." Not with the nightmares and the traffic sounds all night outside her SoHo apartment, and not with the restless voices from the street that she could never be sure weren't meant for her. And not the heat, either. The heat like a living thing to smother her, to hold the world perpetually at the edge of conflagration.

"I'm very sorry," and Dr. Cavanaugh was squinting at her through the gauze of smoke, her stingy smile already traded for familiar concern. Audry Cavanaugh never seemed to sweat, always so cool in her mannish suits, her hair pulled back in its neat, tight bun.

"Did you speak with your friend in London?" Mina asked. "You *said* that you would..." and maybe the psychoanalyst heard the strain in Mina's voice because she sighed a loud, impatient sigh and tilted her head backwards, gazing up at the ceiling,

"Yes," she answered. "I've talked with Dr. Beecher. Just yesterday, actually."

Mina licked her lips, her dry tongue across drier lips, the parched skin of dead fruit. There was a pause, a moment if silence, and then Audry Cavanaugh said, "He was able to find a number of references to attacks on children by a 'bloofer lady', some articles dating from late in September, 1897, in *The Westminster Gazette* and a few other papers. A couple of pieces on the wreck at Whitby, also. But, Mina, I never *said* I doubted you. You didn't have to prove anything."

"I *had* those clippings," Mina mumbled around her dry tongue. "I used to have *all* the clippings."

"I always believed that you did."

There was more silence, then, and only street sounds ten stories down to fill the void, Dr. Cavanaugh put on her reading glasses and opened her yellow stenographer's pad. Her pencil scritched across the paper to record the date. "The dreams, are they still about Lucy? Or is it the asylum again?"

And a drop of sweat ran slowly down Mina's rouged cheek, pooling at the corner of her mouth, offering an abrupt tang of salt and cosmetics to tease her thirst. She looked away, at the worn and dusty rug under her shoes, at the barrister shelves stuffed with medical books and psychological journals. The framed diplomas and, almost whispering, she said, "I had a dream about the world."

"Yes?" and Audry Cavanaugh sounded a little eager, because here was something new, perhaps, something novel in old Mina Murray's tiresome parade of delusions. "What did you dream about the world, Wilhelmina?"

Another drop of sweat dissolved on the tip of Mina's tongue, leaving behind the musky, fleeting taste of herself and fading too soon. "I dreamed that the world was dead," she said. "That the world ended a long, long time ago. But it doesn't know it's dead, and all that's left of the world is the dream of a ghost."

For a few minutes, neither of them said anything more, and so there was only the sound of the psychoanalyst's pencil, and then not even that. Mina listened to the street, the cars and trucks, the city. The sun made blazing slashes through the aluminium blinds, and Audry Cavanaugh struck a match, lighting another cigarette. The stink of sulphur made the insides of Mina's nostrils burn.

"Do you think that's true, Mina?"

And Mina closed her eyes, wanting to be alone with the weary, constant rhythm of her heart, the afterimages like burn-scar slashes in the dark behind her vellum eyelids. She was too tired for confession or memory today, too uncertain to commit her scattered thoughts to words; she drifted, and there was no intrusion from patient Cavanaugh, and in a few minutes she was asleep.

April 1969

After she's swallowed the capsules and a mouthful of plastic-flavoured water from the blue pitcher on her night stand, after Brenda Neufield and her white shoes have left the hospital room, Mina sits up. She wrestles the safety bar wrestled down and her legs swing slowly, painfully, over and off the edge of the bed. She watches her bare feet dangling above the linoleum floor, her ugly yellowed toenails, age spots and skin parchment-stretched too tightly over kite-frame bones.

A week ago, after her heart attack and the ambulance ride from her shitty little apartment, there was the emergency room and the doctor who smiled at her and said, "You're a pip, Miss Murray. I have sixty-year old patients who should be glad to look half so good as you."

She waits, counting the nurse's footsteps—twelve, thirteen, fourteen, and surely Neufield's at the desk by now, going back to her magazines. And Mina sits, staring across the room, her back to the window, cowardice to pass for defiance. If she had a razor, or a kitchen knife, or a few more of Neufield's tranquilliser pills.

If she had the courage.

Later, when the rain has stopped and the crape myrtle has settled down for the night, the nurse comes back and finds her dozing, still perched upright on the edge of her bed, like some silly parakeet or geriatric gargoyle. She eases Mina back, and there's a dull click as the safety bar locks again. The nurse mumbles something so low Mina can't make out the words. So, she lies very still, instead, lies on those starch-stiff sheets and her pillowcase and listens to the drip and patter from the street outside, the velvet sounds after the storm almost enough to smooth the edges off Manhattan for a few hours. The blanket tucked rough beneath her chin and taxi wheels on the street, the honk of a car horn, a police siren blocks away. And footsteps on the sidewalk below her window, and, then, the soft and unmistakable pad of wolf paws on asphalt.

"The blood-dimmed tide is loosed, and everywhere
The ceremony of innocence is drowned..."
—W.B. Yeats, 'The Second Coming'

THE MAMMOTH BOOK OF

BEST NEW HORROR

THE YEAR'S BEST HORROR
STORIES BY SUCH MASTERS
OF DARK FANTASY AS:

**RAMSEY CAMPBELL
HARLAN ELLISON
CHRISTOPHER FOWLER
NEIL GAIMAN
TANITH LEE
PETER STRAUB
and many others**

EDITED BY
STEPHEN JONES

"A must-have, must-read
anthology for horror buffs."
– *PUBLISHERS WEEKLY*

**TENTH
ANNIVERSARY
EDITION**

[1998]

JUST BECAUSE I thought vampires had become a cliché did not mean that the publisher was in any way averse to putting them on the cover. However, it was perhaps unfortunate that they chose to do so with the Tenth Anniversary edition which, unlike the previous volume, did not actually contain any stories featuring the undead.

At least the British Fantasy Award-winning anthology kicked off with four pages of testimonials by the likes of Clive Barker, Peter Straub, Brian Lumley, Neil Gaiman, Ellen Datlow and others, including the redoubtable Ramsey Campbell.

This time I managed to rein the Introduction back to just over sixty pages, while the Necrology held fast at twenty-eight. With the 21st century just around the corner, I predictably looked back over the first decade of *The Mammoth Book of Best New Horror* (as the series was now entitled on both sides of the Atlantic).

Once again featuring just nineteen stories, the tenth volume introduced the incomparable Tanith Lee and astonishing newcomer Kelly Link to the series, and included the novella 'The Boss in the Wall: A Treatise on the House Devil', the last major work by the late Avram Davidson (who died in 1993), completed by Grania Davis.

However, I have chosen another powerful novella to represent this edition. Peter Straub had previously made two appearances in *Best New Horror*, but neither could have prepared us for his International

Horror Guild Award-winning revenge tale 'Mr. Clubb and Mr. Cuff'. Loosely inspired by Herman Melville's story 'Bartleby the Scrivener', this is just about as dark and funny as horror can get...

PETER STRAUB

MR. CLUBB AND MR. CUFF

PETER STRAUB's first supernatural novel, *Julia*, appeared in 1975.
Since then he has published *If You Could See Me Now, Ghost
Story, Shadowland, Floating Dragon, Koko, Mystery, The Throat, The
Hellfire Club, Mr. X, Lost Boy Lost Girl, In the Night Room, A Dark
Matter* and two collaborations with Stephen King, *The Talisman* and
Black House.

His short fiction has been collected in *Houses Without Doors,
Magic Terror: Seven Tales, 5 Stories, The Juniper Tree and Other Stories*
and *Interior Darkness: Selected Stories.* He has also edited the
anthologies *Ghosts, Poe's Children* and two volumes of *American
Fantastic Tales: Terror and the Uncanny from Poe to the Pulps* and
Terror and the Uncanny from 1940s to Now.

Julia was filmed in 1977 as *Full Circle* (aka *The Haunting of Julia*)
starring Mia Farrow and Keir Dullea, while the 1981 movie of *Ghost
Story* featured an impressive cast that included veterans Fred Astaire,
Melvyn Douglas, Douglas Fairbanks, Jr. and John Houseman.

Amongst many literary honours, Straub has won multiple World
Fantasy Awards and HWA Bram Stoker Awards, along with the
International Horror Guild Award and the British Fantasy August
Derleth Award.

About the following powerful novella, the author explains: "I had
been thinking about what I might do with Herman Melville's great

story 'Bartleby the Scrivener' when Otto Penzler asked me to contribute to an anthology based on the theme of revenge. 'All right,' I thought, 'let's do a "Bartleby" about revenge.'

"I had to do something with 'Bartleby', anyhow, as I hadn't been able to think about anything else since I re-read it. Plus the idea of revenge exacted by revenge itself, which is the only kind of revenge interesting enough to write about, seemed to fit pretty well into a story about a man who cannot rid himself of a mysterious employee. Once I started, the entire story seemed to fall happily into place. I should add that the lyrical descriptions of cigar-smoke are jokes about connoisseurship."

I

I NEVER INTENDED to go astray, nor did I know what that meant. My journey began in an isolated hamlet notable for the piety of its inhabitants, and when I vowed to escape New Covenant I assumed that the values instilled within me there would forever be my guide. And so, with a depth of paradox I still only begin to comprehend, they have been. My journey, so triumphant, also so excruciating, is both from my native village and of it. For all its splendour, my life has been that of a child of New Covenant.

When in my limousine I scanned The Wall Street Journal, when in the private elevator I ascended to the rosewood-panelled office with harbour views, when in the partners' dining room I ordered squab on a mesclun bed from a prison-rescued waiter known to me alone as Charlie-Charlie, also when I navigated for my clients the complex waters of financial planning, above all when before her seduction by my enemy Graham Lesson I returned homeward to luxuriate in the attentions of my stunning Marguerite, when transported within the embraces of my wife, even then I carried within the frame houses dropped like afterthoughts down the streets of New Covenant, the stiff faces and suspicious eyes, the stony cordialities before and after services in the grim great Temple, the blank storefronts along Harmony Street— tattooed within me was the ugly, enigmatic beauty of my birthplace. Therefore I believe that when I strayed, and stray I did, make no mistake, it was but to come home, for I claim that the two strange gentlemen who beckoned me into error were the night of its night, the dust of its dust. In the period of my life's greatest turmoil—the month of my exposure to Mr. Clubb and Mr. Cuff, "Private Detectives Extraordinaire," as their business card described them—in the midst of the uproar I felt that I saw the contradictory dimensions of...of...

I felt I saw...had seen, had at least glimpsed...what a wiser man might call...try to imagine the sheer difficulty of actually writing these words...the Meaning of Tragedy. You smirk; I don't blame you: in your place I'd do the same, but I assure you I saw something.

I must sketch in the few details necessary for you to understand my story. A day's walk from New York State's Canadian border, New Covenant was (and still is, still is) a town of just under a thousand inhabitants united by the puritanical Protestantism of the Church of the New Covenant, whose founders had broken away from the even more puritanical Saints of the Covenant. (The Saints had proscribed sexual congress in the hope of hastening the Second Coming.) The village flourished during the end of the nineteenth century and settled into its permanent form around 1920.

To wit: Temple Square, where the Temple of the New Covenant and its bell tower, flanked left and right by the Youth Bible Study Centre and the Combined Boys and Girls Elementary and Middle School, dominate a modest greensward. Southerly stand the shop fronts of Harmony Street, the bank, also the modest placards indicating the locations of New Covenant's doctor, lawyer, and dentist; south of Harmony Street lie the two streets of frame houses sheltering the town's clerks and artisans, beyond these the farms of the rural faithful, beyond the farmland deep forest. North of Temple Square is Scripture Street, two blocks lined with the residences of the reverend and his Board of Brethren, the aforementioned doctor, dentist, and lawyer, the president and vice president of the bank, also the families of some few wealthy converts devoted to Temple affairs. North of Scripture Street are more farms, then the resumption of the great forest, in which our village described a sort of clearing.

My father was New Covenant's lawyer, and to Scripture Street was I born. Sundays I spent in the Youth Bible Study Centre, weekdays in the Combined Boys and Girls Elementary and Middle School. New Covenant was my world, its people all I knew of the world. Three-fourths of all mankind consisted of gaunt, bony, blond-haired individuals with chiselled features and blazing blue eyes, the men six feet or taller in height, the women some inches shorter—the remaining fourth being the Racketts, Mudges and Blunts, our farm families, who after generations of intermarriage had coalesced into a tribe of squat, black-haired, gap-toothed, moon-faced males and females seldom taller than five feet, four or five inches. Until I went to college I thought that all people were divided into the races of town and barn, fair and dark, the spotless and the mud-spattered, the reverential and the sly.

Though Racketts, Mudges and Blunts attended our school and worshipped in our Temple, though they were at least as prosperous as we in town, we knew them tainted with an essential inferiority. Rather than intelligent they seemed crafty, rather than spiritual, animal. Both in classrooms and Temple, they sat together, watchful as dogs compelled for the nonce to be "good", now and again tilting their heads to pass a whispered comment. Despite Sunday baths and Sunday clothes, they bore an unerasable odour redolent of the barnyard. Their public self-effacement seemed to mask a peasant amusement, and when they separated into their wagons and other vehicles, they could be heard to share a peasant laughter.

I found this mysterious race unsettling, in fact profoundly annoying. At some level they frightened me—I found them compelling. Oppressed from my earliest days by life in New Covenant, I felt an inadmissible fascination for this secretive brood. Despite their inferiority, I wished to know what they knew. Locked deep within their shabbiness and shame I sensed the presence of a freedom I did not understand but found thrilling.

Because town never socialised with barn, our contacts were restricted to places of education, worship, and commerce. It would have been as unthinkable for me to take a seat beside Delbert Mudge or Charlie-Charlie Rackett in our fourth-grade classroom as for Delbert or Charlie-Charlie to invite me for an overnight in their farmhouse bedrooms. Did Delbert and Charlie-Charlie actually have bedrooms, where they slept alone in their own beds? I recall mornings when the atmosphere about Delbert and Charlie-Charlie suggested nights spent in close proximity to the pigpen, others when their worn dungarees exuded a freshness redolent of sunshine, wildflowers and raspberries.

During recess an inviolable border separated the townies at the northern end of our play area from the barnies at the southern. Our play, superficially similar, demonstrated our essential differences, for we could not cast off the unconscious stiffness resulting from constant adult measurement of our spiritual worthiness. In contrast, the barnies did not play at playing but actually played, plunging back and forth across the grass, chortling over victories, grinning as they muttered what must have been jokes. (We were not adept at jokes.) When school closed at end of day, I tracked the homebound progress of Delbert, Charlie-Charlie, and clan with envious eyes and a divided heart.

Why should they have seemed in possession of a liberty I desired? After graduation from Middle School, we townies progressed to Shady Glen's Consolidated High, there to monitor ourselves and our fellows while encountering the temptations of the wider world, in some cases then advancing into colleges and universities. Having concluded their educations with the seventh grade's long division and "Hiawatha" recitations, the barnies one and all returned to their barns. Some few, some very few of us, among whom I had determined early on to be numbered, left for good, thereafter to be celebrated, denounced, or mourned. One of us, Caleb Thurlow, violated every standard of caste and morality by marrying Munna Blunt and vanishing into barnie-dom. A disgraced, disinherited pariah during my childhood, Thurlow's increasingly pronounced stoop and decreasing teeth terrifyingly mutated him into a blond, wasted barnie-parody on his furtive annual Christmas appearances at Temple. One of them, one only, my old classmate Charlie-Charlie Rackett, escaped his ordained destiny in our twentieth year by liberating a plough horse and Webley-Vickers pistol from the family farm to commit serial armed robbery upon Shady Glen's George Washington Inn, Town Square Feed & Grain, and Allsorts Emporium. Every witness to his crimes recognised what, if not who, he was, and Charlie-Charlie was apprehended while boarding the Albany train in the next village west. During the course of my own journey from and of New Covenant, I tracked Charlie-Charlie's gloomy progress through the way stations of the penal system until at last I could secure his release at a parole hearing with the offer of a respectable job in the financial-planning industry.

I had by then established myself as absolute monarch of three floors in a Wall Street monolith. With my two junior partners, I enjoyed the services of a fleet of paralegals, interns, analysts, investigators, and secretaries. I had chosen these partners carefully, for as well as the usual expertise, skill and dedication, I required other, less conventional qualities.

I had sniffed out intelligent but unimaginative men of some slight moral laziness; capable of cutting corners when they thought no one would notice; controlled drinkers and secret drug takers: juniors with reason to be grateful for their positions. I wanted no zealousness. My employees were to be steadfastly incurious and able enough to handle their clients satisfactorily, at least with my paternal assistance.

My growing prominence had attracted the famous, the established, the notorious. Film stars and athletes, civic leaders, corporate pashas, and heirs to long-standing family fortunes regularly visited our offices, as did a number of conspicuously well-tailored gentlemen who had accumulated their wealth in a more colourful fashion. To these clients I suggested financial stratagems responsive to their labyrinthine needs. I had not schemed for their business. It simply came to me, willy-nilly, as our Temple held that salvation came to the elect. One May morning, a cryptic fellow in a pin-striped suit appeared in my office to pose a series of delicate questions. As soon as he opened his mouth, the cryptic fellow summoned irresistibly from memory a dour, squinting member of the Board of Brethren of New Covenant's Temple. I knew this man, and instantly I found the tone most acceptable to him. Tone is all to such people. After our interview he directed others of his kind to my office, and by December my business had tripled. Individually and universally these gentlemen pungently reminded me of the village I had long ago escaped, and I cherished my suspicious buccaneers even as I celebrated the distance between my moral life and theirs. While sheltering these self-justifying figures within elaborate trusts, while legitimising subterranean floods of cash, I immersed myself within a familiar atmosphere of pious denial. Rebuking home, I was home.

Life had not yet taught me that revenge inexorably exacts its own revenge.

My researches eventually resulted in the hiring of the two junior partners known privately to me as Gilligan and the Skipper. The first, a short, trim fellow with a comedian's rubber face and dishevelled hair, brilliant with mutual funds but an ignoramus at estate planning, each morning worked so quietly as to become invisible. To Gilligan I had referred many of our actors and musicians, and those whose schedules permitted them to attend meetings before the lunch hour met their soft-spoken adviser in a dimly lighted office with curtained windows. After lunch, Gilligan tended towards the vibrant, the effusive, the extrovert. Red-faced and sweating, he loosened his tie, turned on a powerful sound system, and ushered emaciated musicians with haystack hair into the atmosphere of a backstage party. Morning Gilligan spoke in whispers; Afternoon Gilligan batted our secretaries' shoulders as he bounced officeward down the corridors. I snapped him up as soon as one of my competitors let him go, and he proved a perfect complement to the Skipper. Tall, plump, silver-haired, this gentleman had come to me from a specialist in estates and trusts discomfited by his tendency to become pugnacious when outraged by a client's foul language, improper dress, or other offences against good taste. Our tycoons and inheritors of family fortunes were in no danger of arousing the Skipper's ire, and I myself handled the unshaven film stars' and heavy metallists' estate planning. Neither Gilligan nor the Skipper had any contact with the cryptic gentlemen. Our office was an organism balanced in all its parts. Should any mutinous notions occur to my partners, my spy the devoted Charlie-Charlie Rackett, known to them as Charles the Perfect Waiter, every noon silently monitored their every utterance while replenishing Gilligan's wine glass. My marriage of two years seemed blissfully happy, my reputation and bank account flourished alike, and I anticipated perhaps another decade of labour followed by luxurious retirement. I could not have been less prepared for the disaster to come.

Mine, as disasters do, began at home. I admit my contribution to the difficulties. While immersed in the demands of my profession, I had married a beautiful woman twenty years my junior. It was my understanding that Marguerite had knowingly entered into a contract under which she enjoyed the fruits of income and social position while postponing a deeper marital communication until I cashed in and quit the game, at which point she and I could travel at will, occupying grand hotel suites and staterooms while acquiring every adornment that struck her eye. How could an arrangement so harmonious have failed to satisfy her? Even now I feel the old rancour. Marguerite had come into our office as a faded singer who wished to invest the remaining proceeds from a five- or six-year-old "hit", and after an initial consultation Morning Gilligan whispered her down the corridor for my customary lecture on estate tax, trusts, so forth and so on, in her case due to the modesty of the funds in question mere show. (Since during their preliminary discussion she had casually employed the Anglo-Saxon monosyllable for excrement, Gilligan dared not subject her to the Skipper.) He escorted her into my chambers, and I glanced up with the customary show of interest. You may imagine a thick bolt of lightning slicing through a double-glazed office window, sizzling across the width of a polished teak desk, and striking me in the heart.

Already I was lost. Thirty minutes later I violated my most sacred edict by inviting a female client to a dinner date. She accepted, damn her. Six months later, Marguerite and I were married, damn us both. I had attained everything for which I had abandoned New Covenant, and for twenty-three months I inhabited the paradise of fools.

I need say only that the usual dreary signals, matters like unexplained absences, mysterious telephone calls abruptly terminated upon my appearance, and visitations of a melancholic, distracted daemon forced me to set one of our investigators on Marguerite's trail, resulting in the discovery that my wife had been two-backed-beasting it with my sole professional equal, the slick, the smooth Graham Leeson, to whom I, swollen with uxorious pride a year after our wedding day, had introduced her during a function at the Waldorf-Astoria hotel. I know what happened. I don't need a map. Exactly as I had decided to win her at our first meeting, Graham Leeson vowed to steal Marguerite from me the instant he set his handsome blue eyes on her between the fifty-thousand-dollar tables on the Starlight Roof.

My enemy enjoyed a number of natural advantages. Older than she by but ten years to my twenty, at six-four three inches taller than I, this reptile had been blessed with a misleadingly winning Irish countenance and a full head of crinkly red-blonde hair. (In contrast, my white tonsure accentuated the severity of the all-too-Cromwellian townie face.) I assumed her immune to such obvious charms, and I was wrong. I thought Marguerite could not fail to see the meagreness of Leeson's inner life, and I was wrong again. I suppose he exploited the inevitable temporary isolation of any spouse to a man in my position. He must have played upon her grudges, spoken to her secret vanities. Cynically, I am sure, he encouraged the illusion that she was an "artist". He flattered, he very likely wheedled. By every shabby means at his disposal he had overwhelmed her, most crucially by screwing her brains out three times a week in a corporate suite at a Park Avenue hotel.

After I had examined the photographs and other records arrayed before me by the investigator, an attack of nausea brought my dizzied head to the edge of my desk; then rage stiffened my backbone and induced a moment of hysterical blindness. My marriage was dead, my wife a repulsive stranger. Vision returned a second or two later. The chequebook floated from the desk drawer, the Waterman pen glided into position between thumb and forefinger, and while a shadow's efficient hand inscribed a cheque for ten thousand dollars, a disembodied voice informed the hapless investigator that the only service required of him henceforth would be eternal silence.

For perhaps an hour I sat alone in my office, postponing appointments and refusing telephone calls. In the moments when I had tried to envision my rival, what came to mind was some surly drummer or guitarist from her past, easily intimidated and readily bought off. In such a case, I should have inclined towards mercy. Had Marguerite offered a sufficiently self-abasing apology, I would have slashed her clothing allowance in half, restricted her public appearances to the two or three most crucial charity events of the year and perhaps as many dinners at my side in the restaurants where one is "seen", and ensured that the resultant mood of sackcloth and ashes prohibited any reversion to bad behaviour by intermittent use of another investigator.

No question of mercy, now. Staring at the photographs of my life's former partner entangled with the man I detested most in the world,

I shuddered with a combination of horror, despair, loathing, and—appallingly—an urgent spasm of sexual arousal. I unbuttoned my trousers, groaned in ecstatic torment, and helplessly ejaculated over the images on my desk. When I had recovered, weak-kneed and trembling, I wiped away the evidence, closed the hateful folders, and picked up the telephone to request Charlie-Charlie Rackett's immediate presence in my office.

The cryptic gentlemen, experts in the nuances of retribution, might have seemed more obvious sources of assistance, but I could not afford obligations in that direction. Nor did I wish to expose my humiliation to clients for whom the issue of respect was all-important. Devoted Charlie-Charlie's years in the jug had given him an extensive acquaintanceship among the dubious and irregular, and I had from time to time commandeered the services of one or another of his fellow yardbirds. My old companion sidled around my door and posted himself before me, all dignity on the outside, all curiosity within.

"I have been dealt a horrendous blow, Charlie-Charlie," I said, "and as soon as possible I wish to see one or two of the best."

Charlie-Charlie glanced at the folders. "You want serious people," he said, speaking in code. "Right?"

"I must have men who can be serious when seriousness is necessary," I said, replying in the same code. While my lone surviving link to New Covenant struggled to understand this directive, it came to me that Charlie-Charlie had now become my only true confidant, and I bit down on an upwelling of fury. I realised that I had clamped shut my eyes, and opened them upon an uneasy Charlie-Charlie.

"You're sure," he said.

"Find them," I said. Then, to restore some semblance of our conventional atmosphere, I asked, "The boys still okay?"

Telling me that the juniors remained content, he said, "Fat and happy. I'll find what you want, but it'll take a couple of days."

I nodded, and he was gone.

For the remainder of the day I turned in an inadequate impersonation of the executive who usually sat behind my desk and, after putting off the moment as long as reasonably possible, buried the awful files in a bottom drawer and returned to the town house I had purchased for my bride-to-be and which, I remembered with an unhappy pang, she had once in an uncharacteristic moment of cuteness called "our town home".

Since I had been too preoccupied to telephone wife, cook, or butler with the information that I would be staying late at the office, when I walked into our dining room the table had been laid with our china and silver, flowers arranged in the centre-piece, and, in what I took to be a new dress, Marguerite glanced mildly up from her end of the table and murmured a greeting. Scarcely able to meet her eyes, I bent to bestow the usual homecoming kiss with a mixture of feelings more painful than I previously would have imagined myself capable. Some despicable portion of my being responded to her beauty with the old husbandly appreciation even as I went cold with the loathing I could not permit myself to show. I hated Marguerite for her treachery, her beauty for its falsity, myself for my susceptibility to what I knew was treacherous and false. Clumsily, my lips brushed the edge of an azure eye, and it came to me that she may well have been with Leeson while the investigator was displaying the images of her degradation. Through me coursed an involuntary tremor of revulsion with, strange to say, at its centre a molten erotic core. Part of my extraordinary pain was the sense that I too had been contaminated: a layer of illusion had been peeled away, revealing monstrous blind groping slugs and maggots.

Having heard voices, Mr. Moncrieff, the butler I had employed upon the abrupt decision of the Duke of Denbigh to cast off worldly ways and enter an order of Anglican monks, came through from the kitchen and awaited orders. His bland, courteous manner suggested as usual that he was making the best of having been shipwrecked on an island populated by illiterate savages. Marguerite said that she had been worried when I had not returned home at the customary time.

"I'm fine," I said. "No, I'm not fine. I feel unwell. Distinctly unwell. Grave difficulties at the office." With that I managed to make my way up the table to my chair, along the way signalling to Mr. Moncrieff that the Lord of the Savages wished him to bring in the pre-dinner martini and then immediately begin serving whatever the cook had prepared. I took my seat at the head of the table, and Mr. Moncrieff removed the floral centrepiece to the sideboard. Marguerite regarded me with the appearance of probing concern. This was false, false, false. Unable to meet her eyes, I raised mine to the row of Canalettos along the wall, then the intricacies of the plaster moulding above the paintings, at last to the chandelier depending from the central rosette on the ceiling. More had changed than my relationship with my wife. The moulding, the blossoming chandelier, even Canaletto's Venice resounded with a cold, selfish lovelessness.

Marguerite remarked that I seemed agitated.

"No, I am not," I said. The butler placed the ice-cold drink before me, and I snatched up the glass and drained half its contents. "Yes, I am agitated, terribly," I said. "The difficulties at the office are more far-reaching than I intimated." I polished off the martini and tasted only glycerine. "It is a matter of betrayal and treachery made all the more wounding by the closeness of my relationship with the traitor."

I lowered my eyes to measure the effect of this thrust to the vitals on the traitor in question. She was looking back at me with a flawless imitation of wifely concern. For a moment I doubted her unfaithfulness. Then the memory of the photographs in my bottom drawer once again brought crawling into view the slugs and maggots. "I am sickened unto rage," I said, "and my rage demands vengeance. Can you understand this?"

Mr. Moncrieff carried into the dining room the tureens or serving dishes containing whatever it was we were to eat that night, and my wife and I honoured the silence that had become conventional during the presentation of our evening meal. When we were alone again, she nodded in affirmation.

I said, "I am grateful, for I value your opinions. I should like you to help me reach a difficult decision."

She thanked me in the simplest of terms.

"Consider this puzzle," I said. "Famously, vengeance is the Lord's, and therefore it is often imagined that vengeance exacted by anyone other is immoral. Yet if vengeance is the Lord's, then a mortal being who seeks it on his own behalf has engaged in a form of worship, even an alternate version of prayer. Many good Christians regularly pray for the establishment of justice, and what lies behind an act of vengeance but a desire for justice? God tells us that eternal torment awaits the wicked. He also demonstrates a pronounced affection for those who prove unwilling to let Him do all the work."

Marguerite expressed the opinion that justice was a fine thing indeed, and that a man such as myself would always labour on its behalf. She fell silent and regarded me with what on any night previous I would have seen as tender concern. Though I had not yet so informed her, she declared, the Benedict Arnold must have been one of my juniors, for no other employee could injure me so greatly. Which was the traitor?

"As yet I do not know," I said. "But once again I must be grateful for your grasp of my concerns. Soon I will put into position the bear-traps that will result in the fiend's exposure. Unfortunately, my dear, this task will demand all of my energy over at least the next several days. Until the task is accomplished, it will be necessary for me to camp out in the—Hotel." I named the site of her assignations with Graham Leeson.

A subtle, momentary darkening of the eyes, her first genuine response of the evening, froze my heart as I set the bear-trap into place. "I know, the—'s vulgarity deepens with every passing week, but Gilligan's apartment is only a few doors north, the Skipper's one block south. Once my investigators have installed their electronic devices, I shall be privy to every secret they possess. Would you enjoy spending several days at Green Chimneys? The servants have the month off, but you might enjoy the solitude there more than you would being alone in town."

Green Chimneys, our country estate on a bluff above the Hudson River, lay two hours away. Marguerite's delight in the house had inspired me to construct on the grounds a fully equipped recording studio, where she typically spent days on end, trying out new "songs".

Charmingly, she thanked me for my consideration and said that she would enjoy a few days in seclusion at Green Chimneys. After I had exposed the traitor, I was to telephone her with the summons home. Accommodating on the surface, vile beneath, these words brought an anticipatory tinge of pleasure to her face, a delicate heightening of her beauty I would have, very likely had, misconstrued on earlier occasions. Any appetite I might have had disappeared before a visitation of nausea, and I announced myself exhausted. Marguerite intensified my discomfort by calling me her poor darling. I staggered to my bedroom, locked the door, threw off my clothes, and dropped into bed to endure a sleepless night. I would never see my wife again.

II

Sometime after first light I had attained an uneasy slumber; finding it impossible to will myself out of bed on awakening, I relapsed into the same restless sleep. By the time I appeared within the dining room, Mr. Moncrieff, as well-chilled as a good Chardonnay, informed me that Madame had departed for the country some twenty minutes before. Despite the hour, did Sir wish to breakfast? I consulted, trepidatiously, my wristwatch. It was ten-thirty: my unvarying practice was to arise at six, breakfast soon after, and arrive in my office well before seven. I rushed downstairs, and as soon as I slid into the back seat of the limousine forbade awkward queries by pressing the button to raise the window between the driver and myself.

No such mechanism could shield me from Mrs. Rampage, my secretary, who thrust her head around the door a moment after I had expressed my desire for a hearty breakfast of poached eggs, bacon, and whole-wheat toast from the executive dining room. All calls and appointments were to be postponed or otherwise put off until the completion of my repast. Mrs. Rampage had informed me that two men without appointments had been awaiting my arrival since 8:00 a.m. and asked if I would consent to see them immediately. I told her not to be absurd. The door to the outer world swung to admit her beseeching head. "Please," she said. "I don't know who they are, but they're frightening everybody."

This remark clarified all. Earlier than anticipated, Charlie-Charlie Rackett had deputised two men capable of seriousness when seriousness was called for. "I beg your pardon," I said. "Send them in."

Mrs. Rampage withdrew to lead into my chambers two stout, stocky, short, dark-haired men. My spirits had taken wing the moment I beheld these fellows shouldering through the door, and I rose smiling to my feet. My secretary muttered an introduction, baffled as much by my cordiality as by her ignorance of my visitors' names.

"It is quite all right," I said. "All is in order, all is in train." New Covenant had just entered the sanctum.

Barnie-slyness, barnie-freedom shone from their great, round gap-toothed faces: in precisely the manner I remembered, these two suggested mocking peasant violence scantily disguised by an equally mocking impersonation of convention. Small wonder that they had intimidated Mrs. Rampage and her underlings, for their nearest exposure to a like phenomenon had been with our musicians, and when offstage they were pale, emaciated fellows of little physical vitality. Clothed in black suits, white shirts, and black neckties, holding their black derbies by their brims and turning their gappy smiles back and forth between Mrs. Rampage and myself, these barnies had evidently been loose in the world for some time. They were perfect for my task. You will be irritated by their country manners, you will be annoyed by their native insubordination, I told myself, but you will never find men more suitable, so grant them what latitude they need. I directed Mrs. Rampage to cancel all telephone calls and appointments for the next hour.

The door closed, and we were alone. Each of the black-suited darlings snapped a business card from his right jacket pocket and extended it to me with a twirl of the fingers. One card read:

MR. CLUBB AND MR. CUFF
Private Detectives Extraordinaire
MR. CLUBB

and the other:

MR. CLUBB AND MR. CUFF
Private Detectives Extraordinaire
MR. CUFF

I inserted the cards into a pocket and expressed my delight at making their acquaintance.

"Becoming aware of your situation," said Mr. Clubb, "we preferred to report as quickly as we could."

"Entirely commendable," I said. "Will you gentlemen please sit down?"

"We prefer to stand," said Mr. Clubb.

"I trust you will not object if I again take my chair," I said, and did so. "To be honest, I am reluctant to describe the whole of my problem. It is a personal matter, therefore painful."

"It is a domestic matter," said Mr. Cuff.

I stared at him. He stared back with the sly imperturbability of his kind.

"Mr. Cuff," I said, "you have made a reasonable and, as it happens, an accurate supposition, but in the future you will please refrain from speculation."

"Pardon my plain way of speaking, sir, but I was not speculating," he said. "Marital disturbances are domestic by nature."

"All too domestic, one might say," put in Mr. Clubb. "In the sense of pertaining to the home. As we have so often observed, you find your greatest pain right smack-dab in the living room, as it were."

"Which is a somewhat politer fashion of naming another room altogether." Mr. Cuff appeared to suppress a surge of barnie-glee.

Alarmingly, Charlie-Charlie had passed along altogether too much information, especially since the information in question should not have been in his possession.

For an awful moment I imagined that the dismissed investigator had spoken to Charlie-Charlie. The man may have broadcast my disgrace to every person encountered on his final journey out of my office, inside the public elevator, thereafter even to the shoeshine "boys" and cup-rattling vermin lining the streets. It occurred to me that I might be forced to have the man silenced. Symmetry would then demand the silencing of valuable Charlie-Charlie. The inevitable next step would resemble a full-scale massacre.

My faith in Charlie-Charlie banished these fantasies by suggesting an alternate scenario and enabled me to endure the next utterance.

Mr. Clubb said, "Which in plainer terms would be to say the bed-room."

After speaking to my faithful spy, the Private Detectives Extraordinaire had taken the initiative by acting as if already employed and following Marguerite to her afternoon assignation at the—Hotel. Here, already, was the insubordination I had foreseen, but instead of the expected annoyance I felt a thoroughgoing gratitude for the two men leaning slightly towards me, their animal senses alert to every nuance of my response. That they had come to my office armed with the essential secret absolved me from embarrassing explanations; blessedly, the hideous photographs would remain concealed in the bottom drawer.

"Gentlemen," I said, "I applaud your initiative."

They stood at ease. "Then we have an understanding," said Mr. Clubb. "At various times, various matters come to our attention. At these times we prefer to conduct ourselves according to the wishes of our employer, regardless of difficulty."

"Agreed," I said. "However, from this point forward I must insist—"

A rap at the door cut short my admonition. Mrs. Rampage brought in a coffee-pot and cup, a plate beneath a silver cover, a rack with four slices of toast, two jam pots, silverware, a linen napkin, and a glass of water, and came to a halt some five or six feet short of the barnies. A sinfully arousing smell of butter and bacon emanated from the tray. Mrs. Rampage deliberated between placing my breakfast on the table to her left or venturing into proximity to my guests by bringing the tray to my desk. I gestured her forward, and she tacked wide to port and homed in on the desk. "All is in order, all is in train," I said. She nodded and backed out—literally walked backward until she reached the door, groped for the knob, and vanished.

I removed the cover from the plate containing two poached eggs in a cup-sized bowl, four crisp rashers of bacon, and a mound of home fried potatoes all the more welcome for being a surprise gift from our chef.

"And now, fellows, with your leave I shall—"

For the second time my sentence was cut off in mid-flow. A thick barnie-hand closed upon the handle of the coffee-pot and proceeded to fill the cup. Mr. Clubb transported my coffee to his lips, smacked appreciatively at the taste, then took up a toast slice and plunged it like a dagger into my egg-cup, releasing a thick yellow suppuration. He crunched the dripping toast between his teeth.

At that moment, when mere annoyance passed into dumbfounded ire, I might have sent them packing despite my earlier resolution, for Mr. Clubb's violation of my breakfast was as good as an announcement that he and his partner respected none of the conventional boundaries and would indulge in boorish, even disgusting behaviour. I very nearly did send them packing, and both of them knew it. They awaited my reaction, whatever it should be. Then I understood that I was being tested, and half of my insight was that ordering them off would be a failure of imagination. I had asked Charlie-Charlie to send me serious men, not Boy Scouts, and in the rape of my breakfast were depths and dimensions of seriousness I had never suspected. In that instant of comprehension, I believe, I virtually knew all that was to come, down to the last detail, and gave a silent assent. My next insight was that the moment when I might have dismissed these fellows with a conviction of perfect rectitude had just passed, and with the sense of opening myself to unpredictable adventures I turned to Mr. Cuff. He lifted a rasher from my plate, folded it within a slice of toast, and displayed the result.

"Here are our methods in action," he said. "We prefer not to go hungry while you gorge yourself, speaking freely, for the one reason that all of this stuff represents what you ate every morning when you were a kid." Leaving me to digest this shapeless utterance, he bit into his impromptu sandwich and sent golden-brown crumbs showering to the carpet.

"For as the important, abstemious man you are now," said Mr. Clubb, "what do you eat in the mornings?"

"Toast and coffee," I said. "That's about it."

"But in childhood?"

"Eggs," I said. "Scrambled or fried, mainly. And bacon. Home fries, too." Every fatty, cholesterol-crammed ounce of which, I forbore to add, had been delivered by barnie-hands directly from barnie-farms. I looked at the rigid bacon, the glistening potatoes, the mess in the egg-cup. My stomach lurched.

"We prefer," Mr. Clubb said, "that you follow your true preferences instead of muddying mind and stomach by gobbling this crap in search of an inner peace that never existed in the first place, if you can be honest with yourself." He leaned over the desk and picked up the plate. His partner snatched a second piece of bacon and wrapped it within a second slice of toast. Mr. Clubb began working on the eggs, and Mr. Cuff grabbed a handful of home fried potatoes. Mr. Clubb dropped the empty egg-cup, finished his coffee, refilled the cup, and handed it to Mr. Cuff, who had just finished licking the residue of fried potato from his free hand.

I removed the third slice of toast from the rack. Forking home fries into his mouth, Mr. Clubb winked at me. I bit into the toast and considered the two little pots of jam, greengage, I think, and rosehip. Mr. Clubb waggled a finger. I contented myself with the last of the toast. After a while I drank from the glass of water. All in all I felt reasonably satisfied and, but for the deprivation of my customary cup of coffee, content with my decision. I glanced in some irritation at Mr. Cuff. He drained his cup, then tilted into it the third and final measure from the pot and offered it to me. "Thank you," I said. Mr. Cuff picked up the pot of greengage jam and sucked out its contents, loudly. Mr. Clubb did the same with the rosehip. They sent their tongues into the corners of the jam pots and cleaned out whatever adhered to the sides. Mr. Cuff burped. Overlappingly, Mr. Clubb burped.

"Now, that is what I call by the name of breakfast, Mr. Clubb," said Mr. Cuff. "Are we in agreement?"

"Deeply," said Mr. Clubb. "That is what I call by the name of breakfast now, what I have called by the name of breakfast in the past, and what I shall continue to call by that sweet name on every morning in the future." He turned to me and took his time, sucking first one tooth, then another. "Our morning meal, sir, consists of that simple fare with which we begin the day, except when in all good faith we wind up sitting in a waiting room with our stomachs growling because our future client has chosen to skulk in late for work." He inhaled. "Which was for the same exact reason that brought him to our attention in the first place and for which we went without in order to offer him our assistance. Which is, begging your pardon, sir, the other reason for which you ordered a breakfast you would ordinarily rather starve than eat, and all I ask before we get down to the business at hand is that you might begin to entertain the possibility that simple men like ourselves might possibly understand a thing or two."

"I see that you are faithful fellows," I began.

"Faithful as dogs," broke in Mr. Clubb.

"And that you understand my position," I continued.

"Down to its smallest particulars," he interrupted again. "We are on a long journey."

"And so it follows," I pressed on, "that you must also under-stand that no further initiatives may be taken without my express consent."

These last words seemed to raise a disturbing echo—of what I could not say, but an echo nonetheless, and my ultimatum failed to achieve the desired effect. Mr. Clubb smiled and said, "We intend to follow your inmost desires with the faithfulness, as I have said, of trusted dogs, for one of our sacred duties is that of bringing these to fulfilment, as evidenced, begging your pardon, sir, in the matter of the breakfast our actions spared you from gobbling up and sickening yourself with. Before you protest, sir, please let me put to you the question of how you think you would be feeling right now if you had eaten that greasy stuff all by yourself?"

The straightforward truth announced itself and demanded utterance. "Poisoned," I said. After a second's pause, I added, "Dis-gusted."

"Yes, for you are a better man than you know. Imagine the situation. Allow yourself to picture what would have transpired had Mr. Cuff and myself not acted on your behalf. As your heart throbbed and your veins groaned, you would have taken in that while you were stuffing yourself the two of us stood hungry before you. You would have remembered that good woman informing you that we had patiently awaited your arrival since eight this morning, and at that point, sir, you would have experienced a self-disgust which would forever have tainted our relationship. From that point forth, sir, you would have been incapable of receiving the full benefits of our services."

I stared at the twinkling barnie. "Are you saying that if I had eaten my breakfast you would have refused to work for me?"

"You did eat your breakfast. The rest was ours."

This statement was so literally true that I burst into laughter. "Then I must thank you for saving me from myself. Now that you may accept employment, please inform me of the rates for your services."

"We have no rates," said Mr. Clubb.

"We prefer to leave compensation to the client," said Mr. Cuff.

This was crafty even by barnie-standards, but I knew a counter-move. "What is the greatest sum you have ever been awarded for a single job?"

"Six hundred thousand dollars," said Mr. Clubb.

"And the smallest?"

"Nothing, zero, nada, zilch," said the same gentleman.

"And your feelings as to the disparity?"

"None," said Mr. Clubb. "What we are given is the correct amount. When the time comes, you shall know the sum to the penny."

To myself I said, So I shall, and it shall be nothing; to them, "We must devise a method by which I may pass along suggestions as I monitor your ongoing progress. Our future consultations should take place in anonymous public places on the order of street corners, public parks, diners, and the like. I must never be seen in your office."

"You must not, you could not," said Mr. Clubb. "We would prefer to install ourselves here within the privacy and seclusion of your own beautiful office."

"Here?" He had once again succeeded in dumbfounding me.

"Our installation within the client's work space proves so advantageous as to overcome all initial objections," said Mr. Cuff. "And in this case, sir, we would occupy but the single corner behind me where the table stands against the window. We would come and go by means of your private elevator, exercise our natural functions in your private bathroom, and have our simple meals sent in from your kitchen. You would suffer no interference or awkwardness in the course of your business. So we prefer to do our job here, where we can do it best."

"You prefer," I said, giving equal weight to every word, "to move in with me."

"Prefer it to declining the offer of our help, thereby forcing you, sir, to seek the aid of less reliable individuals."

Several factors, first among them being the combination of delay, difficulty, and risk involved in finding replacements for the pair before me, led me to give further thought to this absurdity. Charlie-Charlie, a fellow of wide acquaintance among society's shadow side, had sent me his best. Any others would be inferior. It was true that Mr. Clubb and Mr. Cuff could enter and leave my office unseen, granting us a greater degree of security than possible in diners and public parks. There remained an insuperable problem.

"All you say may be true, but my partners and clients alike enter this office daily. How do I explain the presence of two strangers?"

"That is easily done, Mr. Cuff, is it not?" said Mr. Clubb.

"Indeed it is," said his partner. "Our experience has given us two infallible and complementary methods. The first of these is the installation of a screen to shield us from the view of those who visit this office."

I said, "You intend to hide behind a screen."

"During those periods when it is necessary for us to be on-site."

"Are you and Mr. Clubb capable of perfect silence? Do you never shuffle your feet, do you never cough?"

"You could justify our presence within these sacrosanct confines by the single manner most calculated to draw over Mr. Clubb and myself a blanket of respectable, anonymous impersonality."

"You wish to be introduced as my lawyers?" I asked.

"I invite you to consider a word," said Mr. Cuff. "Hold it steadily in your mind. Remark the inviolability that distinguishes those it identifies, measure its effect upon those who hear it. The word of which I speak, sir, is this: consultant."

I opened my mouth to object and found I could not.

Every profession occasionally must draw upon the resources of impartial experts—consultants. Every institution of every kind has known the visitations of persons answerable only to the top and given access to all departments—consultants. Consultants are supposed to be invisible. Again I opened my mouth, this time to say, "Gentlemen, we are in business." I picked up my telephone and asked Mrs. Rampage to order immediate delivery from Bloomingdale's of an ornamental screen and then to remove the breakfast tray.

Eyes agleam with approval, Mr. Clubb and Mr. Cuff stepped forward to clasp my hand. "We are in business," said Mr. Clubb.

"Which is by way of saying," said Mr. Cuff, "jointly dedicated to a sacred purpose."

Mrs. Rampage entered, circled to the side of my desk, and gave my visitors a glance of deep-dyed wariness. Mr. Clubb and Mr. Cuff looked heavenward. "About the screen," she said. "Bloomingdale's wants to know if you would prefer one six feet high in a black and red Chinese pattern or one ten feet high, Art Deco, in ochres, teals and taupes."

My barnies nodded together at the heavens. "The latter, please, Mrs. Rampage," I said. "Have it delivered this afternoon, regardless of cost, and place it beside the table for the use of these gentlemen, Mr. Clubb and Mr. Cuff, highly regarded consultants to the financial industry. That table shall be their command post."

"Consultants," she said. "Oh."

The barnies dipped their heads. Much relaxed, Mrs. Rampage asked if I expected great changes in the future.

"We shall see," I said. "I wish you to extend every co-operation to these gentlemen. I need not remind you, I know, that change is the first law of life."

She disappeared, no doubt on a beeline for her telephone.

Mr. Clubb stretched his arms above his head. "The preliminaries are out of the way, and we can move to the job at hand. You, sir, have been most exceedingly, most grievously wronged. Do I over-state?"

"You do not," I said.

"Would I overstate to assert that you have been injured, that you have suffered a devastating wound?"

"No, you would not," I responded, with some heat.

Mr. Clubb settled a broad haunch upon the surface of my desk. His face had taken on a grave, sweet serenity. "You seek redress. Redress, sir, is a correction, but it is nothing more. You imagine that it restores a lost balance, but it does nothing of the kind. A crack has appeared on the earth's surface, causing widespread loss of life. From all sides are heard the cries of the wounded and dying. It is as though the earth itself has suffered an injury akin to yours, is it not?"

He had expressed a feeling I had not known to be mine until that moment, and my voice trembled as I said, "It is exactly."

"Exactly," he said. "For that reason I said correction rather than restoration.

Restoration is never possible. Change is the first law of life."

"Yes, of course," I said, trying to get down to brass tacks.

Mr. Clubb hitched his buttock more comprehensively onto the desk. "What will happen will indeed happen, but we prefer our clients to acknowledge from the first that, apart from human desires being a messy business, outcomes are full of surprises. If you choose to repay one disaster with an equal and opposite disaster, we would reply, in our country fashion, There's a calf that won't suck milk."

I said, "I know I can't pay my wife back in kind, how could I?"

"Once we begin," he said, "we cannot undo our actions."

"Why should I want them undone?" I asked.

Mr. Clubb drew up his legs and sat cross-legged before me. Mr. Cuff placed a meaty hand on my shoulder. "I suppose there is no dispute," said Mr. Clubb, "that the injury you seek to redress is the adulterous behaviour of your spouse."

Mr. Cuff's hand tightened on my shoulder.

"You wish that my partner and myself punish your spouse."

"I didn't hire you to read her bedtime stories," I said.

Mr. Cuff twice smacked my shoulder, painfully, in what I took to be approval.

"Are we assuming that her punishment is to be of a physical nature?" asked Mr. Clubb. His partner gave my shoulder another all-too-hearty squeeze.

"What other kind is there?" I asked, pulling away from Mr. Cuff's hand.

The hand closed on me again, and Mr. Clubb said, "Punishment of a mental or psychological nature. We could, for example, torment her with mysterious telephone calls and anonymous letters. We could use any of a hundred devices to make it impossible for her to sleep. Threatening incidents could be staged so often as to put her in a permanent state of terror."

"I want physical punishment," I said.

"That is our constant preference," he said. "Results are swifter and more conclusive when physical punishment is used. But again, we have a wide spectrum from which to choose. Are we looking for mild physical pain, real suffering, or something in between, on the order of, say, broken arms or legs?"

I thought of the change in Marguerite's eyes when I named the— Hotel. "Real suffering."

Another bone-crunching blow to my shoulder from Mr. Cuff and a wide, gappy smile from Mr. Clubb greeted this remark. "You, sir, are our favourite type of client," said Mr. Clubb. "A fellow who knows what he wants and is unafraid to put it into words. This suffering, now, did you wish it in brief or extended form?"

"Extended," I said. "I must say that I appreciate your thoughtfulness in consulting with me like this. I was not quite sure what I wanted of you when first I requested your services, but you have helped me become perfectly clear about it."

"That is our function," he said. "Now, sir. The extended form of real suffering permits two different conclusions, gradual cessation or termination. Which is your preference?"

I opened my mouth and closed it. I opened it again and stared at the ceiling. Did I want these men to murder my wife? No. Yes. No. Yes, but only after making sure that the unfaithful trollop understood exactly why she had to die. No, surely an extended term of excruciating torture would restore the world to proper balance. Yet I wanted the witch dead. But then I would be ordering these barnies to kill her. "At the moment I cannot make that decision," I said. Irresistibly, my eyes found the bottom drawer containing the files of obscene photographs. "I'll let you know my decision after we have begun."

Mr. Cuff dropped his hand, and Mr. Clubb nodded with exaggerated, perhaps ironic slowness. "And what of your rival, the seducer, sir? Do we have any wishes in regard to that gentleman, sir?"

The way these fellows could sharpen one's thinking was truly remarkable. "I most certainly do," I said. "What she gets, he gets. Fair is fair."

"Indeed, sir," said Mr. Clubb, "and, if you will permit me, sir, only fair is fair. And fairness demands that before we go any deeper into the particulars of the case we must examine the evidence as presented to yourself, and when I speak of fairness, sir, I refer to fairness particularly to yourself, for only the evidence seen by your own eyes can permit us to view this matter through them."

Again, I looked helplessly down at the bottom drawer. "That will not be necessary. You will find my wife at our country estate, Green..."

My voice trailed off as Mr. Cuff's hand ground into my shoulder while he bent down and opened the drawer.

"Begging to differ," said Mr. Clubb, "but we are now and again in a better position than the client to determine what is necessary. Remember, sir, that while shame unshared is toxic to the soul, shame shared is the beginning of health. Besides, it only hurts for a little while."

Mr. Cuff drew the files from the drawer.

"My partner will concur that your inmost wish is that we examine the evidence," said Mr. Clubb. "Else you would not have signalled its location. We would prefer to have your explicit command to do so, but in the absence of explicit, implicit serves just about as well."

I gave an impatient, ambiguous wave of the hand, a gesture they cheerfully misunderstood.

"Then all is... how do you put it, sir? 'All is...'"

"All is in order, all is in train," I muttered.

"Just so. We have ever found it beneficial to establish a common language with our clients, in order to conduct ourselves within terms enhanced by their constant usage in the dialogue between us." He took the files from Mr. Cuff's hands. "We shall examine the contents of these folders at the table across the room. After the examination has been completed, my partner and I shall deliberate. And then, sir, we shall return for further instructions."

They strolled across the office and took adjoining chairs on the near side of the table, presenting me with two identical wide, black-clothed backs. Their hats went to either side, the files between them. Attempting unsuccessfully to look away, I lifted my receiver and asked my secretary who, if anyone, had called in the interim and what appointments had been made for the morning.

Mr. Clubb opened a folder and leaned forward to inspect the topmost photograph.

My secretary informed me that Marguerite had telephoned from the road with an inquiry concerning my health. Mr. Clubb's back and shoulders trembled with what I assumed was the shock of disgust. One of the scions was due at 2:00 p.m., and at four a cryptic gentleman would arrive. By their works shall ye know them, and Mrs. Rampage proved herself a diligent soul by asking if I wished her to place a call to Green Chimneys at three o'clock. Mr. Clubb thrust a photograph in front of Mr. Cuff. "I think not," I said. "Anything else?" She told me that Gilligan had expressed a desire to see me privately—meaning, without the Skipper—sometime during the morning. A murmur came from the table. "Gilligan can wait," I said, and the murmur, expressive, I had thought, of dismay and sympathy, rose in volume and revealed itself as amusement.

They were chuckling—even chortling!

I replaced the telephone and said, "Gentlemen, your laughter is insupportable." The potential effect of this remark was undone by its being lost within a surge of coarse laughter. I believe that something else was at that moment lost...some dimension of my soul...an element akin to pride...akin to dignity...but whether the loss was for good or ill, then I could not say. For some time, in fact an impossibly lengthy time, they found cause for laughter in the wretched photographs. My occasional attempts to silence them went unheard as they passed the dread images back and forth, discarding some instantly and to others returning for a second, a third, even a fourth and fifth perusal.

At last the barnies reared back, uttered a few nostalgic chirrups of laughter, and returned the photographs to the folders. They were still twitching with remembered laughter, still flicking happy tears from their eyes, as they sauntered, grinning, back across the office and tossed the files onto my desk. "Ah me, sir, a delightful experience," said Mr. Clubb. "Nature in all her lusty romantic splendour, one might say. Remarkably stimulating, I could add. Correct, sir?"

"I hadn't expected you fellows to be stimulated to mirth," I grumbled, ramming the foul things into the drawer and out of view.

"Laughter is merely a portion of the stimulation to which I refer," he said. "Unless my sense of smell has led me astray, a thing I fancy it has yet to do, you could not but feel another sort of arousal altogether before these pictures, am I right?"

I refused to respond to this sally but felt the blood rising to my cheeks. Here they were again, the slugs and maggots.

"We are all brothers under the skin," said Mr. Clubb. "Remember my words. Shame unshared poisons the soul. And besides, it only hurts for a little while."

Now I could not respond. What was the "it" that hurt only for a little while—the pain of cuckoldry, the mystery of my shameful response to the photographs, or the horror of the barnies knowing what I had done?

"You will find it helpful, sir, to repeat after me: It only hurts for a little while."

"It only hurts for a little while," I said, and the naïve phrase reminded me that they were only barnies after all.

"Spoken like a child," Mr. Clubb most annoyingly said, "in, as it were, the tones and accents of purest innocence," and then righted matters by asking where Marguerite might be found. Had I not mentioned a country place named Green...?

"Green Chimneys," I said, shaking off the unpleasant impression that the preceding few seconds had made upon me. "You will find it at the end of—Lane, turning right off—Street just north of the town of— The four green chimneys easily visible above the hedge along—Lane are your landmark, though as it is the only building in sight you can hardly mistake it for another. My wife left our place in the city just after ten this morning, so she should be getting there..." I looked at my watch. "...in thirty to forty-five minutes. She will unlock the front gate, but she will not re-lock it once she has passed through, for she never does. The woman does not have the self-preservation of a sparrow. Once she has entered the estate, she will travel up the drive and open the door of the garage with an electronic device. This door, I assure you, will remain open, and the door she will take into the house will not be locked."

"But there are maids and cooks and laundresses and bootboys and suchlike to consider," said Mr. Cuff. "Plus a majordomo to conduct the entire orchestra and go around rattling the doors to make sure they're locked. Unless all of these parties are to be absent on account of the annual holiday."

"My servants have the month off," I said.

"A most suggestive consideration," said Mr. Clubb. "You possess a devilish clever mind, sir."

"Perhaps," I said, grateful for the restoration of the proper balance. "Marguerite will have stopped along the way for groceries and other essentials, so she will first carry the bags into the kitchen, which is the first room to the right off the corridor from the garage. Then I suppose she will take the staircase upstairs and air out her bedroom." I took pen and paper from my topmost drawer and sketched the layout of the house. "She may go around to the library, the morning room, and the drawing room, opening the shutters and a few windows. Somewhere during this process, she is likely to use the telephone. After that, she will leave the house by the rear entrance and take the path along the top of the bluff to a long, low building that looks like this."

I drew in the outlines of the studio in its nest of trees above the Hudson. "It is a recording studio I had built for her convenience. She may well plan to spend the entire afternoon inside it. You will know if she is there by the lights." I saw Marguerite smiling to herself as she fit her key into the lock on the studio door, saw her let herself in and reach for the light switch. A wave of emotion rendered me speechless.

Mr. Clubb rescued me by asking, "It is your feeling, sir, that when the lady stops to use the telephone she will be placing a call to that energetic gentleman?"

"Yes, of course," I said, only barely refraining from adding you dolt. "She will seize the earliest opportunity to inform him of their good fortune."

He nodded with an extravagant caution I recognised from my own dealings with backward clients. "Let us pause to see all 'round the matter, sir. Would the lady wish to leave a suspicious entry in your telephone records? Isn't it more likely that the person she telephones will be you, sir? The call to the athletic gentleman will already have been placed, according to my way of seeing things, either from the roadside or the telephone in the grocery where you have her stop to pick up her essentials."

Though disliking these references to Leeson's physical condition, I admitted that he might have a point.

"In that case, sir, and I know that a mind as quick as yours has already overtaken mine, you would want to express yourself with the utmost cordiality when the missus calls again, so as not to tip your hand in even the slightest way. But that, I'm sure, goes without saying, after all you have been through, sir."

Without bothering to acknowledge this, I said, "Shouldn't you fellows be leaving? No sense in wasting time, after all."

"Precisely why we shall wait here until the end of the day," said Mr. Clubb. "In cases of this unhappy sort, we find it more effective to deal with both parties at once, acting in concert when they are in prime condition to be taken by surprise. The gentleman is liable to leave his place of work at the end of the day, which implies to me that he is unlikely to appear at your lovely country place at any time before seven this evening or, which is more likely, eight. At this time of the year, there is still enough light at nine o'clock to enable us to conceal our vehicle on the grounds, enter the house, and begin our business. At eleven o'clock, sir, we shall call with our initial report and request additional instructions."

I asked the fellow if he meant to idle away the entire afternoon in my office while I conducted my business.

"Mr. Cuff and I are never idle, sir. While you conduct your business, we will be doing the same, laying out our plans, refining our strategies, choosing our methods and the order of their use."

"Oh, all right," I said, "but I trust you'll be quiet about it."

At that moment, Mrs. Rampage buzzed to say that Gilligan was before her, requesting to see me immediately, proof that bush telegraph is a more efficient means of spreading information than any newspaper. I told her to send him in, and a second later Morning Gilligan, pale of face, dark hair tousled but not as yet completely wild, came treading softly towards my desk. He pretended to be surprised that I had visitors and pantomimed an apology which incorporated the suggestion that he depart and return later. "No, no," I said, "I am delighted to see you, for this gives me the opportunity to introduce you to our new consultants, who will be working closely with me for a time." Gilligan swallowed, glanced at me with the deepest suspicion, and extended his hand as I made the introductions. "I regret that I am unfamiliar with your work, gentlemen," he said. "Might I ask the name of your firm? Is it Locust, Bleaney, Burns or Charter, Carter, Maxton, and Coltrane?"

By naming the two most prominent consultancies in our industry, Gilligan was assessing the thinness of the ice beneath his feet: LBB specialised in investments, CCM&C in estates and trusts. If my visitors worked for the former, he would suspect that a guillotine hung above his neck; if the latter, the Skipper was liable for the chop. "Neither," I said. "Mr. Clubb and Mr. Cuff are the directors of their own concern, which covers every aspect of the trade with such tactful professionalism that it is known to but the few for whom they will consent to work."

"Excellent," Gilligan whispered, gazing in some puzzlement at the map and floor plan atop my desk. "Tip-top."

"When their findings are given to me, they shall be given to all. In the meantime, I would prefer that you say as little as possible about the matter. Though change is a law of life, we wish to avoid unnecessary alarm."

"You know that you can depend on my silence," said Morning Gilligan, and it was true, I did know that. I also knew that his alter ego, Afternoon Gilligan, would babble the news to everyone who had not already heard it from Mrs. Rampage. By 6:00 p.m., our entire industry would be pondering the information that I had called in a consultancy team of such rarefied accomplishments that they chose to remain unknown but to the very few. None of my colleagues could dare admit to an ignorance of Clubb & Cuff, and my reputation, already great, would increase exponentially.

To distract him from the floor plan of Green Chimneys and the rough map of my estate, I said, "I assume some business brought you here, Gilligan."

"Oh! Yes—yes—of course," he said, and with a trace of embarrassment brought to my attention the pretext for his being there, the ominous plunge in value of an overseas fund in which we had advised one of his musicians to invest. Should we recommend selling the fund before more money was lost, or was it wisest to hold on? Only a minute was required to decide that the musician should retain his share of the fund until next quarter, when we anticipated a general improvement, but both Gilligan and I were aware that this recommendation call could easily have been handled by telephone. Soon he was moving towards the door, smiling at the barnies in a pathetic display of false confidence.

The telephone rang a moment after the detectives had returned to the table.

Mr. Clubb said, "Your wife, sir. Remember: the utmost cordiality." Here was false confidence, I thought, of an entirely different sort. I picked up the receiver to hear Mrs. Rampage tell me that my wife was on the line.

What followed was a banal conversation of the utmost duplicity. Marguerite pretended that my sudden departure from the dinner table and my late arrival at the office had caused her to fear for my health. I pretended that all was well, apart from a slight indigestion. Had the drive up been peaceful? Yes. How was the house? A little musty, but otherwise fine. She had never quite realised, she said, how very large Green Chimneys was until she walked around in it, knowing she was going to be there alone. Had she been out to the studio? No, but she was looking forward to getting a lot of work done over the next three or four days and thought she would be working every night, as well. (Implicit in this remark was the information that I should be unable to reach her, the studio being without a telephone.) After a moment of awkward silence, she said, "I suppose it is too early for you to have identified your traitor." It was, I said, but the process would begin that evening. "I'm so sorry you have to go through this," she said. "I know how painful the discovery was for you, and I can only begin to imagine how angry you must be, but I hope you will be merciful. No amount of punishment can undo the damage, and if you try to exact retribution you will only injure yourself. The man is going to lose his job and his reputation. Isn't that punishment enough?" After a few meaningless pleasantries the conversation had clearly come to an end, although we still had yet to say good-bye. Then an odd thing happened to me. I nearly said, Lock all the doors and windows tonight and let no one in. I nearly said, You are in grave danger and must come home. With these words rising in my throat, I looked across the room at Mr. Clubb and Mr. Cuff. Mr. Clubb winked at me. I heard myself bidding Marguerite farewell, and then heard her hang up her telephone.

"Well done, sir," said Mr. Clubb. "To aid Mr. Cuff and myself in the preparation of our inventory, can you tell us if you keep certain staples at Green Chimneys?"

"Staples?" I said, thinking he was referring to foodstuffs.

"Rope?" he asked. "Tools, especially pliers, hammers, and screwdrivers? A good saw? A variety of knives? Are there by any chance firearms?"

"No firearms," I said. "I believe all the other items you mention can be found in the house."

"Rope and tool chest in the basement, knives in the kitchen?"

"Yes," I said, "precisely." I had not ordered these barnies to murder my wife, I reminded myself; I had drawn back from that precipice. By the time I went into the executive dining room for my luncheon, I felt sufficiently restored to give Charlie-Charlie that ancient symbol of approval, the thumbs-up sign.

III

When I returned to my office the screen had been set in place, shielding from view the detectives in their preparations but in no way muffling the rumble of comments and laughter they brought to the task. "Gentlemen," I said in a voice loud enough to be heard behind the screen—a most unsuitable affair decorated with a pattern of ocean liners, martini glasses, champagne bottles, and cigarettes—"you must modulate your voices, as I have business to conduct here as well as you." There came a somewhat softer rumble of acquiescence. I took my seat to discover my bottom desk drawer pulled out, the folders absent. Another roar of laughter jerked me once again to my feet.

I came around the side of the screen and stopped short. The table lay concealed beneath drifts and mounds of yellow legal paper covered with lists of words and drawings of stick figures in varying stages of dismemberment. Strewn through the yellow pages were the photographs, loosely divided into those in which either Marguerite or Graham Leeson provided the principal focus. Crude genitalia had been drawn, without reference to either party's actual gender, over and atop both of them. Aghast, I began gathering up the defaced photographs. "I must insist . . ." I said. "I really must insist, you know . . ."

Mr. Clubb immobilised my wrist with one hand and extracted the photographs with the other. "We prefer to work in our time-honoured fashion," he said. "Our methods may be unusual, but they are ours. But before you take up the afternoon's occupations, sir, can you tell us if items on the handcuff order might be found in the house?"

"No," I said. Mr. Cuff pulled a yellow page before him and wrote handcuffs. "Chains?" asked Mr. Clubb.

"No chains," I said, and Mr. Cuff added chains to his list. "That is all for the moment," said Mr. Clubb, and released me.

I took a step backward and massaged my wrist, which stung as if from rope burn. "You speak of your methods," I said, "and I understand that you have them. But what can be the purpose of defacing my photographs in this grotesque fashion?"

"Sir," said Mr. Clubb in a stern, teacherly voice, "where you speak of defacing, we use the term enhancement. Enhancement is a tool we find vital to the method known by the name of Visualisation."

I retired defeated to my desk. At five minutes before two, Mrs. Rampage informed me that the Skipper and our scion, a thirty-year-old inheritor of a great family fortune named Mr. Chester Montfort de M—, awaited my pleasure. Putting Mrs. Rampage on hold, I called out, "Please do give me absolute quiet, now. A client is on his way in."

First to appear was the Skipper, his tall, rotund form as alert as a pointer's in a grouse field as he led in the taller, inexpressibly languid figure of Mr. Chester Montfort de M—, a person marked in every inch of his being by great ease, humour, and stupidity. The Skipper froze to gape horrified at the screen, but Montfort de M—continued around him to shake my hand and say, "Have to tell you, I like that thingamabob over there immensely. Reminds me of a similar thingamabob at the Beeswax Club a few years ago, whole flocks of girls used to come tumbling out. Don't suppose we're in for any unicycles and trumpets today, eh?"

The combination of the raffish screen and our client's unbridled memories brought a dangerous flush to the Skipper's face, and I hastened to explain the presence of top-level consultants who preferred to pitch tent on-site, as it were, hence the installation of a screen, all the above in the service of, well, service, an all-important quality we . . .

"By Kitchener's moustache," said the Skipper. "I remember the Beeswax Club. Don't suppose I'll ever forget the night Little Billy

Pegleg jumped up and..." The colour darkened on his cheeks, and he closed his mouth.

From behind the screen, I heard Mr. Clubb say, "Visualise this." Mr. Cuff chuckled. The Skipper recovered himself and turned his sternest glare up on me. "Superb idea, consultants. A white-glove inspection tightens up any ship." His veiled glance towards the screen indicated that he had known of the presence of our "consultants" but, unlike Gilligan, had restrained himself from thrusting into my office until given legitimate reason. "That being the case, is it still quite proper that these people remain while we discuss Mr. Montfort de M—'s confidential affairs?"

"Quite proper, I assure you," I said. "The consultants and I prefer to work in an atmosphere of complete co-operation. Indeed, this arrangement is a condition of their accepting our firm as their client."

"Indeed," said the Skipper.

"Top of the tree, are they?" said Mr. Montfort de M—. "Expect no less of you fellows. Fearful competence. Terrifying competence."

Mr. Cuff's voice could be heard saying, "Okay, visualise this." Mr. Clubb uttered a high-pitched giggle.

"Enjoy their work," said Mr. Montfort de M—.

"Shall we?" I gestured to their chairs. As a young man whose assets equalled two to three billion dollars (depending on the condition of the stock market, the value of real estate in half-a-dozen cities around the world, global warming, forest fires, and the like), our client was as catnip to the ladies, three of whom he had previously married and divorced after siring a child upon each, resulting in a great interlocking complexity of trusts, agreements, and contracts, all of which had to be re-examined on the occasion of his forthcoming wedding to a fourth young woman, named like her predecessors after a semiprecious stone. Due to the perspicacity of the Skipper and myself, each new nuptial altered the terms of those previous so as to maintain our client's liability at an unvarying level. Our computers had enabled us to generate the documents well before his arrival, and all Mr. Montfort de M—had to do was listen to the revised terms and sign the papers, a task that generally induced a slumberous state except for those moments when a prized asset was in transition.

"Hold on, boys," he said ten minutes into our explanations, "you mean Opal has to give the racehorses to Garnet, and in return she gets the teak plantation from Turquoise, who gets Garnet's ski resort in Aspen? Opal is crazy about those horses."

I explained that his second wife could easily afford the purchase of a new stable with the income from the plantation. He bent to the task of scratching his signature on the form. A roar of laughter erupted behind the screen. The Skipper glanced sideways in displeasure, and our client looked at me blinking. "Now to the secondary trusts," I said. "As you will recall, three years ago—"

My words were cut short by the appearance of a chuckling Mr. Clubb clamping an unlighted cigar in his mouth, a legal pad in his hand, as he came towards us. The Skipper and Mr. Montfort de M— goggled at him, and Mr. Clubb nodded. "Begging your pardon, sir, but some queries cannot wait. Pickaxe, sir? Dental floss? Awl?"

"No, yes, no," I said, and then introduced him to the other two men. The Skipper appeared stunned, Mr. Montfort de M—cheerfully puzzled.

"We would prefer the existence of an attic," said Mr. Clubb.

"An attic exists," I said.

"I must admit my confusion," said the Skipper. "Why is a consultant asking about awls and attics? What is dental floss to a consultant?"

"For the nonce, Skipper," I said, "these gentlemen and I must communicate in a form of cipher or code, of which these are examples, but soon—"

"Plug your blowhole, Skipper," broke in Mr. Clubb. "At the moment you are as useful as wind in an outhouse, always hoping you will excuse my simple way of expressing myself."

Spluttering, the Skipper rose to his feet, his face rosier by far than during his involuntary reminiscence of what Little Billy Pegleg had done one night at the Beeswax Club.

"Steady on," I said, fearful of the heights of choler to which indignation could bring my portly, white-haired, but still powerful junior.

"Not on your life," bellowed the Skipper. "I cannot brook...cannot tolerate...If this ill-mannered dwarf imagines excuse is possible after..." He raised a fist. Mr. Clubb said, "Pish tosh," and placed a hand on the nape of the Skipper's neck. Instantly, the Skipper's eyes rolled up, the colour drained from his face, and he dropped like a sack into his chair.

"Hole in one," marvelled Mr. Montfort de M—. "Old boy isn't dead, is he?" The Skipper exhaled uncertainly and licked his lips.

"With my apologies for the unpleasantness," said Mr. Clubb, "I have only two more queries at this juncture. Might we locate bedding in the aforesaid attic, and have you an implement such as a match or a lighter?"

"There are several old mattresses and bed frames in the attic," I said, "but as to matches, surely you do not..."

Understanding the request better than I, Mr. Montfort de M— extended a golden lighter and applied an inch of flame to the tip of Mr. Clubb's cigar. "Didn't think that part was code," he said. "Rules have changed? Smoking allowed?"

"From time to time during the workday my colleague and I prefer to smoke," said Mr. Clubb, expelling a reeking miasma across the desk. I had always found tobacco nauseating in its every form, and in all parts of our building smoking had, of course, long been prohibited.

"Three cheers, my man, plus three more after that," said Mr. Montfort de M—, extracting a ridged case from an inside pocket, an absurdly phallic cigar from the case. "I prefer to smoke, too, you know, especially during these deadly conferences about who gets the pincushions and who gets the snuffboxes." He submitted the object to a circumcision, snick-snick, and to my horror set it alight. "Ashtray?" I dumped paper clips from a crystal oyster shell and slid it towards him. "Mr. Clubb, is it? Mr. Clubb, you are a fellow of wonderful accomplishments, still can't get over that marvellous whopbopaloobop on the Skipper, and I'd like to ask if we could get together some evening, cigars and cognac kind of thing."

"We prefer to undertake one matter at a time," said Mr. Clubb. Mr. Cuff appeared beside the screen. He, too, was lighting up eight or nine inches of brown rope. "However, we welcome your appreciation and would be delighted to swap tales of derring-do at a later date."

"Very, very cool," said Mr. Montfort de M—, "especially if you could teach me how to do the whopbopaloobop."

"This is a world full of hidden knowledge," Mr. Clubb said. "My partner and I have chosen as our sacred task the transmission of that knowledge."

"Amen," said Mr. Cuff.

Mr. Clubb bowed to my awed client and sauntered off. The Skipper shook himself, rubbed his eyes, and took in the client's cigar. "My goodness," he said. "I believe . . . I can't imagine . . . heavens, is smoking permitted again? What a blessing." With that, he fumbled a cigarette from his shirt pocket, accepted a light from Mr. Montfort de M—, and sucked in the fumes. Until that moment I had not known that the Skipper was an addict of nicotine.

For the remainder of the hour a coiling layer of smoke like a low-lying cloud established itself beneath the ceiling and increased in density as it grew towards the floor while we extracted Mr. Montfort de M—'s careless signature on the transfers and assignments. Now and again the Skipper displaced one of a perpetual chain of cigarettes from his mouth to remark upon the peculiar pain in his neck. Finally I was able to send client and junior partner on their way with those words of final benediction, "All is in order, all is in train", freeing me at last to stride about my office flapping a copy of Institutional Investor at the cloud, a remedy our fixed windows made more symbolic than actual. The barnies further defeated the effort by wafting ceaseless billows of cigar effluvia over the screen, but as they seemed to be conducting their business in a conventionally businesslike manner I made no objection and retired in defeat to my desk for the preparations necessitated by the arrival in an hour of my next client, Mr. Arthur "This Building is Condemned" C—, the most cryptic of all the cryptic gentlemen.

So deeply was I immersed in these preparations that only a polite cough and the supplication of "Begging your pardon, sir" brought to my awareness the presence of Mr. Clubb and Mr. Cuff before my desk. "What is it now?" I asked.

"We are, sir, in need of creature comforts," said Mr. Clubb. "Long hours of work have left us exceeding dry in the region of the mouth and throat, and the pressing sensation of thirst has made it impossible for us to maintain the concentration required to do our best."

"Meaning a drink would be greatly appreciated, sir," said Mr. Cuff.

"Of course, of course," I said. "I'll have Mrs. Rampage bring in a couple of bottles of water. We have San Pellegrino and Evian. Which would you prefer?"

With a smile almost menacing in its intensity, Mr. Cuff said, "We prefer drinks when we drink. Drink drinks, if you take my meaning."

"For the sake of the refreshment found in them," said Mr. Clubb, ignoring my obvious dismay. "I speak of refreshment in its every aspect, from relief to the parched tongue, taste to the ready palate, warmth to the inner man, and to the highest of refreshments, that of the mind and soul. We prefer bottles of gin and bourbon, and while any decent gargle would be gratefully received, we have, like all men who partake of grape and grain, our favourite tipples. Mr. Cuff is partial to J.W. Dant bourbon, and I enjoy a drop of Bombay gin. A bucket of ice would not go amiss, and I could say the same for a case of ice-cold Old Bohemia beer. As a chaser."

"You consider it a good idea to consume alcohol before embarking on . . . " I sought for the correct phrase. "A mission so delicate?"

"We consider it an essential prelude. Alcohol inspires the mind and awakens the imagination. A fool dulls both by overindulgence, but up to that point, which is a highly individual matter, there is only enhancement. Through history, alcohol has been known for its sacred properties, and the both of us know that during the sacrament of Holy Communion, priests and reverends happily serve as bartenders, passing out free drinks to all comers, children included."

"Besides that," I said after a pause, "I suppose you would prefer not to be compelled to quit my employment after we have made such strides together."

"We are on a great journey," he said.

I placed the order with Mrs. Rampage, and fifteen minutes later into my domain entered two ill-dressed youths laden with the requested liquors and a metal bucket, in which the necks of beer bottles protruded from a bed of ice. I tipped the louts a dollar apiece, which they accepted with a boorish lack of grace. Mrs. Rampage took in this activity with none of the revulsion for the polluted air and spirituous liquids I had anticipated.

The louts slouched away; the chuckling barnies disappeared from view with their refreshments; and, after fixing me for a moment of silence, her eyes alight with an expression I had never before observed in them, Mrs. Rampage ventured the amazing opinion that the recent relaxation of formalities should prove beneficial to the firm as a whole and added that, were Mr. Clubb and Mr. Cuff responsible for the reformation, they had already justified their reputation and would assuredly enhance my own.

"You believe so," I said, noting with momentarily delayed satisfaction that the effects of Afternoon Gilligan's indiscretions had already begun to declare themselves. Employing the tactful verbal formula for I wish to speak exactly half my mind and no more, Mrs. Rampage said, "May I be frank, sir?"

"I depend on you to do no less," I said.

Her carriage and face became what I can only describe as girlish—years seemed to drop away from her. "I don't want to say too much, sir, and I hope you know how much everyone understands what a privilege it is to be a part of this firm." Like the Skipper but more attractively, she blushed. "Honest, I really mean that. Everybody knows that we're one of the two or three companies best at what we do."

"Thank you," I said.

"That's why I feel I can talk like this," said my ever-less-recognisable Mrs. Rampage. "Until today, everybody thought if they acted like themselves, the way they really were, you'd fire them right away. Because, and maybe I shouldn't say this, maybe I'm way out of line, sir, but it's because you always seem, well, so proper you could never forgive a person for not being as dignified as you are. Like the Skipper is a heavy smoker and everybody knows it's not supposed to be permitted in this building, but a lot of companies here let their top people smoke in their offices as long as they're discreet because it shows they appreciate those people, and that's nice because it shows that if you get to the top you can be appreciated, too, but here the Skipper has to go all the way to the elevator and stand outside with the file clerks if he wants a cigarette. And in every other company I know the partners and important clients sometimes have a drink together and nobody thinks they're committing a terrible sin. You're a religious man, sir, we look up to you so much, but I think you're going to find that people will respect you even more once it gets out that you've loosened the rules a little bit." She gave me a look in which I read that she feared having spoken too freely. "I just wanted to say that I think you're doing the right thing, sir."

What she was saying, of course, was that I was widely regarded as pompous, remote, and out of touch. "I had not known that my employees regarded me as a religious man," I said.

"Oh, we all do," she said with almost touching earnestness. "Because of the hymns."

"The hymns?"

"The ones you hum to yourself when you're working."

"Do I, indeed? Which ones?"

"'Jesus Loves Me', 'The Old Rugged Cross', 'Abide with Me', and 'Amazing Grace', mostly. Sometimes 'Onward, Christian Soldiers.'"

Here, with a vengeance, were Temple Square and Scripture Street! Here was the Youth Bible Study Centre, where the child-me had hours on end sung these same hymns during our Sunday school sessions! I did not know what to make of the knowledge that I hummed them to myself at my desk, but it was some consolation that this unconscious habit had at least partially humanised me to my staff.

"You didn't know you did that? Oh, sir, that's so cute!"

Sounds of merriment from the far side of the office rescued Mrs. Rampage from the fear that this time she had truly overstepped the bounds, and she made a rapid exit. I stared after her for a moment, at first unsure how deeply I ought to regret a situation in which my secretary found it possible to describe myself and my habits as cute, then resolved that it probably was, or eventually would be, for the best. "All is in order, all is in train," I said to myself. "It only hurts for a little while." With that, I took my seat once more to continue delving into the elaborations of Mr. "This Building is Condemned" C—'s financial life.

Another clink of bottle against glass and ripple of laughter brought with them the recognition that this particular client would never consent to the presence of unknown "consultants". Unless the barnies could be removed for at least an hour, I should face the immediate loss of a substantial portion of my business.

"Fellows," I cried, "come up here now. We must address a serious problem." Glasses in hand, cigars nestled into the corners of their mouths, Mr. Clubb and Mr. Cuff sauntered into view. Once I had explained the issue in the most general terms, the detectives readily agreed to absent themselves for the required period. Where might they install themselves? "My bathroom," I said. "It has a small library attached, with a desk, a worktable, leather chairs and sofa, a billiard table, a large-screen cable television set, and a bar. Since you have not yet had your luncheon, you may wish to order whatever you like from the kitchen."

Five minutes later, bottles, glasses, hats, and mounds of paper arranged on the bathroom table, the bucket of beer beside it, I exited through the concealed door as Mr. Clubb ordered up from my doubtless astounded chef a meal of chicken wings, french fries, onion rings, and T-bone steaks, medium well. With plenty of time to spare, I immersed myself again in details, only to be brought up short by the recognition that I was humming, none too quietly, that most innocent of hymns, 'Jesus Loves Me'. Then, precisely at the appointed hour, Mrs. Rampage informed me of the arrival of my client and his associates, and I bade her bring them through.

A sly, slow-moving whale encased in an exquisite double-breasted black pinstripe, Mr. "This Building is Condemned" C—advanced into my office with his customary hauteur and offered me the customary nod of the head while his three "associates" formed a human breakwater in the centre of the room. Regal to the core, he affected not to notice Mrs. Rampage sliding a black leather chair out of the middle distance and around the side of the desk until it was in position, at which point he sat himself in it without looking down. Then he inclined his slab-like head and raised a small, pallid hand. One of the "associates" promptly moved to hold the door for Mrs. Rampage's departure. At this signal, I sat down, and the two remaining henchmen separated themselves by a distance of perhaps eight feet. The third closed the door and stationed himself by his general's right shoulder. These formalities completed, my client shifted his close-set obsidian eyes to mine and said, "You well?"

"Very well, thank you," I replied, according to ancient formula. "And you?"

"Good," he said. "But things could be better." This, too, followed long-established formula. His next words were a startling deviation. He took in the stationary cloud and the corpse of Montfort de M—'s cigar rising like a monolith from the reef of cigarette butts in the crystal shell and, with the first genuine smile I had ever seen on his pockmarked, small-featured face, said, "I can't believe it, but one thing just got better already. You eased up on the stupid no-smoking rule which is poisoning this city; good for you."

"It seemed," I said, "a concrete way in which to demonstrate our appreciation for the smokers among those clients we most respect." When dealing with the cryptic gentlemen, one must not fail to offer intervallic allusions to the spontaneous respect in which they are held.

"Deacon," he said, employing the sobriquet he had given me on our first meeting, "you being one of a kind at your job, the respect you speak of is mutual, and besides that, all surprises should be as pleasant as this here." With that, he snapped his fingers at the laden shell, and as he produced a ridged case similar to but more capacious than Mr. Montfort de M—'s, the man at his shoulder whisked the impromptu ashtray from the desk, deposited its contents in the poubelle, and repositioned it at a point on the desk precisely equidistant from us. My client opened the case to expose the six cylinders contained within, removed one, and proffered the remaining five to me. "Be my guest, Deacon," he said. "Money can't buy better Havanas."

"Your gesture is much appreciated," I said. "However, with all due respect, at the moment I shall choose not to partake."

Distinct as a scar, a vertical crease of displeasure appeared on my client's forehead, and the ridged case and its five inhabitants advanced an inch towards my nose. "Deacon, you want me to smoke alone?" asked Mr. "This Building is Condemned" C—. "This stuff, if you were ever lucky enough to find it at your local cigar store, which that lucky believe me you wouldn't be, is the best of the best, straight from me to you as what you could term a symbol of the co-operation and respect between us, and at the commencement of our business today it would please me greatly if you would do me the honour of joining me in a smoke."

As they say or, more accurately, as they used to say, needs must when the devil drives, or words to that effect. "Forgive me," I said, and drew one of the fecal things from the case. "I assure you, the honour is all mine."

Mr. "This Building is Condemned" C—snipped the rounded end from his cigar, plugged the remainder in the centre of his mouth, then subjected mine to the same operation. His henchman proffered a lighter, and Mr. "This Building is Condemned" C—bent forward and surrounded himself with clouds of smoke, in the manner of Bela Lugosi materialising before the brides of Dracula. The henchmen moved the flame towards me, and for the first time in my life I inserted into my mouth an object that seemed as large around as the handle of a baseball bat, brought it to the dancing flame, and drew in that burning smoke from which so many other men before me had derived pleasure.

Legend and common sense alike dictated that I should sputter and cough in an attempt to rid myself of the noxious substance. Nausea was in the cards, also dizziness. It is true that I suffered a degree of initial discomfort, as if my tongue had been lightly singed or seared, and the sheer unfamiliarity of the experience—the thickness of the tobacco tube, the texture of the smoke, as dense as chocolate—led me to fear for my well-being. Yet, despite the not altogether unpleasant tingling on the upper surface of my tongue, I expelled my first mouthful of cigar smoke with the sense of having sampled a taste every bit as delightful as the first sip of a properly made martini. The thug whisked away the flame, and I drew in another mouthful, leaned back, and released a wondrous quantity of smoke. Of a surprising smoothness, in some sense almost cool rather than hot, the delightful taste defined itself as heather, loam, morel mushrooms, venison, and some distinctive spice akin to coriander. I repeated the process, with results even more pleasurable—this time I tasted a hint of black butter sauce. "I can truthfully say," I told my client, "that never have I met a cigar as fine as this one."

"You bet you haven't," said Mr. "This Building is Condemned" C—, and on the spot presented me with three more of the precious objects. With that, we turned to the tidal waves of cash and the interlocking corporate shells, each protecting another series of interconnected shells that concealed yet another, like Chinese boxes.

The cryptic gentlemen one and all appreciated certain ceremonies, such as the appearance of espresso coffee in thimble-sized porcelain cups and an accompanying assortment of biscotti at the halfway point of our meditations. Matters of business being forbidden while coffee and cookies were dispatched, the conversation generally turned to the conundrums posed by family life. Since I had no family to speak of, and, like most of his kind, Mr. "This Building is Condemned" C— was richly endowed with grandparents, parents, uncles, aunts, sons, daughters, nephews, nieces, and grandchildren, these remarks on the genealogical tapestry tended to be monologic in nature, my role in them limited to nods and grunts. Required as they were more often by the business of the cryptic gentlemen than was the case in other trades or professions, funerals were also an ongoing topic. Taking tiny sips of his espresso and equally maidenish nibbles from his favourite sweetmeats (Hydrox and Milano), my client favoured me with the expected praises of his son, Arthur Jr. (Harvard graduate school, English lit.), lamentations over his daughter, Fidelia (thrice married, never wisely), hymns to his grandchildren (Cyrus, Thor, and Hermione, respectively the genius, the dreamer, and the despot), and then proceeded to link his two unfailing themes by recalling the unhappy behaviour of Arthur Jr. at the funeral of my client's uncle and a principal figure in his family's rise to an imperial eminence, Mr. Vincente "Waffles" C—. The anecdote called for the beheading and ignition of another magnificent stogie, and I greedily followed suit.

"Arthur Jr.'s got his head screwed on right, and he's got the right kinda family values," said my client. "Straight A's all through school, married a stand-up dame with money of her own, three great kids, makes a man proud. Hard worker. Got his head in a book morning to night, human-encyclopaedia-type guy, up there at Harvard, those professors, they love him. Kid knows how you're supposed to act, right?"

I nodded and filled my mouth with another fragrant draft.

"So he comes to my uncle Vincente's funeral all by himself, which troubles me. On top of it doesn't show the proper respect to old Waffles, who was one hell of a man, there's guys still pissing blood on account of they looked at him wrong forty years ago, on top of that, I don't have the good feeling I get from taking his family around to my friends and associates and saying, So look here, this here is Arthur Jr., my Harvard guy, plus his wife, Hunter, whose ancestors I think got here even before that rabble on the Mayflower, plus his three kids— Cyrus, little bastard's even smarter than his dad, Thor, the one's got his head in the clouds, which is okay because we need people like that, too, and Hermione, who you can tell just by looking at her she's mean as a snake and is gonna wind up running the world someday. So I say, Arthur Jr., what the hell happened, everybody else get killed in a train wreck or something? He says, No, Dad, they just didn't wanna come, these big family funerals, they make 'em feel funny, they don't like having their pictures taken so they show up on the six o'clock news. Didn't wanna come, I say back, what kinda shit is that, you shoulda made 'em come, and if anyone took their pictures when they didn't want, we can take care of that, no trouble at all. I go on like this, I even say, What good is Harvard and all those books if they don't make you any smarter than this, and finally Arthur Jr.'s mother tells me, Put a cork in it, you're not exactly helping the situation here.

"So what happens then? Insteada being smart like I should, I go nuts on account of I'm the guy who pays the bills, that Harvard up there pulls in the money better than any casino I ever saw, and you wanna find a real good criminal, get some Boston WASP in a bow tie, and all of a sudden nobody listens to me! I'm seeing red in a big way here, Deacon, this is my uncle Vincente's funeral, and insteada backing me up his mother is telling me I'm not helping. I yell, You wanna help? Go up there and bring back his wife and kids, or I'll send Carlo and Tommy to do it. All of a sudden I'm so mad I'm thinking these people are insulting me, how can they think they can get away with that, people who insult me don't do it twice—and then I hear what I'm thinking, and I do what she said and put a cork in it, but it's too late, I went way over the top and we all know it.

"Arthur Jr. takes off, and his mother won't talk to me for the whole rest of the day. Only thing I'm happy about is I didn't blow up where anyone else could see it. Deacon, I know you're the type guy who wouldn't dream of threatening his family, but if the time ever comes, do yourself a favour and light up a Havana instead."

"I'm sure that is excellent advice," I said.

"Anyhow, you know what they say, it only hurts for a little while, which is true as far as it goes, and I calmed down. Uncle Vincente's funeral was beautiful. You woulda thought the Pope died. When the people are going out to the limousines, Arthur Jr. is sitting in a chair at the back of the church reading a book. Put that in your pocket, I say, wanna do homework, do it in the car. He tells me it isn't homework, but he puts it in his pocket and we go out to the cemetery. His mother looks out the window the whole time we're driving to the cemetery, and the kid starts reading again. So I ask what the hell is it, this book he can't put down? He tells me but it's like he's speaking some foreign language, only word I understand is 'the', which happens a lot when your kid reads a lot of fancy books, half the titles make no sense to an ordinary person. Okay, we're out there in Queens, goddamn graveyard the size of Newark, FBI and reporters all over the place, and I'm thinking maybe Arthur Jr. wasn't so wrong after all, Hunter probably hates having the FBI take her picture, and besides that little Hermione probably woulda mugged one of 'em and stole his wallet. So I tell Arthur Jr. I'm sorry about what happened. I didn't really think you were going to put me in the same grave as Uncle Waffles, he says, the Harvard smart-ass. When it's all over, we get back in the car, and out comes the book again. We get home, and he disappears. We have a lot of people over, food, wine, politicians, old-timers from Brooklyn, Chicago people, Detroit people, L.A. people, movie directors, cops, actors I never heard of, priests, bishops, the guy from the Cardinal. Everybody's asking me, Where's Arthur Jr.? I go upstairs to find out. He's in his old room, and he's still reading that book. I say, Arthur Jr., people are asking about you, I think it would be nice if you mingled with our guests. I'll be right down, he says, I just finished what I was reading. Here, take a look, you might enjoy it. He gives me the book and goes out of the room. So I'm wondering—what the hell is this, anyhow? I take it into the bedroom, toss it on the table. About ten-thirty, eleven, everybody's gone, kid's on the shuttle back to Boston, house is cleaned up, enough food in the refrigerator to feed the whole bunch all over again, I go up to bed. Arthur Jr.'s mother still isn't talking to me, so I get in and pick up the book. Herman Melville is the name of the guy who wrote it. The story the kid was reading is called 'Bartleby the Scrivener'. I decide I'll try it. What the hell, right? You're an educated guy, you ever read that story?"

"A long time ago," I said. "A bit . . . odd, isn't it?"

"Odd? That's the most terrible story I ever read in my whole life! This dud gets a job in a law office and decides he doesn't want to work. Does he get fired? He does not. This is a story? You hire a guy who won't do the job, what do you do, pamper the asshole? At the end, the dud ups and disappears and you find out he used to work in the dead-letter office. Is there a point here? The next day I call up Arthur Jr., say could he explain to me please what the hell that story is supposed to mean? Dad, he says, it means what it says. Deacon, I just about pulled the plug on Harvard right then and there. I never went to any college, but I do know that nothing means what it says, not on this planet."

This reflection was accurate when applied to the documents on my desk, for each had been encoded in a systematic fashion that rendered their literal contents deliberately misleading. Another code had informed both of my recent conversations with Marguerite. "Fiction is best left to real life," I said.

"Someone shoulda told that to Herman Melville," said Mr. Arthur "This Building is Condemned" C—.

Mrs. Rampage buzzed me to advise that I was running behind schedule and inquire about removing the coffee things. I invited her to gather up the debris. A door behind me opened, and I assumed that my secretary had responded to my request with an alacrity remarkable even in her. The first sign of my error was the behaviour of the three other men in the room, until this moment no more animated than marble statues. The thug at my client's side stepped forward to stand behind me, and his fellows moved to the front of my desk. "What the hell is this shit?" said the client, unable, because of the man in front of him, to see Mr. Clubb and Mr. Cuff. Holding a pad bearing one of his many lists, Mr. Clubb gazed in mild surprise at the giants flanking my desk and said, "I apologise for the intrusion, sir, but our understanding was that your appointment would be over in an hour, and by my simple way of reckoning you should be free to answer a query as to steam irons."

"What the hell is this shit?" said my client, repeating his original question with a slight tonal variation expressive of gathering dismay.

I attempted to salvage matters. "Please allow me to explain the interruption. I have employed these men as consultants, and as they prefer to work in my office, a condition I of course could not permit during our business meeting, I temporarily relocated them in my washroom, outfitted with a library adequate to their needs."

"Fit for a king, in my opinion," said Mr. Clubb.

At that moment the other door into my office, to the left of my desk, opened to admit Mrs. Rampage, and my client's guardians inserted their hands into their suit jackets and separated with the speed and precision of a dance team.

"Oh, my," said Mrs. Rampage. "Excuse me. Should I come back later?"

"Not on your life, my darling," said Mr. Clubb. "Temporary misunderstanding of the false-alarm sort. Please allow us to enjoy the delightful spectacle of your feminine charms."

Before my wondering eyes, Mrs. Rampage curtsied and hastened to my desk to gather up the wreckage.

I looked towards my client and observed a detail of striking peculiarity, that although his half-consumed cigar remained between his lips, four inches of cylindrical ash had deposited a grey smear on his necktie before coming to rest on the shelf of his belly. He was staring straight ahead with eyes grown to the size of quarters. His face had become the colour of raw piecrust.

Mr. Clubb said, "Respectful greetings, sir."

The client gargled and turned upon me a look of unvarnished horror.

Mr. Clubb said, "Apologies to all." Mrs. Rampage had already bolted. From unseen regions came the sound of a closing door.

Mr. "This Building is Condemned" C—blinked twice, bringing his eyes to something like their normal dimensions. With an uncertain hand but gently, as if it were a tiny but much-loved baby, he placed his cigar in the crystal shell. He cleared his throat; he looked at the ceiling. "Deacon," he said, gazing upwards. "Gotta run. My next appointment musta slipped my mind. What happens when you start to gab. I'll be in touch." He stood, dislodging the ashen cylinder to the carpet, and motioned his goons to the outer office.

IV

Of course at the earliest opportunity I interrogated my detectives about this turn of events, and while they moved their mountains of paper, bottles, buckets, glasses, hand-drawn maps, and other impedimenta back behind the screen, I continued the questioning. No, they averred, the gentleman at my desk was not a gentleman whom previously they had been privileged to look upon, acquaint themselves with, or encounter in any way whatsoever.

They had never been employed in any capacity by the gentleman. Mr. Clubb observed that the unknown gentleman had been wearing a conspicuously handsome and well-tailored suit.

"That is his custom," I said.

"And I believe he smokes, sir, a noble high order of cigar," said Mr. Clubb with a glance at my breast pocket. "Which would be the sort of item customarily beyond the dreams of honest labourers such as ourselves."

"I trust that you will permit me," I said with a sigh, "to offer you the pleasure of two of the same." No sooner had the offer been accepted, the barnies back behind their screen, than I buzzed Mrs. Rampage with the request to summon by instant delivery from the most distinguished cigar merchant in the city a box of his finest. "Good for you, boss!" whooped the new Mrs. Rampage.

I spent the remainder of the afternoon brooding upon the reaction of Mr. Arthur "This Building is Condemned" C—to my "consultants". I could not but imagine that his hasty departure boded ill for our relationship. I had seen terror on his face, and he knew that I knew what I had seen. An understanding of this sort is fatal to that nuance-play critical alike to high level churchmen and their outlaw counterparts, and I had to confront the possibility that my client's departure had been of a permanent nature. Where Mr. "This Building is Condemned" C—went, his colleagues of lesser rank, Mr. Tommy "I Believe in Rainbows" B—, Mr. Anthony "Moonlight Becomes You"

M—, Mr. Bobby "Total Eclipse" G—, and their fellow archbishops, cardinals, and papal nuncios would assuredly follow. Before the close of the day, I would send a comforting fax informing Mr. "This Building is Condemned" C—that the consultants had been summarily released from employment. I would be telling only a "white" or provisional untruth, for Mr. Clubb and Mr. Cuff's task would surely be completed long before my client's return. All was in order, all was in train, and as if to put the seal upon the matter, Mrs. Rampage buzzed to inquire if she might come through with the box of cigars. Speaking in a breathy timbre I had never before heard from anyone save Marguerite in the earliest, most blissful days of our marriage, Mrs. Rampage added that she had some surprises for me, too. "By this point," I said, "I expect no less." Mrs. Rampage giggled.

The surprises, in the event, were of a reassuring practicality. The good woman had wisely sought the advice of Mr. Montfort de M—, who, after recommending a suitably aristocratic cigar emporium and a favourite cigar, had purchased for me a rosewood humidor, a double-bladed cigar cutter, and a lighter of antique design. As soon as Mrs. Rampage had been instructed to compose a note of gratitude embellished in whatever fashion she saw fit, I arrayed all but one of the cigars in the humidor, decapitated that one, and set it alight. Beneath a faint touch of fruitiness like the aroma of a blossoming pear tree, I met in successive layers the tastes of black olives, aged Gouda cheese, pine needles, new leather, miso soup, either sorghum or brown sugar, burning peat, library paste, and myrtle leaves. The long finish intriguingly combined Bible paper and sunflower seeds. Mr. Montfort de M—had chosen well, though I regretted the absence of black butter sauce.

Feeling comradely, I strolled across my office towards the merriment emanating from the far side of the screen. A superior cigar should be complemented by a worthy liquor, and in the light of what was to transpire during the evening I considered a snifter of Mr. Clubb's Bombay gin not inappropriate. "Fellows," I said, tactfully announcing my presence, "are preparations nearly completed?"

"That, sir, they are," said one or the other of the pair.

"Welcome news," I said, and stepped around the screen. "But I must be assured—" It was as if the detritus of New York City's half-a-dozen filthiest living quarters had been scooped up, shaken, and dumped into my office. Heaps of ash, bottles, shoals of papers, books with stained covers and broken spines, battered furniture, broken glass, refuse I could not identify, refuse I could not even see, undulated from the base of the screen, around and over the table, heaping itself into landfill-like piles here and there, and washed against the plate-glass windows. A jagged, five-foot opening gaped in a smashed pane. Their derbies perched on their heads, islanded in their chairs, Mr. Clubb and Mr. Cuff leaned back, feet up on what must have been the table.

"You'll join us in a drink, sir," said Mr. Clubb, "by way of wishing us success and adding to the pleasure of that handsome smoke." He extended a stout leg and kicked rubble from a chair. I sat down. Mr. Clubb plucked an unclean glass from the morass and filled it with Dutch gin, or jenever, from one of the minaret-shaped stone flagons I had observed upon my infrequent layovers in Amsterdam, the Netherlands. Mrs. Rampage had been variously employed during the barnies' sequestration. Then I wondered if Mrs. Rampage might not have shown signs of intoxication during our last encounter.

"I thought you drank Bombay," I said.

"Variety is, as they say, life's condiment," said Mr. Clubb, and handed me the glass.

I said, "You have made yourselves quite at home."

"I thank you for your restraint," said Mr. Clubb. "In which sentiment my partner agrees, am I correct, Mr. Cuff?"

"Entirely," said Mr. Cuff. "But I wager you a C-note to a see-gar that a word or two of explanation is in order."

"How right that man is," said Mr. Clubb. "He has a genius for the truth I have never known to fail him. Sir, you enter our work space to come upon the slovenly, the careless, the unseemly, and your response, which we comprehend in every particular, is to recoil. My wish is that you take a moment to remember these two essentials: one, we have, as aforesaid, our methods, which are ours alone, and two, having appeared fresh on the scene, you see it worse than it is. By morning tomorrow, the cleaning staff shall have done its work."

"I suppose you have been Visualising." I quaffed jenever.

"Mr. Cuff and I," he said, "prefer to minimise the risk of accidents, surprises, and such by the method of rehearsing our, as you might say, performances. These poor sticks, sir, are easily replaced, but our work once under way demands completion and cannot be duplicated, redone, or undone."

I recalled the all-important guarantee. "I remember your words," I said, "and I must be assured that you remember mine. I did not request termination. During the course of the day my feelings on the matter have intensified. Termination, if by that term you meant—"

"Termination is termination," said Mr. Clubb.

"Extermination," I said. "Cessation of life due to external forces. It is not my wish, it is unacceptable, and I have even been thinking that I overstated the degree of physical punishment appropriate in this matter."

"'Appropriate'?" said Mr. Clubb. "When it comes to desire, 'appropriate' is a concept without meaning. In the sacred realm of desire, 'appropriate', being meaningless, does not exist. We speak of your inmost wishes, sir, and desire is an extremely thingy sort of thing."

I looked at the hole in the window, the broken bits of furniture and ruined books. "I think," I said, "that permanent injury is all I wish. Something on the order of blindness or the loss of a hand."

Mr. Clubb favoured me with a glance of humorous irony. "It goes, sir, as it goes, which brings to mind that we have but an hour more, a period of time to be splendidly improved by a superior Double Corona such as the fine example in your hand."

"Forgive me," I said. "And might I then request . . . ?" I extended the nearly empty glass, and Mr. Clubb refilled it. Each received a cigar, and I lingered at my desk for the required term, sipping jenever and pretending to work until I heard sounds of movement. Mr. Clubb and Mr. Cuff approached. "So you are off," I said.

"It is, sir, to be a long and busy night," said Mr. Clubb. "If you take my meaning."

With a sigh I opened the humidor. They reached in, snatched a handful of cigars apiece, and deployed them into various pockets. "Details at eleven," said Mr. Clubb.

A few seconds after their departure, Mrs. Rampage informed me that she would be bringing through a fax communication just received.

The fax had been sent me by Chartwell, Munster, and Stout, a legal firm with but a single client, Mr. Arthur "This Building is Condemned" C—. Chartwell, Munster, and Stout regretted the necessity to inform me that their client wished to seek advice other than my own in his financial affairs. A sheaf of documents binding me to silence as to all matters concerning the client would arrive for my signature the following day. All records, papers, computer disks, and other data were to be referred post-haste to their offices. I had forgotten to send my intended note of client-saving reassurance.

V

What an abyss of shame I must now describe, at every turn what humiliation. It was at most five minutes past 6:00 p.m. when I learned of the desertion of my most valuable client, a turn of events certain to lead to the loss of his cryptic fellows and some forty per cent of our annual business. Gloomily I consumed my glass of Dutch gin without noticing that I had already far exceeded my tolerance. I ventured behind the screen and succeeded in unearthing another stone flagon, poured another measure, and gulped it down while attempting to demonstrate numerically that (a) the anticipated drop in annual profit could not be as severe as feared and (b) if it were, the business could continue as before, without reductions in salary, staff, or benefits. Despite ingenious feats of juggling, the numbers denied (a) and mocked (b), suggesting that I should be fortunate to retain, not lose, forty per cent of present business. I lowered my head to the desk and tried to regulate my breathing. When I heard myself rendering an off-key version of 'Abide with Me', I acknowledged that it was time to go home, got to my feet, and made the unfortunate decision to exit through the general offices on the theory that a survey of my presumably empty realm might suggest the sites of pending amputations.

I tucked the flagon under my elbow, pocketed the five or six cigars remaining in the humidor, and passed through Mrs. Rampage's chamber. Hearing the abrasive music of the cleaners' radios, I moved with exaggerated care down the corridor, darkened but for the light spilling from an open door thirty feet before me. Now and again, finding myself unable to avoid striking my shoulder against the wall,

I took a medicinal swallow of jenever. I drew up to the open door and realised that I had come to Gilligan's quarters. The abrasive music emanated from his sound system. We'll get rid of that, for starters, I said to myself, and straightened up for a dignified navigation past his doorway. At the crucial moment I glanced within to observe my jacketless junior partner sprawled, tie undone, on his sofa beside a scrawny ruffian with a quiff of lime-green hair and attired for some reason in a skin-tight costume involving zebra stripes and many chains and zippers. Disreputable creatures male and female occupied themselves in the background. Gilligan shifted his head, began to smile, and at the sight of me turned to stone.

"Calm down, Gilligan," I said, striving for an impression of sober paternal authority. I had recalled that my junior had scheduled a late appointment with his most successful musician, a singer whose band sold millions of records year in and year out despite the absurdity of their name, the Dog Turds or the Rectal Valves, something of that sort. My calculations had indicated that Gilligan's client, whose name I recalled as Cyril Futch, would soon become crucial to the maintenance of my firm, and as the beaky little rooster coldly took me in I thought to impress upon him the regard in which he was held by his chosen financial planning institution. "There is, I assure you, no need for alarm, no, certainly not, and in fact, Gilligan, you know, I should be honoured to seize this opportunity of making the acquaintance of your guest, whom it is our pleasure to assist and advise and whatever."

Gilligan reverted to flesh and blood during the course of this utterance, which I delivered gravely, taking care to enunciate each syllable clearly in spite of the difficulty I was having with my tongue. He noted the bottle nestled into my elbow and the lighted cigar in the fingers of my right hand, a matter of which until that moment I had been imperfectly aware. "Hey, I guess the smoking lamp is lit," I said. "Stupid rule anyhow. How about a little drink on the boss?"

Gilligan lurched to his feet and came reeling towards me.

All that followed is a montage of discontinuous imagery. I recall Cyril Futch propping me up as I communicated our devotion to the safeguarding of his wealth, also his dogged insistence that his name was actually Simon Gulch or Sidney Much or something similar before he sent me toppling onto the sofa; I see an odd little fellow with a tattooed head and a name like Pus (there was a person named Pus in attendance, though he may not have been the one) accepting one of my cigars and eating it; I remember inhaling from smirking Gilligan's cigarette and drinking from a bottle with a small white worm lying dead at its bottom and snuffling up a white powder recommended by a female Turd or Valve; I remember singing 'The Old Rugged Cross' in a state of partial undress. I told a face brilliantly lacquered with make-up that I was "getting a feel" for "this music". A female Turd or Valve, not the one who had recommended the powder but one in a permanent state of hilarity I found endearing, assisted me into my limousine and on the homeward journey experimented with its many buttons and controls. Atop the town-house steps, she removed the key from my fumbling hand gleefully to insert it into the lock. The rest is welcome darkness.

VI

A form of consciousness returned with a slap to my face, the muffled screams of the woman beside me, a bowler-hatted head thrusting into view and growling, "The shower for you, you damned idiot." As a second assailant whisked her away, the woman, whom I thought to be Marguerite, wailed. I struggled against the man gripping my shoulders, and he squeezed the nape of my neck.

When next I opened my eyes, I was naked and quivering beneath an onslaught of cold water within the marble confines of my shower cabinet. Charlie-Charlie Rackett leaned against the open door of the cabinet and regarded me with ill-disguised impatience. "I'm freezing, Charlie-Charlie," I said. "Turn off the water." Charlie-Charlie thrust an arm into the cabinet and became Mr. Clubb. "I'll warm it up, but I want you sober," he said. I drew myself up into a ball.

Then I was on my feet and moaning while I massaged my forehead. "Bath time all done now," called Mr. Clubb. "Turn off the wa-wa." I did as instructed. The door opened, and a bath towel unfurled over my left shoulder.

Side by side on the bedroom sofa and dimly illuminated by the lamp, Mr. Clubb and Mr. Cuff observed my progress towards the bed. A black leather satchel stood on the floor between them. "Gentlemen," I said, "although I cannot presently find words to account for the condition in which you found me, I trust that your good nature will enable you to overlook...or ignore...whatever it was that I must have done...I cannot quite recall the circumstances."

"The young woman has been dispatched," said Mr. Clubb, "and you need never fear any trouble from that direction, sir."

"The young woman?" I remembered a hyperactive figure playing with the controls in the back of the limousine. A fragmentary memory of the scene in Gilligan's office returned to me, and I moaned aloud.

"None too clean, but pretty enough in a ragamuffin way," said Mr. Clubb. "The type denied a proper education in social graces. Rough about the edges. Intemperate in language. A stranger to discipline."

I groaned—to have introduced such a creature to my house!

"A stranger to honesty, too, sir, if you'll permit me," said Mr. Cuff. "It's addiction turns them into thieves. Give them half a chance, they'll steal the brass handles off their mothers' coffins."

"Addiction?" I said. "Addiction to what?"

"Everything, from the look of the bint," said Mr. Cuff. "Before Mr. Clubb and I sent her on her way, we retrieved these items doubtless belonging to you, sir." While walking towards me he removed from his pockets the following articles: my wristwatch, gold cuff-links, wallet, the lighter of antique design given me by Mr. Montfort de M—, likewise the cigar cutter and the last of the cigars I had purchased that day. "I thank you most gratefully," I said, slipping the watch on my wrist and all else save the cigar into the pockets of my robe. It was, I noted, just past four o'clock in the morning. The cigar I handed back to him with the words, "Please accept this as a token of my gratitude."

"Gratefully accepted," he said. Mr. Cuff bit off the end, spat it onto the carpet, and set the cigar alight, producing a nauseating quantity of fumes.

"Perhaps," I said, "we might postpone our discussion until I have had time to recover from my ill-advised behaviour. Let us reconvene at..." A short period was spent pressing my hands to my eyes while rocking back and forth. "Four this afternoon?"

"Everything in its own time is a principle we hold dear," said Mr. Clubb. "And this is the time for you to down aspirin and Alka-Seltzer, and for your loyal assistants to relish the hearty breakfasts the thought of which sets our stomachs to growling. A man of stature and accomplishment like yourself ought to be able to overcome the effects of too much booze and attend to business, on top of the simple matter of getting his flunkies out of bed so they can whip up the bacon and eggs."

"Because a man such as that, sir, keeps ever in mind that business faces the task at hand, no matter how lousy it may be," said Mr. Cuff.

"The old world is in flames," said Mr. Clubb, "and the new one is just being born. Pick up the phone."

"All right," I said, "but Mr. Moncrieff is going to hate this. He worked for the Duke of Denbigh, and he's a terrible snob."

"All butlers are snobs," said Mr. Clubb. "Three fried eggs apiece, likewise six rashers of bacon, home fries, toast, hot coffee, and for the sake of digestion a bottle of your best cognac."

Mr. Moncrieff picked up his telephone, listened to my orders, and informed me in a small, cold voice that he would speak to the cook. "Would this repast be for the young lady and yourself, sir?"

With a wave of guilty shame that intensified my nausea, I realised that Mr. Moncrieff had observed my unsuitable young companion accompanying me upstairs to the bedroom. "No, it would not," I said. "The young lady, a client of mine, was kind enough to assist me when I was taken ill. The meal is for two male guests." Unwelcome memory returned the spectacle of a scrawny girl pulling my ears and screeching that a useless old fart like me didn't deserve her band's business.

"The phone," said Mr. Clubb. Dazedly I extended the receiver.

"Moncrieff, old man," he said, "amazing good luck, running into you again. Do you remember that trouble the Duke had with Colonel Fletcher and the diary?...Yes, this is Mr. Clubb, and it's delightful to hear your voice again...He's here, too, couldn't do anything without him...I'll tell him...Much the way things went with the Duke, yes, and we'll need the usual supplies...Glad to hear it...The dining room in half an hour." He handed the telephone back to me and said to Mr. Cuff, "He's looking forward to the pinochle, and there's a first-rate Pétrus in the cellar he knows you're going to enjoy."

I had purchased six cases of 1928 Château Pétrus at an auction some years before and was holding it while its already immense value doubled, then tripled, until perhaps a decade hence, when I would sell it for ten times its original cost.

"A good drop of wine sets a man right up," said Mr. Cuff. "Stuff was meant to be drunk, wasn't it?"

"You know Mr. Moncrieff?" I asked. "You worked for the Duke?"

"We ply our humble trade irrespective of nationality and borders," said Mr. Clubb. "Go where we are needed, is our motto. We have fond memories of the good old Duke, who showed himself to be quite a fun-loving, spirited fellow, sir, once you got past the crust, as it were. Generous, too."

"He gave until it hurt," said Mr. Cuff. "The old gentleman cried like a baby when we left."

"Cried a good deal before that, too," said Mr. Clubb. "In our experience, high-spirited fellows spend a deal more tears than your gloomy customers."

"I do not suppose you shall see any tears from me," I said. The brief look that passed between them reminded me of the complicitous glance I had once seen fly like a live spark between two of their New Covenant forebears, one gripping the hind legs of a pig, the other its front legs and a knife, in the moment before the knife opened the pig's throat and an arc of blood threw itself high into the air. "I shall heed your advice," I said, "and locate my analgesics." I got on my feet and moved slowly to the bathroom. "As a matter of curiosity," I said, "might I ask if you have classified me into the high-spirited category, or into the other?"

"You are a man of middling spirit," said Mr. Clubb. I opened my mouth to protest, and he went on, "But something may be made of you yet."

I disappeared into the bathroom. I have endured these moon-faced yokels long enough, I told myself. Hear their story, feed the bastards, then kick them out.

In a condition more nearly approaching my usual self, I brushed my teeth and splashed water on my face before returning to the bedroom. I placed myself with a reasonable degree of executive command in a wing-chair, folded my pin-striped robe about me, inserted my feet into velvet slippers, and said, "Things got a bit out of hand, and I thank you for dealing with my young client, a person with whom in spite of appearances I have a professional relationship only. Now let us turn to our real business. I trust you found my wife and Leeson at Green Chimneys. Please give me an account of what followed."

"Things got a bit out of hand," said Mr. Clubb. "Which is a way of describing something that can happen to us all, and for which no one can be blamed. Especially Mr. Cuff and myself, who are always careful to say right smack at the beginning, as we did with you, sir, what ought to be so obvious as to not need saying at all, that our work brings about permanent changes which can never be undone. Especially in the cases when we specify a time to make our initial report and the client disappoints us at the said time. When we are let down by our client, we must go forward and complete the job to our highest standards with no rancour or ill-will, knowing that there are many reasonable explanations of a man's inability to get to a telephone."

"I don't know what you mean by this self-serving double-talk," I said. "We had no arrangement of that sort, and your effrontery forces me to conclude that you failed in your task."

Mr. Clubb gave me the grimmest possible suggestion of a smile. "One of the reasons for a man's failure to get to a telephone is a lapse of memory. You have forgotten my informing you that I would give you my initial report at eleven. At precisely eleven o'clock I called, to no avail. I waited through twenty rings, sir, before I abandoned the effort. If I had waited through a hundred, sir, the result would have been the same, on account of your decision to put yourself into a state where you would have had trouble remembering your own name."

"That is a blatant lie," I said, then remembered. The fellow had in fact mentioned in passing something about reporting to me at that hour, which must have been approximately the time when I was regaling the Turds or Valves with 'The Old Rugged Cross'. My face grew pink. "Forgive me," I said. "I am in error, it is just as you say."

"A manly admission, sir, but as for forgiveness, we extended that quantity from the git-go," said Mr. Clubb. "We are your servants, and your wishes are our sacred charge."

"That's the whole ball of wax in a nutshell," said Mr. Cuff, giving a fond glance to the final inch of his cigar. He dropped the stub onto my carpet and ground it beneath his shoe. "Food and drink to the fibres, sir," he said.

"Speaking of which," said Mr. Clubb, "we will continue our report in the dining room, so as to dig into the feast ordered up by that wondrous villain Reggie Moncrieff."

Until that moment it had never quite occurred to me that my butler possessed, like other men, a Christian name.

VII

"A great design directs us," said Mr. Clubb, expelling morsels of his cud. "We poor wanderers, you and me and Mr. Cuff and the milkman too, only see the little portion right in front of us. Half the time we don't even see that in the right way. For sure we don't have a Chinaman's chance of understanding it. But the design is ever-present, sir, a truth I bring to your attention for the sake of the comfort in it. Toast, Mr. Cuff."

"Comfort is a matter cherished by all parts of a man," said Mr. Cuff, handing his partner the toast rack. "Most particularly that part known as his soul, which feeds upon the nutrient adversity."

I was seated at the head of the table, flanked by Mr. Clubb and Mr. Cuff. The salvers and tureens before us overflowed, for Mr. Moncrieff, who after embracing each barnie in turn and entering into a kind of conference or huddle, had summoned from the kitchen a banquet far surpassing their requests. Besides several dozen eggs and perhaps two packages of bacon, he had arranged a mixed grill of kidneys, lambs' livers and lamb chops, and strip steaks, as well as vats of oatmeal and a pasty concoction he described as "kedgeree—as the old Duke fancied it."

Sickened by the odours of the food, also by the mush visible in my companions' mouths, I tried again to extract their report. "I don't believe in the grand design," I said, "and I already face more adversity than my soul finds useful. Tell me what happened at the house."

"No mere house, sir," said Mr. Clubb. "Even as we approached along—Lane, Mr. Cuff and I could not fail to respond to its magnificence."

"Were my drawings of use?" I asked.

"Invaluable." Mr. Clubb speared a lamb chop and raised it to his mouth. "We proceeded through the rear door into your spacious kitchen or scullery. Wherein we observed evidence of two persons having enjoyed a dinner enhanced by a fine wine and finished with a noble champagne."

"Aha," I said.

"By means of your guidance, Mr. Cuff and I located the lovely staircase and made our way to the lady's chamber. We effected an entry of the most praiseworthy silence, if I may say so."

"That entry was worth a medal," said Mr. Cuff.

"Two figures lay slumbering upon the bed. In a blamelessly professional manner we approached, Mr. Cuff on one side, I on the other. In the fashion your client of this morning called the whopbopaloobop, we rendered the parties in question even more unconscious than previous, thereby giving ourselves a good fifteen minutes for the disposition of instruments. We take pride in being careful workers, sir, and like all honest craftsmen we respect our tools. We bound and gagged both parties in timely fashion. Is the male party distinguished by an athletic past?" Alight with barnieish glee, Mr. Clubb raised his eyebrows and washed down the last of his chop with a mouthful of cognac.

"Not to my knowledge," I said. "I believe he plays a little racquetball and squash, that kind of thing."

He and Mr. Cuff experienced a moment of mirth. "More like weightlifting or football, is my guess," he said. "Strength and stamina. To a remarkable degree."

"Not to mention considerable speed," said Mr. Cuff with the air of one indulging a tender reminiscence.

"Are you telling me that he got away?" I asked.

"No one gets away," said Mr. Clubb. "That, sir, is gospel. But you may imagine our surprise when for the first time in the history of our consultancy"—and here he chuckled—"a gentleman of the civilian persuasion managed to break his bonds and free himself of his ropes whilst Mr. Cuff and I were engaged in the preliminaries."

"Naked as jaybirds," said Mr. Cuff, wiping with a greasy hand a tear of amusement from one eye. "Bare as newborn lambie-pies. There I was, heating up the steam iron I'd just fetched from the kitchen, sir, along with a selection of knives I came across in exactly the spot you described, most grateful I was, too, squatting on my haunches without a care in the world and feeling the first merry tingle of excitement in my little soldier—"

"What?" I said. "You were naked? And what's this about your little soldier?"

"Hush," said Mr. Clubb, his eyes glittering. "Nakedness is a precaution against fouling our clothing with blood and other bodily products, and men like Mr. Cuff and myself take pleasure in the exercise of our skills. In us, the inner and the outer man are one and the same."

"Are they, now?" I said, marvelling at the irrelevance of this last remark. It then occurred to me that the remark might have been relevant after all—most unhappily so.

"At all times," said Mr. Cuff, amused by my having missed the point. "If you wish to hear our report, sir, reticence will be helpful."

I gestured for him to go on.

"As said before, I was squatting in my birthday suit by the knives and the steam iron, not a care in the world, when I heard from behind me the patter of little feet. Hello, I say to myself, what's this? and when I look over my shoulder here is your man, bearing down on me like a steam engine. Being as he is one of your big, strapping fellows, sir, it was a sight to behold, not to mention the unexpected circumstances. I took a moment to glance in the direction of Mr. Clubb, who was busily occupied in another quarter, which was, to put it plain and simple, the bed."

Mr. Clubb chortled and said, "By way of being in the line of duty."

"So in a way of speaking I was in the position of having to settle this fellow before he became a trial to us in the performance of our duties. He was getting ready to tackle me, sir, which was what put us in mind of football being in his previous life, tackle the life out of me before he rescued the lady, and I got hold of one of the knives. Then, you see, when he came flying at me that way all I had to do was give him a good jab in the bottom of the throat, a matter which puts the fear of God into the bravest fellow. It concentrates all their attention, and after that they might as well be little puppies for all the harm they're likely to do. Well, this boy was one for the books, because for the first time in I don't know how many similar efforts, a hundred—"

"I'd say double at least, to be accurate," said Mr. Clubb.

"—in at least a hundred, anyhow, avoiding immodesty, I under-estimated the speed and agility of the lad, and instead of planting my weapon at the base of his neck stuck him in the side, a manner of wound which in the case of your really aggressive attacker, who you come across in about one out of twenty, is about as effective as a slap with a powder puff. Still, I put him off his stride, a welcome sign to me that he had gone a bit loosey-goosey over the years. Then, sir, the advantage was mine, and I seized it with a grateful heart. I spun him over, dumped him on the floor, and straddled his chest. At which point I thought to settle him down for the evening by taking hold of a cleaver and cutting off his right hand with one good blow.

"Ninety-nine times out of a hundred, sir, chopping off a hand will take the starch right out of a man. He settled down pretty well. It's the shock, you see, shock takes the mind that way, and because the stump was bleeding like a bastard, excuse the language, I did him the favour of cauterising the wound with the steam iron because it was good and hot, and if you sear a wound there's no way that bugger can bleed anymore. I mean, the problem is solved, and that's a fact."

"It has been proved a thousand times over," said Mr. Clubb.

"Shock being a healer," said Mr. Cuff. "Shock being a balm like salt water to the human body, yet if you have too much of shock or salt water, the body gives up the ghost. After I seared the wound, it looked to me like he and his body got together and voted to take the next bus to what is generally considered a better world." He held up an index finger and stared into my eyes while forking kidneys into his mouth. "This, sir, is a process. A process can't happen all at once, and every reasonable precaution was taken. Mr. Clubb and I do not have, nor ever have had, the reputation for carelessness in our undertakings."

"And never shall." Mr. Clubb washed down whatever was in his mouth with half a glass of cognac.

"Despite the process under way," said Mr. Cuff, "the gentleman's left wrist was bound tightly to the stump. Rope was again attached to the areas of the chest and legs, a gag went back into his mouth, and besides all that I had the pleasure of whapping my hammer once and once only on the region of his temple, for the purpose of keeping him out of action until we were ready for him in case he was not boarding the bus. I took a moment to turn him over and gratify my little soldier, which I trust was in no way exceeding our agreement, sir." He granted me a look of the purest innocence.

"Continue," I said, "although you must grant that your tale is utterly without verification."

"Sir," said Mr. Clubb, "we know one another better than that." He bent over so far that his head disappeared beneath the table, and I heard the undoing of a clasp. Resurfacing, he placed between us on the table an object wrapped in one of the towels Marguerite had purchased for Green Chimneys. "If verification is your desire, and I intend no reflection, sir, for a man in your line of business has grown out of the habit of taking a fellow at his word, here you have wrapped up like a birthday present the finest verification of this portion of our tale to be found in all the world."

"And yours to keep, if you're taken that way," said Mr. Cuff.

I had no doubts whatsoever concerning the nature of the trophy set before me, and therefore I deliberately composed myself before pulling away the folds of towelling. Yet for all my preparations the spectacle of the actual trophy itself affected me more greatly than I would have thought possible, and at the very centre of the nausea rising within me I experienced the first faint stirrings of enlightenment. Poor man, I thought, poor mankind.

I refolded the material over the crab-like thing and said, "Thank you. I meant to imply no reservations concerning your veracity."

"Beautifully said, sir, and much appreciated. Men like ourselves, honest at every point, have found that persons in the habit of duplicity often cannot understand the truth. Liars are the bane of our existence. And yet, such is the nature of this funny old world, we'd be out of business without them."

Mr. Cuff smiled up at the chandelier in rueful appreciation of the world's contradictions. "When I replaced him on the bed, Mr. Clubb went hither and yon, collecting the remainder of the tools for the job at hand."

"When you say you replaced him on the bed," I broke in, "is it your meaning—"

"Your meaning might differ from mine, sir, and mine, being that of a fellow raised without the benefits of a literary education, may be simpler than yours. But bear in mind that every guild has its legacy of customs and traditions which no serious practitioner can ignore without thumbing his nose at all he holds dear. For those brought up into our trade, physical punishment of a female subject invariably begins with the act most associated in the feminine mind with humiliation of the most rigorous sort. With males the same is generally true. Neglect this step, and you lose an advantage which can never be regained. It is the foundation without which the structure cannot stand, and the foundation must be set in place even when conditions make the job distasteful, which is no picnic, take my word for it." He shook his head and fell silent.

"We could tell you stories to curl your hair," said Mr. Clubb. "Matter for another day. It was on the order of nine-thirty when our materials had been assembled, the preliminaries taken care of, and business could begin in earnest. This is a moment, sir, ever cherished by professionals such as ourselves. It is of an eternal freshness. You are on the brink of testing yourself against your past achievements and those of masters gone before. Your skill, your imagination, your timing and resolve will be called upon to work together with your hard-earned knowledge of the human body, because it is a question of being able to sense when to press on and when to hold back, of, I can say, having that instinct for the right technique at the right time you can acquire only through experience. During this moment you hope that the subject, your partner in the most intimate relationship which can exist between two people, owns the spiritual resolve and physical capacity to inspire your best work. The subject is our instrument, and the nature of the instrument is vital. Faced with an out-of-tune, broken-down piano, even the greatest virtuoso is up Shit Creek without a paddle. Sometimes, sir, our work has left us tasting ashes for weeks on end, and when you're tasting ashes in your mouth you have trouble remembering the grand design and your wee part in that majestical pattern."

As if to supplant the taste in question and without benefit of knife and fork, Mr. Clubb bit off a generous portion of steak and moistened it with a gulp of cognac. Chewing with loud smacks of the lips and tongue, he thrust a spoon into the kedgeree and began moodily slapping it onto his plate while seeming for the first time to notice the Canalettos on the walls.

"We started off, sir, as well as we ever have," said Mr. Cuff, "and better than most times. The fingernails was a thing of rare beauty, sir, the fingernails was prime. And the hair was on the same transcendent level."

"The fingernails?" I asked. "The hair?"

"Prime," said Mr. Clubb with a melancholy spray of food. "If they could be done better, which they could not, I should like to be there as to applaud with my own hands."

I looked at Mr. Cuff, and he said, "The fingernails and the hair might appear to be your traditional steps two and three, but they are in actual fact steps one and two, the first procedure being more like basic groundwork than part of the performance work itself. Doing the fingernails and the hair tells you an immense quantity about the subject's pain level, style of resistance, and aggression/passivity balance, and that information, sir, is your virtual bible once you go past step four or five."

"How many steps are there?" I asked.

"A novice would tell you fifteen," said Mr. Cuff. "A competent journeyman would say twenty. Men such as us know there to be at least a hundred, but in their various combinations and refinements they come out into the thousands. At the basic or kindergarten level, they are, after the first two: foot soles; teeth; fingers and toes; tongue; nipples; rectum; genital area; electrification; general piercing; specific piercing; small amputation; damage to inner organs; eyes, minor; eyes, major; large amputation; local flaying; and so forth."

At mention of "tongue", Mr. Clubb had shoved a spoonful of kedgeree into his mouth and scowled at the paintings directly across from him. At "electrification", he had thrust himself out of his chair and crossed behind me to scrutinise them more closely. While Mr. Cuff continued my education, he twisted in his chair to observe his partner's actions, and I did the same.

After "and so forth", Mr. Cuff fell silent. The two of us watched Mr. Clubb moving back and forth in evident agitation before the paintings. He settled at last before a depiction of a regatta on the Grand Canal and took two deep breaths. Then he raised his spoon like a dagger and drove it into the painting to slice beneath a handsome ship, come up at its bow, and continue cutting until he had deleted the ship from the painting. "Now that, sir, is local flaying," he said. He moved to the next picture, which gave a view of the Piazzetta. In seconds he had sliced all the canvas from the frame. "And that, sir, is what is meant by general flaying." He crumpled the canvas in his hands, threw it to the ground, and stamped on it.

"He is not quite himself," said Mr. Cuff.

"Oh, but I am, I am myself to an alarming degree, I am," said Mr. Clubb. He tromped back to the table and bent beneath it. Instead of the second folded towel I had anticipated, he produced his satchel and used it to sweep away the plates and serving dishes in front of him. He reached within and slapped down beside me the towel I had expected. "Open it," he said. I unfolded the towel. "Are these not, to the last particular, what you requested, sir?"

It was, to the last particular, what I had requested. Marguerite had not thought to remove her wedding band before her assignation, and her...I cannot describe the other but to say that it lay like the egg perhaps of some small shore bird in the familiar palm. Another portion of my eventual enlightenment moved into place within me, and I thought: Here we are, this is all of us, this crab and this egg. I bent over and vomited beside my chair. When I had finished, I grabbed the cognac bottle and swallowed greedily, twice. The liquor burned down my throat, struck my stomach like a branding iron, and rebounded. I leaned sideways and, with a dizzied spasm of throat and guts, expelled another reeking contribution to the mess on the carpet.

"It is a Roman conclusion to a meal, sir," said Mr. Cuff.

Mr. Moncrieff opened the kitchen door and peeked in. He observed the mutilated paintings and the objects nested in the striped towel and watched me wipe a string of vomit from my mouth. He withdrew for a moment and reappeared holding a tall can of ground coffee, wordlessly sprinkled its contents over the evidence of my distress, and vanished back into the kitchen. From the depths of my wretchedness, I marvelled at the perfection of this display of butler decorum.

I draped the towelling over the crab and the egg. "You are conscientious fellows," I said.

"Conscientious to a fault, sir," said Mr. Cuff, not without a touch of kindness. "For a person in the normal way of living cannot begin to comprehend the actual meaning of that term, nor is he liable to understand the fierce requirements it puts on a man's head. And so it comes about that persons in the normal way of living try to back out long after backing out is possible, even though we explain exactly what is going to happen at the very beginning. They listen, but they do not hear, and it's the rare civilian who has the common sense to know that if you stand in a fire you must be burned. And if you turn the world upside down, you're standing on your head with everybody else."

"Or," said Mr. Clubb, calming his own fires with another deep draft of cognac, "as the Golden Rule has it, what you do is sooner or later done back to you."

Although I was still one who listened but could not hear, a tingle of premonition went up my spine. "Please go on with your report," I said.

"The responses of the subject were all one could wish," said Mr. Clubb. "I could go so far as to say that her responses were a thing of beauty. A subject who can render you one magnificent scream after another while maintaining a basic self-possession and not breaking down is a subject highly attuned to her own pain, sir, and one to be cherished. You see, there comes a moment when they understand that they are changed for good, they have passed over the border into another realm, from which there is no return, and some of them can't handle it and turn, you might say, sir, to mush. With some it happens right at the foundation stage, a sad disappointment because thereafter all the rest of the work could be done by the crudest apprentice. It takes some at the nipples stage, and at the genital stage quite a few more. Most of them comprehend irreversibility during the piercings, and by the stage of small amputation ninety per cent have shown you what they are made of. The lady did not come to the point until we had begun the eye work, and she passed with flying colours, sir. But it was then the male upped and put his foot in it."

"And eye work is delicate going," said Mr. Cuff. "Requiring two men, if you want it done even close to right. But I couldn't have turned my back on the fellow for more than a minute and a half."

"Less," said Mr. Clubb. "And him lying there in the corner meek as a baby. No fight left in him at all, you would have said. You would have said, that fellow there is not going to risk so much as opening his eyes until his eyes are opened for him."

"But up he gets, without a rope on him, sir," said Mr. Cuff, "which you would have said was beyond the powers of a fellow who had recently lost a hand."

"Up he gets and on he comes," said Mr. Clubb. "In defiance of all of Nature's mighty laws. Before I know what's what, he has his good arm around Mr. Cuff's neck and is earnestly trying to snap that neck while beating Mr. Cuff about the head with his stump, a situation which compels me to set aside the task at hand and take up a knife and ram it into his back a fair old number of times. The next thing I know, he's on me, and it's up to Mr. Cuff to peel him off and set him on the floor."

"And then, you see, your concentration is gone," said Mr. Cuff. "After something like that, you might as well be starting all over again at the beginning. Imagine if you are playing a piano about as well as ever you did in your life, and along comes another piano with blood in its eye and jumps on your back. It was pitiful, that's all I can say about it. But I got the fellow down and jabbed him here and there until he was still, and then I got the one item we count on as a surefire last resort for incapacitation."

"What is that item?" I asked.

"Dental floss," said Mr. Clubb. "Dental floss cannot be overestimated in our line of work. It is the razor wire of everyday life, and fishing line cannot hold a candle to it, for fishing line is dull, but dental floss is both dull and sharp. It has a hundred uses, and a book should be written on the subject."

"What do you do with it?" I asked.

"It is applied to a male subject," he said. "Applied artfully and in a manner perfected only over years of experience. The application is of a lovely subtlety. During the process, the subject must be in a helpless, preferably an unconscious, position. When the subject regains the first fuzzy inklings of consciousness, he is aware of no more than a vague discomfort like unto a form of tingling, similar to when a foot has gone to sleep. In a wonderfully short period of time, that discomfort builds itself up, ascending to mild pain, severe pain, and outright agony. Then it goes past agony. The final stage is a mystical condition I don't think there is a word for which, but it closely resembles ecstasy. Hallucinations are common. Out-of-body experiences are common. We have seen men speak in tongues, even when tongues were, strictly speaking, organs they no longer possessed. We have seen wonders, Mr. Cuff and I."

"That we have," said Mr. Cuff. "The ordinary civilian sort of fellow can be a miracle, sir."

"Of which the person in question was one, to be sure," said Mr. Clubb. "But he has to be said to be in a category all by himself, a man in a million you could put it, which is the cause of my mentioning the grand design ever a mystery to us who glimpse but a part of the whole. You see, the fellow refused to play by the time-honoured rules. He was in an awesome degree of suffering and torment, sir, but he would not do us the favour to lie down and quit."

"The mind was not right," said Mr. Cuff. "Where the proper mind goes to the spiritual, sir, as just described, this was that one mind in ten million, I'd estimate, which moves to the animal at the reptile level. If you cut off the head of a venomous reptile and detach it from the body, that head will still attempt to strike. So it was with our boy. Bleeding from a dozen wounds. Minus one hand. Seriously concussed. The dental floss murdering all possibility of thought. Every nerve in his body howling like a banshee. Yet up he comes with his eyes red and the foam dripping from his mouth. We put him down again, and I did what I hate, because it takes all feeling away from the body along with the motor capacity, and cracked his spine right at the base of the head. Or would have, if his spine had been a normal thing instead of solid steel in a thick india-rubber case. Which is what put us in mind of weightlifting, sir, an activity resulting in such development about the top of the spine you need a hacksaw to get even close to it."

"We were already behind schedule," said Mr. Clubb, "and with the time required to get back into the proper frame of mind, we had at least seven or eight hours of work ahead of us. And you had to double that, because while we could knock the fellow out, he wouldn't have the decency to stay out more than a few minutes at a time. The natural thing, him being only the secondary subject, would have been to kill him outright so we could get on with the real job, but improving our working conditions by that fashion would require an amendment to our contract. Which comes under the heading of Instructions from the Client."

"And it was eleven o'clock," said Mr. Cuff.

"The exact time scheduled for our conference," said Mr. Clubb. "My partner was forced to clobber the fellow into senselessness, how many times was it, Mr. Cuff, while I prayed for our client to do us the grace of answering his phone during twenty rings?"

"Three times, Mr. Clubb, three times exactly," said Mr. Cuff. "The blow each time more powerful than the last, which, combined with his having a skull made of granite, led to a painful swelling of my hand."

"The dilemma stared us in the face," said Mr. Clubb. "Client unreachable. Impeded in the performance of our duties. State of mind, very foul. In such a pickle, we could do naught but obey the instructions given us by our hearts. Remove the gentleman's head, I told my partner, and take care not to be bitten once it's off. Mr. Cuff took up an axe. Some haste was called for, the fellow just beginning to stir again. Mr. Cuff moved into position. Then from the bed, where all had been lovely silence but for soft moans and whimpers, we hear a god-awful yowling ruckus of the most desperate and importunate protest. It was of a sort to melt the heart, sir. Were we not experienced professionals who enjoy pride in our work, I believe we might have been persuaded almost to grant the fellow mercy, despite his being a pest of the first water. But now those heart-melting screeches reach the ears of the pest and rouse him into movement just at the moment Mr. Cuff lowers the boom, so to speak."

"Which was an unfortunate bit of business," said Mr. Cuff. "Causing me to catch him in the shoulder, causing him to rear up, causing me to lose my footing what with all the blood on the floor, then causing a tussle for possession of the axe and myself suffering several kicks to the breadbasket. I'll tell you, sir, we did a good piece of work when we took off his hand, for without the nuisance of a stump really being useful only for leverage, there's no telling what that fellow might have done. As it was, I had the devil's own time getting the axe free and clear, and once I had done, any chance of making a neat, clean job of it was long gone. It was a slaughter and an act of butchery with not a bit of finesse or sophistication to it, and I have to tell you, such a thing is both an embarrassment and an outrage to men like ourselves. Turning a subject into hamburger by means of an axe is a violation of all our training, and it is not why we went into this business."

"No, of course not, you are more like artists than I had imagined," I said. "But in spite of your embarrassment, I suppose you went back to work on . . . on the female subject."

"We are not like artists," said Mr. Clubb, "we are artists, and we know how to set our feelings aside and address our chosen medium of expression with a pure and patient attention. In spite of which we discovered the final and insurmountable frustration of the evening, and that discovery put paid to all our hopes."

"If you discovered that Marguerite had escaped," I said, "I believe I might almost, after all you have said, be—"

Glowering, Mr. Clubb held up his hand. "I beg you not to insult us, sir, as we have endured enough misery for one day. The subject had escaped, all right, but not in the simple sense of your meaning. She had escaped for all eternity, in the sense that her soul had taken leave of her body and flown to those realms at whose nature we can only make our poor, ignorant guesses."

"She died?" I asked. "In other words, in direct contradiction of my instructions, you two fools killed her. You love to talk about your expertise, but you went too far, and she died at your hands. I want you incompetents out of my house immediately. Begone. Depart. This minute."

Mr. Clubb and Mr. Cuff looked into each other's eyes, and in that moment of private communication I saw an encompassing sorrow that utterly turned the tables on me: before I was made to understand how it was possible, I saw that the only fool present was myself. And yet the sorrow included all three of us, and more besides.

"The subject died, but we did not kill her," said Mr. Clubb. "We did not go, nor have we ever gone, too far. The subject chose to die. The subject's death was an act of suicidal will. While you are listening, sir, is it possible, sir, for you to open your ears and hear what I am saying? She who might have been in all of our long experience the noblest, most courageous subject we ever will have the good fortune to be given witnessed the clumsy murder of her lover and decided to surrender her life."

"Quick as a shot," said Mr. Cuff. "The simple truth, sir, is that otherwise we could have kept her alive for about a year."

"And it would have been a rare privilege to do so," said Mr. Clubb. "It is time for you to face facts, sir."

"I am facing them about as well as one could," I said. "Please tell me where you disposed of the bodies."

"Within the house," said Mr. Clubb. Before I could protest, he said, "Under the wretched circumstances, sir, including the continuing unavailability of the client and the enormity of the personal and professional letdown felt by my partner and myself, we saw no choice but to dispose of the house along with the telltale remains."

"Dispose of Green Chimneys?" I said, aghast. "How could you dispose of Green Chimneys?"

"Reluctantly, sir," said Mr. Clubb. "With heavy hearts and an equal anger. With the same degree of professional unhappiness experienced previous. In workaday terms, by means of combustion. Fire, sir, is a substance like shock and salt water, a healer and a cleanser, though more drastic."

"But Green Chimneys has not been healed," I said. "Nor has my wife."

"You are a man of wit, sir, and have provided Mr. Cuff and myself many moments of precious amusement. True, Green Chimneys has not been healed, but cleansed it has been, root and branch. And you hired us to punish your wife, not heal her, and punish her we did, as well as possible under very trying circumstances indeed."

"Which circumstances include our feeling that the job ended before its time," said Mr. Cuff. "Which circumstance is one we cannot bear."

"I regret your disappointment," I said, "but I cannot accept that it was necessary to burn down my magnificent house."

"Twenty, even fifteen years ago, it would not have been," said Mr. Clubb. "Nowadays, however, that contemptible alchemy known as Police Science has fattened itself up into such a gross and distorted breed of sorcery that a single drop of blood can be detected even after you scrub and scour until your arms hurt. It has reached the hideous point that if a constable without a thing in his head but the desire to imprison honest fellows employed in an ancient trade finds two hairs at what is supposed to be a crime scene, he waddles along to the laboratory and instantly a loathsome sort of wizard is popping out to tell him that those same two hairs are from the heads of Mr. Clubb and Mr. Cuff, and I exaggerate, I know, sir, but not by much."

"And if they do not have our names, sir," said Mr. Cuff, "which they do not and I pray never will, they ever after have our particulars, to be placed in a great universal file against the day when they might have our names, so as to look back into that cruel file and commit the monstrosity of unfairly increasing the charges against us. It is a malignant business, and all sensible precautions must be taken."

"A thousand times I have expressed the conviction," said Mr. Clubb, "that an ancient art ought not be against the law, nor its practitioners described as criminals. Is there a name for our so-called crime? There is not. GBH they call it, sir, for Grievous Bodily Harm, or, even worse, Assault. We do not Assault. We induce, we instruct, we instil. Properly speaking, these cannot be crimes, and those who do them cannot be criminals. Now I have said it a thousand times and one."

"All right," I said, attempting to speed this appalling conference to its end, "you have described the evening's unhappy events. I appreciate your reasons for burning down my splendid property. You have enjoyed a lavish meal. All remaining is the matter of your remuneration, which demands considerable thought. This night has left me exhausted, and after all your efforts, you, too, must be in need of rest. Communicate with me, please, in a day or two, gentlemen, by whatever means you choose. I wish to be alone with my thoughts. Mr. Moncrieff will show you out."

The maddening barnies met this plea with impassive stares and stoic silence, and I renewed my silent vow to give them nothing—not a penny. For all their pretensions, they had accomplished naught but the death of my wife and the destruction of my country house. Rising to my feet with more difficulty than anticipated, I said, "Thank you for your efforts on my behalf."

Once again, the glance that passed between them implied that I had failed to grasp the essentials of our situation.

"Your thanks are gratefully accepted," said Mr. Cuff, "though, dispute it as you may, they are premature, as you know in your soul. Yesterday morning we embarked upon a journey of which we have yet more miles to go. In consequence, we prefer not to leave. Also, setting aside the question of your continuing education, which if we do not address will haunt us all forever, residing here with you for a sensible period out of sight is the best protection from law enforcement we three could ask for."

"No," I said, "I have had enough of your education, and I need no protection from officers of the law. Please, gentlemen, allow me to return to my bed. You may take the rest of the cognac with you as a token of my regard."

"Give it a moment's reflection, sir," said Mr. Clubb. "You have announced the presence of high-grade consultants and introduced these same to staff and clients both. Hours later, your spouse meets her tragic end in a conflagration destroying your upstate manor. On the very same night also occurs the disappearance of your greatest competitor, a person certain to be identified before long by a hotel employee as a fellow not unknown to the late spouse. Can you think it wise to have the high-grade consultants vanish right away?"

I did reflect, then said, "You have a point. It will be best if you continue to make an appearance in the office for a time. However, the proposal that you stay here is ridiculous." A wild hope, utterly irrational in the face of the grisly evidence, came to me in the guise of doubt. "If Green Chimneys has been destroyed by fire, I should have been informed long ago. I am a respected figure in the town of—, personally acquainted with its chief of police, Wendall Nash. Why has he not called me?"

"Oh, sir, my goodness," said Mr. Clubb, shaking his head and smiling inwardly at my folly, "for many reasons. A small town is a beast slow to move. The available men have been struggling throughout the night to rescue even a jot or little portion of your house. They will fail, they have failed already, but the effort will keep them busy past dawn. Wendall Nash will not wish to ruin your night's sleep until he can make a full report." He glanced at his wristwatch. "In fact, if I am not mistaken..." He tilted his head, closed his eyes, and raised an index finger. The telephone in the kitchen began to trill.

"He has done it a thousand times, sir," said Mr. Cuff, "and I have yet to see him strike out."

Mr. Moncrieff brought the instrument through from the kitchen, said, "For you, sir," and placed the receiver in my waiting hand. I uttered the conventional greeting, longing to hear the voice of anyone but...

"Wendall Nash, sir," came the chief's raspy, high-pitched drawl. "Calling from up here in—. I hate to tell you this, but I have some awful bad news. Your place Green Chimneys started burning sometime around midnight last night, and every man jack we had got put on the job and the boys worked like dogs to save what they could, but sometimes you can't win no matter what you do. Me personally, I feel terrible about this, but, tell you the truth, I never saw a fire like it. We nearly lost two men, but it looks like they're going to come out of it okay. The rest of our boys are still out there trying to save the few trees you got left."

"Dreadful," I said. "Please permit me to speak to my wife."

A speaking silence followed. "The missus is not with you, sir? You're saying she was inside there?"

"My wife left for Green Chimneys yesterday morning. I spoke to her there in the afternoon. She intended to work in her studio, a separate building at some distance from the house, and it is her custom to sleep in the studio when working late." Saying these things to Wendall Nash, I felt almost as though I were creating an alternative world, another town of—and another Green Chimneys, where another Marguerite had busied herself in the studio, and there gone to bed to sleep through the commotion. "Have you checked the studio? You are certain to find her there."

"Well, I have to say we didn't, sir," he said. "The fire took that little building pretty good, too, but the walls are still standing and you can tell what used to be what, furnishing-wise and equipment-wise. If she was inside it, we'd have found her."

"Then she got out in time," I said, and instantly it was the truth: the other Marguerite had escaped the blaze and now stood, numb with shock and wrapped in a blanket, unrecognised amidst the voyeuristic crowd always drawn to disasters.

"It's possible, but she hasn't turned up yet, and we've been talking to everybody at the site. Could she have left with one of the staff?"

"All the help is on vacation," I said. "She was alone."

"Uh-huh," he said. "Can you think of anyone with a serious grudge against you? Any enemies? Because this was not a natural-type fire, sir. Someone set it, and he knew what he was doing. Anyone come to mind?"

"No," I said. "I have rivals, but no enemies. Check the hospitals and anything else you can think of, Wendall, and I'll be there as soon as I can."

"You can take your time, sir," he said. "I sure hope we find her, and by late this afternoon we'll be able to go through the ashes." He said he would give me a call if anything turned up in the meantime.

"Please, Wendall," I said, and began to cry. Muttering a consolation I did not quite catch, Mr. Moncrieff vanished with the telephone in another matchless display of butler politesse.

"The practice of hoping for what you know you cannot have is a worthy spiritual exercise," said Mr. Clubb. "It brings home the vanity of vanity."

"I beg you, leave me," I said, still crying. "In all decency."

"Decency lays heavy obligations on us all," said Mr. Clubb. "And no job is decently done until it is done completely. Would you care for help in getting back to the bedroom? We are ready to proceed."

I extended a shaky arm, and he assisted me through the corridors. Two cots had been set up in my room, and a neat array of instruments—"staples"—formed two rows across the bottom of the bed. Mr. Clubb and Mr. Cuff positioned my head on the pillows and began to disrobe.

VIII

Ten hours later, the silent chauffeur aided me in my exit from the limousine and clasped my left arm as I limped towards the uniformed men and official vehicles on the far side of the open gate. Blackened sticks that had been trees protruded from the blasted earth, and the stench of wet ash saturated the air. Wendall Nash separated from the other men, approached, and noted without comment my garb of grey homburg hat, pearl-grey cashmere topcoat, heavy gloves, woollen charcoal-grey pin-striped suit, sunglasses, and malacca walking stick. It was the afternoon of a midsummer day in the upper eighties. Then he looked more closely at my face. "Are you, uh, are you sure you're all right, sir?"

"In a manner of speaking," I said, and saw him blink at the oozing gap left in the wake of an incisor. "I slipped at the top of a marble staircase and tumbled down all forty-six steps, resulting in massive bangs and bruises, considerable physical weakness, and the persistent sensation of being uncomfortably cold. No broken bones, at least nothing major." Over his shoulder I stared at four isolated brick towers rising from an immense black hole in the ground, all that remained of Green Chimneys. "Is there news of my wife?"

"I'm afraid, sir, that—" Nash placed a hand on my shoulder, causing me to stifle a sharp outcry. "I'm sorry, sir. Shouldn't you be in the hospital? Did your doctors say you could come all this way?"

"Knowing my feelings in this matter, the doctors insisted I make the journey." Deep within the black cavity, men in bulky orange space suits and space helmets were sifting through the sodden ashes, now and then dropping unrecognisable nuggets into heavy bags of the same colour. "I gather that you have news for me, Wendall," I said.

"Unhappy news, sir," he said. "The garage went up with the rest of the house, but we found some bits and pieces of your wife's little car. This here was one incredible hot fire, sir, and by hot I mean hot, and whoever set it was no garden-variety firebug."

"You found evidence of the automobile," I said. "I assume you also found evidence of the woman who owned it."

"They came across some bone fragments, plus a small portion of a skeleton," he said. "This whole big house came down on her, sir. These boys are experts at their job, and they don't hold out hope for finding a whole lot more. So if your wife was the only person inside . . . "

"I see, yes, I understand," I said, staying on my feet only with the support of the malacca cane. "How horrid, how hideous that it should all be true, that our lives should prove such a littleness . . . "

"I'm sure that's true, sir, and that wife of yours was a, was what I have to call a special kind of person who gave pleasure to us all, and I hope you know that we all wish things could of turned out different, the same as you."

For a moment I imagined that he was talking about her recordings. Then I understood that he was labouring to express the pleasure he and the others had taken in what they, no less than Mr. Clubb and Mr. Cuff but much, much more than I, had perceived as her essential character.

"Oh, Wendall," I said into the teeth of my sorrow, "it is not possible, not ever, for things to turn out different."

He refrained from patting my shoulder and sent me back to the rigours of my education.

IX

A month—four weeks—thirty days—seven hundred and twenty hours—forty-three thousand, two hundred minutes—two million, five hundred and ninety-two thousand seconds—did I spend under the care of Mr. Clubb and Mr. Cuff, and I believe I proved in the end to be a modestly, moderately, middlingly satisfying subject, a matter in which I take an immodest and immoderate pride. "You are little in comparison to the lady, sir," Mr. Clubb once told me while deep in his ministrations, "but no one could say that you are nothing." I, who had countless times put the lie to the declaration that they should never see me cry, wept tears of gratitude. We ascended through the fifteen stages known to the novice, the journeyman's further five, and passed, with the frequent repetitions and backward glances appropriate for the slower pupil, into the artist's upper eighty, infinitely expandable by grace of the refinements of his art. We had the little soldiers. We had dental floss. During each of those forty-three thousand, two hundred minutes, throughout all two million and nearly six hundred thousand seconds, it was always deepest night. We made our way through perpetual darkness, and the utmost darkness of the utmost night yielded an infinity of textural variation, cold, slick dampness to velvety softness to leaping flame, for it was true that no one could say I was nothing.

Because I was not nothing, I glimpsed the Meaning of Tragedy.

Each Tuesday and Friday of these four sunless weeks, my consultants and guides lovingly bathed and dressed my wounds, arrayed me in my warmest clothes (for I never after ceased to feel the blast of arctic wind against my flesh), and escorted me to my office, where I was presumed much reduced by grief as well as by certain household accidents attributed to grief.

On the first of these Tuesdays, a flushed-looking Mrs. Rampage offered her consolations and presented me with the morning newspapers, an inch-thick pile of faxes, two inches of legal documents, and a tray filled with official-looking letters. The newspapers described the fire and eulogised Marguerite; the increasingly threatening faxes declared Chartwell, Munster, and Stout's intention to ruin me professionally and personally in the face of my continuing refusal to return the accompanying documents along with all records having reference to their client; the documents were those in question; the letters, produced by the various legal firms representing all my other cryptic gentlemen, deplored the (unspecified) circumstances necessitating their clients' universal desire for change in re financial management. These lawyers also desired all relevant records, disks, etc., etc., urgently. Mr. Clubb and Mr. Cuff roistered behind their screen. I signed the documents in a shaky hand and requested Mrs. Rampage to have these shipped with the desired records to Chartwell, Munster, and Stout. "And dispatch all these other records, too," I said, handing her the letters. "I am now going in for my lunch."

Tottering towards the executive dining room, now and then I glanced into smoke-filled offices to observe my much-altered underlings. Some of them appeared, after a fashion, to be working. Several were reading paperback novels, which might be construed as work of a kind. One of the Skipper's assistants was unsuccessfully lofting paper airplanes towards his wastepaper basket. Gilligan's secretary lay asleep on her office couch, and a records clerk lay sleeping on the file room floor. In the dining room, Charlie-Charlie Rackett hurried forward to assist me to my accustomed chair. Gilligan and the Skipper gave me sullen looks from their usual lunch-time station, an unaccustomed bottle of Scotch whisky between them. Charlie-Charlie lowered me into my seat and said, "Terrible news about your wife, sir."

"More terrible than you know," I said.

Gilligan took a gulp of whisky and displayed his middle finger, I gathered to me rather than Charlie-Charlie.

"Afternoonish," I said.

"Very much so, sir," said Charlie-Charlie, and bent closer to the brim of the homburg and my ear. "About that little request you made the other day. The right men aren't nearly so easy to find as they used to be, sir, but I'm still on the job."

My laughter startled him. "No squab today, Charlie-Charlie. Just bring me a bowl of tomato soup."

I had partaken of no more than two or three delicious mouthfuls when Gilligan lurched up beside me. "Look here," he said, "it's too bad about your wife and everything, I really mean it, honest, but that drunken act you put on in my office cost me my biggest client, not to forget that you took his girlfriend home with you."

"In that case," I said, "I have no further need of your services. Pack your things and be out of here by three o'clock."

He listed to one side and straightened himself up. "You can't mean that."

"I can and do," I said. "Your part in the grand design at work in the universe no longer has any connection with my own."

"You must be as crazy as you look," he said, and unsteadily departed.

I returned to my office and gently lowered myself into my seat. After I had removed my gloves and accomplished some minor repair work to the tips of my fingers with the tape and gauze pads thoughtfully inserted by the detectives into the pockets of my coat, I slowly drew the left glove over my fingers and became aware of feminine giggles amid the coarser sounds of male amusement behind the screen. I coughed into the glove and heard a tiny shriek. Soon, though not immediately, a blushing Mrs. Rampage emerged from cover, patting her hair and adjusting her skirt. "Sir, I'm so sorry, I didn't expect…" She was staring at my right hand, which had not as yet been inserted into its glove.

"Lawn-mower accident," I said. "Mr. Gilligan has been released, and I should like you to prepare the necessary papers. Also, I want to see all of our operating figures for the past year, as significant changes have been dictated by the grand design at work in the universe." Mrs. Rampage flew from the room. For the next several hours, as for nearly every remaining hour I spent at my desk on the Tuesdays and Fridays thereafter, I addressed with a carefree spirit the details involved in shrinking the staff to the smallest number possible and turning the entire business over to the Skipper. Graham Leeson's abrupt disappearance greatly occupied the newspapers, and when not occupied as described I read that my arch rival and competitor had been a notorious Don Juan, i.e., a compulsive womaniser, a flaw in his otherwise immaculate character held by some to have played a substantive role in his sudden absence. As Mr. Clubb had predicted, a clerk at the—Hotel revealed Leeson's sessions with my late wife, and for a time professional and amateur gossipmongers alike speculated that he had caused the disastrous fire. This came to nothing. Before the month had ended, Leeson sightings were reported in Monaco, the Swiss Alps, and Argentina, locations accommodating to sportsmen—after four years of varsity football at the University of Southern California, Leeson had won an Olympic silver medal in weightlifting while earning his MBA at Wharton.

In the limousine at the end of each day, Mr. Clubb and Mr. Cuff braced me in happy anticipation of the lessons to come as we sped back through illusory sunlight towards the real darkness.

X The Meaning of Tragedy

Everything, from the designs of the laughing gods down to the lowliest cells in the human digestive tract, is changing all the time, every particle of being large and small is eternally in motion, but this simple truism, so transparent on its surface, evokes immediate headache and stupefaction when applied to itself, not unlike the sentence "Every word that comes out of my mouth is a bald-faced lie". The gods are ever laughing while we are always clutching our heads and looking for a soft place to lie down, and what I beheld in my momentary glimpses of the meaning of tragedy preceding, during, and after the experience of dental floss was so composed of paradox that I can state it only in cloud or vapour form, as:

The meaning of tragedy is: All is in order, all is in train. The meaning of tragedy is: It only hurts for a little while. The meaning of tragedy is: Change is the first law of life.

XI

So it took place that one day their task was done, their lives and mine were to move forward into separate areas of the grand design, and all that was left before preparing my own departure was to stand, bundled up against the non-existent arctic wind, on the bottom step and wave farewell with my remaining hand while shedding buckets and bathtubs of tears with my remaining eye. Chaplinesque in their black suits and bowlers, Mr. Clubb and Mr. Cuff ambled cheerily towards the glittering avenue and my bank, where arrangements had been made for the transfer into their hands of all but a small portion of my private fortune by my private banker, virtually his final act in that capacity. At the distant corner, Mr. Clubb and Mr. Cuff, by then only tiny figures blurred by my tears, turned, ostensibly to bid farewell, actually, as I knew, to watch as I mounted my steps and went back within the house, and with a salute I honoured this last painful agreement between us.

A more pronounced version of the office's metamorphosis had taken place inside my town house, but with the relative ease practice gives even to one whose step is halting, whose progress is interrupted by frequent pauses for breath and the passing of certain shooting pains, I skirted the mounds of rubble, the dangerous loose tiles, more dangerous open holes in the floor, and the regions submerged under water and toiled up the resilient staircase, moved with infinite care across the boards bridging the former landing, and made my way into the former kitchen, where broken pipes and limp wires protruding from the lathe marked the sites of those appliances rendered pointless by the gradual disappearance of the household staff. (In a voice choked with feeling, Mr. Moncrieff, Reggie Moncrieff, Reggie, the last to go, had informed me that his final month in my service had been "as fine as my days with the Duke, sir, every bit as noble as ever it was with that excellent old gentleman.") The remaining cupboard yielded a flagon of jenever, a tumbler, and a Monte Cristo torpedo, and with the tumbler filled and the cigar alight I hobbled through the devastated corridors towards my bed, there to gather my strength for the ardours of the coming day.

In good time, I arose to observe the final appointments of the life soon to be abandoned. It is possible to do up one's shoelaces and knot one's necktie as neatly with a single hand as with two, and shirt buttons eventually become a breeze. Into my travelling bag I folded a few modest essentials atop the flagon and the cigar box, and into a pad of shirts nestled the black lucite cube prepared at my request by my instructor-guides and containing, mingled with the ashes of the satchel and its contents, the few bony nuggets rescued from Green Chimneys. The travelling bag accompanied me first to my lawyer's office, where I signed papers making over the wreckage of the town house to the European gentleman who had purchased it sight unseen as a "fixer upper" for a fraction of its (considerably reduced) value. Next I visited the melancholy banker and withdrew the pittance remaining in my accounts. And then, glad of heart and free of all unnecessary encumbrance, I took my place in the sidewalk queue to await transportation by means of a kindly kneeling bus to the great terminus where I should employ the ticket reassuringly lodged within my breast pocket.

Long before the arrival of the bus, a handsome limousine crawled past in the traffic, and glancing idly within, I observed Mr. Chester Montfort de M—smoothing the air with a languid gesture while in conversation with the two stout, bowler-hatted men on his either side. Soon, doubtless, he would begin his instructions in the whopbopa-loobop.

XII

What is a pittance in a great city may be a modest fortune in a hamlet, and a returned prodigal might be welcomed far in excess of his true deserts. I entered New Covenant quietly, unobtrusively, with the humility of a new convert uncertain of his station, inwardly rejoicing to see all unchanged from the days of my youth. When I purchased a dignified but unshowy house on Scripture Street, I announced only that I had known the village in my childhood, had travelled far, and now in my retirement wished no more than to immerse myself in the life of the community, exercising my skills only inasmuch as they might be requested of an elderly invalid. How well the aged invalid had known the village, how far and to what end had he travelled, and the nature of his skills remained unspecified. Had I not attended daily services at the Temple, the rest of my days might have passed in pleasant anonymity and frequent perusals of a little book I had obtained at the terminus, for while my surname was so deeply of New Covenant that it could be read on a dozen headstones in the Temple graveyard, I had fled so early in life and so long ago that my individual identity had been entirely forgotten. New Covenant is curious—intensely curious—but it does not wish to pry. One fact and one only led to the metaphoric slaughter of the fatted calf and the prodigal's elevation. On the day when, some five or six months after his installation on Scripture Street, the afflicted newcomer's faithful Temple attendance was rewarded with an invitation to read the Lesson for the Day, Matthew 5:43–48, seated amid numerous offspring and offspring's offspring in the barnie-pews for the first time since an unhappy tumble from a hayloft was Delbert Mudge.

My old classmate had weathered into a white-haired, sturdy replica of his own grandfather, and although his hips still gave him considerable difficulty his mind had suffered no comparable stiffening. Delbert knew my name as well as his own, and though he could not connect it to the wizened old party counselling him from the lectern to embrace his enemies, the old party's face and voice so clearly evoked the deceased lawyer who had been my father that he recognised me before I had spoken the whole of the initial verse. The grand design at work in the universe once again could be seen at its mysterious business: unknown to me, my entirely selfish efforts on behalf of Charlie-Charlie Rackett, my representation to his parole board and his subsequent hiring as my spy, had been noted by all of barnie-world. I, a child of Scripture Street, had become a hero to generations of barnies! After hugging me at the conclusion of the fateful service, Delbert Mudge implored my assistance in the resolution of a fiscal imbroglio that threatened his family's cohesion. I of course assented, with the condition that my services should be free of charge. The Mudge imbroglio proved elementary, and soon I was performing similar services for other barnie-clans. After listening to a half-dozen accounts of my miracles while setting broken barnie-bones, New Covenant's physician visited my Scripture Street habitation under cover of night, was prescribed the solution to his uncomplicated problem, and sang my praises to his fellow townies. Within a year, by which time all New Covenant had become aware of my "tragedy" and consequent "reawakening", I was managing the Temple's funds as well as those of barn and town. Three years later, our reverend having in his ninety-first year, as the Racketts and Mudges put it, "woke up dead", I submitted by popular acclaim to appointment in his place.

Daily, I assume the honoured place assigned me. Ceremonious vestments assure that my patchwork scars remain unseen. The lucite box and its relics are interred deep within the sacred ground beneath the Temple where I must one day join my predecessors—some bony fragments of Graham Leeson reside there, too, mingled with Marguerite's more numerous specks and nuggets. Eye patch elegantly in place, I lean forward upon the malacca cane and, while flourishing the stump of my right hand as if in demonstration, with my ruined tongue whisper what I know none shall understand, the homily beginning, It only... To this I append in silent exhalation the two words concluding that little book brought to my attention by an agreeable murderer and purchased at the great grand station long ago, these: Ah, humanity!

INDEX TO THE FIRST TEN YEARS
OF *BEST NEW HORROR*

I: Index by Contributor

II: Index by Title

Note: There are no artist credits for the US cover of volume #3 or the covers for volume #4 and #9.

III: Contents of Previous Omnibus Editions

In the early 1990s, Robinson Publishing's bargain imprint Magpie Books published two omnibus editions of Best New Horror *in budget trade paperback editions. The details of the contents are listed below.*

THE GIANT BOOK OF BEST NEW HORROR (1993)
Edited by Stephen Jones and Ramsey Campbell
Cover by Luis Rey

THE GIANT BOOK OF TERROR (1994)
Edited by Stephen Jones and Ramsey Campbell
Cover by Luis Rey

ABOUT THE EDITOR

STEPHEN JONES lives in London, England. A Hugo Award nominee, he is the winner of four World Fantasy Awards, three International Horror Guild Awards, five Bram Stoker Awards, twenty-one British Fantasy Awards and a Lifetime Achievement Award from the Horror Writers Association. One of Britain's most acclaimed horror and dark fantasy writers and editors, he has more than 155 books to his credit, including *The Art of Horror Movies: An Illustrated History*, the film books of Neil Gaiman's *Coraline* and *Stardust*, *The Illustrated Monster Movie Guide* and *The Hellraiser Chronicles*; the non-fiction studies *Horror: 100 Best Books* and *Horror: Another 100 Best Books* (both with Kim Newman); the single-author collections *Necronomicon* and *Eldritch Tales* by H.P. Lovecraft, *The Complete Chronicles of Conan* and *Conan's Brethren* by Robert E. Howard, and *Curious Warnings: The Great Ghost Stories of M.R. James*; plus such anthologies as *Terrifying Tales to Tell at Night: 10 Scary Stories to Give You Nightmares!*, *The Mammoth Book of Nightmare Stories*, *The Mammoth Book of Halloween Stories*, *The Lovecraft Squad* and *Zombie Apocalypse!* series, and thirty volumes of *Best New Horror*. You can visit his web site at www.stephenjoneseditor.com or follow him on Facebook at "Stephen Jones-Editor".